The Rio Grande:
A River with a Thousand Tales

Mom,
You are my Hero!
my True North...
You gave me my direction.
I love you,
your daughter... Mary J

Edited by Don Clifford and Frank Cortazo
Title by John Rogans M.D.
Cover Courtesy of Cowboy Zone Enterprises

Published by Rio Grande Valley Byliners

2101 E. Bowie Ave
Harlingen, TX 78550

www.rgvbyliners.org

ISBN 978-0-9960972-0-8
Ebook ISBN 978-0-9960972-1-5

Library of Congress Control Number: 2014906433

Printed in the United States of America

Also by the Valley Byliners:

Collected Tales from the Rio Grande
Tales Told at Midnight Along the Rio Grande
Rio Grande Roundup
Roots by the River
Gift of the Rio

Anthology Selections

Editor's Note: The asterisk indicates a winner in Jack's Writing Challenge

FOREWORD:

The stories in *The Rio Grande: A River with a Thousand Tales* are the result of a challenge. In early 2009, then Valley Byliners President Jack King sought for a way to stimulate the members to write. He felt, Valley Byliners is an organization devoted to writing and to the encouragement of would be authors. "So, why aren't we writing?" he asked. Besides, an anticipated new anthology needed many more stories.

The rules were simple. The challenge was open to members only. Any member could submit via eMail a short story, poem, essay, memoir, stage script, or whatever, in 1500 words or less. Jack then provided the challenge entry to the membership who voted on which submission was thought to be the best piece of writing -- no editing or criticism was allowed.

In September 2009, Jack's Writing Challenge produced its first winner -- Don Clifford for his short story, *The Outhouse*. The prize was an elaborate bookbinding press, which Jack made. Clifford declined the prize because he had two presses already. Runner-up Judy Stevens earned the press for her short story, *A Cup of Humility*.

As the Challenge progressed from month to month, the prize changed to a ten-dollar bill for the author of the submission that received the most votes -- at first, paid for out of Jack's pocket, later, from Club funds.

The submissions were slow in coming. A couple of months early on, the Challenge had only one or no submissions, so the prize was carried over until a subsequent month had a decent number of entries. When it was realized that the cash prize was real, and that there was a certain kind of reward from peers who read each other's manuscripts, the quantity of manuscripts received soon increased. More importantly, the quality of the writing became better and better.

As more and more Byliners submitted entries, the Challenge evolved. Every third month, a member could submit a 4000 word entry -- an opportunity to increase one's writing skill. May and November were set aside for poetry only.

The collection contained in *The Rio Grande: A River with a Thousand Tales* is a sampling of the many contest entries on file. Jack's Writing Challenge will continue in the foreseeable future, and perhaps, not too far down the road, The Valley Byliners will have another anthology ready for publication.

Metaphors be with you!

Don Clifford
President 2009-2010
Chairman of the Board 2013-2016

INTRODUCTION
Why Writers Write

A writer died and was given the option of going to heaven or hell.
She decided to check out each place first.
As the writer descended into the fiery pits, she saw row upon row of writers chained to their desks in a steaming sweatshop. As they worked, they were whipped repeatedly with thorny lashes.
"Oh, my," the writer said. "Now let me see heaven."
A few moments later, as she ascended into heaven, she saw rows of writers chained to their desks in a steaming sweatshop. As they worked, they, too, were whipped with thorny lashes.
"Wait a minute!" said the writer. "This is just as bad as hell!"
"Oh, no, it's not," an unseen voice said.
"Here, your work gets published."

Writing, for many of us, is a form of self-expression. And because self-expression among individuals differs, I see writing as more of an artistic endeavor with flexibility and freedom instead of working within a binding, rigid or scientific formula.

Writers write because they have to. For some of us, writing is our profession. We are paid to write.

Then, there are writers who write to express themselves in the same way that artists reveal themselves in painting, sculpture and photography. A writer's passion for words opens a portal that allows others into his/her world. Writing is a passion open to all, and not limited to merely a few.

Bernard Shaw believed he had ideas to give to the world. At first, he tried the medium of a novel. When he found that the medium was ineffective, he turned to drama. In drama, he found the medium he needed and decided to write plays for propagating his views.

Surely, there must be motivational forces other than the desire to communicate one's ideas, views, and so on, to others -- such as the need for money. As Juvenal says, "The incurable itch for money possesses many."

According to George Orwell, there are four great motives for writing, besides money and the ones mentioned above. He said that these motives exist in different degrees in every writer, and that in any one, the proportions will vary from time to time according to the atmosphere in which s/he is living.

Creativity also plays a part in writing. For instance, creative writing blends and integrates one's creativity with one's love for words. Novels are one form of creative writing. When we are creative and share a love for writing, we can create worlds of our own and invite readers into them. Movies adapted from novels are the perfect example of how feature films translate words into moving images.

Some of the more important reasons why writers write are to self-reflect; to clarify their understanding of certain subject matters; to share knowledge, to educate, to inform and/or to entertain.

And the most important reason of all?
To learn more about ourselves and the world we live in.

Sue Groves
President 2011- 2014

A BLOOD SACRIFICE
Hugh Barlow

I met Bean (pronounced Bayan) McCann when I was hired by Captain Stark. After boarding the *Wayward Sun*, I was shown my berth by the First, and upon stowing my gear, I was brought to Captain's Quarters. I was quick to notice that the ship seemed short handed, and when asked, the First confirmed my observations.

"Welcome aboard, Haley." the Captain says from his chair with a smile and an outstretched hand. Grasping the offered appendage firmly while I stand before him, I smile back and reply, "It's good to be here, Captain, Sir."

"I want you to meet my Chief Engineer, Bean McCann. Bean, Haley Brennen." The Captain informally waves his hand at both me and McCann. McCann takes that as his cue to extend his scarred fist in my direction. From his seat, he clasps my hand in a bone crushing display of dominance. No stranger to pain, I do not let the discomfort of his grip show on my face as I attempt to at least place for show in this contest of strength. McCann's scowl lightens somewhat and a glimmer of surprise shows in his eyes as we grip each other for what seems like a short eternity. When he releases my hand, I put it behind my back and work the circulation back into my fingers. Bean grunts tersely, "You'll do, I suppose."

"Haley, you will be working under Bean as an apprentice engineer. Bean, Haley has had no formal training, but his aptitude scores are off the charts. I found him working in a maintenance garage at a dump recycling location on the border of Mexico and Texas. He is young, but seems to know his way around machines. Claims his father was Irish from the asteroids. I met his mama. She's Mexican Catholic. Haley is the eldest of eight. His Papa's nowhere to be found. You, Bean, are to be his surrogate, understand? Teach the boy everything he needs to know." The Captain turns to face me and says, "Having said that, do not expect to be coddled by Bean. He is a mean bastard, but what he doesn't know about ships does not bear mentioning. He has saved my life, and the life of everyone on board this ship more times than I care to mention with his knowledge and ability. I do not expect him to treat you like a child. I do expect him to treat you with respect," A telling glance is cast toward McCann. Looking back at me the Captain says, "I expect you to study in your off hours. You will take every course you can from Luna U that you can cram into your schedule. You seem to have an innate ability with machines, but that will only take you so far on a space ship. You will need to learn the math and engineering to back up your skills. You fail a course twice, and I will bounce you off the ship in a safe port with your pay and a one way ticket in steerage back to Earth, understood?"

I reply, "Yes, Sir." The Captain turns to McCann and says, "Show him the boat, Bean, and keep him out of my hair." Bean's grimace passes for a salute and he grunts, "Yessir. Follow me, boy." McCann swivels his chair from the table and wrestles his bulk out of it. He is surprisingly short and broad, and I notice that his left arm is a ceramic replacement from the elbow down. The coloration is close to his own, but the arm does not flex like a natural arm or even a modern inexpensive replacement. I follow McCann out the door and into the passageway. He gestures to the right and says, "I'm gonna take ya to the most important part of the ship first. Down the hall to the lift, an' press th' call button."

The Captain's Quarters are closest to the bridge and the main airlock. Crew quarters are not far from both, so I have had little opportunity to see the ship I have hired on with. Everything I see so far is bright and polished, but our footfalls echo hollowly in the passageway as we walk along. I reach the elevator and press the button. The door cycles open immediately, and McCann says, "Engineering." I look at the control panel and McCann comments, "Voice activation. Captain installed it as an upgrade when he refitted the NavComs. Triple redundancy, so there is plenty of spare processing power. This scow may be old, but she has all the modern conveniences." The trip to Engineering takes longer than I expect, and we ride in silence the rest of the way.

The tour is uneventful, but I do notice that the public areas of the ship are much more polished than the working areas. Engineering seems clean and functional, but the section has not seen paint for more than a few years. McCann notices me looking at the walls and states, “Cap'n prefers to put th' effort where it matters in maintenance. Paint in Engineering is a low priority. Might get around to it on this trip though if we have enough crew. The public areas need to shine for the customers. Makes the passengers and shippers feel better if things look new and bright.”

“We have passengers?” I ask. “I thought the *Wayward Sun* was a freighter.”

“Freighter, passengers, and manufacturing. Sometimes salvage. We do whatever we need to to make ends meet. There ain't no first class, but sometimes we freight people with the merchandise. Passenger cabins can double for fragile storage when re-configured. The Sun was built as a military supply ship in it's day, so we have room for more people than we usually carry.

"This here will be your tool box.” McCann stops in front of a row of robotic tool bins and points at the one closest to him. “I'll set you up with a password once you get settled in. Minor cosmetic mods are OK on th' unit without checking with me first. Major mods that affect function, and reprogramming will need to be cleared with me before you can do anything.”

I look at the other boxes secured in the area and notice that each has been customized with paint or stickers so that no two tool boxes look alike. Mine is obviously new and still has a nice shine on the paint. The wheels and clamps have no wear on them.

“We make these in house.” McCann's gesture takes in all the boxes clamped to the wall. “Last apprentice I had shipped out when he graduated. Cap'n let him take his box with him as a gift when he transferred to his new ship. Keep in his graces, and he'll likely do the same for you, come your turn to go. Hopefully, you'll decide to stay when your hitch is up. I'm getting' tired of trainin' you pups just to watch you up an' run off.” The perpetual scowl deepens slightly. “C'mon, shake a leg. I gotta show ya the rest of th' ship before shift ends. Don't want to be late for dockside. I got some drinkin' to catch up on. Need to spend some money before we shove off. Let's head to the engine room."

The maze of machinery, pipes, and cables is daunting in the engine room. What I see is far beyond what I had ever worked on back in the garage. The crawlers, cats, and haulers that I repaired there were all standardized, and the electrics had been tried and tested over centuries. The poorest mechanics in the shop could still manage to do basic maintenance on the machines after a few lessons on the job. Heck, even trained monkeys were able to do some basic work if someone was willing to take the time to show them what to do. People were much cheaper than monkeys, though, so the company would not use them unless they can absolutely not get humans to do the job.

What I see in the belly of the *Wayward Sun* is much more complicated than the E9 Cats and the electric flatbeds that I am accustomed to working on. Nothing that I see seems to be standard, most looks to be military castoffs or complete custom fabrications. Still, there is much that I recognized without being told what it is. McCann is succinct in his description of the workings of the engine room and explains that he will give much more detail when I have "settled in."

The tour of the ship ends in the mess hall. McCann introduces me to one of the navigators and asks her to show me how to use the mess. He then disappears, and I will not see him for several days. Angela shows me how to contact the First using my pad, and after I eat, the First sets me up in my bunk.

I spend the next few days meeting my crew mates, calling my friends and family to say goodbye, and missing my mother. I am ashamed to say I am feeling lost, overwhelmed, and rather pathetic. I am also a bit excited, since I am starting out on the adventure I have always dreamed of. Most of the crew seems to go out of their way to include me in their activities, but I have to decline participation if anything they do cost more than a few credits. I have sent most of my signing bonus on to my mother so that she can pay off some of the debt that my father left her in when he disappeared. The kids need to eat, and clothing and school supplies are not free. Between the homesickness, the activities and the excitement, I do not get much sleep while the ship is in port.

McCann comes bursting in to the work room in Engineering and blasts out, "Brennen! Get your box, and follow me!" Without pausing, he heads for the Engine Room, and I have to scurry to order the box to follow and keep him in sight. We tread through the maze between the pipes and cables and McCann stops in front of a rather large capacitor, points at it, and says, "This cap feeds power to the main engine. It blew during pretest, and I need you to remove it and replace it with a new one from stores before we take off."

McCann's usual scowl was replaced by a look of anticipation. I grab a wrench from the tool box and reach over to disconnect the main feed from the cap when I am hit with what felt like a bolt of lightning. The shock kicks me back into the toolbox, almost knocking it over, and bruising my back. I land on the deck plates, temporarily stunned. After a minute or so, I manage to get back on my feet and look at McCann.

"What the hell, HAPPENED?"

I see an evil gleam in his eye as McCann says, "This is your first lesson. Always check a cap before replacing it. If it is charged, bleed it off. If you do not do this, the cap can bite you on the ass! You were lucky this time that the cap was bad. Had it a full charge, you would likely be dead. Never assume that someone else has done this for you. Always check things for yourself. Do you need to see the medic?"

My anger and my pride made me answer through gritted teeth, "No, I do not need medical attention at this time. I'll check in with the medic when my shift is over."

"Good, see that you do. In the mean time, bleed off what is left in that cap and replace it with one from stores."

"Yes, sir." I growl as I reached into the tool box to get a shunt coil. McCann leaves, and I fume until the end of my task.

Up until the attack, I spend most of my work time repairing and maintaining the manufacturing robots on board the ship. The Captain has outfitted several of the cargo areas with automated machinery that takes raw materials he purchases at many of his ports of call. These automated factories print parts and then assembles them into the machines and tools that we both use on board ship, and sell at some of our remote destinations. The Captain gets orders from customers, and if he can't find what the customer wants at a port of call for less than he can manufacture it, he will program one of the robots to assemble what he needs. These parts are made of plastics, ceramics, or whatever metals we have on hand. My job is to see that these machines ran smoothly and to ensure that they have all the supplies needed to do the job. I maintain them and fix whatever breaks down. I rarely actually see the parts of the ship that the rest of the crew and I rely upon to keep us moving and alive. The task of maintaining these parts of the ship are left to the more experienced crew. It is expected that I will only ask for help if I can not figure out what is wrong myself. I rarely ask for help, because if I do, I am ridiculed by McCann if he hears about it. He pretty much leaves me to my own devices and leaves engineering education to his subordinates. This suits me, since I do not much care for him and do not want to see him anyway.

I am awakened by the klaxon announcing "All Hands."

The ship's computer announces, "The Captain wants all available crew members to meet him in the mess. Those whose jobs are considered essential to ship's operations are to remain at their posts. These people will be linked via com to the meeting."

After everyone has arrived at mess, the Captain stands at one end of the room and announces, "OK, folks, I have tried to avoid this, but it looks like we are going to have to go to Ceres Station." Groans and puzzled looks meet his statement.

“For those who do not know, Ceres Station is surrounded by the 'Ceresian Triangle.' This area of space is known to be treacherous. It is a sphere of space that spans a few weeks travel time in all directions out from Ceres Station. For those who noted that I said a 'sphere' and not 'triangle,' it is called the Ceresian Triangle in memory of an area of Earth once known as the Bermuda Triangle or Devil's Triangle. Many old sea vessels and aircraft were lost in this section of the Atlantic Ocean under mysterious circumstances. That area of the sea was also known to be rife with pirates. I suspect that many of the same circumstances surround Ceres Station as were present in the Bermuda Triangle.

"In the old days before NavSats on Earth, many ships reported mysterious electronic and magnetic anomalies in the Devil's Triangle just before the crafts were lost with all hands. Some of the same types of reports come from the Ceres area of space. Most of the ships making these reports are never heard from again. Occasionally, merchandise and parts from these ships end up on the black and gray markets in and surrounding Ceres Station. Officials there are lax in enforcing space salvage laws, and many of the 'salvage ships' in the area have tools that could be used for either ship salvage, ship's defense, or offensive attack. I suspect that many of the ships lost in this area are 'salvaged' before all hands are lost. The anomalies could be caused by electronic jamming. We should all keep our eyes open for anything unusual, and we should be prepared for unwelcome guests.

"We have an advantage that most other ships do not. The *Wayward Sun* was once a military vessel. As such, she is hardened against electro/magnetic tampering from opposing forces. We have standard NavSystems and drives listed as installed on official records, but we also have non-standard systems as backups that are not on the records. If you see any anomalies in the standard systems, check the backups. If something doesn't look right, contact me or the First at any time. It is much better to be safe than sorry. All hands will be required to participate in emergency drills. I will leave the details to be given by your section heads.” With that, the Captain leaves the room and we disperse to our sections for briefing.

When the alarm sounds, it's at the worst possible time. The ship is in an asteroid cluster that is unusually thick making navigation tricky. I awake with a start and slam my head into the padded underside of the bunk above mine. Opening the seals of my bunk, I curse the Captain and his officers. I expect to hear the announcement of even more drills. I turn cold with the rush of adrenaline as I hear the words, “All hands to emergency stations, this is not a drill.” repeated several times.

I feel the bitter taste of bile in my mouth as I rush to my station in Engineering. I am immediately directed by McCann to don my space suit and take my box to the Engine Room. McCann is more agitated than usual, and he keeps up a running commentary as we wait. “Keep your helmet and gloves on unless you absolutely have to remove them. These blighters are likely to come from behind and try to disable our drives to make their work easy. If they do, they may puncture the walls of the engine room, and that will cause us to lose atmosphere.”

McCann restlessly paces the Engine Room from one monitor to another watching the drives as they fire outside the hull. He redirects a camera to watch a section of space in our wake. All we can see is the glint of sunlight reflected from an asteroid that we have passed, or the cloud of reaction mass turning to vapor, then to ice, and reflecting sunlight as it slowly disperses behind us. One of the asteroid glints behind us proves false, and nickle slugs take out our rear defensive guns before we are even aware that we were targeted.

The pirates do not use targeting lasers or radar to direct their fire, and so the attack is a surprise. Old fashioned optics are their guidance system, and the ammunition is not self guiding missiles, but slugs from a rail gun. No-one has used such tactics for hundreds of years, and so we are not prepared for the attack. The *Wayward Sun* is armored, but certain areas are still vulnerable, including the missile tubes, lasers, and the reaction ports on the engines. A lucky shot can easily take out one or several engines and leave us at the mercy of the attacking foe.

We watch as an asteroid behind us splinters and a powerful salvage tug emerges from the wreckage. The pirate ship wastes reaction mass prolifically as it attempts to come up behind us. We watch as a line of nickel slugs glints as the forward gunner on the attacking ship searches our backside for vulnerabilities.

I had been studying the ship's drives in class, and I ask McCann, “What are we using for reaction mass?”

He looks confused and replies, “Water, of course. We are not going fast enough to use metals. We can't maneuver through the asteroids at high speed.”

“Are we still fueled with metals?”

“Yes,” McCann said. “Why do you want to know?”

“Can we burn one of the engines cold, and run metals through it?”

“Sure, but it would not make us go any faster, and if it could, we could not control the ship to get through this tangle.”

“I don't want to make the ship faster, I want to turn one of our engines into a weapon.”

“I don't think that'll work.” McCann says. "The orifices in the plasma tube are too small to emit molten metals. The firebox usually atomizes the metals and turns them into plasma before the magnetic fields accelerates them out the reaction ports.”

“What if we install an oversized orifice, and run the reactor cold?”

“By all the spirits that are holy, that might just work!” McCann shouts. “Go to Engineering and get a fresh orifice. Drill it out quickly. It doesn't matter what size, just make sure that you leave enough ceramic to thread into the port. I'll reprogram the computer to allow the reactor to run cold, and then start removing the orifice so that we can replace it. Get a move on, boy!”

McCann rushes over to one of the monitoring stations and begins to quickly re-write code as I hurry out the airlock and on my way to Engineering.

Upon my return, I notice McCann hunched over an idled engine with his helmet and gloves off. "Quick, boy! Over here! Hand me the spanner!"

I fumble the adjustable wrench from my box and almost drop it because of my suit's gloves. McCann lights a torch and plays the flames over the orifice until it glows white hot. "Need to weaken the weld before I can remove the orifice."

I hear him grumble. "Quick, give me the spanner!" I hand him the wrench. Still playing fire on the orifice, McCann gingerly places the wrench on it. Finding the wrench too large, he removes the fire and adjusts the jaws of the wrench. The burled knob is hot, and I can hear the flesh sizzle as he spins the knob. Once the wrench is adjusted, he briefly sticks his fingers in his mouth and then grabs the torch again.

Getting the ceramic back to the desired temperature, McCann begins to put pressure on the wrench with his artificial hand. The pressure is not enough, and he shuts the torch off, and uses his right hand to assist. When the wrench finally moves, the pressure is released in an instant. McCann's hand impacts a protrusion on the magnetic accelerator, skinning his knuckles. "Shit!" he snaps, "Oh, good! Blood sacrifice to the machine gods. This is sure to work now."

McCann quickly reassembles the engine with the larger orifice. "No time to weld the new orifice." he mutters. "Go start the reactor!"

I head to the monitoring station and I hear McCann talking to himself, "Won't be able to aim, but shouldn't have to. The bastards are right behind us. Gonna cut right through their hull like a hot knife through butter."

I watch as he scrambles out from the engine bay. “What ya waitin' for? Light 'er up!” he glares at me.

“Just waiting for you to close up and get out of the way,” I say.

“To hell with that, I'll be fine. We're runnin' cold, remember? I don't plan on havin' any kids in the near future anyway, and I still have most of my suit on. If it makes you feel better, I'll put on my gloves and helmet as you light the candles.”

McCann wipes the blood from his hand on the front of his suit as I start the program that fires the engine. In mere seconds we watch in the monitor as a fireball blooms behind us. We cheer, and I turn off the engine that we have converted into a cannon.

“The machine gods require a blood sacrifice to ensure that any repair will work,” McCann informs me as we stare at the remains of the ship that was attacking us.

Now I know why his hand is so scarred.

A BLOOMING IDIOT*
Hugh Barlow

"Brennan! Get your ass to hydroponics! It is flooding again!" Bean blasts over the intercom.

"Hydroponics." I say with resignation to the tool box, and it trundles after me. My job on board ship is to repair and maintain non-essential machinery while I get the training to do more important work. I am the most junior mechanic, and as such, I get all the "scutt work." Before our trip to Ceres Station, the chief mechanic seemed to hate me. Since the battle with the pirate ship, he seems to have warmed up a bit. Now he just finds me annoying. I do not know why. It is nothing that I have done, or so I am told. The other crew members tell me that he treats me better than any other apprentice he has had. I find this difficult to believe. He goes out of his way to make my life miserable. I get to hydroponics and discover that the water regulator has failed again. The place is swamped. I shut down the crop watering system, replace a faulty valve, and proceed to start mopping up. One would think that after all the centuries that technology has been around someone would have found a better way to clean up water than with synthetic fibers on the end of a metal pipe, but, no. Here I am, a space ship mechanic, and the best way to clean up this mess is to use my muscle instead of my brain.

As I swab the decks like the seamen of antiquity, I hear a muted buzzing that tickles my memory. The tinny hum fades in and out, and I strain to find where the noise is coming from. I try to place where I have heard the noise before but fail. Suddenly, the noise stops and I feel something sting the back of my neck. Autonomic responses kick in, and I slap myself, hard. I bring my hand to my face and look to see a spot of blood surrounding the splayed corpse of a mosquito. I shudder, and wipe my hand on my uniform. Bugs give me the willies, and I hate mosquitoes more than most.

Having spent most of my life near garbage dumps, I have seen all kinds of bugs. Most of them are disgusting. I had not heard so much as a whisper of an insect since coming on board the Wayward Sun, and I found the presence of one now to be somewhat disconcerting.

"Uh, Mister McCann, Sir?" I sputter on the intercom.

"You get that mess cleaned up boy?" Bean replies.

"Almost," I say. "Is there any reason that we would have mosquitoes in hydroponics?"

"No, why?"

"Because I just killed one." I state.

"WHAT?" Bean roars. "Wait right there. Don't lose the bug, I want to see."

I carefully search my uniform for the mangled corpse, pluck it off, and stare at it in revulsion as it sits on the tip of my finger. In a few minutes I am surrounded by several of the ship's officers. The Captain comes in with Bean. "What's this I hear that you have found a mosquito." the Captain inquires.

"Yessir," I bring my hand up with the bug displayed on my fingertip.

"Lemme see, is it real? You sure it's not a surveillance device?" The Captain takes his own finger and gently wipes the corpse from mine. He flips his hand over and places the finger next to his eye.

"Yep, looks like it's a mosquito," he says banally as he shows the insect to McCann.

"Bean, go double check to make sure it is not artificial. Astra, I need you to check the records of where we got our last water. I want to know it's point of origin."

The ship's avatar responds with a curt, “Yes Sir,” and begins her records search. “Ceres Station was the last place we took on water. The water was sold to us as asteroid ice, but there are anomalies. Chemical composition shows organics that are not common to asteroid water. The composition is more like Earth based water.”

“Crap! I should have tested the water myself before we bought it. Where would Ceres Station get Earth water?” the Captain queries.

“There was a research vessel that was lost in the vicinity of Ceres Station a few months ago. The stated purpose of the ship was to set up a base where contamination vectors of disease causing insects was studied in a controlled environment. There were some especially virulent strains of disease on board that ship. The water may have come from there.”

“Oh, Lord” the captain drones, “I'm not your garden variety idiot, I'm a blooming idiot. We need to seal off hydroponics and get rid of these bloody nuisances! Astra, contamination protocols. Everyone gets suited up until we can figure out how bad the contamination is. We need to see if anyone is infected, and we need to clean these buggers out!”

My shipmates scuttle out of hydroponics like roaches exposed to light, and I go back to Engineering to get my ship suit.

At night, after a long day of panic and decontamination, I dream about home. Mama and Papa are there, and I am roughly about 7 years old. I remember that the family was still pretty small, since only 4 of my siblings had been born at this time. The trailer we live in is parked next to a swamp where the company has set up the “reclamation center.” The swamp was used as a dumping ground by one of the local cities, and it is my father's job to supervise the men who repair the machines used to remove the trash and reclaim the metals, plastics and chemicals that previous generations had carelessly disposed of.

Most of the time, the swamp is dry, but after a rare rainfall, the swamp comes to life. Unfortunately, it had rained earlier in the week, and the mosquitoes woke from their collective slumber with a vengeance. The mosquitoes act like the fabled vampires of old and congregate to find involuntary donors. Mama has tied water bags around the trailer in an attempt to rid us of the pests, but the smell of water just seems to lure more of the creatures to us.

We had run out of citronella, and Papa growls as he slaps another blood sucking nuisance, "Females! You know the male mosquito does not suck blood?" Papa looks at me and continues. "They sip nectar from flowers. The females need the protein in blood to make their babies. Just like a human female, all they want is to suck you dry."

He gets up and looks at Mama, "I'll be back in a minute." and he wanders off. He returns after a while with several cans of starting fluid that he has stolen from the service garage.

"Here," he hands a can to Mama. "Spray this about. It will knock them out." Both Papa and Mama spray the trailer with the starting fluid. The smell is sweet and cloying. I like it. Shortly afterward we all fall asleep. I awake in the morning to find myself covered in mosquito bites. Looking at my siblings and then at myself, I discover that we are all covered with swollen, itchy spots, We look like we have the chicken pox, or some exotic disease.

"Damn!" I hear Papa curse. "Looks like the starting fluid knocked US out, but did nothing to affect the bugs. We ended up becoming a smorgasbord." In my dream I think to myself, "Blooming idiot, indeed."

We spend the next few weeks running blood tests and decontaminating the ship. All the tests come up negative for new contagions of the crew members. All the water reserves are treated with radiation, and run through the Wayward Sun's own water treatment system to kill organics. I thought I had it bad when I had to clean up the spilled water in hydroponics. I have spent most of my time the last few days in a shipsuit scrubbing the storage areas for water with a sponge and a bottle of Decon. Every surface and area that contains water or comes into contact with it on board the ship is wiped down or otherwise decontaminated. The Captain does NOT use starting fluid to anesthetize the crew, and I am grateful. I do wish that I could get a whiff now and again when I go to bed. My dreams have become disturbingly filled with insects, and the dreamless sleep of anesthesia would be welcome. One of the nice things about living in space is the lack of bugs. I hate them. They give me the willies.

A CAT TALE*
Marge Flado

Seeking closure for my disappointment leads me to write about this incident in the hope that sharing it may assuage my frustration with my cat. Mrs. Gray, my cat, has an interesting history. Over the objections of my more intelligent friends, I decided I needed a cat to bring joy to my life. So I went to the "kitten room" at the local Humane Society to look at all the little kittens waiting for homes. All were appealing. All were noisy. My heart ached that so many would end up here with only a slim chance of being placed in a secure, loving environment.

I went from cage to cage, and in the last one was a half grown gray cat sitting quietly and elegantly staring out at me with emerald colored eyes. I asked the attendant if I could hold her, and she opened the cage and handed her to me. I sat down and looked her over. The first impression was that she had very unusual fur. It was softer and thicker than any cat pelt I had ever felt. She continued to sit upright, no purring, no meowing. My thought: What a remarkable animal this is! I told the attendant I would adopt her.

Papers were drawn up, many papers. I could have adopted a child with fewer papers to sign. But I had a cat. And home we went. I was prepared for her arrival and she inspected her new quarters in a disinterested manner.

I soon discovered she was quite sensitive to verbal commands. She readily learned not to climb up the blinds, claw the furniture or walk on the tables and cupboard tops. She also decided not to walk close to my feet since each time she did so, she had a free "flying lesson". This may sound mean to some, but old people frequently stumble over their pets and break bones, so I decided, if she was so darn smart she could learn to stay away from my walking feet. And she did. She walks near me, never within touching distance, because in her wee cat brain she has learned that touching my feet hurts her. How smart is that, then?

She also learned the word "outside", for when I say it she runs to the back door. She learned to come inside when I gently slam the back door. She flattens when I scold her and best of all she is mat trained. She will rest, sleep or sit only on a mat well imbued with her scent. This is her best quality. She has a mat on my bed, one in the living room and one on a director's chair by the big window in the dining room. At night, she stays on her mat on my bed until the alarm goes off at 7 A.M., at which time she comes over and tromps up the length of my body and peers into my face as if to say, "didn't you hear the alarm, old girl?" Then she scoots off. Not a cuddler by nature, her affectionate periods are short and transient. She has an uncanny ability to read my mind, and act upon it. She knows when I am going to medicate her ears BEFORE I pick up the medicine. She knows when I leave the room, if I am returning immediately or if I am staying out of the room and moves accordingly.

She hides when people visit, and doesn't warm to people generally. Aside from her unusual intelligence, I began to notice other things about her that set her apart from the cat-dom I had always known.

During this time I was still teaching my exercise classes four days a week at Park Place Estates. One day I mentioned to the class that I had adopted a cat from the Humane Society and that she was gray with four white feet. A woman in the class asked me if she had a tiny white streak down the middle of her face and when I said yes, she showed great emotion and I thought she was going to start crying right then and there. After class she rushed up, hugged me and really lost it!

It seems she had found a stray gray kitten close to the R.V. park where they lived in their winter vacation trailer home. She began feeding and taking care of the kitten. When her granddaughters came to visit for several weeks they cared for the little stray and became very attached to it. The children lived in Ohio and there was no way they would be allowed to bring the cat home with them. The grandmother already had two cats in her house trailer so after her grandchildren returned to Ohio she sadly decided to take the stray kitten to the Humane Society. That is how Mrs. Gray ended up where I found her.

After living with me for about a month she went missing. I put up signs and notices, notified the local police and my daughter drove the golf cart all around Palm Valley searching for her. Nothing. Three days later I received a call from my grandson's wife and she said that Mrs. Gray showed up on their patio and they had taken her into the house while she made the phone call. She had shown up very close to where she had first been picked up by the grandmother and her grandchildren. The fact that she was four miles and across two highways away from where I live was the greatest mystery of all. I never will figure that one out, so I am calling it divine intervention. Nothing else could explain a young cat making that trek.

A friend from Florida had come to visit and when she saw Mrs. Gray, she exclaimed, "Oh, you have a Russian Blue"! I said, "a Russian what"? It seems she was a cat lover and her favorite cats were a breed called Russian Blue. She told me a little about them and I promptly forgot about it.

One day I randomly Googled Russian Blue cats and read some very interesting things about the breed. They came from Angel Island, were favorites of the Czars in Russia, were known for their intelligence, their dislike of strangers, their loyalty to one person, their ability to learn how to fetch on command, and their unusually soft fur. The under fur and the guard hairs are the same length and accounts for its thick softness. The guard hairs are tipped with white which makes them look "blue", almost iridescent. They also have emerald colored eyes and their mouth turns up at the corners which make them look like they are smiling. They have faintly visible rings in the coloring of their tails. Mrs. Gray has all of these characteristics. Russian Blues are fairly rare in this country...

At one time breeders tried to develop a White Russian by interbreeding to achieve this genetic goal. But it didn't work out and the bloodlines became tainted with white genes that crop up in litters to this day. The white chested Russian blue has what is termed "locket" coloring and of course is a throw away to a breeder when it appears in a litter of kittens.

So I conjured up some additions to my cat's history. She was in a litter of "Blues", but had the unfortunate genetic throw back of the "locket". The breeder gave her away. She ran away from her new home, she was rescued by the kind grandmother and her grandchildren, then taken to the Humane Society and ultimately rescued by me. She in turn ran back to her second home from which I retrieved her. Now isn't it nice to know all that!!!

Lately when I travel, I hire someone to cat-sit in my home because I can't bear leaving her alone for days at a time. I travel often, sometimes for a period of two weeks. Having a cat is very inconvenient. My two friends who advised me against getting a cat were so right. All the others who thought I should have a cat were so wrong.

Julie, my household helper, has kept her twice while I was away from home. However, each time I found her at home when I arrived back. Knowing Julie to be the efficient person she is, I figured she deposited Mrs. Gray back here so she would be in the house to welcome me back home. (Oh, how naïve of me to think that.) When I asked how Mrs. Gray behaved at her house, she always said, "Fine".

I hired a tutor to get me over the bumps with my new Windows 7.0 operating system, which I consider user-unfriendly. Sandie, my tutor, was very taken with Mrs. Gray and vice versa. Mrs. Gray was abnormally friendly when Sandie was here and I asked if she and her husband would consider adopting my cat. They were delighted to do so. They bought cat toys, they built her a perch to sit on and a fancy cat box that rakes the poop, places it in a gift box and ties it with a bow....I jest...but it was one fancy litter box! They built a beautiful custom screen to shield the litter box from stranger's eyes, and I said, "Thank you, Lord, for sending me these people to take my cat and love her". I told them she was almost a "perfect cat", that she had stayed with Julie while I was gone and had done very well. They brought her an Easter card and gift. Sandie brought her husband and mother over to meet "Mittens" (They changed her name.). They brought a friend over to meet their new "baby". The clincher was Sandie's mother and her friends were planning a "kitty shower" for Sandie and Mittens. I continued to be so thankful!

I wrote a Cat Contract, stating what she did, what she didn't do, what she liked and didn't like, that I would cat-sit her when and if they traveled and that if she failed to bond and adjust to her new home, I would take her back. I put the contract in a large envelope with her medical record and put it with her schtuff. Before transfer, I took her paraphernalia, her feeder, her drinker, her toys and her mats over and Sandie placed them in her home. I then filled two coffee cans with some of the contents of her litter box and told them to sprinkle it around outside their townhome so if she should get out, she could "smell" her way back home. I thought to myself, "This is going to be such a neat transfer". I am so happy, no more cat sitting bills, no more veterinary bills, no more concern about her being lonesome. She will be with people who want her and will love her, I am free at last!!

The transfer moment arrived. I delivered Mrs. Gray in her carrier, we went in, I turned her out and she proceeded to calmly prowl around the place looking and sniffing about. Sandie and her husband served wine and we toasted the event. Mrs. Gray (Mittens) was acting cute and jumped up on Dick's lap and was rubbing on Sandie. (Thank you, Lord). I left. I called Bill and told. Him, "I AM CAT-FREE!!

One day later, Sandie called and told me Mittens was friendly but seemed restless. She said, "I don't think she likes us". I told her to give her time to adjust. Day two arrived and Sandie called and told me Mitten's tail never stops swishing and she sits on her perch looking out, and paces and meows. Meows? This is a cat that rarely meowed and when she did it was the tiniest meow in the whole wide world. Meows?

I decided to call Julie and ask her about the times she had kept Mrs. Gray, and I wanted the facts. There was a momentary silence. Julie then admitted that my cat had been very naughty, that she had climbed up her fireplace chimney and sat on a ledge among the soot and cinders and came down only to eat and defecate, after which she would return to her perch. She was mean to Julie's cat and she told me she brought her home after three days because she didn't want her around anymore. I wanted to euthanize Julie about this time; I told her she had made a big liar out of me because I had assured Sandie and Dick that Mrs. Gray had been a good kitty away from home. Julie said, "She wasn't".

Day Three: Sandie called and said Mittens had urinated a large puddle right beside her fancy litter box with the screen. She also said Dick scolded her and yelled, "Naughty kitty" at Mittens. So Sandie was mad at Dick for doing that. The cat was mad at Dick for doing that.

Day Four: The phone rang. It is Sandie, she is crying. She tells me the cat doesn't like Dick, because he yelled at her, and they were supposed to be friends by this time. Mittens was still swishing her tail, pacing and had begun to pee and poop all over the house. Sandie said her mom was mad at her husband for alienating the cat, her father was mad at her (Sandie) for getting the cat in the first place, her mom was mad at her husband for being mad at Sandie for getting the cat. Dick was still mad at the cat, Sandie was mad at Dick and the cat was mad at everyone. She said, "We are all mad at each other, my family is falling apart". Tears…Tears. I said, "Give it one more day, and if she doesn't shape up, I will come and get her.

Day five: The phone rings, it is Sandie in tears. Mittens had bitten Dick and scratched Sandie and they were not minor injuries, they were wounds! Sandie had a hunk torn out of her finger. I said, "Pack her up, I will come get her". I wanted to bring a euthanasia kit and do her in on the spot. They put all of Mrs. Gray's schtuff in a big basket and placed it by the front door, at which time she sat down beside it and didn't move. No tail swish. No meow. And she held her urine. She waited.

When I arrived she skittered away. And skittered some more. No one can catch a skittering cat inside a house. We all tried. I knew she knew I was angry with her. She has always been able to read my mind. Always. This time she was scared, she knew I was furious. I told Sandie and Dick to take a seat and let me handle it. Mrs. Gray had gone under the dining room table and was hunkered down with her feet folded under. Her eyes didn't leave my face. I told her quietly, "You will not move. If you do I will kill you. I am picking you up and taking you home." I slowly walk across the room, staring into her face, and her face turned up toward mine as I drew closer. She did not move. Some feral neurological instinct told her she was in danger of becoming extinct. When I leaned over to pick her up, I was amazed to see that her eyes were solid black, pupils totally dilated. She was a black-eyed cat. No green showing. She didn't move. I picked her up, put her in her carrier, Dick carried her basket of schtuff to the car and we returned home.

I released her from her carrier, placed her mats about in their usual places, set up her feeder and her waterer, emptied the two coffee cans that contained contents from her litter box (Yes, I got those back, too.) and she curled up on a mat and went sound asleep. She had won the day. I was out-witted and out-maneuvered by a cat with a brain the size of a lima bean.

> Now my cat is back home, happy as a clam and I feel like I have re-married. I am married to my cat. She shares my bed!! She still reads my mind. She has lapsed back into Miss Perfect Cat.

A PASSING THOUGHT...
Mary Jo Bogatto

Afraid..

Commitment...

Life..

Love..

Loss...

Afraid..

New ...

Beginnings...

Life..

Love..

Loss..

Breathe...

Apprehensive..

Scared...

Fearful...

Frightened...

Life...

A PEACEFUL WORLD?
Nellie Venselaar
(In Memoriam 1919-2013)

What are we doing for the Earth?
Let's enjoy the serenity of this world
Without devastation of people, countries or towns;
Without destruction of esthetic ancient buildings,
Castles, acropolis, museums.

Destroying nature in wartime is horrible enough,
But deforestation, oil spills,
With its loss of sea life and birds, is
The most important unleashing destruction of nature.

As Michael Jackson expresses so beautifully in his Earth Song:
Where is that Peace forever?
Where is that wonderful world without borders?

No thundering, blustering guns and war machines disturbing land and life,
Tranquil music only Mozart or Mendelssohn could create,
With now and then happy rhythms for little tykes to dance on,
Or teenagers to enjoy in upbeat cheerful jazz.

When humans can get their own act together for the ultimate harmony,
Only then may we start putting our soul
Into making joyful relaxing music together.

And form a world of freedom and peace
So the children in this wonderful world
May succeed With Flying Colors.

Maybe we should start with ourselves,
With energy, enthusiasm,
As well as an attitude of faith,
May we rise over all earthly problems
Or soar above it like the eagle.

A PRAYER TO THE PORCELAIN GOD
By Hugh A. Barlow

Mark Anthony stares at his reflection in the mirror behind the bar. Twining tendrils of smoke hang thick in the room. A few stools down sits a mousy woman who has ALMOST everything right. She is just a bit too short. Her eyes are just a bit too big, a bit too far apart, and are just a shade off from being green. They are almost a muddy brown. Her ears are a bit too large, her lips a bit too full. Her dirty blonde hair is a bit too stringy and does not really cover her ears well. Her breasts? Well, they are far too big for her slender frame. In short, while not ugly, by no stretch of the imagination would she be considered beautiful. Mark fingers the golden emblem of his god while he waves two fingers in the air to get the bartender's attention. The tender comes, and Mark yells out over the noise of the crowd.

"ANOTHER JACK FOR ME, AND ONE OF WHATEVER THE LADY IS HAVING."

The tender nods without saying a word, pours two fingers into Mark's glass, and mixes up another fruity concoction for the target of Mark's attentions. The bartender passes the drink on to the woman, and points to Mark when she asks who it is from. After a minute or so, the woman moves down and sits next to him.

"Thanks for the drink." she purrs as she leans forward to speak into his ear, "I'm Diana." She puts out her hand in greeting.

Mark clasps her hand gently and simply says, "Mark."
In her cleavage, Mark is able to discern a golden heart with the image of an arrow piercing it. A bow is super-imposed over both.

"I see you are a devotee of Cupid." Mark says.

“I notice that you are a follower of Bacchus.” Diana winks.

Mark fingers the little gold plated toilet seat that hangs from the chain around his neck. It is one of several symbols that Mark uses to inform strangers of his affiliation. In choosing this symbol, Mark shows that he is less a traditionalist than the conservative lyre symbol would imply. Both have a similar shape, but the toilet seat is more associated with “praying to the porcelain god” than actually praying to Bacchus. Mark hopes this will convey more of the “party spirit” that is part of his life than the other aspects of Bacchanalia. He glances toward the hallway that leads to the private rooms at the back of the meeting house. He raises his eyebrows a bit and inclines his head toward the back of the room.

“Wanna go somewhere where we can talk in private?” he asks.

“Sure.”

Mark again signals the bartender and yells, “A FIFTH AND A PITCHER.”

A short time later, the bartender hands him a flask and a pitcher filled with Diana's drink. Mark again motions toward the back to Diana after paying the tab. Diana leads as they walk to the desk at the entrance of the hallway. She insists on paying for the room. Mark takes this as a good sign. It means that she is not a temple prostitute or slave, but is merely a follower of Cupid/Eros. He may get out of this encounter spending less than he had expected.

As they walk down the dim hallway, Mark spies a huddled form on the floor. The sound of retching and the smell of alcohol laced vomit are overpowering, and he and Diana gingerly step around the growing puddle.

“I'm glad our room is on the second floor.” Diana said. “The worst of the drunks can't climb the stairs.”

The comment makes Mark a little uncomfortable, but he decides to press on despite his discomfort. He does not plan to make the relationship permanent, so it really doesn't matter what Diana thinks about his past-time. As they walk along, Mark admires

Diana's form from behind. He is a bit startled when Diana stops and inserts a key into the door. He was distracted by the scenery, and had lost track of where he was going. The door opens to show a spacious room with a low table. Couches line one wall, and near the open window and facing it is a love seat. On the wall opposite the couches is a day bed that could be used for sitting or for sleeping. It is large enough to accommodate two comfortably.

Mark flips the switch near the door, turning on the "Do not disturb" sign, and locks the door. He places the tray with the pitcher, the flask, and his glass on the low table. Diana places her glass next to his, and motions to him to join her on the love seat. They sit making the kind of small talk that two strangers who are interested in each other make, and after a short time, Diana begins to remove Mark's clothing and leads him toward the day bed. As they rest, after their communion, there is a commotion outside the window.

"Repent, for the kingdom of God is at hand!" comes the cry from outside. "Turn away from your false gods and follow the one TRUE God!"

Looking out of the window and down, Mark sees a lone figure in a pool of light across the street from the meeting house. Spotlighted is a man of indiscriminate age. Mark can see that he is wearing an expensive business suit and a scarlet colored silk tie with a white cross emblazoned in it.

"Gods, damned Christians!" Mark spits. "No WAY would I become a slave to ANY man, not even a god. Those stupid silk ties they wear denote their bondage to their god, did you know that?" Mark looks back at Diana. "Ties used to be a symbol of slavery in Rome during the ancient days." he continues.

"I did not know that." Diana shows her disinterest.

"Yeah," Mark says, "It used to be that the slaves in ancient Rome would wear a tie to symbolize the noose of a rope. This way, you could tell who was a freeman, and who was a slave. The Christians adopted this symbolism to show that they were slaves to their god. The habit gradually fell out of favor with the rest of Roman society because of this co-opting of symbolism. The true slaves did not want to be mistakenly identified as Christians. Gods, how I wish it were still legal to feed those fanatics to the lions!"

Mark's veins pulse purple on his neck and forehead. 'Why would anyone want to give up his god to follow some religious fanatic?" he spat. "Give up all this fun for WHAT? What do they get out of the suffering?"

Diana motions to Mark to sit next to her on the love seat. She slowly begins to smooth his dark hair and to softly croon, "There, there. Settle down. You don't have to listen to those nuts, you know."

"I know, yeah, I know. It just bugs me that they consider their god to be better than mine."

A commotion outside draws Mark to the window again. A Centurion has arrived with his ceremonial spear and horse hair plume. He is brocaded in a scarlet tunic as a sign of his office. Having braced the Christian and pinned him to the wall, the Centurion begins the process of binding his hands behind his back.

"May you ROT in HADES!" Mark shouts out the window to the Christian as he is being arrested.

"Gods!" Mark looks back to Diana and says, "He is likely to just get a slap on the wrist by the magistrate and a fine for disorderly conduct. What has happened to our society?"

Diana rises from the love seat and joins Mark as the disorderly protester is frog marched away. "Well, I for one would never be like one of them." Diana informs Mark. "I like being a follower of Eros too much. No way would I give up all of this! I have considered converting to following my namesake, however."

Mark starts at that. "The goddess Diana? Isn't she also known as Artemis?"

“Yes.”

“Lord Bacchus, Dionysus, help me!” thinks Mark in a short prayer. “Artemis is the huntress and the goddess of childbirth... maybe I should have used protection instead of assuming that a follower of Cupid would want to protect herself! I'll bet she's an Artemisian using Cupid as camouflage. What do I do now?” Mark stares at Diana with the startled look of a deer caught in a spotlight.

A telling smile crosses Diana's face.

A REVERSAL OF FATE
Jack King

Little Akeem cried when his parents died. He was only six. He cried again when the authorities took him away to a madrasa, a home for orphaned and abandoned boys on the outskirts of Islamabad. His duty and purpose in the ensuing years would be to learn Arabic and to rock back and forth in a chair for hours on end reciting verses from the Koran. When he wasn't praying, or reciting, or listening to lectures about the necessity of total submission to the will of Allah, he was on a busy sidewalk or street corner begging for money to take back to his teachers. There were occasions when they said he collected less than he should have, and they beat him. One day a teacher wielding a cricket bat beat him so badly that he was left with a broken leg, and when it healed it was crooked and he walked with a limp.

By the age of ten, he was too old to beg. A ten-year-old does not elicit sympathy from those who give coins to raggedy little beggars. A ten-year-old is capable of demanding physical work. Akeem still had to pray, and recite verses, and listen to lectures, but he also had chores to do. He swept and mopped floors, did dishes and laundry, and helped to tend the vegetable garden at the madrasa. Occasionally he was hired out as day labor to paint houses or fill potholes in driveways or parking lots.

When he was fourteen, Akeem became friends with a seventeen-year-old called Farook, who was the personal chauffeur and manservant for Mullah Samarra, the cleric in charge of all the madrasas in the Taliban-controlled sector of the city. Every morning Farook would load some of the little ones into the back of the Mullah's Japanese-made pickup and drop them off on downtown street corners to beg for money. At the end of the day, he would go and pick them up and bring them back to their respective madrasas where they would turn in the money they had collected. Farook would put the bills and coins in a bag and then have the little ones turn pockets inside out and take off their shoes, if they happened to be wearing any, to make sure they weren't concealing rupees for themselves. He warned them that the punishment for stealing was the chopping off of the offending hand, that stealing from a madrasa was equivalent to stealing from Allah. Farook would then give the bags of money to Mullah Samarra and from whichever madrasa the mullah had spent the day, he would drive the old man back to his house. The mullah was responsible for paying the bills and the teachers at his schools, but Farook suspected that the man spent more on his own personal luxuries, as no luxuries whatsoever were visible at the schools.

One day Farook asked Akeem if he could keep a secret. Akeem nodded, and his friend confided in him that he had met a girl in a downtown shop, and they had fallen in love, and he planned to run away with her and get married. He would need money, so he had decided that he would take the moneybags from each madrasa at the end of the day and make his escape in the Mullah's pickup to a distant part of the country. Akeem was dumbfounded but agreed not to say a word. He did, however, ask how Farook was going to support himself and his bride. Farook said he was going to sell the pickup and buy a vending cart like the ones you see downtown offering portions of roasted meat wrapped in flatbread.

Akeem had seen those pushcarts many times when he was out begging on the sidewalks. The only meat the boys found on their plates at the madrasa was a few flecks in the rice, and so the aroma of roasted chicken, beef, or water buffalo wafting from those carts was tantalizing to say the least. Some of the boys, when they had collected a generous amount while begging, had furtively patronized those vendors and gobbled down their purchase in nearby alleys or other hiding places.

Farook told Akeem that when he got his pushcart, he would sell the meat at half price when his customer was a little beggar.
The following day was marked by a shocking event. While making his getaway with the money, Farook barreled into a turn much too fast, skidded into a tree, wrecked the pickup, and knocked himself out. He regained consciousness in police custody and was returned to the madrasa in handcuffs for the mullah to decide his

punishment. The teachers locked him in a storage room while the mullah walked down the street to look for a surgeon. The next morning, the surgeon came and removed Farook's right hand while the teachers held him down. All the children heard his screams. An hour later, the mullah drove up in a newly acquired, late model Nissan pickup and drove Farook away. All the children saw the bloody bandage at the end of the stricken boy's right forearm, and nobody at the madrasa ever saw him again.

When Akeem was sixteen, Mullah Samarra sent him and the other boys his age off to a military training camp near the Afghan border where young men were trained to fight with the Taliban. The trainers at the camp rejected him because of his bad leg. They sent him back to the madrasa, and later that day Mullah Samarra dropped by in his pickup. He told Akeem to get in the back of the truck and he took the boy home with him. The trip took less than ten minutes.

Mullah Samarra's house was a big cream-colored stucco affair built in the Arabic style. It sat on top of a hill, and to get up there from the street on foot, visitors obviously had to struggle about a hundred meters up a rather steep slope, something that would have been difficult for a boy with a crooked leg. Fortunately, there was a driveway, and Mullah Samarra put the pickup in first gear, roared up the hill, and parked behind an ornate wrought-iron gate at the side of his big house. There was a side entrance, but the mullah led the boy around to the front of the house because he wanted to show Akeem the impressive main entrance. It was framed by a fancy filigreed ogee arch, and above the arch in the flowing curves of Arabic script was the word Samarra molded in relief into the stucco; Mullah Samarra was obviously quite proud of his name. Akeem knew that Samarra was also a city in Iraq not far from Bagdad. He was also familiar with an old story about a man who fled Bagdad for Samarra to escape death, and in Samarra, the man ran straight into the arms of death. One of his young friends at the madrasa had smuggled the story in, and although they were forbidden to read anything except the Koran, all the boys had read the story in secret and sometimes, when they were not being watched, they engaged in animated discussions about free will versus fate.

Inside the house, Mullah Samarra told the boy to sit down at a table in a small room that opened off the main hallway, and soon another man came in to join them. Akeem immediately recognized the man as the teacher who had beaten him with a cricket bat and broken his leg. His name was Abdul. The mullah sat down first and then Abdul sat down, and they faced the boy across the table.

The mullah smiled amiably at Akeem and began to speak. "I know you are disappointed that you are unable to fulfill your duty as a valiant Taliban soldier, but there are other ways to serve Allah that are just as honorable, if not more so. Allow me to describe the situation outside my domicile. When you walk out my front door, and go down the slope to the street and then look to the right, you will see a bus stop about a block away. It is on the near side of the street. Every morning about seven thirty, a busload of students approaches from the left, passes my house, and halts at the bus stop to pick up more students. The students on the bus are not virtuous students of Islam like you but unholy infidels who come from an enclave a mere kilometer west of our own neighborhood. They are vile creatures who eat the unclean flesh of pigs, sleep with dogs, and allow their wives and daughters onto the sidewalks unescorted, bareheaded, and barelegged. The infidel men blatantly flout the commandments delivered to us by the Prophet, may peace be with him, and the infidel women are nothing but filthy whores. Many of the sinful youth aboard that bus are about your age and you will appear to fit right in at the bus stop … provided you wear a backpack."

Mullah Samarra paused for a moment, and smiled again at Akeem, who now looked pale and nervous. The mullah continued, "When we were in the hallway a moment ago you may have noticed that along the north wall is a row of photographs of young men, some of whom were once your classmates at the madrasa. It is the Wall of Martyrs, and it honors the faithful who have given their lives to advance our holy cause. They are happy in Paradise now, and are each served eagerly and faithfully by seventy beautiful young virgins who cater to their every desire. When you board the bus and detonate your backpack, you, too, will promptly be made whole again in your own joyous Paradise. So, Akeem, if you will put a smile on your brave young face, Abdul will now take your photograph for display tomorrow and forever on the Wall of Martyrs."

Akeem's face went white. He looked vacantly at the mullah and then into the camera that Abdul was pointing at him. The shutter clicked and he was momentarily blinded by the flash. He gagged for an instant and then threw up on the table.

Mullah Samarra jumped up from his chair, and for a moment Akeem could see the hot glare of anger in his eyes. Abdul fled toward the kitchen and came back with a damp towel. As he cleaned up the mess, the mullah stepped out of the room and unlocked another room across the hall. He returned with a black canvas backpack and hoisted it onto the table. It was firmly stuffed, and Akeem knew full well that its contents were not books or school supplies.

"This is nothing to be frightened of," said the mullah, patting the backpack with his right hand. "The weapons grade explosive is powerful, quick, and painless. When you push the detonator button you will experience not even a millisecond of this world, only the euphoria of coming fully alive in a perfect new body in the next. And you will thank me eternally for what I have done for you."

The mullah unzipped the backpack and pulled out a short metal tube about the size of a fat stick of chalk. On one end was the detonator button and on the other end was a pair of wires that extended downward into the backpack. Akeem felt a sickening urge to grab the device and push the button right then and there in the company of his tormentors. But he held back, and after a few seconds of silence, he whispered, "Very well, I will do it."

The mullah replied, "And you will never regret it, my boy. Abdul will now show you to your room where you can get some rest." As Akeem followed Abdul out into the wide hallway, he looked up at the Wall of Martyrs and recognized the face on one photo as that of his old friend, Farook, and he felt a sharp pang of ineffable sadness.

Later, Akeem lay on his bed staring at the ceiling and racking his brain for a way to escape. Maybe Farook had nothing to live for or maybe everything to die for, but he, Akeem, was not going to voluntarily throw his life away and snatch other lives away while doing it. He looked at the window but saw steel bars on the outside. After sundown, he tried his door and happily found it open. He stepped out into the hallway. The hall nightlight was on. Across the hall, the bathroom door next to the bomb room was open and he entered. He saw a flush toilet, a lavatory, a towel bar, and a waste basket half full of soiled toilet tissue. He left the bathroom and quietly tested other doors. The front door was locked with a keyed deadbolt and could not be opened. The back door was similarly configured. Akeem tried every door in the house and all of them were securely locked except his own bedroom and the bathroom that he had recently inspected. All the windows were like the ones in his room, secured with steel bars on the outside. He went back to his bed and lay awake in the darkness. An hour later, he heard footsteps and pretended to be asleep. Someone with a flashlight looked in on him, but he didn't open his eyes to see who it was. When the door closed, he waited till he heard the sound of departing footsteps, then got up and cracked the door and peeped out. The hall nightlight was still on, and he saw the mullah go into the bathroom across the hall and close the door. Akeem left his room and made his way quietly to the mullah's room. The door was now unlocked. Akeem went in quickly and removed the keys from the pocket of the robe on the chair near the bed. He closed the door on his way out and slipped silently back to his room. He heard footsteps again and heard the sound of the mullah's door closing, followed by the rasping groan of bedsprings as the old man got back into bed.

Minutes later, Akeem removed the blanket from his bed and slipped out into the hallway with the mullah's keys in his right hand and the rolled blanket under his left arm. He opened the door to the room from which the mullah had earlier retrieved the backpack. Once inside, he placed the rolled blanket on the floor across the bottom of the door so that light could not escape and betray his presence. He slid a hand across the wall next to the door until he found the light switch. He turned on the light and carefully surveyed the room. On a counter he saw the backpack bomb, and beside it was a cell phone lying on a piece of paper with a phone number printed on it. He unzipped the backpack and the first thing he saw was the detonator tube with the push button on one end and the wires coming out the other. He pulled the backpack open as far as he could and traced the pair of wires down to the end where they were knotted and sewn securely to the bottom of the backpack, not imbedded in the explosive. Realizing that the detonator mechanism was phony, he searched further until he found the tip of an antenna sticking out of the plastic explosive. He then realized that the mullah was planning to trigger the bomb himself remotely with the cell phone. He would probably do it from outside the front door of the house from where he could see the bus as it drove away with its newly boarded passengers. Akeem opened a cabinet door and saw a dozen empty backpacks of various colors. He took a black one like the one that held the bomb. He opened a tall floor cabinet and saw blocks of plastic explosive stacked on the shelves. He opened the cabinet under the counter and found a large padlocked chest inside. He found its key on the mullah's key ring and opened the chest. It was full of cash, a thick layer of bills on top and several kilos of coins beneath. "So this is where the money goes after the little boys spend the day begging on the hot, hard sidewalks." He stuffed his black backpack with large-denomination bills and added just enough coins to give it the right heft. He carried it to the bathroom, dumped out the wastebasket, put the backpack of cash inside, picked up the soiled paper, and tossed it back in, concealing the dummy bomb from view. He washed his hands, went back to the bomb room, retrieved his blanket, closed the door, and went back to his bedroom hoping that the old mullah had a prostate problem. Apparently, he did; a half hour later he heard footsteps, and while the mullah was in the bathroom again, Akeem hastily returned the keys to the old man's room.

Abdul woke Akeem at 6:50 a.m. and took him back to the table across the hall from the bomb room. Mullah Samarra emerged from the room carrying the lethal backpack by the top strap. "The bus will be here in about thirty minutes," he said, "and it will take you about twenty minutes to make it to the bus stop with your bad leg, so we better get you ready. Stand up, and we'll help you with your load." In seconds the bomb was in place, centered behind

Akeem's shoulders. "When you find a seat on the bus, make sure it is next to the window and no one is sitting next to you that might interfere with your holy mission. Remove the backpack and sit down with it in your lap. Don't unzip it until you are ready to push the button."

At this point, Akeem began to retch and gag and suddenly darted across the hall and into the bathroom. Abdul and the mullah heard more retching followed by the sound of the toilet flushing, and then the boy emerged looking pale and sick. They noted that he was still wearing the backpack. Abdul took him by the hand and said, "We haven't much time, boy; let's get going."

Because of Akeem's crooked leg, the descent to the street was somewhat slow, even with Abdul holding his hand to steady him. Then once they were at the bottom of the hill and on the sidewalk, Abdul jerked his hand away as if he'd been holding something unclean and disgusting. "One block to go," he sneered. "And now you can surely walk without my help."

"Just enough time for me to recite to you a cautionary tale, "said Akeem.

"I don't want to hear it," said Abdul.

"If you won't listen to it, I won't get on the bus."

"Then I'll drag you to the bus and throw you in."

"And before I'm inside, I'll start screaming about the bomb."

Abdul stopped in his tracks and looked at Akeem. "All right, tell me the tale, but make it quick."

"It's about a man in Bagdad who saw Death look at him and make a gesture. The man concluded that Death intended to take him, so he fled Bagdad and went to Samarra to hide from Death. What he didn't know was that Death had intended all along to take him in Samarra. Is that quick enough for you?"

"Quite, and it's the stupidest story I ever heard.

"I told you it's a cautionary tale. And I'm telling you now that you have to read between the lines."

"I don't have time for such nonsense. Look, the bus is coming."

A boy and a girl, each wearing backpacks were waiting at the bus stop when Akeem and Abdul arrived. As the bus approached, they all looked at the banner above the windshield to assure themselves it was the right bus. Bagdad Heights was spelled out on the banner. They all boarded the bus except Abdul. As soon as the door closed behind the youngsters, he turned back in the direction from whence he had come and began to walk very fast. He knew that Mullah Samarra was holding the cell phone and that the mullah was a very impatient, impulsive man who might detonate the bomb any second. As soon as the bus pulled away from the curb, Abdul began to run. He knew he was running from death, and it made him think about Akeem's cautionary tale. He remembered that the word Bagdad was on the bus banner. When he got to the path that led up the hill, he turned left and began his ascent. He was more than halfway up when he saw the mullah come out the front door and stop under the entry arch, cell phone in hand. The mullah gazed out in the direction of the bus, which was now almost two blocks away. Abdul could see the word Samarra above the arch and suddenly it all clicked. Akeem had somehow managed to switch backpacks, and the bomb was still in the house along with an additional huge cache of explosives! Abdul watched in horror as Mullah Samarra lifted the phone to get a clear view of the keypad and then began to type in the numbers. "No!" screamed Abdul, but the mullah appeared not to hear. "Stop! Stop!" screamed Abdul, but the mullah's thumb was already on the talk button.

Akeem was kneeling on the back seat of the bus looking out the rear window. Under his breath, he whispered, "This one's for you, Farook." All in the searing flash of an instant, the entire hilltop behind the bus disintegrated and the atmosphere fulminated with billowing spears of black smoke and flying debris. The bus driver floored the gas pedal and the bus lurched forward, its acceleration boosted by the shock wave that overtook it from behind. Akeem almost fell off the seat as he swung his legs around to sit down. He was shaking and simultaneously suppressing a smile. For the first time ever, he was free to direct his own life and had the resources to do it. He took off the backpack and hugged it tightly as visions of new dangers and opportunities danced fiercely before his eyes.

A SOLUTION
Eunice Greenhaus

The differences between me and thee
Are oh so easy for me to see
I'm so rounded, pleasingly plump
You're just a big fat ugly lump
I can giggle hardly moving my jaw
You sound like a jackass with a hearty hee-haw

Isn't it amazing how we can't agree
On how I should be like you, or you be like me
Wouldn't the world be a better place
If all those insults we could replace
With kindly words and gracious deeds
To meet each person's daily needs

A TROUBADOR'S LAMENT
Don Clifford

There was a time when I with rhyme
Could sing a song so fair,
Of Kings and Queens, of simple Beings,
Of Maidens tressed in flaxen hair.

My song was told 'bout Knights of old,
Who roamed a troubled land.
They fought with might to set things right,
Then gently kissed a Damsel's hand.

Alack, alas. Those days are passed.
Chivalry is all but dead.
No more good deed. Because of greed
The crude and guile now rule instead.

My song near died, my sight dim eyed.
Adrift in ebbing sands of time
My voice was still; I had no will,
No muse, no dream nor word to rhyme.

But then I heard a quickened word
Far off from a Western Shire.
Lassies and Lads, some dressed in plaids,
Did deeds I so much admire.

With trembling hope, I searched to ope'
A lost but not forgotten door.
To see first hand some unknown band
Bring couth to this most "sauvage" shore.

In Edin-town, a burg renowned,
There found upon the green,
Were homespun vests, the gaily dressed,
And burly Knights in armor sheen.

From whence they came or what their name
I knew not right away,
Until I asked a comely Lass.
She said they were the S.C.A.

A Herald cried with mien of pride,
"Now, hearken back to days of yore,
For 'tis not fit that we forget
The task, the skill, the passed on lore."

A mighty shout! I whirl about…
A brave Knight smacked another bold!
'Twas all in fun, and one by one
Each feigned a wound and slipped his hold.

Inside the Hall a Fair Trade Mall
Contained all sorts of craft to see…
The Armorour, a Bookbinder,
And skills in Hand Calligraphy.

From wire to coil, each link with toil
Was soon wrought forth a suit of mail.
A sheet of writ was stitched a bit,
Then glued into a Book of Tale.

Ah! So much more was there in store
For all those wishing to behold.
But time was o'er, my feet were sore,
The warming clime had turned to cold.

A cheering thought that what I sought
Had not yet died away -
Just hid from sight 'till time was right
To re-appear another day.

The Torch was passed, the Age at last
Is twisting hard to re-align
With new found zeals and great ideals…
Can Camelot be far behind?

ADDICTED*
Frank Cortazo

Twenty-year old Norma Ramber felt uncomfortable in the dimly-lit room full of strangers. She agreed to accompany her mother to this place because, at the time, it seemed like a good idea. Now, she regretted it. Almost everyone around her squirmed and mumbled.

"Mom, I can't stand it anymore!" Norma fidgeted and twitched on the edge of her seat.

"This...this place! Why didn't you tell me it would be like this? I'm going crazy! I've got to have it! I've got to or---!"

She opened her purse.

"No!" Mrs. Ramber said. "I don't want to hear it."

Inside the purse, Norma's mother saw a pack of cigarettes next to some folded one-dollar bills. A small container of pills rested beside them. *This is not good*, she thought. She looked at the empty soft drink cup in her daughter's hand. *How many of those things did she drink today already?*

"You're...so nervous...playing with that empty cup. The caffeine must be very strong."

"I like soft drinks," Norma said. "They're as good as beer and wine."

"And you drink too much of those. They're...not doing your health any good."

Norma sulked. She looked at the people around them. Everyone else was just as restless and nervous as she was. The only calm person in the room was her mother.

Mrs. Ramber also looked at the other people around her and shook her head in disbelief. *They're just as bad, if not worse than Norma. I wonder how many of them are hardcore alcoholics?*

After a while, Norma said "This is not the type of place I want to spend time in. You knew this would happen."

"Norma, you agreed to come here with me. I brought you here, at this particular time, so you could spend some time without it. I've told you many times already, you've...you've become addicted to it. You're obsessed with it, just like so many people your age. Just like those who are here. It's...it's not---"

"It's not what?" interrupted Norma. "It's not normal? It's not healthy? It's not the 'in' thing? Just because you never got to experience it when you were my age?"

"That's not...you're not being fair," her mother said. "Not to me and, certainly, not to yourself. Why must you continue doing it just because everybody else does? Your brother Jeffrey doesn't--"

"I'm not Jeffrey! He's so busy with his writing and with his stripper girl friend, he doesn't even know we exist anymore."

"Well, at least he outgrew his obsession with pla---"

"Mom, this is a different time!" For no apparent reason, she scratched her arm. "It's a different world. We need things like this to survive. I need it. And...even you."

"I don't need something like that to give me thrills," her mother said. "There was a time when life was simpler. One didn't have to become dependent upon unnecessary---"

"Mom!" Norma cut her off. She rolled her eyes and said. "You're...you're so...old-fashioned! That was way back during the 'old ages.' Times have changed."

She could not believe how her mother still tried to fill her with old-fashioned ideas. What would one expect, though, from someone her age? Her mother was truly old! And not just because of the grayness in her hair nor the wrinkles around her eyes.

She set aside the empty cup and scratched her arm again.

"You know," Mrs. Ramber said. "You're going to get that arm infected. Every time you're without that...thing...you scratch that same area. Those marks...they're...they're becoming...."

Norma looked at her arm. "I don't know why I do that," she said, as she pushed back her long, wavy chestnut-colored hair. "It's just...a habit."

"Yes, it is," her mother agreed. "You've become so… addicted...you need help."

Norma gritted her teeth and held her temper, especially here in this place.

"MOTH-er!" Her sarcastic grin matched the sarcasm in her voice. "Open your eyes. I'm as normal as you and everyone else in here. They just happen to be as nervous and perturbed as I am. Many of them for the same reason as me. At least one person is anxious for a smoke. Maybe twice as many are wishing they could drink a beer. And maybe half of those around us are craving a little roll in the hay!"

"Norma! Stop being vulgar! And...what you're saying...it's not the same thing!"

"I'm not being vulgar! And it is the same thing! They're probably just as 'addicted' to those 'vices' as much or worse than what you claim I am!"

Her mother sighed while she gained control of her emotions. "Norma," she said in a softer tone. "Listen to yourself. That…that...thing, it...it's taken control of your life. All throughout the day. Why, even on the way over here, you couldn't stop yourself. You had to have it. It's...affected your mind. If the police ever...and, especially while driving...! I... and...those marks on your arm! They look bad!"

"Mom! Stop! It's my life. I'm not a little girl anymore. Neither are most of the people here with us. Look around you. Most of them are just as perturbed as I am and --."

At that moment, the dim lights in the room brightened. For one brief second, Norma thought one of them flashed and showed a human figure. *A trick of the light... If Mom thinks I'm seeing things, I won't hear the end of it!*

The figure materialized as a tall man who walked up the aisle to the front of the room. How similar his well-pressed business suit was to those worn by her father! The grayness of his hair clashed with the black-framed eye glasses he wore. *Another old-fashioned know-it-all. Will it never end?*

"Welcome everyone!" the man announced, in a loud voice. "We will begin in a few minutes. I see a lot of you are uncomfortable and nervous. It is to be expected. However, rules must be followed. And, during a special premiere engagement such as this one, absolutely no recording devices are allowed. And that includes cell phones. No calling or texting during the show. You were asked to turn them in at the front lobby. You may retrieve them when you exit the theatre after this special event concludes. Thank you and enjoy the show."

The man left the room. The lights dimmed.

Norma and her mother sat waiting for the show to begin. They said no more to each other. However, just before the event began,

Norma decided to have the last word.

"I'm not addicted to texting on my cell phone," she mumbled, "anymore than Jeffrey used to be addicted to playing video games. Nor, even, anymore than your addiction to soap operas on TV. Nor, I might add, to your coming here, almost every other day."

Her mother did not respond. Already her attention was engrossed in the images that flashed across the big screen.

AND YER LITTLE DAWG, TOO*
Judy Stevens

The year I turned six I knew nothing could ever scare me, 'cause I had brothers. My best friend disagreed though, saying she just knew witches were scarier—especially the green ones. But I couldn't see it. All they did was stand around cackling, stirring big pots and casting spells—like in some school cafeteria. Anyway, I figured if my best friend really believed that, well then she needed to borrow one of my brothers to toughen herself up.

Obviously, we both knew it was prudent to be wary of things like bullies, bad storms and dogs that bite, but witches? Let's just say I was unconvinced.

Turns out I just hadn't met the right witch.

On that fateful day I was busy with the job of being a kid when Mom commanded me to attention. Since she spoke my middle name only under grave circumstances, I knew she must have discovered my latest breach of protocol, and prepared for the worst. Instead I saw her smile and heard her ask if I'd like to see a movie with her—just us girls. We were going to a movie alone without men! This was unprecedented! Mom said the boys couldn't come because it was too scary for them. At last she had recognized my incredible bravery at being the only girl among boys!

As Mom walked to the movie theater I skipped merrily alongside, barely paying attention to her explanation of the movie we were about to see: a little girl and her dog and a big storm and a place over the rainbow and the witch would be scary but everything would turn out fine in the end.

Adults make such a big deal out of words.

Mom halted just short of the theater. She bent down, looked me sternly in the eye; then, with a skeptical look, said she was taking a chance on me being old enough to sit through a serious movie without talking, whining, carrying on or having to go to the bathroom, and did I think I could do all that?

I hate direct questions, particularly demanding answers to things I hadn't paid attention to. But I tell you, when a mom looks at you that way, the operative answer is, "Yes, ma'am."

No talking, bathroom, and what was the rest? I was still trying to remember the details of her order as we entered a wonderland of thick carpeting, plush seats and the mouth-watering smell of popcorn. Excitement swept through me: Mom and I were suddenly part of a bigger world of movie patrons and, best of all, this movie would be in color: the poster said so!

But maybe not: I overheard two old ladies saying this was the tenth anniversary of this movie. Ten years was ancient! It couldn't be in color! I looked up at Mom. She had a happy to be here expression on her face that told me she must have been unaware of how old and out-of-date this film was.

I asked her the obvious question which she answered briskly with a new word for my vocabulary—Technicolor. That did it; I had to know all about that new thing. Her answers were not as scientific as I preferred, but I loved her anyway for trying. She seemed to give a sigh of relief as we joined the crowd shuffling into the theater.

I clutched my bag of popcorn close as we made our way to our seats and thought, how bad could an old movie about a little girl and a dog be, if it was in Technicolor?

The crowd hushed; the movie started.

Right off the bat I broke one of the terms of my agreement with Mom by loudly proclaiming the hype of Technicolor had been a sham. The movie started out black and white; or rather, an old fashioned sepia and cream, like those Victorian-era photos

Grandpa had in his musty old book. My outburst brought titters of laughter from the old ladies and a stern rebuke from Mom, who ordered me to be patient and there'd be color. With a sour disposition I smushed down in my seat, munched my popcorn and tried on patience for size.

It was an ill fit.

On the screen the stupid girl's sappy little song lasted forever, relieved only by the cuteness of her little black dog. I was grateful when the crotchety old lady finally had it with that brat of a girl and confiscated her dog, saving it from a life of drabness.

The tornado was neat, even though it wasn't in color. But it didn't blow that girl away. If it had, I'm sure even my brothers would have cheered.

I'd about had it with this sepia-tinted world just as the house went thump and the girl woke up and grabbed the dog. I let out a whine and got a shush not only from Mom but the elderly ladies, too, who seemed to really be enjoying this old-fashioned movie. I fell silent, my popcorn almost gone, along with my patience.

Well, the girl opened the door and shazam! Vivid color everywhere, saturating the screen and my senses.

At last! Even though it looked artificial and cartoony and not natural, it was color. You have no idea how starved my eyes were for it. It shut me up, all right. I sat mesmerized as the story progressed.

The infamous witch that Mom warned me about turned out to be some wimpy princess-type dressed in pink chiffon riding inside a bubble. Oh please, I thought sarcastically. Where was a real, dyed-in-the-wool Halloween witch to break up all this—niceness?

Just then I got the fright of my life! A deafening thunderclap, blinding flash of red fire and green smoke announced the arrival of the witch to end all witches. Alas, I did not see her, as I was temporarily wedged into the area directly beneath my theater seat.

Mom's head appeared above my hidey-hole. Failing to hide her grin, she said I was missing the show. Reluctantly, I re-entered the world of Technicolor and soon lost myself in the rest of the movie.

I flinched a little but held my ground when the witch to end all witches reappeared. I even felt at the end that the girl was justified in throwing water on her.

Later I told my best friend all about it, except for that brief interlude playing "duck and cover." Mom said that would be our secret, which made me feel grown-up.

Thereafter though, Mom and her sisters would smile and titter at the oddest moments whenever I was around.

ANOTHER DAY
Judy Stevens

I stand in front of an antique store called "Another Day." The name intrigues me. I peer through dusty front windows. It looks deserted, like this street—but cooler. The afternoon sun is hot on my neck.

The bell above the door tinkles a welcome as I enter. No one says Hello. Dust fills my nostrils and I sneeze. I drag a tissue from my pocket. No one says *Bless You.*

I blink my watery eyes in the subdued light. Dust swirls in the air: I have disturbed the dust of centuries. I look around. Nothing else moves. The muffled weight of years has ground the interior of this place to dust.

The light enters hesitantly, as if it doesn't belong. I hesitate too: I don't belong. I think of leaving. I glance at the little bell atop the door then shrug: I can always leave.

I move slowly through the clutter. I look at my watch: five minutes have fled into eternity. I glance around, fingering my watch as if it will guard my reality. No one says *Hello.*

I study a paperweight then gingerly set it back in its exact spot, the spot without dust. I wonder who would take my money, should I want to buy it. I strain my ears: off to the side a clock tick-tocks. No one says *May I Help You.*

Lifetimes are embedded here. I cast aside unease and wander the eras like a time-traveler, imagining those who once had owned these artifacts.

A line of shelves halts me. I look back across the clutter to the far windows and the door I came through. I see the little bell above the door. Suddenly it seems too far. My back crawls: I have gone too far. Annoyed, I shrug it off. I can always leave.

I look at my feet. They are covered with dust.

I turn back to the shelves. I glance at book titles and objects smothered in dust. If I stand here long enough will this dust smother me too? My deep breath turns into a ragged cough. No one responds.

Then I see it.

I am five again. I hold it in my hand and the years dissolve, and I am that child. Memory sharpens. The world is young again. It terrifies me.

Can memory be purchased? Can I be five again every time I touch this—object?

No.

With shaking hands I set it back on the shelf. I look around this—mausoleum for objects. I look across centuries of clutter to the door I once came through from the world beyond. I know what I must do.

The bell above the door tinkles as I open it to the harsh heat and glare of late afternoon. I hungrily breathe in the heavy, humid air, grateful to not be five.

I close the door. No one says *Goodbye.*

ADDENDUM HAIKU:

Beyond the bookcase
A crack of light
The back door opens.

ARE YOU A BAD EGG OR GOOD EGG
Edna Ratliff

Are you a metaphor or do you eat metaphors? A metaphor is used for something that is not the real meaning. A metaphor can be a word, or group of words. It is a figure of speech.

BAD EGG: Are you a bad egg? A bad egg is old and rotten. You can smell a bad egg without cracking it. If you are a bad egg, you are a bad person just like a rotten egg you stink.

BEAR HUG: Did someone give you a bear hug? When a bear hugs you, the bear comes up from behind you. It puts its arms around your body and holds your arms down. Also, the bear hug is a wrestling hold too. Did you give your friend a bear hug?

BIRDS OF A FEATHER FLOCK TOGETHER: Birds like to be with birds that are like them. Like a Robin only flies and stays with other Robins. They are called birds of a feather flock together. People who do the same things together are also known as birds of a feather flock together. Do you and your friends like the same things? People may say you and your friends are like birds of a feather flock together?

BIRD LEGS: Do you have bird legs? Storks, cranes and heron have long thin bird legs. These birds can fish in deep water because of their long legs. If you have long thin legs you may have bird legs.

BOOKWORM: Are you a bookworm? An insect larva can't stop eating the paste and the binders of books. The insect is a bookworm. Do you read all the time and can't stop reading? You are a bookworm.

BUG OFF: People do not like bugs to land on them. They swat at the bugs, and tell them to bug off. Are you like a bug? Did you pester someone and would not stop. Did they tell you to bug off?

BUSY AS A BEE: Are you busy as a bee? A bee is always in motion. The forager bees collect the nectar. They move the nectar to the house bees. The house bees change the nectar into honey to feed all the bees. Do you rush around trying to get things done? Then you are busy as a bee.

BUTTERFLIES IN YOUR STOMACH: Does your stomach feel funny when you are taking a test, or when you speak in front of the class? You may have butterflies in your stomach. Do you feel the flapping of the wings like butterflies in your stomach?

CLAM UP: Are you like a clam? When a clam is afraid it pulls in its foot and siphon into its shells. A siphon is the clam's neck. Then the clam closes its shells tightly together. When you are scared do you clam up? Are your lips closed tightly together like a clam?

DOG-TIRED: A herding dog is a working dog. A herding dog works all day on a ranch or farm or stock yards. The dog guards sheep, or cows, or goats, or ducks, or reindeer. At the end of the day, the dogs are too tired to eat. The dogs curl up in their beds and sleep. They are dog tired. Do you work hard all day? Are you so tired you can't eat? Do you curl up in bed and sleep? Are you dog tired?

EGGHEAD: Are you an egghead? In 1952, Adlai Stevenson entered the race to become president of the United States. Adlai Stevenson was very smart. His head was bald, and looked like a chicken egg. He was the first egghead. Are you bald? Do you have a head like a chicken egg? Your friends may call you egghead.

ELEPHANT EARS: Do you like to eat elephant ears? You can buy elephant ears at fairs, festivals, and carnivals. The elephant ear is like a yummy thin pastry crust. It has sugar and cinnamon on it. They are shaped like an African Elephant ear. But they are smaller like an Asian elephant ear. Do you eat elephant ears?

EYE LIKE AN EAGLE: Do you have an eye like an eagle? An eagle has very good eyes. When the eagle flies, the eagle can see a mile away. They can see a mouse moving on the ground. An eagle can even see a fish swimming. If you see things your friends don't see, you may have an eye like an eagle.

FROG IN YOUR THROAT: Does your throat feel dry? Do you want to cough? Your voice may squeak like a frog. People may say you have a frog in your throat.

GOOD EGG: Are you a good egg? To check for a good egg hold the egg up to a bright light. You can see if the yellow part of the egg is round, and the white is runny. If no blood spots, cracks, or baby chick starting to form, it is a good egg. If you are a good person, you are a good egg?

HUNGRY AS A BEAR: Are you hungry as a bear? A bear hibernates by sleeping through the winter months without eating. The bear hibernates because it cannot find enough food to eat in the winter. When spring comes the bear wakes up. It is very hungry. The bear cannot wait to find food to eat. When you wake up in the morning are you hungry as a bear?

LIKE A FISH OUT OF WATER: Are you like a fish out of water? When a fish is out of the water it flops all over. The fish is trying to get back into the water. Because a fish cannot breathe oxygen from the air, the fish it is out of its element. When you are in a strange place, you are out of your element. Do you feel like a fish out of water and cannot breathe?

LOOK LIKE A BOILED LOBSTER: A lobster from the state of Maine has a green shell. When the lobster is put in a pot of boiling water the shell turns red. When you sit in the sun too long your skin will turn red. You have a sun burn. People may say you look like a boiled lobster.

MULE EARS: Do you eat mule ears? Mule ears are a pasty (pronounced past-y). You can carry it in your hand. It is beef stew put into a soft dough pouch. They are shaped to look like a mule ear. They are big, because a mule ear is larger than a horse ear. Miners in the Upper Peninsula of Michigan take them down into the mines to eat. Miners like to eat mule ears. Do you eat mule ears?

NIGHT OWL: Are you a night owl? The owls can see better in the dark. That is why an owl stays up all night hunting and sleeps all day. Do you stay up at night watching TV, or playing games on the computer? Do you sleep in the day time? Then you are a night owl?

PACK RAT: Are you a pack rat? The wood rat is known as a pack rat. The rat gathers paper, shiny things, anything it can find. The wood rat drags everything back to its nest. It keeps it forever. Do you keep everything like pizza boxes, pop cans and junky junk in your room? And you never throw anything away. Then you are a pack rat.

PLAY POSSUM: Do you play possum? A possum will play possum if it is afraid. The possum will fall over on the ground. Then the possum will lay there like it is dead. The possum will not move until the danger is gone. Do you try to trick people? Do you pretend you are a sleep and play possum?

QUIET AS A MOUSE: Are you like a mouse? A mouse will sit still and not move. They make no noise. Do you sit still and not move, and don't make a sound? Are you quiet as a mouse?

RED AS A BEET: Have you been out in the sun and red as a beet? A beet is dark red in color because the beet has betalain pigments in it. If you feel embarrassed, or up set your face may turn red. People may say you are as red as a beet.

SLOW AS A SNAIL: Are you slow as a snail? A snail moves very slow. A snail has no legs and only one foot. It moves just over an inch in one minute. It takes a year for the snail to go four miles. Do you walk as slow as a snail?

SQUEAL LIKE A PIG: Do you squeal like a pig? A pig squeals out of fear, hunger, and if the pig is picked up. One pig can squeal louder than an average rock concert. If you scream in a high-pitch voice people may say you squeal like a pig.

TEXAS TURKEY: Do you eat Texas Turkey for Thanksgiving? Back in 1930's during the Great Depression almost all the people were poor. The Texas people found they could eat armadillo. They ate armadillo for Thanksgiving dinner. That's how the armadillo got the name of "Texas turkey." Do you eat Texas Turkey?

WISE AS AN OWL: People think owls are wise because they sit and stare. They make no noise. Do you sit and watch, and say nothing like an owl? Your friends may say you are wise as an owl.

I made up my own metaphor. My metaphor is. Do you work with a mouse? My answer is. Do you work with a mouse on the computer?
How many metaphors can you make up?

How to cook Elephant Ears (with the help of an adult)

2 cups flour
2 tablespoon sugar and1 teaspoon sugar
1/2 teaspoon salt
1 teaspoon baking powder
2 tablespoon shortening
1/2 cup water
Oil (for frying)

TOPPING: mix together 1 cup sugar and 1 teaspoon cinnamon

Mix flour, the sugar, salt, baking powder together. Blend in shortening with fork until it is like crumbs. (It's like making a pie crust.) Add water and shape into a ball. Add a few more drops of water if all the dough doesn't stick together. If the dough is too sticky, add a little more flour. Divide the dough into 10 even balls. Roll each ball out to 9 to 10 inch circle. Cook dough in the hot oil until brown. Flip the elephant ear over to brown the other side. Remove it from the skillet. Place it on a cookie sheet. Sprinkle the elephant ear with the topping. If the elephant ear is thick it will be soft. If the elephant ear is thin it will be crispy. Enjoy your elephant ear.

BARGE PILOT
Rudy H. Garcia

Navy sailor W.W.II
Landing barge pilot
This ode is for you.

Never wavering against the monstrous, soulless, reaping, tempest
Scything towards you, as an incarnated weapon from the other side of the earth,

Steaming, full open throttle, you charge the hostile beach carpeted with corpse red,
The preferential red carpet treatment of war,

Your shell-shocked barge, drops its battled jaw at such homicidal reception
And out of its mouth, spews, languishing, dreadful pleads for absolution,

Boys made men…
Yell, scream, and cry out, No! Not yet! Not now! Don`t send me out there just yet!

But fate prevails and Marines!
Not recruits splash unto the deadly shore amidst a deluge of life siphoning, ripping bullets.

And you… you landing barge pilot, Captain of your boat, your soul
Scream to every angel you can muster

Get them off my deck!

Take these freshly initiated leathernecks off this floating iron casket!

Carry these liberators
And cast them unto that wrinkled, pleated, crimson carpet woven U.S.A. tight, with mangled arms and legs.

Then with empty hull, full throttle in reverse but never retreating!
Never turning your back on the enemy, you bayonet the foam crested breakers, splitting them with grit and rage.

Back to the mother ship, to reload your barge, to re-cock yourself, with nameless, faceless warriors
You do not look to see their faces, what for?

You do not see a color, it`s all a blur, you do not know a single seamans` name
It doesn`t matter.

All that matters is your transport, your delivery, to the fight, to the kill!
But not surrendering to death! Because from killing returns life!

Back and forth, back and forth, killing and killing, death and more death!
Killing for the sake of living!

Ship loads of mothers sons of liberty!
Disembarked armed, fighting missionaries of freedom, human wonders take the beach,

Mission completed…
Until, an untranquil silence permeates the warring burnt powdered air.

Finally!
The only sound you hear is the morbid, idle, sputtering exhausted exhaust of your barges` expended motor.

Huddled, fawning, suckling, next to your ships` bosom
You raise your blood curled eyes to her and wait… she sends down nothing,

Realizing that she has nothing else to give, nothing else to send and die
The combat battle is over.

Wearied, you do not turn to look to shore, no part of you returns there ever more
No part of you can, you left it all on the blood soaked sand, there on foreign land.

Every piece of you…
Was taken by every Marine that plunged into the swallow shoal with the bottomless pit for the dead,

Exasperated and fatigued you curse away moribundity!
Sepulchering the horror, the explosive, the obtrusive
Nightmarish noise of battle to the profoundness depth of your minds` abyss

Hero!

You decommission your barge and march on solid ground, carpeted for you with parade and ticker tape

The biggest public promenade you've ever seen, lined by nameless, cheering, waving, grateful civilians
Red, White and Blue pride engulfs you.

Sparkling, jingling medal and ribboned citations
Adorn your robust, expanded chest. The war is ended and you`re the Victor!

And on your Herculean upper arm…Tattooed
An Eagle, Magnificently perched upon a cactus, wings extended mightily,

A snake, dangles from its beak, a symbol of strength and patriotism - your Badge of Courage!

BEACH SCENE
Travis M. Whitehead

I was at Boca Chica beach near Brownsville one Sunday afternoon for a day of fishing and outdoor cooking with my cousin, Claudine Wells, who was visiting from Minnesota. When we arrived, I was a bit disconcerted to find it packed full of people parked bumper to bumper in their monster trucks; I was even more annoyed with Claudine's attitude.

"What's the matter with these people! They've got a whole beach!" she screeched. She adjusted her flowered dress and floppy hat as we pulled into an area that hadn't filled up yet with people.

"Why do they have to park so close to each other! This is ridiculous!" she bellowed as we walked up into the dunes.

I planned to make some carne guisada in a Dutch oven the way my good friend Art Garza had taught me. I dug a hole into the sand, put in a layer of river rock I had bought at the garden center, then built a charcoal fire.

"You better move back, this is going to flare up big," I said.

"What?" she asked. "What are you going to do?"

"Just get up," I said.

I poured some lighter fluid onto the charcoal, then threw in a lit match causing a huge fire to erupt on the coals.

"What are you trying to do, kill me?" she said.

"No," I said. "I just need to speed things up and get these coals to burn down."

I watched the fire and carefully fed more coals until I was sure I had generated some heat. I started for the car and Claudine snapped, “You’re not leaving me here, are you?”

“I’m just going to fish in the surf a few minutes,” I said.

“You’re leaving me here by the fire?” she caterwauled. “By myself? What if somebody comes over here?”

“Just sit in the car then, I’ll just be a few feet away,” I said.

“Uh!” she said, shaking her head as she pulled up her dress and walked her sandaled feet down from the dunes.

“I’ll watch the fire from here,” she said as I gathered my rod and reel and went into the surf.

I had just cast my line when a Hispanic man parked his white truck right up next to mine and his three daughters bailed out and went swimming right where I was fishing.

I could just picture Claudine getting ready to explode so I came back in and marched her into the dunes.

“Didn’t that man teach his daughters any manners?” Claudine chirped once we were out of hearing range.

“Just let it go,” I said. “They won’t be there that long. I can fish later.”

“You just can’t stand up to ‘em, can you?” she asked. “If it was me I’d go tell ‘em off.”

‘Yes, Claudine, I believe you would,’ I thought as I fed the fire with more charcoal.

Art Garza had emphasized to me the importance of keeping an extra special watch on my fire at the beach, because the moisture could quickly creep in and put out your fire.

"I found that out the hard way," he'd said. "I was out with my friends and we buried some beans and some meat, and we thought we'd have a meal ready in a few hours, but when we came back, it was still raw."

He was right. A fire on the beach, especially when you're building one in a pit, is like a baby. You have to protect it from the wind and the water, and you have to feed it frequently. It's an art in itself, almost as fun as the actual cooking. I sat there and watched as the first layer of coals slowly turned white, then I spread them out a little with a small shovel and added another layer. Slowly the heat increased.

Meanwhile, I became even more annoyed when another car pulled in close on the other side of my car. I frowned at the occupants to let them know I didn't like it, but they stayed anyway. I couldn't understand why they felt it was O.K. to pull in so close to me, and I was appalled when still another car pulled in between them and me. I had never before seen such blatant rudeness. When I used to go to Padre Island near Corpus Christi, I always found some solitude. There were miles and miles of beach, and usually people gave each other their space, unless it was Memorial Day, July 4, or Labor Day, and then anyone with any sense knew better than to look for solitude there.

However, that was 20 years ago, and now I was on Boca Chica Beach and things were apparently different. I couldn't figure it out. And on top of that, I had Claudine's Mid-West Yankee crap to put up with.

"I can't believe those people!" she said. "Who do they think th-"

"Sssshhh, keep your voice down," I said. "They'll hear you."

"Good!!!" she said. "I want them to hear me! Maybe they'll learn how to act. Sarah warned me about the Meskins down here and their attitude."

Sarah warned me about your attitude, too, I thought. *Why didn't I listen....*

I acted like I was looking out at the water so they wouldn't know I was looking at them. The young man in the first car, a light tan four-door, wore loose beach shorts and a maroon shirt. The woman with him wore blue shorts and a bikini top and she unfolded a chair as the man spread out a large blue umbrella.

The other couple had a small boy with them who squealed as he ran along the water's edge. They seemed unconcerned about being parked so close to me, and I was perplexed.

"They're just out here for a Sunday afternoon, just like us," I said as I fed the fire.

"That doesn't mean they have to park right next to us, they've got a whole beach out here," she said. I was glad the strong wind was blowing away from them.

"You're too nice," she said. "I would never let them do that. You just let people walk all over you. You're never going to get anywhere in life if you don't stand up for yourself."

More cars pulled in on the other side, and I began to wonder if someone would actually try to pull in between me and the man in the white truck who was now grilling meat on a small stove on the tailgate.

"Kyle, I wouldn't be surprised if they tried to pull in on the other side," Claudine said. She could be so telepathic it was scary. I must admit I was getting angry thinking about the possibility.

"Oh, shit, I can't believe that," Claudine butted in. "Look."

Four three-wheelers had veered off the beach and were racing into the dunes.

"They're just tearing up the beach," she said. "They don't even care! I thought this was supposed to be a wildlife refuge."

"No, it's not," I said.

“That’s what the sign said,” she said, referring to our drive along 281 to get here. “How long have you been here and you don’t even know!?”

I was looking at the space between my car and the white truck. If I didn’t do something, someone was going to have the audacity to pull in next to me and Claudine was going to explode.

‘I know how to take care of this,’ I said to myself as I walked down to my car. I pulled my ice chest, two bags of charcoal, my rod and reel, and my tackle box out into the area to mark my territory. That should get the idea across.

“That’s good,” Claudine said as I brought back the Dutch oven and a small ice chest with the meat and the vegetables. “Now you’re taking charge. That’s what you have to do.”

The fire was getting hotter now, with a good bed of coals underneath. I put the Dutch oven on top of the fire in the first pit, poured in a little oil, then dropped in the chunks of boneless chuck I had cut up the night before. I had also ground up some Serrano pepper, several garlic cloves (Art only used one but I like it a little more garlicky), peppercorns and *comino* in a *mocajete*; I had put it all in a small Tupperware container with some water. Now it was ready to go into the oven.

“What did you say this was called?” Claudine asked.

“*Carne guisada*,” I said.

“What does that mean?” she said.

“It’s meat with spices and some onions and tomatoes,” I said. “It’s made a lot of different ways. Depends on what you like.”

“I don’t like onions,” Claudine said. “You’ll have to take ‘em out.”

“That’s part of it,” I said. “That’s how I cook it. I like the onions.”

“Kyle, they make me sick,” she said. “Don’t you even care about me? I’m your cousin.”

“O.K., fine, I’ll take ‘em out,” I said. “You never told me onions made you sick.”

By now the meat was sizzling. I stirred it around, browning it on all sides.

“Hey!” someone shouted from where the other cars were parked next to mine.

“Oh, God, I can’t believe-” Claudine muttered.

One of the men was standing next to a dark red suburban that had just pulled up. He looked at me and said, “Can we?” and motioned with his hand to indicate he wanted the suburban to pull in next to my car, in the space where I had already marked my territory.

“Tell him no, tell him no!” Claudine whispered loudly.

“No, you can’t!” I said, as I had planned to do. This was the epitome of rudeness. They wanted to surround my car.

“You can’t, move?” he asked, motioning toward my stuff.

“No,” I said. “That’s my space. It’s too crowded!”

I turned back to my fire at this point, not wanting to show my irritation.

“What is the matter with these people!” Claudine said. “I can’t believe the nerve! Oh , look!”

I turned to see the suburban moving slowly toward my stuff.

“They’re going to move in there anyway!”

The man in the white pickup pulled my pole out of the way, and the suburban stopped. He had me blocked in so I couldn't back out even if I wanted to.

"Look, now they're messing with your stuff!" she said. "Aren't you going to do something? We were here first!"

"What do you want me to do?" I asked. "There's more of them than us. We're outnumbered."

"You're just scared of them," Claudine scoffed. "I would go over there and tell that son-of-a-bitch to take a hike." "Yes, Claudine, I believe you would," I said, aloud now. I poured the spices onto the meat in the Dutch oven, then gingerly picked out the onions, leaving in a few bits just for spite before dumping in the tomatoes. I started to drop in the cut up *tomatillo* but Claudine caught me.

"What's that?" she said.

"*Tomatillo*," I said. "I don't want any of that in there either," she said.

If she'd had her way, the meat wouldn't have had any flavor at all. I didn't dare tell her about the Serrano peppers. We would not have even had a meal.

I must admit I was pretty hot about this whole scene with the other beachgoers. I couldn't figure out how they could be so absurd about all this. I also wished I had not brought Claudine along.

"They are right next to our car," she said. "Our windows are rolled down. They're going to steal everything we've got. I'm going down there-"

"No, you're not," I said. "You're going to sit right there, all that's going to do is provoke them."

"You're just scared of them," she said.

“They’re not going to take anything, we’re sittin’ right here, they know we’ll see ‘em,” I said.

The man in the white pickup left. “I’m gonna go move the car,” I said.

“Good luck trying,” she said. “They’re not gonna let you out, you already pissed them off.”

I got in my car and tried to move forward and around to where the white truck had been parked. However, as soon as I put on the gas, I knew I wasn’t going anywhere. The sand was too soft. I would have to back out.

“You’re moving out?” asked the man in the maroon shirt, politely.

“I thought I’d move over there and you can move in here,” I said.

Everyone quickly moved their things around, and one of them backed the red suburban out of the way. The man with the wide face stationed himself to the rear of my car and guided me out. I nodded to him in a gesture of thanks and he nodded back. I glanced at the woman in one of the cars and forced a smile. She smiled back.

I walked back into the dunes to where Claudine was sitting.

“Did you see that guy that helped you back out!?” She said. “He had an earring! In his ear!”

“Where do you want him to wear it, on his shirt?” I asked, feeling gobsmacked now by her whining.

“No, I don’t want him to wear it on his shirt,” she mumbled. “They’re a bunch of thugs is what they are.”

I stirred the carne guisada some more, then lifted the oven out of the hole. Claudine and I ate silently then I went back into the surf to fish.

Away from all the crowds, I could hear nothing but the wind and the pounding surf. A roll of churning white-brown water built up and pounded me, then the end of my rod doubled over. I reeled in some line, raised it up, and saw a clump of Sargasso weed hanging on the line. I bounced it up and down two or three times to knock it off. I kept my line in the water, and more Sargasso weed and some kind of trash fish or crabs played games with me for awhile. It didn't matter. The important thing was to be in the surf away from Claudine, the crowds and the noise.

"Excuse me," said a friendly voice to my right. "We got crossed with the line."

It was the man who had helped me back out.

"It's no problem," I said, laughing a little.

"Sorry," he said, chuckling as he walked under my line with his fishing pole.

Suddenly a rig with a small weight came riding up my line. I turned to see the first man with his companion.

"I guess I put too light a weight on it," the other man said.

"No, not – well, these currents are really strong," I said casually. "I always put a spider weight on mine."

"That's what we're gonna put right now," said the first man.

They left. I reeled my line in. It still had the bait on it and I cast again. I reeled it in quickly when it doubled back over. I stopped and saw that something was still tugging on it. I reeled it in, halfway expecting to see a clump of Sargasso weed, until up popped a small gaff top catfish. I waited for it to stop squirming, then grasped it, being careful not to let its fins stick me, and tossed it back.

I went back up on shore.

“You caught a catfish?” said the man in the maroon shirt.

“A small one,” I said. “I just let it go. Did you fish?”

“No,” he said. “There’s too many people. I was gonna fish, but I didn’t. It’s better if you go down to the river, over on the other side. You can walk across. But it’s kind of dangerous because you’ve got people coming and going. I don’t like to go over there.

"But you can go to Isla Blanca, they’ve got some jetties. It’s better, they’ve got cops going up and down. That’s why everybody comes over here. There’s no cops.”

So that was it. Maybe I wasn’t here first. I was the newcomer. They knew the code of ethics on this particular beach because they’d been here before. I hadn’t.

The cars were disappearing from the beach, and I began to relax.

We packed up and loaded everything in the car, and as we drove away, Claudine frantically searched the car to find out what had been stolen.

“Finally, we’re gone,” she said. “I’m gonna check my purse. Where’s my purse! Oh there it is. My wallet. Where’s my wallet! I knew it! They got my wallet with all my money and my credit cards, they’re going to be maxed out by midnight! And it’s all your fault because you couldn’t stand up to them!”

I reached under her seat and pulled out her wallet where she had left it.

“Oh, that’s right, I put it under the seat. They didn’t take my wallet. My jewelry. I took my necklace off – oh there it is. Right there. Well, what did they take? They had to take something.”

She stopped and just glared around her, holding out her arms as she exhaled sharply.

"What did they do? Did they just let my stuff sit here in plain sight for two hours and they didn't even take anything? Who do they think they are not stealing from me? I've got stuff to steal! Sarah, she got her jewelry stolen. And Jennifer, they stole her wallet and her credit cards, and they stole Alice's car. And they didn't even steal anything from me!?"

"Sarah never knew for sure what happened," I said, hoping to cut her off.

"It was only obvious!" she said, shaking her head, grimacing as she leaned against the window in disbelief.

Neither one of us spoke on the way home, and she just brooded the rest of the evening. I took her to the airport the next morning and she flew back to Minnesota with a broken wing never to return, deeply, eternally wounded that the Mexicans didn't even have the courtesy to steal from her.

BOXCARS*
Judy Stevens

When I think back on it—Charley and me, we weren't far off. Charley's gone now and I ship out tonight. I think we're still the only ones t'know 'bout this. Believe me, it ain't somethin' you want to know, anyway. Can't do anything about something you can't do anything about.

Pour a stiff one, will ya? Thanks.

Tell you what, I like you. You hear everything and you don't laugh, I like that. Maybe I'll give you a heads up on this before I go. You're different. You see all types in here. Who knows, one of these days you might even see one of them. Yeah, let's get this out in the open so it can stay invisible.

I know, I know: you don't understand. Just hit me again. Thanks; keep 'em coming.

That kid down the block worries me. Too bright; around my age when I found out about the boxcars.

But what's the diff? Can't do anything about something I can't do anything about.

It was different back then. People half-believed in stuff like that. What year was it—nineteen fifty what? I was nine. It was summer. Mom said, "Get out and play, and don't come back till supper."

You know those boxcars at the rail yard—the ones all decorated with weird writing and drawings? Yeah, graffiti, they call it. Well, they fascinated me. I always thought those boxcars were message-boards. Not the usual, "Look at me, I can write swear-words," but something like, "Dear So-and-So at the other end of the world." Most of it was indecipherable so I would make up what it said—

aliens from Mars writing to aliens from Venus while they vacationed here on Earth.

If Mom knew I was down there my head would have come off.

One thing about being nine back then: I was invisible; no one ever looked twice at me as I wandered around town checking out other invisible things—like mysterious designs on boxcars. If anyone noticed them it was only to "tsk-tsk" at the way such vulgarity was destroying our culture. Same thing went for hobos—bums, tramps, vagrants, knights of the highways; whatever you want to call 'em—hiding in plain view. Nobody wants to see 'em, so nobody does.

Brilliant—in your face and invisible at the same time—ain't that a wild way to run things?

I know, I know: you don't get it. Well, let me tell you: some of those hobos—they're aliens.

No, not that kind of alien—aliens.

That's how they communicate: graffiti on boxcars—wild, huh?

Hit me again.

I'll tell you how Charley and I found out back then, and why nobody knows about this. What harm can it do—I'm drunk and I'm shipping out.

Back then I should'a listened. Mom said to never go near strangers—especially bums. I was nine, what did I know? Charley—my cousin—was thirteen. He knew all about girls: I thought he was god. We'd sit and try to read the sides of boxcars. I was convinced some of the scribbles were messages, but I couldn't crack the code, and neither could Charley. We knew boxcars went all over the country. All you had to do is mark 'em and your message got delivered. I sent several, myself. Bums went all over, too: they did what we couldn't do: roamed around carrying their lives on their backs. We had moms and dads and school and chores. They had the world. We always wondered what they really were up to, besides getting drunk. Getting drunk looked like a cover.

We sort of hit upon the theory together. We figured the boxcars carried coded messages for aliens roaming around gathering data on us humans. Now all we had to do was find a bum who was an alien, and ask him—or it—to teach us the code.

We spent the next two weeks—minus Sundays and chore days—observing the ramshackle men and one lady as they came and went, but none of them looked alien enough. Several times we got yelled at and once we were chased, but you know at nine you can outrun the devil himself.

That summer was nearly gone into school when we found one of the aliens. There's not that many, you know. He was sitting at the rim of an open boxcar in a secluded part of the train yard. And his bones didn't look right, like they were assembled by someone who didn't know how to build a human. It creeped me out, but Charley just grinned.

I know, I know—those sordid things like abduction and rape never occurred to us back then. Now, kids are snatched straight out of their beds, but back then, well—the world was naïve.
It was Charley who marched right up to the man and said, "Hi. I'm Charley. What planet you from?"

I gotta hand it to him—the man never dropped his sandwich. He took another bite, then a swig from his bottle and wiped his mouth with his sleeve. "What one you from, Shorty?" he countered in a thick accent.

We'd found our alien.

It's weird nobody—I mean nobody—knows about this, believe me: I've been around the world a few times, mister. These aliens, they're from all over the galaxy, places you can never imagine. To them, we're Disneyland. We're the safari of their lifetime.

"You got a cigarette?" the man asked Charley. I knew Charley had one, and he did—he was my god.

The man lit up, took a long drag and blew a perfect smoke circle. Then he said to no one in particular, "There's balloon writing and there's block writing. Two separate languages. You use the balloons when you want to contact your base ship and the blocks when you want to contact another traveler. The rest of the markings are from the natives. I have no idea what they mean."

He turned his bloodshot eyes to us. "Get me a beer and I'll tell you the rest," he said.

I'd never stolen anything in my life, but I'm sure it didn't count then, 'cause it was a national security issue. Besides, it looked like Charley's dad had plenty of brew.

Now that I remember, the man's hands looked weird grasping the can and he drank like it was something he wasn't used to. But he looked really satisfied by the time he finished. He handed the can back to Charley. Weird: a guy handing contraband back. Anyone else would'a thrown it. He gave us a strange look then mumbled something like who's gonna believe kids anyway; and then he told us everything about the Grid.

Charley and me, we were right. There's a network of "nature preserves" all over the world for thrill-seekers from other planets who want to experience being human. Difference is, the aliens' "wild kingdom" isn't out there in the jungles but here, in the cities. These aliens, they do the best they can to look like us, but some of them look a lot more human all grimed up—hiding in plain view.

Charley and me, we made a pact never to tell anybody, and we decided not to disturb the alien's vacations no more. Besides, it wasn't long after that Charley got a girlfriend and we split up naturally anyway. And I got cynical.

I used to think the bum had handed us a line of crap for a cigarette and beer, but then I got laid off and started roaming around looking for work, and I started to notice them again. You know: a few slip-ups along the way; a few subtle things that tipped me off to those who were just pretending to be human. I caught a few conversations on the sly—that kind of stuff. They were always surprised a “native” had caught on to them. Once I actually helped a beggar in Bangladesh; he was new to Earth and I gave him some pointers.

Some of ‘em still creep me out, but I guess I’ve learned to take it in stride. It gripes me, though, that humans won’t believe me. Charley was the lucky one. Fifteen years ago tomorrow he got to go on the trip of his lifetime. Some clear night in July look straight up and you’ll see it hiding in plain sight.

Here—no, keep it: you’ve earned the tip. Thanks for listening. You have no idea how good it feels to have that off my chest.

Well, it’s time to ship out.

Where?

Vacation of a lifetime. Sent the application out last week on the Union Pacific car eight—got accepted today. Be back in a hundred-fifty years, local time. Don’t know how that works, but who cares?

Be kind to the vagrants. You never know which ones are just visiting.

BUBBLES IN THE BATHTUB
Don Clifford

Owen Grimes squirmed in his seat. "What are we s'posed to tell the priest?" He snuffled up his nose and scrunched himself as small as possible behind his desk.

Father Ryan and the nuns had less than a week to cram into us first-timers the mysteries of Penance and Holy Communion. "Obviously, you don't go around and rob banks or shoot people," he said. "So just think of those things you are too embarrassed to talk about. If you are that bothered, chances are you committed a sin, and you should confess it."

I racked my brain for sins to confess as I didn't want to disappoint Father Ryan, but the only thing I was embarrassed about was watching bubbles in the bathtub.

"Remember," he said. "It's O.K. to tell the priest your sins because he is commanded by God never to tell a living soul what you told him."

I can't say that made me feel any better because the Saturday morning before First Communion Sunday, we all assembled in the classroom where Sister Mary Mercy took charge of us and trooped us into the church. Our heads hung low. I saw the dread that I felt on the faces of my sinful mates, not sure of what to expect. Except for Owen Grimes. In between snuffles, he sauntered into the church as though his first confession was a daily event. Sometimes I wondered, did he ever own a handkerchief?

Added to the misery was the click of a nun's cricket that manipulated us like robots. A cricket is a tension device of two pieces of tin cleverly clamped together and contrived to 'click-' when pressed and '-et' when released.

‘Click-et.’ Halt!

‘Click-et.’ Genuflect!

‘Click-et.’ Sit!

By the time we were seated an urgent need demanded immediate relief. I waved and got Sister Mary Mercy’s attention. “S’ster, I gotta go to the bathroom.”

“Just hold it. We won’t be here long.”

“But, S’ster, I can’t hold it much longer.”

She ignored my plea and glided down the aisle to where Mary Jane McGinnis sat, giggling and gossiping about who knows what. In spite of my pressing need, I daydreamed about what sins she might confess.

My turn took forever. I pushed aside the heavy velvet curtain and crept into the confessional booth. With hands in my pockets, I held back my body’s desperate demand and knelt before a crosshatched grill that covered a small window. The sliding privacy panel behind the grill snapped open. In the dim light I could see Father Ryan’s head lean toward me. Like a fellow conspirator, he said, “Begin your confession.”

I grunted. “Bless me, Father, for I have sinned.”

"And how have you sinned, my son?"

The urge was intense. I moaned. “I watched bubbles in the bathtub.”

“What?”

I twisted and groaned. “Bubbles in the bathtub!”

Father Ryan shook his head as though to say, I don't get paid enough for this. He sighed and said, "Your penance is one Our Father and three Hail Marys. Now say the Act of Contrition."

He blessed me after I recited the Act and said, "Go and sin no more."

The panel snapped shut. I struggled to get off my knees when the dam burst. The more I tried to hold back, the faster the flow. I whimpered, helpless. My bladder emptied. The booth was awash.

I burst out of the confessional and bumped into Owen and Mary Jane next in line. The nearest exit seemed farther away than the football goal post in the recreation yard outside the church. My legs ran fast but they pumped in slow motion until a frantic push opened the heavy oaken door. I heard Owen sneeze. He cried out, "S'ster! It's all wet in here!"

First Communion Sunday came and went without a hitch, but now I had two embarrassments. For some unknown reason, no one grabbed me aside to chew me out for drowning the confessional. I reckoned the nuns were embarrassed about it, too. Peeking at bubbles in the bathtub, though, was something else. I never did tell Father Ryan that Mary Jane's nickname was…Bubbles.

CANADIAN PRAIRIE*
Joan Soggie

Prairie Grass

The sod house perches on the brow of a low knoll, its earthen walls rising like a natural extension of the prairie. It faces an undulating slope of rippling grass, sweeping down to a broad plain. At its back the hills rise, ridge upon ridge, to the western horizon. No tree shades it, no fence surrounds it. Its own dirt walls and turf roof blooming with scarlet mallow provide the family's only protection from sun or wind, rain or snow, scorching heat or mind-numbing cold.

A strange twosome appears from behind the soddie and pauses in dark silhouette for a moment against the sunlit sky. The rider is dwarfed by the horse he is riding. The mare, better paired with a heavy-wheeled hay rack than a four year old child, ponderously navigates the hillside, placing her hooves with exaggerated care. The child shifts his position from side to side, his skinny legs gripping tightly but scarcely able to span the animal's broad, slippery back.

Half hidden in the shadow of the doorway, his mother watches. A slim, erect figure, she stands with shoulders squared and chin high, hands folded in her apron.

A baby cries, and the young woman disappears into the dim interior. Her son is barely into his fourth summer, but already there are two younger than he. Back in Minneapolis, she would not have dreamt of sending a child his age on an errand by himself. In this raw land, necessity dictates. The old rules no longer apply

Horse and boy have reached the bottom of the grassy slope. The land is as yet mostly unbroken, still an almost intact sea of flowers and grass interspersed by small islands of willows and chokecherry. Trails worn deep by Indian travois and later by Metis carts now serve the settlers' wagons. It is not unusual to find a bison skull bleaching among the cactus on a windy hillside. The last shaggy herds grazed here only forty years earlier.

The boy gazes around, wide-eyed and sober-faced, clutching the reins and a hank of coarse mane in both hands. His destination, a soddie like his own home, is just across the flat and up another small hill. But directly in his path lies a complication in the form of a placid blue mirror ringed by tall reeds. Already the mare has quickened her pace, pulling against the reins. His face screws into a grimace. How can he get his huge mount to go around instead of through that slough? He yanks on the reins and kicks his puny heels into the mare's sides.

"Come on, Pet! This way, girl!" he coaxes, in feeble imitation of the hearty tone he has heard his father use. "You don't need water right now."

But he might as well try steering the wind. Unmoved by his now frantic pleas, the mare calmly continues on her path. Straight into the slough she ambles, squelching through mud-rooted reeds until, knee-deep, she bends her shaggy head to drink. Slowly but inexorably, Ernest slides down her neck. He hangs for a moment on her coarse mane, struggles frantically to maintain his grip, and finally, with a despairing yelp, slips over her head and into the water.

He flounders to free himself from the clay sucking him down, bare toes desperately scrabbling for a foothold in the slime. Gagging on soupy water he has already inhaled, he is barely aware of a mounted figure approaching. Immensely tall he seems to Ernest's tear-filled eyes, towering above him, black against the afternoon sun. Leaning forward in the saddle, the man grasps Ernest's thin arm and easily lifts him free of the muck, swinging him into the shallows. The child stumbles to solid ground with a hiccupping sob.

“Dat some big horse you got dere, boy.”

Ernest scrubs a muddy fist across his face and stares up at the stranger. Who is he?

Where did he come from? He does not speak like anyone Ernest knows … not like his parents or grandparents or the even Mrs. Urwin.

"So, dat horse, he want a drink ... dat’s alright. Next time, bes dat you lead him to drink first ting. Den he not play dat trick again, eh?"

The child stands gazing up at the stranger. In his confusion, he has forgotten the dictum to “speak when spoken to,” and remains silent, staring up at the tall figure.

The man pushes back his floppy-brimmed hat, a long lock of gray hair sliding over his forehead. He speaks in a low, slow voice, with grave courtesy, yet his eyes twinkle with amusement.

“Where you headin’ to, mon petit?”

"Mama told me to take this to Mrs. Urwin."

From the pocket of his overalls, the boy pulls a folded and now sodden piece of notepaper.

"Then I will help you back up on dis horse. Dat’s good, you do as your mama say."

Remembering just in time to say "Thank you" and to wave a solemn good-bye to his rescuer, Ernest continues his half-mile journey.

The note delivered, the reply written by Mrs. Urwin while he devours the plate of cream and bread she has set before him, he is boosted back up on his mount and sets off for home again. Upon his return, he gives a full and accurate account of his misadventure to his mother. Accurate in every detail, that is, except one. He makes no mention of his rescuer. This is with no intention of deceiving her, but rather, from feeling at a loss to know what to say. He does not know the man's name, nor how he fits into their small community. How could he begin to describe him? His horse was not like their farm horses, yet he could not explain what the difference was. His clothes had looked like no coat and pants the boy had ever seen before. Even the odour that surrounded him was unique, reminding the boy of woodsmoke and something else, different from the usual man-smell of sweat and dirt.

So, rather than attempting to explain the unexplainable, the boy says nothing about the stranger.

His mother, more than a little alarmed at the incident, takes comfort in the fact that he seems to have avoided any real danger. She is amazed that the child somehow managed to climb back up on the horse without a mounting block, but accepts with secret pride this evidence of her son's self-reliance.

She would have felt more amazement, maybe even a little consternation, if she had known a stranger had chosen to pass so near her home without stopping to make himself known. In this country, newcomers sought one another's company. Therein lay their safety. To neglect that courtesy would excite suspicion, even alarm.

But, since Ernest told no one of his rescuer, it did neither. His little accident passed into the realm of family lore, a story to be told with laughter that softened the unspoken boast,

"See how brave and resourceful is this boy of ours!"

CHARLIE HAMBURGER

Rudy H. Garcia

I remember Charlie Hamburger. I miss him.
He never hurt anybody.
In fact, the opposite is true.

If you knew or didn`t know Charlie,
That was fine by him.
Somehow, for some mystic reason,
Charlie knew you.

He never a stranger was…
He was the curious type.
He had green eyes.
He used to say,
He had intriguing cat eyes.

So I used to trap and capture stray alley cats
Assorted wily cats, young cats mostly,
Just to look into their mystical dilated feline eyes,
To see if their eyes were emerald in color
Like Charlie`s…
Many did.

Charlie was an excellent story teller.
The best I ever knew.
And every one who heard
Him tell his fantastic tales
Will agree with me.
That no one could spin
A taller tale
Than Charlie.

He possessed a special gift,
A rare ability to mimic many different

Kinds of wild jungle animals.
He did the mighty Tarzan yell the best.
The Ape man from Africa!
He was Charlie`s almost very good best friend
And he learned a lot from Tarzan.
Except, that I never saw Charlie
Fight and kill any alligators, tigers, giant river anacondas nor lions.

Charlie could walk, run, jump up and down and spin exactly like Tarzan`s
Chimpanzee and constant companion Cheetah.
Cheetah and Charlie shared many Congo secrets between them.
Charlie could trumpet and
Float-walk, just like the great tusk elephant from the cradle of man`s Africa.
At play he pounded his powerful chest and growled like the mighty giant King Kong.
He often talked to the animals and the animals talked to him.

Charlie attended daily Mass regularly,
Almost on a daily basis and was partial to Saint Francis of Assisi
He lit small candle offerings for him every time he had a spare dime.

Charlie loved to play and frolic
By the water`s edge of the nurturing Laguna Madre.
Much to his fathers' dismay,
He loved the sea shore so much
That he was willing to suffer his fathers` brutal spankings
And stern commanding demands forbidding him
From venturing to the bay waters to explore.
I do not want to see you there anymore! His father scolded.

Charlie would plead and cry to his father
To cease the painful beating, promising
That he would go there never more.
But of course, the very next day
As sure as the tide rolled in,
There was Charlie waist deep
In the refreshing cool blue-green water of the
Laguna Madre.
Pocking for crabs and diving after darting fish
With his home made broom stick gigging spear.

Charlie wasn`t an early riser
In fact he loved sleeping in late, covered with the
comforting warmth
Of the blanket nest his mother Catarina, bedded for
him every night.
But when his altar boy scheduled turn came
To ring the morning church bells
Calling the parish faithful to mass
Charlie was there at six a.m. (sharp)
Pulling down strong on the bell cord
Stirring roosting pigeons into early morning flight
from their belfry steeple coops.
He looked forward to performing the church altar
ritual of lighting the altar candles,
Preparing the water and wine, for the priest to
drink, burning the sweet smelling incense

And laying out the colorful ceremonial robes and
vestments for the priest to wear
He did however prefer to serve during evening
mass, weddings and funerals.
And best of all he always felt especially honored
when asked by Father McDermit,
To be one of the altar servers during Christmas
midnight Mass.

Because God created Charlie, a right, quite smart boy
He was donned by the creator with the gift of healing.
He was constantly being sought out by the injured and afflicted
To place his mending hands on them
The result, was usually relief, followed by wellness.

He wasn`t into school books
As far as he was concerned
They couldn`t teach him much.
He did like going to school however.
Charlie, was a very sociable lad
And loved being around people
And people loved being around him.

Many folk, in his home town of Port Isabel
Will attest and also tell
That if you came down with a muscle sprain,
An aching neck or back spasms,
Or if a body bone cracked or broke
Or happen to pop out of place,
Charlie was summoned to examine
And return the break back to its rightful place.

He did this by spiritually placing his gifted hands
On the injured part of the body.
Then with a trance like concentration, he gently rubbed,
And felt his way until he came upon the injured part of the body.
Once his fingers found and pin pointed the exact spot
That was hurting, he would stop, come out of his trance
And give you his diagnosis and explain to you how he
Was going to treat you.

Charlie, had great bed side manner
And the ability to relax his patients.
Before starting his treatment he would
Tell you if it was going to hurt a little
Or hurt a lot. Many times, while he was
Telling how much it was going to hurt,
He would give you a quick jerk or snap
And before you knew what had happened,
He was done, and you felt better.

He would return again
The following day, as a follow-up visit
Just to make sure you were
Healing the right way. He was just that way.

Charlie, never saved a single dollar
Even though he earned thousands,
God gave Charlie a special mission
During his life here on Earth.
He was born to heal,
To bring joy, comfort and good health.
He brought smiles, laughter and happy feelings
And he certainly fulfilled his mission well.

We all remember Charlie, the Bone Setter,
Charlie, the healer, Charlie, the story Teller...
The one who spoke with the animals
And the animals spoke with him,
The Boy with endless suspense and adventure stories
The Boy sent by God to make sick people well.

Many of us have fond memories of Charlie,
The boy who grew up with the nick name "Charlie Hamburger"
Because his mother owned and operated, a small hamburger stand,
When we were growing up, she worked the stand from
Mid-morning till late at night, consequently, Charlie was

Often seen eating the best hamburgers in town.

As often is the case, with kids growing up, nick names are used
As a source of identifying one another…
“Hamburger Charlie” was his.
Word spread about his healing nature. For many years after that
Charlie was visited by hundreds of people asking him to please
Treat them or their children, because they had an aching back,
Neck, leg, arm or a dislocated bone somewhere on their body.

Charlie never turned anyone away. He's gone now, called to Heaven,
Charlie, the boy from Port Isabel who grew up being called
“Charlie Hamburger”, lives on…famous as the man known
For healing and making people well again.
I knew him as “Chale”… my special friend.

CINÉ EL REY
"Preserving the past for the future"
Sue Groves

Following a woman with a dog out of the movie theater, a man stopped her and said, "I'm sorry to bother you, but I was amazed that your dog seemed to get into the movie so much. He cried at the right spots, moved nervously at the boring spots, and laughed like crazy at the funny parts. Don't you find that unusual?"

"Yes," she replied. "I find it very unusual. Especially considering that he hated the book!"

As you read this, there may not be a scheduled 'dog-and-pony show' at the Ciné El Rey, but with the diverse events on the venue's calendar, you never know.

In the heart of McAllen's historic 17th Street downtown district the Ciné El Rey, ("The King Cinema"), stands as an eclectic beacon unparalleled in the Rio Grande Valley. When the theater originally opened many years ago on May 1, 1947, the El Rey was the first movie theater to exclusively offer Spanish-language motion pictures, beginning with films from Mexico's sigio de oro (golden age) of cinema. The facility was originally built to capitalize on the demand for Spanish-language entertainment created by the influx of Mexican Braceros into the United States during World War II.

The Braceros were named after the U.S.-Mexican Braceros program established during the war was created to help with a shortage of agricultural workers in the United States by recruiting more almost 5 million Mexican nationals to labor on U.S. farms. Many Hispanics who were participants in the Bracero Program were refused entry or services at some movie theaters, while other theaters tried to segregate them by only showing Mexican movies after midnight, or only allowing Mexicans to sit in the balcony.

The Ciné El Rey, originally built by Texas Consolidated Theaters and initially owned by RKO Studios, insured that Hispanics of that time had a place that they could enjoy Mexico's Golden Age of Cinema. They took great pride in the theater. *"Esta cine de nosotros"* ("This was our theater").

Over the years, many celebrities and personalities from Mexico made personal appearances on the El Rey stage, including German Valdes ("Tin Tan"), a comic Mexican actor of legendary stature, who portrayed the streetwise pachuco ("Zoot Suter") in 103 films between 1944 and 1977. Mario Moreno (Cantinflas), Pedro Infante, Sara Garcia, Antonio Aguilar and Lucha Villa also graced the El Rey's stage and screen to the delight of local patrons.

The theater continued to serve as the entertainment center for the city's Hispanic community for the next 40 years, but by the mid-1980s, the Mexican motion picture industry slowed down considerably, and the theater turned to showing second-run American features. Finally closing in 1988, the former theater was used as a religious outreach center from 1996 - 1998.

Since its renovation and reopening in 2002, the theater has not only provided many people with the opportunity to see films not found anywhere else in the Valley, or view cult classics at its Tuesday free-movie nights (including fresh, hot popcorn - gratis), but its repertoire of events has expanded to include a hugely-popular comedy night on Wednesdays, live pro wrestling on Thursdays, and a mix of live concerts and other events on the weekends.

Issac and Bert Guerra, local entrepreneurs with professional expertise in both restaurant ownership, (Issac), and the entertainment industry, (Bert), fought hard to maintain the architectural integrity as the technical upgrades and renovations continue for the multilevel complex and historical landmark that they bought in 2007.

“Some locals have wanted to pigeonhole us ‘The Mexican Apollo’, or McAllen’s attempt to replicate the success of Austin’s Sixth Street entertainment district, “ Issac Guerra said, “but why limit ourselves?

“[In the past] you basically had to be brown and broke to come here. It was a theater of segregation. Now, the theater has evolved, and it’s a gift to experience performing arts, and to be able to bring those experiences to the ‘regular’ guy. That’s beautiful.”

Mike Ochoa, who remembers coming to the movies as a youngster with his grandfather, comes to the El Rey as often as he can. He is a part-time reggae musician who volunteers as a DJ “This is definitely not a cookie-cutter venue,” Ochoa said.

When a Tuesday night screening of the Brad Pitt cult classic FIGHT CLUB, “Ash” and three of his UTPA buddies, decided to drop in on a whim after noting the film’s schedule on the El Rey’s Facebook page. He, too, remembered that as a young boy, "For five dollars, they’d give you a wrist band, and you could go in-and-out of the theater and see films throughout the day”.

Ash and his friends not only stayed for the free screening, but also were “pleasantly surprised” when the Guerra brothers dimmed the amber lights above the bar, threw open the French doors, placed cafe tables and lounge chairs under the marquee, and transformed the forward part of the venue into a live rock-performance domain. The house band was fronted, no less, by the multi-talented Issac on vocals and brother Bert on a “thrashin’” lead guitar. “We’re all about being authentic,” Bert Guerra said between songs.

The Guerras also saw the importance of giving back to the community, and in 2010 they formed the Ciné El Rey Foundation. The mission statement of the foundation emphasizes the promotion and education of the history of regional entertainment artists, as well as the "...traditions that illustrate the diverse nature of the American experience - one that rejoices in the existence of the human spirit”.

Foundation's reason for existence is to underwrite a program similar to Teach America, to support the education of local doctors and other medical professionals who commit to return to the Valley to practice.

A movie series “Fooducation” supports the RGV Food Bank, and helps people “Get Fooducated” so they can make informed food choices that positively affects their lives and health.

The Ciné El Rey also features lease options for corporate or private events at the theater that include state-of-the-art audio and lighting production as well as video presentations. It can even include tailored menus catered exclusively by España Mediterranean Cuisine.

The Ciné El Rey - definitely not your grandfather’s movie theater - is the epitome of the brothers’ Guerra motto: “Preserving the past for the future.”

COME ON-A MY HOUSE
(Written on a Father's Day)
Marianna Nelson

My father had high-brow tastes. On Sunday afternoons (his only free time) he would recline on our gray sofa as sounds of classical symphonies burst from our little Emerson radio courtesy of WQXR in New York, a station which aired classical music all day, every day. By the time Beethoven's 5th filled the room, his mind was immersed in the volume of War and Peace perched on his chest.

One of my early childhood delights was my father reading to me while I sat on his bouncing knee. In his southern drawl, he would rhythmically chant the plight of the oysters as they were being tricked and then eaten by "The Walrus and the Carpenter" in Lewis Carroll's poem. My favorite poem was A.A. Milne's "Rice Pudding" which started like this: "What is the matter with Mary Jane? She's crying with all her might and mane..." and so on to the fifth and final verse when it seemed to me that her parents still hadn't figured out what I knew was the obvious answer – Mary Jane hated rice pudding as much as I did. I would ask him to read it again and again.

Although my father was raised in Appalachia, not one note of Blue Grass or any other non-classical music was played in our house during the 1930s and 40s. Then came 1951, the year that Rosemary Clooney revived Come On-A My House, a song written in 1939 based on an Armenian folk melody and composed by two Armenian-Americans. The repetitive, rollicking tune and lyrics conveyed the hospitality Armenians liked to lavish on their family and friends by inviting them in and feeding them "figs and dates and grapes and cakes."

At that time, we were living in Chester, Vermont, where my parents had opened an inn and restaurant in our home. My father's listening choices were greatly curtailed because the WQXR signal no longer reached us, Public Radio had not yet come into existence, and we didn't own a record player. So, as he cooked and baked and served up food for his customers, his only option was to tune in to disc jockeys playing the hits of the day. When Rosemary Clooney belted out Come On-A My House, he was ready for it and acted out the song when she sang it. Why he got caught up in its infectious beat and zany words always puzzled me until I started writing this piece. Now I realize he identified with the lyrics because the work he loved doing was what Rosemary Clooney seemed to have so much fun singing about – serving up delicious food for others to enjoy.

Thank goodness my father lived in the pre-Internet and Google age and was protected from the surprising truth about Rosemary Clooney: she hated "Come On-A My House." Even though the song became her biggest hit, she claimed she had to force her voice to sing it. Had he known this, his disappointment would have been hard to bear – both for him and for me.

Notes:

"The Walrus and the Carpenter" was published in *Through the Looking Glass and What Alice Found There.*

"Rice Pudding" was published in *When We Were Very Young*.

The Armenian-American composers of "Come On-A My House" were Ross Bagdasarian and William Saroyan.

DINNER AT DIXIE'S*
Jose A. Alvarez

On Friday morning I set out to explore Tel Aviv armed with a map of the city and the English version of the Israeli newspaper Haaretz. I walk leisurely to the heart of the commercial district, already full of people shopping on the first day of the weekend. The smell of freshly brewed coffee lures me to a small café where I order orange juice, croissants and a large espresso. Thankfully, most everyone speaks perfect English. The freshly squeezed orange juice is sweet, the croissants are hot, and the coffee strong; a perfect beginning to my first weekend in Israel.

I sit at a small outdoor table in front of the café to have my breakfast and read the newspaper, and I realize how much this city reminds me of Havana, the city where I was born and bred until I left for an unexpected exile in 1960. It does not surprise me; to this day almost everything reminds me of Havana. The climate in Tel Aviv is hot, and so are its people. Cubans don't have conversations they have shouting matches, and so do the Israelis. We interrupt each other during arguments, and so do the Israelis. We wave our arms as we speak, and so do the Israelis. Tel Aviv borders the Mediterranean Sea and Havana the Straits of Florida. Even the architecture of Tel Aviv seems vaguely familiar; houses are painted in light colors, and both cities show the influences of Modernism in their Twentieth Century architecture.

After breakfast I continue exploring the city. Hidden in an alley off Allenby Street, I find a small bookstore selling books in Spanish and in Hebrew. The owner, Daniel Cohen, tells me he immigrated to Israel from Uruguay in the early sixties. He joined the Israeli army and fought in the Six Day war. We talk about his life in Israel and about his love for Spanish literature. He loves the poetry of José Martí, and admires his influence in Latin American literature. I tell him how much I enjoyed studying Martí´s *Versos Sencillos* in high school, now popularized forever in the song *Guantanamera*. Once he finds out I was born in Cuba and I like crime stories he suggests books by Daniel Chavarria, a Uruguayan author whose stories take place in Havana. I choose *Adios Muchachos* and *Lo Que Dura Dura*. New customers arrive and Daniel switches to Hebrew. I continue browsing through his eclectic book collection and choose another couple of books: A Tale of Love and Darkness, a memoir by Amos Oz –an Israeli – and *Misterios de La Habana*, by Zoé Valdés – another Cuban exile born in Havana who now lives in Paris.

Happy with my successful expedition, I find my way to the beach. I take off my shoes and amble into the shallow water to my ankles. The water feels cool and refreshing as I walk back to my hotel on Tel Aviv's shoreline.

At night I take the elevator to the restaurant on the ground floor to have dinner. I am disappointed to find a very limited menu, all kosher, in observance of the Sabbath which began at sundown. I ask the clerk behind the front desk, who wears a holster with a handgun, where I could get some non-kosher food. She recommends a restaurant called Dixie, on Igal Alon Street. I take a cab to the restaurant accompanied by one of the books I bought earlier in the afternoon *–Misterios de La Habana*. The book is a collection of whimsical stories about real people and events from our Cuban folklore, embellished by the author's fertile imagination.

After the guard frisks me at the door, I enter the restaurant. Dixie is full of young people and I feel like the oldest person in the restaurant. There are no tables available so I find a stool at the bar. I order a glass of red wine and roast pork, the closest I can find to "*lechón asado y arroz con frijoles,*" my favorite Cuban dish. Sitting next to me, a young couple enjoys a shrimp dinner. They carry on an animated discussion, full of guttural Hebrew sounds; accompanied by hand waving that nearly tips my glass of wine. I find a certain pleasure in ignoring the dietary laws, just like my dining neighbors. The background music – Billy Joel,

Bruce Springsteen, Whitney Houston, and others I don't recognize – distracts me from the cacophony of sounds in the busy restaurant.

While I sip my wine waiting for dinner, Zoé Valdés reminds me of many characters I know from my childhood. Matías Perez lifts off from Havana on a hot air balloon, drifts to sea over the north coast and disappears forever, anticipating by a hundred years the balseros leaving Cuba on makeshift rafts during the second half of the twentieth century. Cirilo Villaverde, one of the best known Cuban writers of the nineteenth century, rides through the streets of Havana in a horse drawn carriage accompanied by his wife, by Cecilia Valdes – the main character of his novel by that name published in 1882 – and by Eugène Sue a nineteenth century French novelist. Jose Maria Heredia, whose poem Oda al Niagara we studied in high school, returns to Havana from exile but is denied entry into the country and is only allowed to speak for a few minutes with his friend Domingo Del Monte who was waiting for him at the pier.

Sitting at the bar of the restaurant Dixie in downtown Tel Aviv, surrounded by loud voices I don't understand, and reading stories of real and fictional Cuban characters so familiar to me and yet unknown outside Cuban culture I feel alone and isolated. I feel that my country of birth, described by Christopher Columbus as the "most beautiful land human eyes have ever seen," has been, and continues to be a cradle of nomads and exiles.

My dinner arrives while I read another story about Jose Martí. I put down my book and start eating the pork. Just then, the background music changes to Caribbean rhythms. A male voice sings in a distinct Cuban accent:

"Guantanamera, guajira Guantanamera.

Guantanameeeeera, guajira Guantanamera.

Yo soy un hombre sincero de donde crece la palma,

Yo soy un hombre sincero de donde crece la palma,

Y antes de morirme quiero echar mis versos del alma.

Guantanamera, guajira Guantanamera.

Guantanameeeeera, guajira Guantanamera...."

And I laugh. Cuba may be a cradle of nomads and exiles, but Cuban music is enjoyed all over the world. Here in Israel, I am home again.

DOVETAIL DONE IN DOWNTURN
Kamala Platt

The Ivy House Market was finally calm, but as its proprietor surveyed the locked shop from her work desk, the vendors' stalls still held the aura of commotion that characterized the flea market-art & antique mall on a Saturday afternoon. The sunny day had been especially busy for late January though few cut tags marked "sold" had been added to the box of vendor-numbered envelopes beside her. It had been a year since disposable income had disappeared around town, she thought. Pocket change went first, the substance of its jangle hardly noticed, metal coins shafted in the age of plastic money and electronic funds transfer. She'd seen trouble coming when the students on their way home from the school down the street stopped coming in for the "three for three"--75 cent bag of homemade cookies--from the jar on her desk that one of the vendors kept stocked.

The dust and determination of the frenzy of shoppers, craftspeople and shabby-sheik treasure hunters had settled. So much more was at stake when there was only one-of-a-kind or one batch to sell or buy. Unlike the rows of identical items in Wal-Mart or Target, the Ivy House Market rarely had more than one of a particular item—except perhaps a few identical cigar boxes, from the homes of sophisticated but addicted aficionados who bought their product only in cedar or mahogany boxes with dovetail grooves holding perfectly square corners together by sheer force—no glue. Odd, how boxes built as temporary housing for a small supply of quickly exhumed items were still the epitome of handcraft garnering the attention to detail that no longer held a secure spot in the global commoners' marketplace. It was the name of the 21st century game though that the boxes' value increased as they were discarded.

Like other Ivy House items the cigar boxes (among them the rarest of the rare—Cuban-made, banned here since before her birth) were caught in the economic hiatus that stretched to the ends of the earth, where, she imagined, other women like herself were, also burning candles, figuratively, if not in practice. Two ocher glows eclipsed into one from a head-on perspective—it was the only way to get what you needed, anymore. But there was something more than survival at stake here, she thought.

She figured the singularity of the work was just part of the process. The dolls, pillows, and skirts she stitched, each followed a single pattern, but not one was ever identical. Her partner's woodworking produced one-of-a-kind pieces, which, in another venue, might have been considered fine art furniture garnering top dollar. But here they sold slowly, even when the price tags barely covered the cost of materials, even before the downturn. People were not even buying books, let alone bookcases—and it was only a few who had replaced a book in one's lap with a Kindle. Despondency—her partner's natural response—slowed the woodworking to a near standstill, while the doll-maker responded to the downturn with a frenzy of production. What she didn't sell, she gave away to those who could never purchase them. Neither partner was ever fairly compensated for the cost of labor, not to mention for the creative ingenuity involved. In that injustice to the makers, alone, the Ivy House Market was like Wal-mart, she thought, wryly, looking down at her task at hand.

Shiny black eyes stared up from her lap, as she admired the permanent red smile—held without a quiver, even after the work-day ended. Fingering the stitched toes on the pair of brown feet that stuck out from the tiny overalls, she pictured the children's faces, pressed against the cold windowpanes, waiting for her to arrive with another basket of her lifelike, homemade gifts. They were the children of decades ago, the victims of a school bus crash that had never been reported in print. They still hung out at the railroad tracks on San Anto's south side, near the missions, and on summer nights, they gently rolled the cars of their human peers, tipsy with youth, across the tracks, as if the act, befuddled in the interlude of decades, could somehow go back and save them from the train. They left perfect fingerprints in the talcum powder that expectant revelers had sprinkled on their once chrome—but over the years turned plastic or rubber—bumpers before entering the neighborhood near the old mission, built stone by stone by indigenous craftspeople done in, caught in the bind of enslavement. The children's fingerprints that resembled the paisley filigree of human prints held no matches, no identifiable DNA. The children coveted the dolls they'd received of late, for their physical presence—for their ability to transcend the glass tomb of happenstance. Few living people understood that. The secret held by the woman who gifted the dolls to them was unclear to the children.

The last strand of hair was finally in place. As she gently inserted the needle to tie a knot, the small body lurched in her hand just as she heard a high-pitched, desperate voice say, "Don't send me out, again. You love me too much."

Surprised by the voice, the woman looked out past the doll to see her partner standing in the doorway of the Market. "Nonsense," she answered absently, to no one in particular. "Anyhow, we're already done in."

DR. ROBERT SULLIVAN
A Country Doctor, La Marque, Texas
Mary Jo Bogato

His voice unique…recognized anywhere…
Stature strong… determined… true….
Smile that could melt your heart…
Laugh that could make you smile…
Warmth that made you feel safe…
Stood his ground…
Made house calls in the middle of the night…
Had GIANT DOUBLE BUBBLE GUM in his office…
It was serious if you were in "the" office and not the exam room…
But the bubble gum looked so good…
The needles looked as large around as the double bubble…
But the bubble gum looked good…

He brought me into this world…
Visiting Dr. Sullivan for my checkups…illness and shots…
Then came my brother and it was my duty to catch and deliver him for his shots…
Chasing him down Yucca Street, across Amburn, and through Aunt Pauline's cow fields…
Then tackle and deliver my brother to Dr. Sullivan …
Michael was not tempted by the double bubble..
Told him to keep his treasure chest of goodies…and the shot…
Dr. Sullivan would talk to him for hours…
Then get his shot and I would get the double bubble gum…

I remember a pretty nurse by his side…
Her name is Ruth she was so dedicated…professional…and caring…

It was settled …they were a team…

The adults called him Sully…seemed silly to me…
He was Dr. Sullivan…
In his office…on the right you faced a large wall of paper files …
Sometimes you would hear, see, or smell the cigar of Dr. Kolb…
The long walk down the corridor and the chairs lined along the wall…
A corner office where they would always say,” this is only going to be a prick”
A red bubble appeared on your finger…scooped up by a glass tube…and band of aid…
Next door to Fullers Pharmacy for a coke float and chicken salad sandwich…
Served on a large white ceramic plate… huge greasy crunchy potato chips…
The world was good sitting on top of those red cushioned spinning stools…
My dad said I sounded like a bull in a china cabinet…
Tall and lanky… my feet were echoing on the tile floors of Mr. Fullers pharmacy walls…
A hop and skip across the railroad tracks to the Grocery…

Dr. Sullivan was the doctor for my entire family…
His family has roots in our family tree…
Invited to family celebrations…
Treated great grandparents, parents, kids and grandchildren…
Dr. Sullivan laid hands on six generations of my family…living…teaching…healing…
He lives on in the lives of my family and childhood friends through stories…
You hear them say, “Remember when Dr. Sullivan, Sully said...,” with big smiles and laughs…

Dr. Sullivan at my side in the delivery room…
Coaching me through natural childbirth…

I can hear his response to me on my last pushes of natural child birth…
Changed my mind doc…
I want that shot doc…
To late …push…push…
And instead of double bubble ….
He handed me the most precious gifts of my life…
A daily double…a son and a daughter...

Heaven just got a daily double bubble…
Whenever I see the bubble gum…I smile and can hear that wonderful voice…beautiful smile… Calming and secure…

ENOUGH

Joan Soggie

The fifties in rural America was a time of comfort, change coming in small bites, gratefully swallowed. The switch from horse to tractor power, from outdoor to indoor plumbing, from dirt roads to gravel and from gravel to hard-top, were welcome improvements. Life on the prairies had never been easier.

But with that easier life came other less palatable changes, unruly teenagers and their rock-n-roll attitude being one of the most upsetting.

"It doesn't even look like dancing," Eric complained as he stirred cream into his morning coffee. Catherine buttered his toast at the kitchen counter and smiled sympathetically. He shook his head, recounting for her the events of the night before. When he'd left Joanne and Kathy at their "record hop" before going to his Co-op board meeting in town, he'd been clear that he would pick them up at ten sharp. That would give them almost two hours of dancing. But there he'd stood in the doorway of the Legion Hall, the quiet summer night behind him, confronted by the primitive beat of drums and guitars as teenagers spun and stomped in a crazy swirl of hair oil and ponytails and crinolines. Instead of being able to just walk in, greet a few neighbors, collect his daughters, and go home, he had waited there for nearly half an hour. It seemed to him that the boys had an air of devious insolence about them, with their turned up collars and greasy ducktail haircuts. And the girls were not much better. Although the skirt length was mid-calf, when the seven-yard hemline swung upwards, held aloft by yards of net, it left very little to the imagination. For the first time, Eric felt alarmed about the younger generation in general and his daughters in particular.

"Well, I suppose your parents felt the same way about us. Even after we were married, your Mother did not like to hear that we had been at a school-house dance."

Catherine sat down at the table and sipped her black coffee, nibbled on her dry toast.

Eric scowled. "That was different - Mother disapproved of dancing on principle. Your parents felt the same way. But those schoolhouse dances we went to were just neighborly parties. With real music ... violin and piano ... not like that racket they call music today!"

"I guess it's the same for every generation," Catherine mused. "We try to bring up our kids to live in the world we have lived in. But it's not the one they will inhabit, so they end up having to find their own way."

"I hope you didn't put that thought in the thing you wrote for Mother and Dad's fiftieth anniversary party."

"Of course not!"

The unspoken thought passed between them in a quick glance, half wink, almost smile. After all, Mother's way is – in her mind – the only right way. Any time. Any place.

"Times do change, but people are still basically the same, even if they live in different ways. Farming methods change, but the land never changes. And some values never go out of style."

Perhaps it was that conversation that was in Eric's mind when he drove to Prairie City the next week with his teenage daughter. Joanne would attend a Young Co-operators camp for a week as the delegate from Jonesville, an honour offered annually to an offspring of one of the local Co-op members. Glancing at her, silent as she gazed out the window at the fields flashing past, it occurred to Eric that he really had no idea what his children would do with their lives. What were their dreams, their goals? He didn't know. His eyes had, by necessity, been on the farm, its day to day needs and demands, the unexpected breakdown of machinery or hike in interest rates, the need to plan ahead for the next season.

Seeing that his children were fed, clothed, schooled, and taught to be decent human beings had seemed like a big enough task. Dealing with their personal idiosyncrasies was Catherine's domain.

"What do you think ..." he began, then paused, "about life?"

Joanne looked at him, startled and a little alarmed. "What do you mean?" she stuttered.

"Well - what about life after death? Do you believe in eternal life?"

"Yes, I think so," she replied. Then, seeming to feel that was an inadequate response to such an open-ended question, she added, "But I don't know if I believe everything about heaven and hell that's taught in church. It seems to me that life is a lot bigger and more complicated than it seemed when I was little. Maybe a lot bigger than I can imagine now, too."

Silence, as Eric digested that.

"What do you think, Daddy?"

"I guess that a lot of things are bigger than we can imagine. When I think back to when I was a boy – well, the world has changed a lot over the years. But some things never change. The seasons, seedtime and harvest, the land, that doesn't change. And honesty, integrity, that will always be important. You can count on that not changing. Just be true to what you believe, okay?"

"Okay," she murmured.

The pause this time was so long this time that it seemed the conversation was over. The fields rolled by, the green wheat swayed in the wind, clouds of dust hid the gravel road behind them. Finally he spoke again, choosing his words with care.
"It seems to me that our lives must count for more than just our few years. They will continue on, somehow, in everything that we do or say. Whether we think it matters or not. We are a part of

something bigger. At the very least, our atoms will go into the soil, the grass and trees. Changing every year, but still there. Part of the land. That would be enough for me."

Joanne echoed his words. "I think that would be enough for me, too."

EXODUS

Jose A. Alvarez

María pulls out a clean sheet of paper and tries to solve Professor León's homework problem one more time. But the results of her calculations still make no sense; the fluid flow is too slow. She crumples the sheet of paper, tosses it in the waste basket and slams her fist on the desk shouting to no one in particular "Damn Bernoulli and his equation. I am running out of time." The final exam is in three days and she is not ready.

She gets up from the desk and walks into the kitchen where she finds Caridad getting ready to leave for the afternoon. She tells her "Cachita, I need a break. Do you have time to prepare me some lunch before you leave?"

"Sure Missy," Caridad replies. "I will bring it to you in the dining room."

Caridad prepares a ham and cheese sandwich with mustard and mayonnaise, slices of mango in heavy cream and a glass of cold milk. She sets the tray on the dining room table and asks María.

"Do you want anything else? If not, I will be leaving to see my grandchildren. I will be back later tonight."

María replies. "Thank you Cachita, I've been working all morning preparing for my final in Fluid Dynamics but I am still not getting it and I'm getting very frustrated. This is a perfect time for me to take a break. Thanks so much."

Cachita adds, "Perhaps you should call Matilde for some help. You know she's always been good at math and science."

"You're right at that, I know she's shined in math and science since we were in grade school. And now she's one of the few students who can keep up with Professor León's lectures at the University asking him probing questions. She should be able to help me." Cachita replies, "If anyone can help you I am sure Matilde can."

"I'd better call her right now."

María dials Matilde's number, but the line is busy.

"I'll have to call her later, Cachita" she says, "I still need a break anyway; perhaps a little Verdi will distract me, and provide some inspiration."

María gives Caridad an affectionate hug at the front door. After Caridad leaves, María walks over to the stereo to find her favorite recording of Rigoletto. She stacks the two LP's on the spindle, and turns the music on. Bernoulli will have to wait.

While María enjoys her lunch the music turns brooding and dark halfway through the first act. With a crescendo of foreboding music Count Monterone places a curse on the Duke of Mantua and Rigoletto. The curse scares María, it always does. She knows that Gilda, Rigoletto's daughter, dies in her father's arms in the opera's last scene as he screams at the fulfillment of the curse "*Ah, la maledizione.*"

The front door swings open smashing into the coat rack. Luis rushes into the house, slams the door shut and yells at María,

"You've got to stop whatever you are doing. I need your help right now."

María springs out of her chair. "Luís you're supposed to be in class. Why are you here? What's the matter?"

"I don't have time to explain. You must drive me to Gisela's house right away."

"What's going on? What's the rush?"

"Just do as I say. I'll have to ride in the trunk of the car."

"You've got to be kidding. What's wrong with you?"

"Let's go, let's go. There's no time to waste. It's a matter of life and death."

She gets her car keys. They walk into the garage and María opens the trunk of her MGB.

"See, I warned you, you won't fit in there, it's too small for you," she says.

"I'll have to fit," he replies as he clambers in. "Drive carefully; we don't want to be stopped," he says before she closes the trunk.

She opens the garage door, starts the car and drives off. She turns the radio as loud as she can and tunes in Radio Progreso. She eases into the afternoon traffic on Fifth Avenue, across the tunnel under the *Almendares* River into *El Vedado*. She knows the route well and soon they reach Gisela's house where she's already waiting for them and opens the garage door. In the darkness of the garage, María opens the trunk; Luís jumps out, and runs into Gisela's arms.

"Will somebody tell me what's going on?" asks María.

"The less you know the better. We won't be seeing each other for a while."

"Why? Where are you going?"

"You better drive back and not tell anyone that you drove me here today. It will be better for both of us. Promise?"

"All right I promise."

María hugs her brother, kisses Gisela and gets back into her car. She turns off the radio and drives back in silence. When she arrives back at their house she wipes off the tears flowing gently down her cheeks. She walks to the table where she had left her books and her half eaten sandwich, stashes Bernoulli away in her school bag and stores her unfinished lunch in the refrigerator. She wishes Cachita were here, but she knows she's gone. María is all alone in the big house.

A torrent of ideas flow through her mind, but she can't think straight. Should she tell anyone in the family about the secret trip to Gisela's? Are they are eloping? That's not likely though; they've been planning a big wedding. Something else is going on.
Seeking peace and comfort she kneels in front of the large Crucifix that once hung over the altar in the Chapel at their sugar mill, *Portugalete*. She prays softly. The rhythmic cadence of the Hail Mary's soothes her as she handles the rosary beads.

Her parents, Don Jacinto and Isabel, arrive after night fall. They find María sitting in the dark on the old wooden rocking chair listening to Rigoletto.

"Mom, Dad, I am so glad you are home. I've been alone all afternoon. Where have you been?"

Don Jacinto replies "We were at church, meeting with Monsignor García. Like us, he's disgusted with the Revolution. But he's going to take action. He will voice his concerns from the pulpit at the ten o'clock Mass this Sunday and he encouraged us to be there."
María adds, "I am upset too. I was mocked at school yesterday for voicing my opposition to the Agrarian Reform that confiscated *Portugalete*."

"Who mocked you?" Isabel asks.

"Pedro Ramírez the leader of the Revolutionary Council at the School of Engineering. You know him; he's a friend of Matilde's. He told me I should leave the country because the Revolution does not need, nor want, people like me. But I don't want to leave. I told him to mind his own business."

"Soon we may all have to leave," says Jacinto.

"Not me. I am staying."

"Young lady, you'll do as I say."

"Dad! I was born here and I want to live here and die here. I have no desire to leave. Why do you insist?"

"I am only thinking of you María. You are bright and have a wonderful future ahead of you. Why would you want to throw all of that away living in a communist country? There is no future here."

"I see you don't understand."

Isabel joins the fray. María, your father is only thinking of what is best for you. Try to understand what he is saying."

"And who will try to understand me?"

Jacinto continues: "Look, this has gone far enough. Let's wait to see what happens after Monsignor García's sermon on Sunday. I hope his sermon will have the intended effect."

Isabel adds, "Have you heard from your brothers today?"

"I haven't seen Carlos but Luis stopped by for a few minutes and then he left."

Jacinto asks "He stopped by? Doesn't he have classes?"

"I don't know. He didn't tell me where he was going."

"I hope he's not neglecting his school work."

"I'm sure he's not. But it looked to me like he had a lot on his mind."

"Perhaps he does, but he should be focused on his studies. He's got only one year left. I'll talk to him when he arrives. In the meantime let's have some supper."

Isabel warms up the black beans Cachita prepared the night before, cooks some rice, and fries steaks for the three of them. The familiar smell of the *sofrito*, sautéed onions with a chopped clove of garlic, wafts into the dining room. They sit down to say grace before dinner. Carlos walks in after the Amen.

"Hi Carlos, come on and join us," says Jacinto. "Your mother will cook another steak. Have you seen Luís today?"

"No Dad. Not since Mass this morning. I thought he'd be here."

"María saw him earlier when he stopped by. What's he doing skipping class in the middle of the term? I am worried about his grades."

"Don't worry dad. He's got straight A's going into finals. He'll do all right."

After dinner Don Jacinto sits on his rocking chair to read the morning newspaper while waiting for Luís. He enjoys reading *El Diario de la Marina*, the oldest newspaper in Cuba and the most critical of the policies of the new government. However, he hates reading the "*coletillas*." These brief summaries, written by the union leadership, challenge the viewpoint of the editors of the newspaper and are appended to any articles with which the union disagrees.

He vows to skip all *coletillas* and picks up a *Montecristo No. 4* from his cigar box, squeezes it between his thumb and his index and middle fingers to ensure it is fresh, and lights it with a wooden match. He calms down puffing on his cigar and reading about the exploits of Cuban players in the Major Leagues in the sports pages: Pedro Ramos had won the game for the Washington Senators against the Yankees in relief of Camilo Pascual striking out the side in the bottom of the ninth, and Minnie Miñoso was 2 for 4 playing left field for the Chicago White Sox. He falls asleep in the rocking chair waiting for Luís. When the first rays of the morning sun awake him the cigar, still unfinished, rests in the ashtray.

His anger at Luís turns to fear. It's not like him to disappear overnight. Jacinto fears the worst - Luís could be dead, killed by the secret police. How many times has he told the boys to leave politics to the politicians and to finish their studies?

He remembers his often quoted advice "There will be plenty of time to rebuild the country when the ebb and flow of Cuban politics gets rid of these interlopers"

Friday's breakfast is a gloomy affair. Cachita serves freshly squeezed orange juice, café con leche, and slices of buttered French bread. But nobody wants to talk. Only Luis's empty chair speaks, loudly, of the anguish permeating the room. María struggles with her secret. She decides to wait till evening to break her promise, not before.

María drives to school, parks her car on San Miguel Street, and walks briskly in front of the Havana Hilton, before crossing the street to stop at the kiosk on the corner of 23rd and L. Matilde sees María crossing the street and waits for her at the kiosk while ordering for both of them.

"Two coffees please, with lots of sugar."

"Coming right up."

"Good morning María," says Matilde. "I'm glad to see you."

"Hello Matilde. I'm glad to see you too. It's been a rough day."

They exchange kisses and sip their coffee quietly. Matilde breaks the ice.

"We need to talk," she says.

"Why? What's up?"

"Let's walk to the park across the street."

"We don't have much time before class starts."

"It'll only take a couple of minutes María. We need some privacy."

They cross 23rd Street and stroll into the park till they reach one of the wooden benches, where they sit. They can see the Radio Centro building, partly hidden by the trees, where the rebels took over the radio station for a few hours during Batista's regime before being killed or captured. María hates the olive drab uniform that Matilde wears daily as an officer in the *Ejercito Rebelde*, but she still feels close to her childhood friend.

"Why the mystery Matilde?"

"The police are after your brothers. They are going to arrest them."

"What?"

"Luis and Carlos are in trouble, and so is the rest of your family. Perhaps you should think about leaving the country."

"Are you crazy? I haven't done anything." She wonders about her drive to Gisela's house.

"I don't want to leave."

"Look María, you know that I love you like a sister, and if I tell you to leave I am doing it for your own good."

"You are the second person in the last twenty four hours to tell me to leave my country for my own good. My dad told me last night he wants me to leave too. Doesn't anyone believe I can think for myself?"

"You know Manuel would have wanted you to join the fight against Batista, but now he would also tell you, for your own good, to leave."

"That's not fair Matilde. You don't know what your brother would have felt, or what he would have said. You know I would have followed him to the end of the earth, even against my family's wishes, and I hate Batista and all he stood for. It was his goons that beat Manuel to death when they captured him near our house after the attack on the fort. But this government is much worse than I expected."

"Please, please be careful and don't get involved with the *contrarevolucionarios*. I don't want anything to happen to you."
"Don't worry Matilde. I haven't done anything wrong, nor do I intend to. I think this phase will pass and all I want is to get my engineering degree. I'll be ready to run *Portugalete* when my family gets the sugar mill back."

"You may have to wait a long time."

"I'm willing to wait."

"Let's go to class."

"Let's."

They walk in silence back along L Street and climb the steps, past the statue of the Alma Mater, to the main entrance of the University. When they reach the top, María turns around under the Greek columns and gazes down *San Lázaro Street*. Traffic congestion, as usual, clogs the street. A line of buses at the corner of *Infanta* and *San Lázaro* swaps riders and pedestrians. The local shops overflowing with customers sell coffee, orange juice, sandwiches, beer, books, and just about anything one wants to buy. She turns around and goes to class.

That night, dinner is a disaster at the Aróstegui household. Isabel cries quietly in her room. No one knows where Carlos is being held after his arrest at the house in mid afternoon. Jacinto declares his intention to leave immediately with the family for the United States. Luís calls from the Brazilian Embassy to let the family know that he has been granted political asylum. María tells the family about her trip to Gisela's house with Luis in the trunk of her

MG. She insists she does not want to leave. Even Cachita's *bacalao a la vizcaína*, the family's favorite dish, is overcooked and nobody wants to taste it, adding to the mood of despair in the house.

The police return to the house searching in vain for evidence of additional conspirators in the family. Tía Julia shows up after dinner. She has heard rumors about arrests of student leaders at the University and wants to offer her brother Jacinto's family whatever support she can. Soon she is drowning in gloom with the rest of the family. Jacinto breaks the somber mood stating that the best thing they can do is to go to the Mass at the Cathedral on Sunday morning in support of Monsignor Garcia.

The Cathedral is overflowing for the ten o'clock Mass. Monsignor García's sermon is eagerly awaited and he does not disappoint his flock. After the sermon a standing applause interrupts the Mass for several minutes. He has certainly struck a chord with the people in Church. Some of the phrases echo in Jacinto's ears as they leave the Cathedral:

"The Revolution that began so auspiciously has taken a wrong left turn..."

"Expropriation of private property…"

"Kangaroo trials of officers from the Cuban Army and Air Force..."

"Closing down newspapers critical of the policies of the government..."

"Unwarranted searches of private homes…"

Don Jacinto is excited and shares his enthusiasm with his wife and daughter as they drive along *El Malecón* back to *Miramar.*

"He hit the nail on the head. I hope the newspapers will publish his sermon tomorrow morning. This will have a strong impact on public opinion."

"I am not so sure Dad," says María.

"Everything he said is absolutely true," Jacinto replies.

Isabel joins in: "That may be so, but those who think like Monsignor Garcia are leaving the country, and those who don't agree with him are running the country. I don't think there will be any good coming out of the sermon."

"We'll see," says Jacinto.

María adds, "Dad, before climbing on the plane to Miami or New York, perhaps you can get in touch with some of your friends who have contacts with the government to see if there is anything that can be done."

"That's a good idea," he responds. "I will call Alberto Goicoxea and Lourdes Martín. Their lives were in danger when they emigrated from Spain after Franco won the civil war, and then they made a fortune in Cuba. He is a financial advisor to the government and has contacts with the highest levels in the revolution."

Three days later Monsignor García is arrested and placed on the steamship *Magallanes* on his way to Spain. Alberto Goicoxea calls Jacinto with news that Carlos is being held in *La Cabaña* prison awaiting trial, and that he would probably get twenty to thirty years for sedition. That same afternoon, Jacinto buys airline tickets for Isabel, María and him. Once they declare their intention to leave the country, Jacinto and Isabel have to sign papers giving away their properties and the money in their bank accounts to the Cuban government. But their investments in the United States were safe from confiscation by the Cuban Treasury. *La tía* Julia will be able to stay at the house, safeguarding it for the expected return of the family in a few weeks, or at most a few months, to their house in *Miramar*.

The following Friday, Julia drives them to the airport in Jacinto's car, a 1959 Ford Fairlane that she also will be able to keep. They hug, kiss and cry at the airport before handing the travel documents to the Frontier Police who inspect the passports and visas meticulously. They are searched in a separate room before being allowed back in line and on to the tarmac to climb the steps of the KLM Super G Constellation on its flight to Miami.

As the plane flies around scattered afternoon thunderclouds, María can see the coast line recede behind them, until it disappears below the horizon. "I will be back," she vows in silence. "I will be back."

FOG
Bruce Nelson

Where the hell is the other boat? A minute ago it was just a few boat lengths ahead of me. For that matter, where the hell am I? More importantly, where the hell is that rocky breakwater.

Standing at the tiller, I could just barely make out the bow pulpit of my 26 foot sailboat, *Summertime.*

Shortly after motoring out into Block Island Sound, the light mist had become dense fog. We had followed a larger sail boat through the gap in the stone breakwater that surrounds the Harbor of Refuge at Point Judith. I couldn't see the other boat and wasn't sure where we were in relation to the opening in the now invisible breakwater. My first thought was to turn the boat around and try to scoot back to the harbor. But what if the other boat is turning too? We might be seconds away from a collision! I have to warn them off! In a panic, I grabbed the compressed air horn from the locker under the cockpit seat, raised it over my head and pushed the button.

"Ouch!" cried Marianna, unprepared for the blast of sound a foot or so from her head. "Why didn't you warn me?" she shouted. "You blew that horn right in my ear!"

Clearly, I'm not handling this well. I musn't panic, gotta think things through, stick to my plan, stay the course. Yes, that was it, stay the course. And keep a good lookout.

"Marianna, take the tiller. I'm going to go up on the bow. You just keep us going in the same direction. Use the autopilot, but be ready to change course in a hurry if you have to."

Standing at the bow, holding on to the fore stay with one hand and clutching the horn in the other, I tried to remember what we had been taught in the coast guard boating course. I had my radar reflector hanging from the masthead. My small boat didn't have radar but the aluminum foil-covered, triangular cardboard construction, about a foot long on each side, was supposed to help make my boat visible to other boats, and ships, that had active radar. I had my can of compressed air with its little red plastic horn attached. *Was I supposed to blow it every two minutes? Or was it every 5 minutes? How much air is left in the can? I should listen for other boats.*

It was really quiet up at the bow of the boat. The "thump, thump, thump" of our single cylinder Yamaha diesel engine was not nearly as loud here as it was standing in the cockpit right over the engine compartment. The fog seemed to swallow up all the sound. I felt like I had cotton in my ears. I could hear a foghorn, probably the horn at the harbor entrance. It seemed to be coming from the astern. That was a good thing, I was pretty sure it wasn't coming from in front of us. Below me, I could hear the "swishing" sound as *Summertime* pushed through the water. We were moving slowly, just fast enough to let the rudder control the direction of the boat.

The world had shrunk. I could look up and see the top of the mast moving through a dark mist. I looked back and saw Marianna standing by the tiller with a gray wall of mist at her back. Looking ahead and to the left and the right, I was in the middle of a 20 or 25 foot circle of gray water and beyond that was nothing but a soft gray wall, A soft, gray and dark wall.. *Hark! Was that a noise off to my left, a sort of "clunk"? Maybe a voice? I blew the air horn...No reply. It seems darker off to my left. Is something there? No, it's gone now.*

Today was the last day of our nine day odyssey. We had owned *Summertime*, a 26 foot, 20 year-old fiberglass, bathtub of a sailboat for five years and had rarely sailed beyond Fishers Island Sound. This trip was our first real sailing adventure. We had sailed, mostly motored as it turned out, all the way to the Martha's Vineyard by way of Newport Rhode Island, 130 miles one way from our mooring in Pine Island Bay at the yacht club at Groton, Connecticut. On our way we anchored overnight in Newport,

Rhode Island and again at Cuttyhunk Island, off the coast of Massachusetts. We stayed two days at the Vineyard and returned by way of Cuttyhunk. From Cuttyhunk, we cut across the mouth of Narragansett Bay and spent the previous night in the protected "Harbor of Refuge" at Point Judith, Rhode Island.

Earlier this morning we had charted our course for today. Our plan was to take a heading of 265 degrees for 19 miles to the Watch Hill Passage into Fishers Island Sound. We would be traveling parallel to the Rhode Island Shore and did not expect too much traffic, certainly not much crossing traffic. Once we got into Fishers Island sound it would be a different story. There would be a lot of boat traffic, tricky currents, lobster pot buoys to look out for and reefs to avoid. There are more navigational hazards in Fishers Island Sound than in any other part of the United States Coast, or so I have been told. But that is where we learned to sail and they were our home waters.

In preparation for our adventure, we bought up to date charts of the areas and equipped ourselves with an autopilot and the latest modern navigational device, LORAN.

The autopilot was a box with a long stick coming out of it and a few knobs and buttons on top. One end of the box was attached to a swivel in one of the cockpit seats and the end of the stick was attached to the tiller. (The tiller is the lever that moves the rudder and steers the boat.) The box had a compass and an electric motor in it. When the boat is steered in the direction you want it to go, you push a button to set the autopilot and the stick pushes or pulls on the tiller to keep the boat pointing in that direction.

LORAN is a navigational device with a radio receiver and a computer in it. It picks up signals from shore based installations and calculates the boats position. The operator enters the longitude and latitude of the point he wants to go, a waypoint, and the computer calculates the distance and direction to that point. You can expect accuracy of about a quarter of a mile when the "way-point" is entered from the latitude and longitude. However, if you are actually, physically at a place you want to return to later on and tell your LORAN to enter your present location as a waypoint, repeat accuracy is supposed to be within yards. When we started our trip, I entered all the important waypoints of our route when we were actually at the points. So far, on our return trip the LORAN had been right on the money.

Time to blow the horn again. ... No reply. I think I see something! There is definitely something out there! Just within the gray wall in front of me, I could make out a dim outline of the hull of a boat passing directly in front of me. It looked like the boat that I followed out of the harbor. In a few heartbeats the boat was out of sight again. *What a Jerk. He could have run into me. He never even blew his horn to let me know he was there. The damned fool shouldn't be out here on a day like this.*

OK, lets think this out. I can't see where I am going. I'm not sure how to get back to where I just came from. There is a nut-cake out here in, a bigger boat then mine, who doesn't know where he is going and apparently doesn't know the rules, and is wandering all over. I don't know where he is but he's probably trying to go back to the harbor and I don't want to get in his way. I am pretty sure that I know exactly where Watch Hill Passage is and how to get there. Almost every day of this trip we have had mist and drizzle and it's always burned off after an hour or so. Decision made! We stay the course...were going home!

We motored on through the fog. The boat's top speed under power was about 7 miles per hour and we were creeping along at about 2-3 miles per hour. I stayed at the bow as the look out and periodically blew the horn. Marianna stayed by the tiller and monitored the compass. After an uneventful hour or so, the visibility got a little better. I could probably see about a quarter mile in front of us. With the increased visibility I felt it was safe enough to go back to the cockpit and keep Marianna company.

Several more hours went by and in the early afternoon I sensed a change in the air. Perhaps a breeze was stirring. The haze around us assumed a golden glow and, off our starboard beam, and we could just barely make out the Rhode Island Shore. It seemed to be just where it should be. I was bored and decided to set the sails. We pulled up the mainsail and turned off the motor. And we sat.

And we sat. There was no breeze. *Time to start the engine again.* I pushed the start button. Nothing happened. Now we were dead in the water. *Time for plan C.* Somewhere in the cabin there was a crank to hand start the engine. It was supposed to be a simple process but I had never done it and the crank was pretty rusty. I climbed down into the cabin. The engine was accessible by a hatch behind the cabin stairs. To get to the engine you must remove the stairs and remove the hatch. When cranking the engine, you are facing the cockpit, and cannot get back into the cockpit, where the engine controls are, until you replace the stairs.

The engine started on the first crank, but the crank handle did not release from the engine shaft because of all the rust on the crank handle. There it was, spinning at a high rate of speed between me and the cockpit controls, trapping me inside the cabin. At that moment I remembered how my grandfather had broken his arm when he was cranking up his old model t ford.

"Stop the Engine!" I cried. Wham! Bang! The crank flew off and hit the cabin roof. "No! Wait! Let it Run!"

By the time we got the mainsail down, the fog was back to a quarter mile visibility and we motored on. According to the LORAN, Watch Hill passage was now 5.3 miles away and we should be hearing the fog horn in an hour or so. Eight days ago, on our way out, I had set the waypoint for Watch Hill when we were half way between Red bell buoy number "2," off watch hill, and Green Gong buoy number "1" that marked Watch Hill Reef. The passage is about a quarter mile wide and there is a red and green buoy, "WH," right in the middle of the passage. If the visibility stayed the same and we were on course, all three buoys should be visible when we got closer. If the fog closed back in we would have to use our ears.

"Listen for the bell and the gong. The bell should to be on our right and the gong should be on our left." I told Marianna as we reviewed the charts... *and we will be in a world of hurt if both of them are on the same side.* "Steer to the left of the bell and to the right of the gong."

The minutes crawled by. The fog would thicken and the gray wall would get closer and then it would lighten for a while and the visibility would get better and then worse and then better again.

"I hear a Foghorn."

"Yeah, it must be the Watch Hill Coast Guard station. It won't be long now."

"Check the Compass. Is the autopilot plugged in?"

"Do you hear a bell?"

"I don't think so, all I can hear is the foghorn."

"Wait! Yes, I do hear a bell."

"Left or right?"

"I can't tell."

"I'm going to go forward and listen. Be ready to steer the boat. Remember keep the bell on your right and the gong on your left."

It is definitely getting brighter, the fog is starting to roll back and my circle of visibility is getting larger. There, straight ahead. A buoy. But what color is it? There are no colors. Everything is gray or black.

Seeing heaven for the first time must be something like this. The fog simply lifted up. There were three buoys near us. We were halfway between the bell on our right and the gong on our let and we were going to pass abeam of the red and green buoy in the center of the channel.

Spread out before us, under a translucent pearl sky, was the entirety of Fishers Island sound, the water a sheet of glass broken only by our small bow wave. There was no sun. The pewter colored light seemed to come from every part of the sky and from no place in particular.

There were no shadows. To our left we could see the length of Fishers Island. At the far end of the sound seven miles away, the New London lighthouse marking the entrance to the Thames river looked like a toy. Beyond the lighthouse, on the far side of the river we could make out the thin line that was Ocean Beach Park. On our right, was the Connecticut shoreline, the towns of Groton, Noank, Mystic and Stonington. Between the shore and Fishers Island were countless smaller islands and rock reefs and a multitude of lobster pot buoys, looking like cherries on toothpicks stuck In a silvery gelatin. In an area teeming with marinas and yacht clubs, not a single boat could to be seen on the whole of Fishers Island Sound. Nobody was foolish enough to go sailing on a day like today, nobody but us.

As we picked up our mooring at the yacht club, the setting sun broke through the overcast.

We were home.

FOR THE LOVE OF RAIN
Travis Whitehead

I remember when I first knew that my mother loved the rain. Hurricane Beulah blew in, and my mother pulled me close by a window and told me to look at the wind throwing sheets of water sideways. The storm was a living, breathing entity, tossing trees and garden furniture, ripping shingles off the house and tossing them playfully into the yard.

My mother was making sure I would never be afraid of storms. This one was like a dancing clown that had descended from the Heavens to frolic among mortals. "My goodness, listen!" she said. "Listen to the rain. Hear how it's hittin' the house? Isn't that somethin'? Nothin' else could make that except God! It's just too beautiful!"

And after the worst part of the storm passed she stood out on the front porch where the rain filled the air with its sweet moist breath and fell through the drain spouts in thick waterfalls, and she said "Ooooooo-Weeeee! Look at that rain!"

"You never saw rain before?" my father said with a snicker, his face turning to stone.

"Everybody knows it's raining," he said. "You don't have to broadcast it."

My mother just laughed and ignored him. When the rain slowed to a slight drizzle, she brought me outside, and I was awed to discover the street flooded like a river. The smell of wet concrete and earthworms and drenched cottonwood settled like a thick blanket over its bubbling surface, and she told me to run and get my tricycle. I quickly rode my red trike into the flooded streets, fascinated by the novelty, and then she rolled up her pants legs and dashed into the water, splashing about in circles as if she were mashing wine grapes, and then she was kicking water on me with her slender lily-white legs as mist collected on her thick mound of coal black hair.

“Come on!” she said. “Splash me back! Feel the water in your toes!”

And I laughed with great exuberance at this new game and began throwing big loads of water at her, and she at me, all the while laughing for the sake of laughing and for the ecstasy of storms.

“Rachel, you crazy girl what are you doing?” a voice called from across the street, and then I saw Yoli in her window, her large round face with the laughing brown eyes looking through the torn screen.

“I’m swimmin’ in the street! Come on out!”

Yoli laughed her husky, infectious laugh as she stepped away from the window, muttered, “She wants us to go out there,” and then there she was, she and her three grandchildren – Pepe, Felix and Anna - running across their flooded yard, she with her pants rolled up to reveal moles and varicose veins, her heavy firecracker chuckle revealing her gold front tooth, while spirals of amber curls waved about her wrinkled neck. Her grandchildren followed close behind in blue jean cutoffs, pearly white teeth shining against a backdrop of chestnut skin, jet black hair matted by the wet air.

They charged up to us, bending over and throwing big globs of water at us, me getting off my tricycle and kicking water, Pepe hopping on and erupting in squeals of delight as he peddled through the flooded street. Yoli and my mother laughed and kicked water until they fell in big splashes and then they laughed even more.

Suddenly my father stepped onto the porch and broke the spell. “Rachel, you silly thing, get back in here, the whole world can see you!” he barked.

"I don't care if they see me, they can think anything they want to!" my mother snapped back, never letting up in her laughter and splashing. "You go on back in the house!"

"The whole neighborhood's gonna be talkin' about this, and I'll never hear the end of it. 'Mr. McCormick, your wife's crazy!' Now get back in the house!"

"You get back in the house. They can say anything they want to," she answered, "and I am crazy. I married you, didn't I?"

And Yoli just laughed louder, and he just grimaced, shook his head and grumbled something under his breath, and my mother danced gleefully as the rain fell again in thick, skin-soaking sheets of joy.

GOING BACK TO RUBY*
Frank Cortazo

Albert Gudinez stood with eyes closed. He heard a voice call out to him.

"Come back!"

He opened his eyes.

Beside him stood Ruby, his sixteen year-old girl friend. She smiled at him with full, inviting lips. Her attractive face was as bright as the long, red wavy hair flowing down her shoulders.

“Wakey, wakey,” she told him. “You looked like you were on another planet.”

Albert blinked. Both he and Ruby were at the annual Spring dance at their local high school gymnasium. Almost everyone from school was there. Music played as other teenage couples danced nearby.

“Was I...daydreaming?” he responded. “I heard a voice...telling me to...’come back?’”

“Well, it wasn’t me,” said Ruby, perplexity filling her freckle-filled face. “ Was it male or female?”

“I...” he began but paused and smiled at her. “Forget it. Come on. Let’s dance and show everyone how it should be done.”

Ruby smiled at him. He was such a show off but...who cared? Such things needed to be tolerated by the girlfriend of the best dancer in school. And... senior year only came once within a lifetime.

For a while, they danced to several songs.

This local group of musicians is good, thought Albert.

He felt everyone's eyes upon them with every step, sway, and underarm turn they performed. Nervousness was not a problem . He "tuned out" all persons around him. As he danced, they became mere images, not to be focused upon. Of course, he would be aware of the ones upon the dance floor.

He truly enjoyed leading Ruby and maneuvering his way around without bumping into anyone. It was all a matter of...angles.

And, to think, he hated geometry class!

He and Ruby enjoyed dancing. They were "the perfect couple," both dressed in matching country western attire, the norm of their area of residence.

At times, while upon the dance floor, he would look into Ruby's happy, youthful face. They would both smile at each other.

She was all he ever wished for. He was fortunate she was his high school sweetheart. The fact she chose him over some athlete was a fortune in itself.

They were just about to conclude their third dance in a row when Albert heard the voice once more.

"Concentrate!" it told him. "Please! Come back!"

For one brief instant, the music went silent and the silhouettes of only five people filled his line of vision. He blinked and they vanished as he found himself still dancing with Ruby.

The music, meanwhile, still played within the crowded gymnasium floor.

“What are you thinking of? “ she asked him after the music stopped and they walked off to their seats. “You seem to be far away again.”

“I...," he stammered. “I heard it again.”

“Heard what?”

“The voice of earlier. It...called to me again to... ‘come back.’ I also saw...”

Before he could finish, he felt someone approaching.

“You two are the best couple on the dance floor.”

They turned and saw the smiling face of tall, thin Ms. Rayburn, Albert’s high school geometry teacher. She looked different with her long, auburn hair falling back over the long, maroon gown she wore.

After thanking her, they walked away but Albert made an abrupt stop.

“What’s the matter?” asked Ruby, concerned.

“I...I don’t know. I... feel dizzy.”

“Too many fancy turns,” she said, smiling. “I can handle them better than you. Come on. Let’s get some air.”

They exited the air-conditioned gym into the moonlit vastness of a humid, late Spring evening.

“Let’s not stay out here too long,” he said. “It’s cooler inside.”

As soon as he finished speaking, Ruby kissed and hugged him. A tingle ran through his body at the warmth of her lips and the scent of her perfume.

“Let’s get married!” he exclaimed afterward. “It’s only a few weeks until graduation and we can...”

“...But...” she interrupted, frowning, “that would be a...very big step. You know I love you but...how would we live?”

“We’ll manage,” he said. “I love you very much. Ever since freshman year. We were made for each other and...”

Before he could continue, he felt the dizziness overtake him. At the same time, the voice he heard earlier, spoke to him.

“Yes!” it exclaimed. “Fight it! You’re coming back!”

The dizziness became greater. Everything began spinning.

Albert held on to Ruby’s hand with a very tight grip.

“What’s wrong??!!” she cried, concern filled her face. “You’re...you’re scaring me!”

Albert could not focus. He felt her handhold diminish as the moonlight faded into the night’s darkness. She went spinning, along with everything else around her, into the blackness as well.

“I’m...falling!” Albert cried. “No! Take me back! Take me back!”

“Don’t go!!!’ her fading voice cried out to him. “Come back to me!!! I love you.........”

He closed his eyes.

And the darkness, thick and vast and impenetrable, swallowed everything. Only a lonesome silence remained, a silence soon broken by his own raspy voice.

“Take... me back,” he pleaded. “Take me back...to Ruby!”

He opened his eyes. For one moment, he saw a flash of light with the silhouette of a human figure. It was replaced by several people standing around him as he lay upon...a bed? A white sheet covered his body whose feeble physique was garbed in...a hospital gown!

At a far wall, he saw his reflection upon a large, mirror. The image of a white-haired, wrinkle-skinned old man stared back. Thin, plastic tubes were attached to specific parts of his body. The scent of ammonia intermingled with rubbing alcohol and spilled medicine lingered everywhere.

He remembered! The night he phoned for an ambulance to take him to...

Was this place where he was taken? Corville Medical Center? How long...?

“Uncle!” exclaimed a soft, feminine voice by his side. “You came back!”

A young woman garbed in a white blouse and black skirt hovered by his bedside. The shades of grayness were yet to appear upon the short, dark black hair covering her head. She bore a striking resemblance to her father, Mario, Albert’s long-deceased older brother.

“Carla?” he asked.

“Yes, Uncle Albert,” she said, tears running down her face. “It’s me. You’re going to be well! Soon, you’ll be...”

“No...!” he heard his feeble voice cry out. “I...I have to go back. She ...she waits for me! Ruby! Please! Take me back...to Ruby!”

As he closed his eyes, he concentrated upon willing his mind to return.

To go back...

...to Ruby!

In doing so, sleep overcame him and he, once more, became unconscious.

“No, Uncle Albert!” he heard his niece’s voice cry out from far away. “Come back! Come back!”

As he slept, he was unaware of the other figures standing beside his niece. They were those of the doctor and nurses who attended to him.

“It’s no use,” said the doctor to Carla. “He’s gone under again, this time maybe for good. It’s only a matter of time until Father Joe Silvero is called in to perform...”

“No,” Carla said, weeping into a white tissue. “I refuse to accept it. He came out of it this time...”

“This time,” the doctor agreed, “but...a massive stroke can be very debilitating and.. he wanted...he wanted to go back. Back...to where? And...who is this ‘Ruby’ person he mentioned? A figment of his imagination?

“There was someone named Ruby,” Carla said. “Once, a very long time ago. My father told me about her. Ruby Fuentes, a very attractive girl whom my uncle knew in high school, but only from a distance. She was a very good dancer since her parents ran a dance school. She didn’t pay attention to boys like my uncle who was much of an introvert and never learned to dance. He went through life never marrying nor fathering any children. Oh, he had his little flings with women but, much later in life. Ruby, however, he once told my father, was the love of his life.”

“What became of her?” asked the doctor.

Carla paused.

“On the night of the Spring senior dance,” she continued, “she became ill. A strange paralysis overcame her. The doctors never discovered what caused it and she died just days prior to graduation day. Uncle Albert never forgave himself for not ever attempting to even meet her. Perhaps...Perhaps now..."

She paused as the tragedy of her uncle's situation flooded her mind. As she turned toward him, she saw a smile forming upon his pale, ancient face. She wondered what it meant. What would be occurring within his mind?

If she knew, she would see a teenage boy back upon the dance floor of the school gymnasium. He would be enjoying the music of the annual Spring dance.

And, there, he would be dancing, forever, with Ruby, the love of his life.

GOLIATH
Ann Greenfield

"Mom, do I have to take Sam fishing?"

"Yes, John," Mom said. She handed me two fishing poles and nodded toward the door.

I carried the poles outside where my friends waited for me. "Sorry, guys. I can't go to the movies with you today. I have to take my brother fishing."

"Geez, John, Brenda is going to be there," said Jake, my best friend.

I took a deep breath. "There's nothing I can do about that."

"But Brenda really wants to sit with you in the balcony," said one of the other guys.

"Yeah, and it's a scary movie," said Jake.

Phil nudged me in the side and said, "You could put your arm around her." My friends nodded and laughed. Jose made smooching sounds and wiggled his eyebrows.

I sighed, looked around at my friends and said, "Sorry, guys."

"Can't you go after the movie?" asked Jake.

"No," I said. "Tell Brenda I'll call her later." Jake slapped me on the back.

Sam nudged his way into the center of our circle. He looked around at us and declared, “I’m going to catch Goliath today.”

All of my friends snickered. Then Jake said, “People have been trying to catch Goliath for years. It’s just a legend. There’s not really a forty pound catfish in Cedar Creek.”

“Oh, yes, there is!” insisted Sam.

I shook my head and poked my thumb to my chest. “If anyone is going to catch Goliath, it’s me,” I bragged. “Besides, you’re only ten. He’s too big for you to reel in.”

“No. He’s not!”

“Then you’re too small,” I said and pushed him out of the way so I could talk to my friends. Sam lowered his head and kicked the dirt.

“Fishing sounds more fun than the movies,” said Jake. “Maybe we should blow off the movies. Can we come?”

“No!” shouted Sam. “It’s just me and John.” When my brother looked at me, his eyes gleamed with anticipation, and he had a huge grin on his face. He couldn’t stand still. Sam put his hand over his pocket, and said, “And I’m not telling any of y'all my cat fishing secret.”

I stared at Sam and laughed. “You have a cat fishing secret?”

Sam nodded, but didn’t say anything. He grabbed one of the poles from me, pushed his way clear of me and my friends, and skipped toward the path down to the creek. I waved good-bye to my friends, grabbed the handle of our blue wagon holding our fishing supplies and the sack lunches Mom had prepared for us, and reluctantly followed Sam.

About four-thirty that afternoon, Sam and I returned to the house. I pulled the wagon, and Sam skipped beside me wearing a grin to match the size of Goliath.

I had texted my friends the news about Goliath, but hadn't said who had caught him. They were waiting for us. So was a reporter.

My friends surrounded me and patted me on the back with their congratulations. They all wanted pictures with the legendary Goliath of Cedar Creek. They paid no attention to Sam. He stood to the side and didn't say a word.

After the slaps on the back and congratulations were over, my friends and the reporter wanted to know, "How did you do it?" I looked at the ground and kicked the dirt. Then, I glanced at my brother.

Sam looked at me with such admiration, then surprisingly said, "John used cornbread and a spinner."

I squinted my eyes at Sam. He grinned back at me.

I couldn't let this go on. "Guys," I said. "Sam is being modest. He's really the one who caught Goliath. He deserves all the credit. I only helped him load Goliath into the wagon."

My friends gasped. The reporter took notes. Jake ruffled Sam's hair and said, "Hum, cornbread and a spinner."

Sam moved next to me and whispered, "Why'd you tell them?"

I bent down to look him in the eyes. "I appreciate you trying to help me save face in front of my friends, but the honor of catching the legendary Goliath is rightfully yours."

Sam threw his arms around my neck and said, "I love you."

I said nothing, but hugged him tightly.

The next morning there was a picture of Sam, me and Goliath in the town newspaper. The caption read:

Goliath, 42 pound catfish caught by Sam Smith and his brother John.

GUADALUPE ADVENTURE
Verne Wheelwright

Summer on the Guadalupe River in South Texas is tubing time. People come to New Braunfels from all over to float down the Guadalupe in inner tubes. Big inner tubes, from inside truck tires. All along the river, small shops rent the large, inflated inner tubes to tourists and visitors who want to float the river. The rental fee also includes rides back up the river, usually in the back of a truck or an old school bus. Not fancy, just fun. And that's why so many people come here to float the river…it's fun.

Of course, the fun is floating in cool water on a hot day, splashing often enough to keep comfortable, looking at all the other floaters in their swim suits, sipping a cold drink, laughing because you're having a good time with friends, and generally enjoying life. Maybe getting too much sun or a little too much beer, but having a good time.

My grandson started floating the Guadalupe with his parents when he was about seven years old, so he was experienced with the floating life and looked forward to at least a few days on the river each year. Now, he was out of school and independent. A man!

With two good friends, they rented a camp site, then went to buy groceries. Their grocery budget, to which everyone had contributed, was $100, with which they bought $95 worth of beer and $5 worth of food, mostly potato chips. They locked the beer safely away in the large tool box in the back of my grandson's pickup, except for several six packs of cans that they took with them (no bottles allowed on the river) for a few trips down the river before dark.

Dinner that evening was more beer. My grandson doesn't remember much about that evening, like when he went to sleep,

and is not even certain where he slept, because…well, he just doesn't remember. But he's certain he had a good time!
But he does remember waking up, feeling terrible and smelling worse. He couldn't believe he could smell so bad. And he was still feeling the influence of all that beer. He groaned, searched around for a towel and his bar of soap then stumbled off toward the campground showers. That's what he really needed -- a hot shower.

The shower building had a primitive look, as though it had been thrown together with whatever materials were available cheap, but in spite of the general appearance, the showers were great. He'd expected a row of shower heads on a wall, like in the boy's gym at his high school. These were individual showers, plywood stalls with shower curtains. But he wasn't really interested in all that, he just wanted lots of hot water. Which he got. Big shower heads with lots of hot water. The hot water and soap were starting to wash off the effects of yesterday's beer binge, when he heard the voices. Women's voices. He realized the plywood walls were thin, and there was a big gap between the top of the wall and the ceiling, but he was surprised that the voices sounded clear, not muffled, and they seemed to be getting nearer...they sounded like they were right beside him.

"Someone's wearing men's underwear!"

Panic! That was underwear and shorts! What were these women doing here? Then it hit him. Where was he? Was he in the women's shower? He must be. "Oh, no! This can't be happening!"

He didn't waste time thinking, he acted.

"Ladies," he called out, "I'm afraid I've made a mistake. I'm in the wrong shower. If you'll cover up, I'll grab my stuff and get out. Okay?"

A pause, some whispers, then, "Just a minute!" Another pause.

"Okay, we're covered."

And they were, one towel each. Grandson only had a closely held wash cloth, but he was quick, out of the shower and into his shorts. Then, he turned and apologized again. They were both young, his age, and very attractive. He didn't waste time. He was gone.

Giggles followed him.

Back on the river, grandson and friends were letting their hangovers slowly fade away, assisted by a little "hair of the dog." They were all laughing.

"You should have put that washcloth over your face! They can still ID you!" More laughter.

They were on their second trip down the river that morning when he heard.

"There he is! The guy in the dark gold trunks. That's the guy that was in the shower!"

He knew the voice before he looked and felt a chill. One of the girls in the shower. They were both there in a cluster of tubes near the shore. It looked like they had a football team with them. Well not that many, but they all looked big. Really big.

Grandson's buddies sensed trouble and already seemed to be drifting apart from him. Maybe it was just his imagination. He could visualize a running fight down the river. Or an ambush at the landing spot. Not sure what to do, he waved!

From the large cluster of tubes went up a cheer. "Really cool, man! Really cool!" They raised beer cans in a salute.

Laughter followed the two clusters of tubes as they floated on down the Guadalupe.

HANDYMAN*
Pete Gray

It used to be I could do it all,
Plug the leak and patch the wall.
Now I can't get off the floor.
I ain't no handyman no more.

Hard work never did bother me,
Crawlin' on hand or bending my knee,
Reachin' up high to change a light,
Getting' on down to lift a bight.

Up in the attic to change a fan,
Down in the cellar with the router man,
Put a new faucet in the sink.
Change the filter, pure water to drink.

Out in the cold shovelin' winter's snow,
Sweatin' the heat for the fires glow.
Mowin' the lawn to keep it low.
Pullin' them weeds so they won't grow.

Nail that drywall, tape and spackle.
Sand it smooth so there ain't no crackle.
Wire those outlets, change those breakers.
Be glad this lot ain't got more acres.

Assemble that cabinet, hang that hinge,
Homeowners watchin', don't make 'em cringe.
Clean the dirt from the old sump pump.
Take the garbage off to the dump.

Paint the walls, the ceiling and floor.
Careful with the trim around that door.
Vacuum the carpet and sweep the kitchen.
Fix whatever else needs fixin'.

Clean out garage and sweep the drive.
Beginnin' to feel more dead than alive.
Back is achin' and my calves are sore.
I ain't no handyman—no more.

HEAVEN
Eunice Greenhaus

My dreams come true at every turn
My life is full of joy
I've got each thing for which I yearn
Each day a brand new toy
I wake each morn so full of life
I leap right out of bed
In my life there is no strife
It must be that I'm dead

HISTORY LESSON*
Caroline Steele

Listen! Hoof beats of horsemen near,

And lilting barks accompany

Jingling bridles, stirrups, trumpets clear,

Announcing royal company.

Hever Castle rises from the field,

Surrounded by a moat carp-filled.

Doomed queen's childhood laughter pealed

'Till she was courted, wooed, then killed.

Henry's visits were for some years vexed.

A clever lass paid price too high,

Was accused of having Henry hexed,

Imprisoned briefly, went to die.

Feel the history seeping from the gate.

Imagine pageantry therein.

Stop a minute – hesitate.

Shed a tear for Anne Boleyn.

HOMER AND OL' JACK*
LeRoy Overstreet

In the beginning I hated ol' Jack. Back in 1939, I went to work on a 40,000 acre cattle ranch whose owner was named Joel Yates. This was before the USDA implemented the screw worm eradication program. Almost every calf that was born got screw worms in its navel and had to be roped and treated.

Joel said: "Homer, I'm going to let you ride ol' Jack. He's lazy and cantankerous but he knows how to take care of himself. The others are sort of high strung and inclined to get exhausted if you have to work 'em real hard."

The very first day when I was working in one of the far pastures, he ran off and left me. One of my boots had a little hole in the sole and the thorns and grass stubble stuck my feet as I limped the six miles back to headquarters. My feet were sore and bloody and I swear ol' Jack was laughing at me there in the barn lot as I led him over to the tack room to take the saddle off. I whispered in his ear. "Ol' Jack you won the first round but I've got a surprise for you tomorrow."

The next morning when I roped a calf I tied the rope to a mesquite tree. Ol' Jack looked around at me with the whites of his eyes showing and started sidling off toward the barn. I jumped up, ran towards him and yelled, "WHOA JACK!"

When he got to the end of the rope, he turned a complete flip over backwards and landed on the back of his head. It knocked him out. He shuddered and I thought he was dying.

By the time I got the calf treated, he came to and struggled to his feet with his legs all spraddled out and his head hanging down. I told him, “Ol’ buddy, it looks like we’re stuck with each other. You may not like it any more than I do, but you and I are going to do just as good work as the other hands on this ranch from now on and you’re not going to embarrass me anymore."

Three or four days later he tried it again but wasn’t running quite so fast. After that, he never tried to leave me again.

Joel had three sons. Clayton and Little Joe lived on the ranch. Cecil was a cattle trader and lived in town. Cecil was continually sending cattle to fatten, and about once a week we gathered a load or two to sell. There was a corral on one side of the cow pens about the size and shape of a football field. We put the herd in one end and Cecil and Joel rode in on their cutting horses to separate the ones they wanted to sell. The rest of us lined up on the fifty yard line to keep the two herds separated.

Ol’ Jack drag-assed around and let one get by us every once in a while so everybody cussed me out and told me how sorry I was. I felt lower than a snake’s belly. He knew what to do and how to do it. He was just plain lazy.

I started really working on him. If a cow turned back to the left and he didn’t turn back fast enough, I stuck him in the right shoulder with my spur really hard. If it turned back to the right and he wasn’t fast enough, I stuck him in the left shoulder really hard. If he didn’t jump out fast enough I stuck him in the flanks really hard. If he did good I said, “Good boy, Jack.” And when his shoulders and flanks got good and sore he decided that he liked “Good boy, Jack” a whole lot better than the spurs.

It wasn't long before Ol' Jack and I began to get a little respect from the other hands. They could depend on us to do our share of the work.

Cecil's cutting horse was a sorrel mare quarter horse. She was really good. Cecil didn't let anybody else ride her but himself, not Joel, not Clayton, not Little Joe. Not even Jesus Christ would have been allowed to ride her if He had been there. Cecil was afraid she might pick up some bad habits.

One day, while we were eating dinner, Little Joe looked out the window and exclaimed, "Looka yonder! What a dust cloud coming down the road!" It was being led down the dirt road by Cecil's pickup. He must have been doing at least 60!

He slammed on the breaks and slid to a stop in the yard. We all ran out to see what the emergency was about. Cecil said, "You know that special order I've been putting together for that buyer from Amarillo? Well, he wants 'em right now. The truck's right behind me. We've got to get 'em up and get 'em loaded."

The yearlings were in a small holding pasture but there were about 100 head of other cattle in there with them. Cecil's mare was nowhere to be found. We always turned her out in one of the big pastures when he was not planning to be there.

Joel said: "Cecil, why don't you ride Ol' Jack? Homer has been helping me cut some lately and Ol' Jack is working real good. There's a couple of colts in the lot he's breaking. He can ride one of them."

Cecil said, "Papa, Ol' Jack's so sorry. If he's the best we've got then this ranch is getting in awful bad shape."

We started working the cattle and Ol' Jack worked like a seventeen jewel Swiss watch. He wasn't making any mistakes. Cecil started really enjoying it. He started pushing Ol' Jack just a little bit. He cut out a wild yearling and decided to crowd it a little to see what Ol' Jack would do. He spurred him pretty hard and Ol' Jack knew that was the signal that if he messed up he would get spurred in the shoulder real hard. He decided that he would rather have a "Good Boy Jack", so he got ready for some serious cutting horse work.

The yearling cut back to the left as fast as lightning, right through his rear end. Ol' Jack pointed his ears at the yearling, planted his front feet and turned back even faster.

Cecil kept going straight!

The yearling got back in the herd. Ol' Jack looked around with the whites of his eyes showing at Cecil sitting on the ground with his face as red as a beet. All the rest of us had our hands over our mouths because we couldn't keep a straight face but didn't dare laugh out loud.

Cecil got up, dusted himself off and climbed back on Ol' Jack. He made another pass at the wild yearling. This time Cecil was ready and Ol' Jack outmaneuvered the yearling. The yearling cut to the left but couldn't get away because Ol' Jack was there. He cut to the right but Ol' Jack was there too! Everything that yearling tried Ol' Jack was ahead of him.

Cecil said, "ALL RIGHT!"

After the yearlings were loaded and headed toward town, Cecil came over to where we were sitting on the cow pen fence in the shade and said, "Homer, you've been working Ol' Jack pretty hard here lately and I think he needs a rest. Why don't you ride my sorrel mare for a while?"

I felt like I was 9 feet tall!

HUMMINGBIRDS
Mary Jo Bogato

Hope Migrating

The wind was like my mother's voice, soothing and calming, telling me it was okay to go and play beneath the trees and upon the soil. Her voice would encourage me to go and look for buried treasure and fasten forts from vines and limbs and built fires to cook my china berries.

Today, as I lay in this hammock, the sounds of birds singing and tree limbs tapping remind me of my youth. My mother Mary, with the support of Mother Nature, parented me jointly within the outdoors. Living along the sandy beaches of the Gulf of Mexico to the rolling plains of Colorado County. Ice cold water filled the river streams, curved earth of mountain ledges and the caverns where I played as I grew into a young woman.

Today, the hummingbirds arrived and I opened the door for my morning coffee break. To my surprise, there must have been forty hummingbirds. I spent the morning watching them as they flickered, suspended around two feeders. They love the new, shiny bases to the feeders of past years. They prefer the feeders that have the perches to those without.

The hummingbird show went on for hours, interrupted by a wasp, woodpecker and mocking bird.

My mind wanders and I think how wonderful it would be to have a hummingbird Christmas tree. My Christmas tree would have little red feeders and lots of yellow perches outlined in white lights.

My mind wanders again, "The garden must be a manger for the raccoon's in this drought as the flowers are all matted from them sleeping in them last night."

The quail flush and sounds of tiny prop-propelled engines fill the air as the hummingbirds move from feeder to feeder and I watch as a wood ant scurries down my dress.

My eyes and body are full of the weight of my world. Exhausted by reality and relaxed by hope. How hard I try to make a difference in the outdoor world, protecting, educating, and passing on my passion, respect and wonder.

Purple Flowers dance in the shadow of the mesquite trees.
The treetops howl as the mesquite forest protects me and I am swung in my hammock surrounded by green.

Tiny chirps from hummingbirds surround me and, if you listen, you will hear four chirps, followed by one more in a higher pitch as they hasten from feeder to flower and favorite perch.

They climb to the highest limb and, then, watch anxiously, turning their heads from side to side. What are they looking and watching for with such intent?

Maybe it is to guard their precious nectar. But, now, there are so many and they sit almost shoulder to shoulder, all staring upward and heads moving from side to side.

What are they searching for?

What is the sign, the one that says it is time to move with this Autumn wind? What is the key? Is it the change in pressure or in the degrees of the northern wind, pushing, guiding them? Why do they let me sit so close just feet away and share their cycle of life?

The cat lies beneath my feet and they are not afraid, or are they so confident in their abilities and just worn from their travel?
They are newborn, young and old, all on the same journey. Migrating through life and to life!

I am not sure why today, but the sounds, smells, and caressing touch of wind have taken me back to my favorite childhood memories. They are the memories of the outdoors where I felt safe.

The sound of the wind through the mesquites reminds me of the ocean rising to the shore and then retreating. The tides are calming and then fierce with the return of the waves. I wonder if Mother Nature intended us to hear and feel the same in the woods and upon the sands of the ocean's door.

Mother Nature has created lullabies to help us feel free and safe. My precious memories and Mother Nature's daily gifts of wonder supply our hearts and souls with poetry that helps us understand.

The Hummingbird Tree

This tree, so rich with the shimmers of green, white and red feathers, glistens to the sway of the wind and boughs of trees dancing.

I have not felt this weight of comfort for many years and, possibly, not since I was a child. A child filled with hope, hope for my future and hope for the future of my feathered friends.

The hummingbirds and I came together today and, as I shared my wealth of water and nectar, they trusted and shared their life. I feel as though they have brought back my youth.

The sight of their beauty and the frailness of their size combined with the determination to survive.

So tiny and the only thing they seem to fight is each other? I wonder if our Creator sees the same in us.

The leaf reaches for the sun as if to waltz.

A hummingbird flutters level to my eye and stays for 60 seconds, looking at me with questions, and I return the stare with no answer.

Exhausted by reality and relaxed by hope.

"IF YOU DON'T FINISH, IT WON'T BE THE END OF THE WORLD."

Janice Workman

For several years I heard that on December, 2112, the world, as we know it, would come to a screeching halt. To what did we owe for this cataclysmic action? Back then, the Mayan calendar was coming to an end.

I remember glancing at the cavorting cats and diving dogs on my own calendar and made a mental note to pick up a new one at the Dollar store, just in case we were still here when 2013 came around. As the end of the year rapidly approached, I thought, "Humm. If aliens came down tomorrow, ready to conquer the world, they would take one look at our calendar and return to the mother ship explaining, 'Don't bother, their world ends in a few days. We can move in afterwards to create our piece of paradise.'"

As the date of destruction became more specific, I saw anxiety grow in some folks around me. I heard talk of "Day will become night for three turns of the Earth."

"The electronic grid will be fried and nothing will work." (Seems I'd heard that before, like when the Millennium came around the corner.)

"The planet will undergo a massive shift and the poles change. Gravity won't work for a time and we'll all float off into space."

I've been told "If you aren't part of the solution, you are part of the problem." Mind working quickly, I came up with the perfect answer. Bungee cords. Yup. On E-Bay or late night info-mercials I could rake it in. "For today only, you can buy two twenty foot bungee cords for $25 and get two more three mile long ones for free. Those are perfect for family and friends who always wanted to take a space flight, but never had the finances. But wait, if you order now, we will toss in a handful of our 'imperfect' collection for that special mother-in-law or ex-husband that could benefit from your generosity. Color coding? Not a problem. What easier way is there to keep track of your group when chaos is happening all around you. Worried about 'Rex the wonder dog'? We have several options, including a bungee that snaps to yours so he thinks he is going for a walk. Call now. All purchases must be paid in full by December 20th."

In an attempt to reason with a particularly 'concerned' individual, I explained what Jimmy Buffet meant when he said "It's 5:00 somewhere."

"Look," I said, "When you cross a 'date line', you are in a different day than you were two minutes ago. So how is the world going to end on the 21st if it is already the 22nd or still the 20th someplace else?"

The concern in her eyes changed to hope. "You mean, I can go to one of those date lines and run back and forth so I don't have to go through the 21st?"
"Well, no, I don't think it works like that. But look at it this way. If the world ends, we'll all be gone and there won't be anything to worry about," I said in a quiet, soothing tone.

"You're not helping!" she said.

Looking back through my life, I recall three full scale global destructions predicted internationally with matching books, merchandise and multiple web sites. (should have gone with those bungee cords). I've lost count of prognostications by lesser individuals, never mind those that were revealed to be frauds by "Snopes"-- an on-line hoax alert site.

On a recent tour that included a Mayan ruin, our native guide discussed the forth-coming prediction with great pride. Locals thought it amusing that the world was basing it's future on a calendar folks didn‘t understand. That was okay though, tourist industry and souvenir sales were through the roof!

Some folks will use any excuse to celebrate, and there were plenty of “End of the World” parties. I hope none of the revelers did anything they regretted the next day.

The end of the world came and went with neither a whimper nor a bang. My explanation is that the Mayan Calendar maker was dyslexic. He really meant 12/12/12 not 12/21/12. Everyone was so excited about 12/12/12 being a really special, lucky date that the end of the world slipped by without notice.

Another explanation, received by E-Mail showed two Mayans: one says to the other “You want to grab a beer?”

The other guy says “I’m working on this calendar."

"Well, if you don’t finish, it won’t be the end of the world.”

So, when’s the next one?

JOURNEY OF AN EMPTY SOUL
Travis Whitehead

A vacant soul, dark-shrouded

Suffocated by false apparitions

Sanctified delusions

Devouring the human senses

Lost humanity wandering

Speechless through the human journey

Life without drama, tragedy or comedy

Blinded from ecstasy, robbed of transgressions

Struggling, aching, longing, dreaming,

Agonized by lost memories

Tortured by sacrificed passions

Restless for humanity dreaming, laughing,

Crying,

A bland world

Of smells without fragrance

Visions without color

Tastes without flavor

Music without melody

Leaping from the precipice

Thrashing, flailing, terrified falling

Clinging to nothingness

Hungering for sanity.

Safety abandoned, dogma discarded
Death desired over breathless life
Falling, crying, laughing, senses absorbing
A butterfly emerging
Diving into a sea of color
A breath of ecstasy, a timeless wonder
Smells with fragrance
Tastes rich with flavor
Music dancing with harmony
Scented dancers beneath flowering trees
Winds intertwined with perfume and laughter
Twisting shorelines of rocky beaches
Stars whirling, moon beckoning
Warm breath, sweet kisses, a passionate embrace,
Lovers twisting and turning, rising and falling
A heart beating, enthralled with life
Beckoning an anguished soul
To laugh, to cry, to breathe, to dream.

JUANITO THE COWBOY WINS
Frank Cortazo

Juanito the cowboy sat upon his horse
Until his time had, at long last, run its course
And then, to the ground, he went when he was thrown
Near the big corral where he lay, all alone.

In due time, he stood and, the dust, shook away
To keep clean his denim pants whose hue that day
Outlined with blue, now looked much faded and worn,
Their brightness, that garment, no more to adorn.

His determination to win, not yet spent,
Enhanced his will power, for Juanito went
Contented, then, with courage as his great guide
Of faith in himself, that untamed horse, to ride.

With no time to spare, that horse, he rode once more,
Beginning, his body, to feel stiff and sore,
Outwitting, though, his fear of failure which, nought
Yet, of his persistence, to take command, sought.

Win, Juanito did, the grand prize of that day,
In time for a trophy to put in display
Next to a framed picture of him that would be
Set upon a wall, with pride, for all to see.

(read each first letter of the first word of each line downward to reveal the four words of a secret message)

LETTERS FROM MY FATHER*
Jose A. Alvarez

My father's side of the family was a complete mystery to me until I was nearly thirty years old. My father, Baldomero, was the third of nine brothers and sisters born to my grandparents Santos and Vicenta in Luces, a small village on the rugged coast of Asturias in northern Spain. He was the only one of the nine siblings to emigrate; the others lived the rest of their lives within walking distance from the place where they were born. In 1924, at age seventeen my father sailed across the Atlantic on the Reina Maria Cristina to seek fame and fortune in Cuba, leaving Luces and the rest of his family behind. He settled in Havana, where he met my mother Isel. They married in 1940 and had two children. I was born in 1943 and my brother, Raul, in 1947.

We enjoyed an idyllic childhood growing up in a closely knit family centered on my mother and her relatives. We spent our summers and weekends at the house my parents built on a hill overlooking a beautiful beach in Santa Maria del Mar. On Sundays the house, "La Casa de la Playa," was full of friends and relatives who came to spend a day at the beach and to enjoy the afternoon meal my grandmother Panchita, an excellent cook, prepared every Sunday. Yet we knew very little about my father's side of the family, only what we could glean from occasional conversations at the dinner table about news received in the infrequent letters arriving from across the Atlantic. At the dinner table my father referred to *Luces as La Aldea*, The Village.

The triumph of Fidel Castro´s Revolution on January 1st, 1959 changed everything. A few months later the family split up and we would not see each other for several years. On August 12th, 1960, when I was seventeen, I left Havana for college in the US. On March 22nd 1961, a few weeks before the Bay of Pigs invasion on April 17th, my brother sailed in the steamship *Covadonga* for Spain to live with our father's side of the family and wait for the Revolution to run its course. He was thirteen years old. Our idyllic existence had been shattered. My parents stayed behind thinking that Fidel Castro would not last long. Little did they know!

During the next few years I seldom spoke with my relatives. Phone calls were very expensive and difficult to arrange. Calls to my parent's house in Cuba had to be scheduled days in advance, and often could not be completed. My relatives in Luces had no phones in their houses so I had to call *El Espacio*, the local pub, to ask someone to pass the word to my brother for him to call back. But he also had scarce means so we did not call each other, we used the mail.

After 1964, my parents had lost their business, confiscated by the Revolution. They realized the Revolution was there to stay and decided to leave Cuba. But by then it was difficult to escape. After college I started working and tried –unsuccessfully- to get visas for my parents to enter the United States. The only country willing to accept my parents was Spain, because my father was born there. They flew to Spain in 1967 to stay with Laureano and Lola, my father's brother and sister in law, in their tiny house in Luces. While spending a year in Spain they obtained US visas. They flew to New York in April 1968, arriving in the United States shortly after Martin Luther King's assassination in April of that year. They settled in Red Bank, New Jersey, near where I lived. My maternal grandparents and great aunt arrived in the United States shortly thereafter reuniting the matriarchy once again. In a few years my parents became citizens of the United States.

Still, I knew very little of my relatives in Spain. I finally took my first trip to Spain in May 1971 when I went to visit my brother and meet my father's side of the family. When I met them I had trouble remembering the names of so many cousins, uncles and aunts. We stayed at Laureano and Lola's house. The kitchen was the largest and warmest room in the house, with a wood burning stove that Lola kept going all day long. A string of home-made sausages hung from the ceiling inviting everyone to eat. The meals were plentiful, earthy, hearty and long.

The street where they lived was not paved. My relatives wore traditional Asturian wooden shoes with three tiny feet, called *madreñas*, to walk in the muddy fields and streets. I was invited to walk on them and found them incredibly uncomfortable.

The family lived off the land. They grew some vegetables and raised a few cows to sell the milk. They also had several chickens and a couple of pigs. Laureano walked his cows every morning to lush local pastures, *"prados,"* to feed on the plentiful grass, and he walked them back home in the evening to sleep in the barn adjoining the house. He told me the body heat from the cows helped to warm up their house. That night, I kept waking up when I heard the cows stumping their hoofs in the barn next to the house. In the morning I woke up to the sound of Laureano sharpening his scythe.

Once I had met my cousins and my aunts and uncles. I thought I would visit them again frequently, but I found many reasons to keep postponing my next trip. I was raising a family, my parents were living in the US close to where I lived, and crossing the Atlantic by plane was expensive. I did not return for another fifteen years.

After medical school in Salamanca, my brother settled in Gijon, the largest city in Asturias, nearly an hour away from La Aldea via a hilly country road full of curves that was often covered by dense fog. For the next thirty years I visited my brother in Spain half a dozen times, always spending a day at La Aldea to visit the relatives.

After my wife Ana and I moved to Europe in 2004 we visited the family more often. My brother, his wife Pilar, my cousins Agustin, his wife Maxi, and my cousin Isel, also visited us in The Netherlands. Over time, the stories my cousins told me about my father's generation gave me a good idea of Baldomero's life before he sailed to Cuba. But the stories of why he left Spain were still shrouded in mystery.

My brother knew that our father had been working in another village –La Isla– when he left for Cuba. Agustin had heard that my grandmother Vicenta had sent my father to work with relatives in La Isla who needed help with their farm. Cousin Isel thought that it was Tio Jose who encouraged him to emigrate. She even showed me the house in La Isla where Jose's family lived at the time.

Michael, my son, was very close to my father. He also became interested in searching for Baldomero's family history and I relayed to him many of the stories my cousins had told me. We wanted to find out why my father had settled in Cuba and decided to plan a trip with my brother to La Aldea the next time we were together in Spain. We wanted to dispel the mystery and search for the real story.

We did not have long to wait. Last Spring my cousin Manolo, the son of Laureano and Lola, invited Ana and me to the wedding of his youngest daughter Marta, on September 11, 2010, in Asturias. I called him during the summer to ask him if my son, Michael, could come too. He was delighted and told me that Michael would be more than welcome.

Ana and I were very happy to go to Marta's wedding. We had met her during one of our previous trips to Spain when we ate a wonderful meal at Isel's house in Luces. Manolo contributed *"pulpo a la gallega,"* a delicious snack he had prepared with an octopus Marta had pulled out of the water earlier that morning at a rocky beach near their house.

At the wedding reception we sat at a table with several of the cousins. One of them suggested we meet with a distant relative - Pepin el de La Isla - who was sure to have some knowledge about my father and his travel to Cuba. My brother made a few phone calls and arranged a meeting with Pepin the following weekend in Colunga, where he lived.

On Saturday, Ana and I drove to Colunga with my brother and Pilar, to meet Pepin. The roads are better now and the drive only took us fifteen minutes. Michael drove back from Bilbao, where he had met some friends, and met us there. Agustin, the self-appointed family historian, also came to Colunga. While Ana and Pilar went off to do some shopping, the rest of us met at a local bar to dig into the past, armed with sketches of the family tree.

Over a couple of beers Pepin told us that, as far as he knew, the uncle who had encouraged Baldomero to go to Cuba was Casimiro, not Jose like we had thought. He also told us that Casimiro´s son Javier, who also lived in Colunga, could provide us with more first-hand details about Baldomero´s immigration to Cuba. Someone had told my brother that Javier´s health had been failing and his memory of events from eighty years ago was not very reliable, but Pepin assured us that Javier was lucid enough to talk to us. He said, "I talked with Javier earlier this week and, while he may forget some things, he still remembers many details and will be able to tell you more about the events from that period than anyone else alive today." We decided it was worth a try.

Raul called Javier and arranged a visit to his apartment in about thirty minutes. Michael, Raul and I finished our beers and walked a couple of blocks to Javier's apartment on the second floor of a building still showing signs of damage dating back to the Spanish Civil War. Javier and his wife Teresa received us gladly. She offered us some wine and we sat at the dining room table to hear Javier's stories about Casimiro and Baldomero.

He confirmed that by 1920, when my father was working in La Isla, some relatives of Casimiro had already lived in Cuba for several years and that it was his father who had encouraged my father to go to Cuba. I remembered then that my father had spoken occasionally, while we still lived in Cuba, about some relatives who lived in Oriente province, at the eastern end of the island miles away from Havana.

We asked Javier many questions and he provided us with as much information as he could remember. His memory had been stretched as far as it could go and the conversation was winding down when suddenly he said: "Perhaps you'd be interested in some of the correspondence between Casimiro and Baldomero. I think we have a stack of letters here in one of the drawers."

"Yes, of course," said my brother. We became very excited as Teresa went searching for the letters. She looked in a couple of drawers and finally found a folder full of old letters in one of the dining room cabinets. She gave Javier the folder. He glanced at a few of the letters and said, "Yes these are the letters," as he gave the folder to Raul.

Immediately we began reading some of the letters from the small treasure trove we had stumbled upon. The letters were dated from 1937 through 1957, a span that included the last couple of years of the Spanish Civil War, World War II, and reached nearly to the Cuban Revolution.

There were letters including medical prescriptions my father was sending for his relatives. There were letters itemizing the contents of his shipments of clothing and food for individual relatives. Reading these letters I became aware that my father in Cuba had become a bulwark against hunger and poverty for his family in Spain during a very difficult period.

There were letters talking about the ups and downs of the clothing store my mother and father owned in Cuba. There were letters expressing their desire to travel to Spain to visit the family, but facing the grim reality that crossing the Atlantic in time of war was unsafe and undesirable.

I found a letter from April 1940 announcing the forthcoming wedding, on May 17th, of my mother and father. Raul started reading a letter from early December 1947, but suddenly he stopped. In the letter, my father quaintly says, “The stork is coming to deliver us a package later this month.” My brother, holding back some tears, said, “He is talking about me. I am that package.” Raul was born on Christmas day 1947. We had to stop. It was more than we could handle in just one afternoon.

Javier gave us the letters for us to keep. He also gave us some pictures that made us laugh; especially a picture of my father, his cousin Angel, my godfather Pepe, and Raul’s godfather Antonio taken in the 1930’s. The clothes they wore made them look like extras from The Untouchables.

My father’s letters rekindled memories of my happy childhood. I felt closer to him. They opened my eyes to an aspect of his life as an immigrant that was new to me. I was surprised how he remained so close to his family in spite of the years and the distance that separated them.

In 1995, in deteriorating health and afraid of the exorbitant costs of American health care, my parents settled in Gijon to be near my brother and under his medical care. My father died three years later at age ninety one. We scattered his ashes into the sea off a cliff by El Faro de Lastres, a lighthouse overlooking the Bay of Biscay, less than half a mile from the house where he was born. Thomas Wolfe says “You can’t go home again.” Yet, after searching for his roots and finding his letters, I think that my father, who lived most of his life far from the place where he was born, did not yearn to go home again. He had never left.

LITTLE GREEN REDNECKS
Hugh Barlow

Terra = Terror.

This was the message that I spray paint on the red rocks of the Valles Marineris. The green paint stands out well against the stone, It matches my skin, and I'm sure that others will appreciate the message fer years ta come.

Me an' Earl (my buddy-Earl is short for Earliariaxxzzz) is on our way ta the Tharsis Montes ta hunt fer chitterblax. They is gettin' harder to find, an' we had ta bring the snellacs along ta sniff 'em out. If you ain't never hunted chitterblax using snellacs, I feel sorry fer you. Theys ain't nothin' more excitin' than the brayin' of a snellac as she scents a chitterblax. The pack gets excited, an' we set 'em loose ta chase the critter to its lair. Once holed, the chitterblax is quite dangerous, but my lead hunter is sharp. She knows how ta dodge in ta keep the chitterblax in the lair without gettin' close enough ta be gored.

We is usin' Earl's suburban because my all terrain vehicle doesn't have enough room for me an' Earl ta sprawl out fer a nap. It's quite a drive ta the mountains of Tharsis from Xanthe. Between me, Earl, an' the snellacs, we need all the room we c'n git. We tanked up at Charlie's Bait-N-Bullets. Charlie's is the last stop on the route ta the mountains where you c'n git both ammo and fuel, an' Earl's suburban only gits about 6 clicks ta the liter. It's a good thing that Earl has a big tank! We also have cans strapped ta the roof in case we run out.

The slickers from Ophir Planum kept givin' me an' Earl dirty looks as we drove through town. I overheard a couple of 'em comment that we shoulda got us a new vehicle since

Earl's old 'burban uses too much fuel an' is contributing ta the greenhouse gasses in the atmosphere. Them pantywaists was all drivin' Beamers an' wearing pretty clothes. The uppity bastards even went so far as to cover the red stripe on the back of their necks. There ain't no ROOM in a Beamer for a pack of snellacs, an' if we was to bag a chitterblax, we would NEVER be able ta bring it home-not even if we used the ROOF of the vehicle! Earl's fender's just about right fer carrying an adult chitterblax. Nope, we ain't buyin' no fancy-pants econo-box! Gimme room an' POWER!

Ennyways, me an Earl headed ta the trench an' made that pit-stop for freedom of expression. Earl kept a look out for the fuzz whilst I left my mark, an' once I was done expressin' myself an' takin' a whizz, we loaded back up an' put a few clicks between us'n' home. A few days trapped in a suburban with a pack of snellacs will make a fella come ta appreciate the great outdoors. Even taking potty breaks, it was gettin' rank inside the 'burban by the time we got ta Syria Planum. By then, we could see the mountains in the distance, an' me, Earl, an' the snellacs was gettin' antsy. The snellacs was tired of kibble. I knew the feelin'. Dry rations was startin' ta taste like cardboard.

Arsia Mons has the biggest crater with a huge glacier in the middle. They's more area to hunt for chitterblax there, but it is also the most popular with the pantywaists from the city. Most of the chitterblax has been hunted out, and if the rangers even think you is there ta bag one without a permit, you will get fined. The pretty-boys can afford the permits. Me an' Earl cain't.

The next most popular spot to hunt fer chitterblax is Pavonis Mons. It is closest to the base camp and has a nice deep crater. The ice gets very little sunlight, and has not receded as much as the glacier on Arsia Mons, but the glacier is much smaller. We chose ta go to the most difficult hunting ground, Ascraeus Mons. You don't have to pay for a permit there. Few folks actually bag anything, an' most don't want ta climb the tallest of the three mountains just hopin' to get somethin'. We was desperate, so's we went even though the glaciers on all three mountains is evaporatin'.

The shrinkin' habitat o' the chitterblax perplexes me. I keeps hearin' about how all this global warmin' is man made, and I sure as hell wish them Terran bastards would stop pollutin' the atmosphere. I mean, here we are on Mars, an' them bastards hasn't even left HOME an' they's messin' things up fer us! The smarty-pants back on Terra have been sending all kinds of junk our way, though, an' we keep hidin' so's they cain't find us. We sure don't want ta encourage 'em ta come an' visit in person. We got most folks on Terra convinced that we don't exist, an' we aim ta keep it that way. Look at what theys done ta Venus, after all!

Chitterblax is about ta us what bears is to Terrans. They ain't the same, but they's occupy about the same nitch in the ecology. They's about as big as a polar bear, but they's got eight feet insteada four. They's ain't got no pelt ta speak of, but theys shell is quite useful fer household utensils. Until we discovered Terran radio an' Terran TV, theys was the main source fer our kitchen goods. The meat is quite tasty too. Now we make pots an' pans outa metal like you all, an' we make plates an' cups outa ceramic. Mosta the city folks eat food that is growed on farms run by families like mine. Theys a few o' us who perfer to do things the old fashioned way, and me, Earl, an' our families is some o' 'em. We still prefer ta hunt. Course, it is sure too far to go huntin' by thraxiz like we used ta, but the SUV works well instead.

“Hey. Bubba!” (my name is Bubbaliariaxxzzz an' me an' Earl is kinda cousins) Earl yells out.

“Tell me ag'in how all this warmin' is the fault of the Terrans.” Earl ain't too bright, an' sometimes you has to repeat yourself ta git him ta unnerstan'.

“I was listenin' ta one o' them Terran religious broadcasts 'bout Mother Earth when they up an' says that global warmin' was all the fault o' mankind, an' they had ta make the non-believers see that all the drivin' they did, an' all the stuff they bought was causin' the planet ta warm up. This was makin' the oceans rise an' killin off whole species o' critters just like it is doin' ta the chitterblax. Some folks got ta fightin' 'gainst the faithful by sayin' how Terra has been warmer than it is now, an' it was likely that the warmin' they was goin' thru was due to somethin' other than man. Some even went so far as ta say that it may be ole Sol who is responsible and point out that our planet and Pluto was experiencin' the same type o' effect, but the preacher done said not ta believe 'em 'cause the science was settled. He said there was some kinda consensus among scientists an' that this proved the existence o' 'Man Made Global Warming.' The sceptics replied that in no way was the science settled, an' that this 'Global Warming' scam was nothing but 'Watermellon Politics.' They say it is green on the outside, but red inside. I don't quite know what that means, but I think it has something to do with growin' watermellons, which the Terrans love ta eat. Ennyhows, I kinda think that the preacher was right. I just wish them damned Terrans would get their act together and quit polutin' the atmosphere 'round here. I heard there was a group that called themselves 'Earth Firsters,' and that their motto was. 'Earth First.' I think I'ma Firster. Earth First! Let'em mess up the OTHER planets later! Maybe they will do themselves in before they get ta us. You ready ta go huntin'?”

MISFITS
Georgia Tuxbury

Barney was dead at fifty-eight. Millicent sat under the canopy staring at her lap while an oversize coffin was lowered into the grave. One hand fluttered to her chin, almost as if she were waving goodbye.

Millicent, who was never called Millie, and Barney, whose death certificate revealed his name to be Bernard, had been an unlikely couple. He was a brown grocery bag while she was tissue paper. Barney was a candy maker, overfed and sloppy; Millicent, a librarian, was meticulous and hunched over. Both of them had spent their lives over-indulging in their wares.

Barney dipped and rolled and swirled his chocolates with fingers that, in contrast to the rest of him, were tapered and deft. Quite regularly a candy would flip into his mouth, and a finger would fly across the already chocolate-splotched apron covering his great expanse of belly.

And Barney would burp. Deep, resounding burps that were too deliberate to ask for pardon. But his rich, delicious candies were works of art that he praised as much as he sampled. "Food that gratifies more than the stomach," he would say. Tasting to him was a sensuous pleasure that fulfilled something within him that perhaps could have been called his soul.

Millicent, on the other hand, felt tears arise when a new book by a favorite author crossed her desk. The excitement of anticipation would cause her pale face to take on the tones of a cherry bon-bon. She savored descriptive phrases and would re-read them a dozen times, letting them play around in her mind, licking their flavor clean.

What capricious Cupid had brought these two together? And what feeble Fate had kept them there? Millicent, as a young lady in her twenties, was soft and fragile as icing. Barney, at the same age, was solid as a novel by Dostoevsky.

Barney resembled Orson Welles. His voice, though, was hoarse and unpolished and his conversation was blotched with "bullshits" and "ain'ts."

As a young lady, Millicent's slumping of shoulders put her head on a slight angle so that when she looked up she appeared coy and bashful .Her voice was as fresh as peppermint and words like "doth" and "perchance" were sprinkled like powdered sugar through her speech.

So there she sits, with her shoulders bent, now in a dowager's hump, peering up at the preacher with a look more questioning than coy. What were the years with Barney like?

Did he at times curl up beside her in bed with a book? Did the two of them ever share chocolate-covered cherries, letting the pink filling dribble over their chins? Wouldn't a man like Barney crush her pretzel ribs? Millicent's thoughts, like nougat, were thick and impenetrable.

"Goodbye, Barney, goodbye." Millicent reached into her purse for a handkerchief.

Were those tears really real? Were their years together truly fulfilling? Did they ever read each other's souls ? Together, did they share the sweet, fresh fruit of Paradise?

Millicent dabbed at the corner of first her right eye and then her left. Then, spreading the delicate, embroidered hanky over her lap, revealed it to be—not clean as one would expect, but smeared with something that looked suspiciously like . . . chocolate.

MISSING AGAIN*
Frank Cortazo

It happened again! Madalyn was gone! Her side of the bed had not even been slept in!

Seventy-five year old veteran Joe Sanderson shook away the sleepiness of a forgotten dream. He got up and put on his robe and house shoes. Not bothering to comb his unruly, white hair, he walked over to the window and looked outside. The fog had settled in quite well over the darkness of the night.

His mind raced with the possibility of where Madalyn could be. Maybe she had insomnia and decided to wander somewhere around the trailer park. That could be dangerous at her age, out there alone at that hour, with her bad knees. That was probably what she did, but...no! She must have gone over there to them again! Over there, where she felt safe...safe...from him!

He took a flashlight from the kitchen and opened the front door of his tiny motor home. As he stepped out into the darkness the coldness of the fog touched his face and pierced through the robe and flimsy sleeping clothes he wore underneath

He headed straight over to Estelle and Fred's. They were good people who became their closest friends since moving to this senior citizen trailer park. Lately, Madalyn got into the habit of going over there after putting up with one of his drunken binges. Maybe he should phone them. But...wait! He did not have his cell phone. He would have to knock on their door and wake them.

When he got to their nearby motor home, he stopped.

No light shone from inside. Estelle and Fred were probably asleep, as they would be at that late hour. Madalyn could not be in there. Maybe he SHOULD go back and call the police or 9-1-1!

No, not yet! First, he must talk to Fred. It could be nothing. Fred would be willing to help, even at this late hour. He was a good friend.

He ignored the tug of the bushes that surrounded their yard and pushed through to the entry. He flashed his light through the window of the door and knocked.

"Fred!" he called out. "It's me, Joe!"

After several more knocks, a light switched on inside. A moment later, the front door opened. Fred's tall, dark shape stood outlined against the glare of the light behind him. Joe could see the locks of Fred's uncombed, gray hair as his friend rubbed the sleepiness out of his eyes.

"Fred!" stammered Joe. "Madalyn is missing again! I'm certain she came over here again! I...was...drinking again tonight and I... I...but..., never mind! Please! Let me talk to her! Let me tell her I didn't mean the awful things I said!"

Fred realized what was happening and opened the screen door. He stepped outside. "Calm down, Joe," he said, softly. He placed a comforting left hand upon his friend's right shoulder.

Joe began to panic. "You don't understand! I need to tell her everything is fine!"

Fred continued to reassure Joe as he walked with him outside. He could smell the faint odor of liquor on this old man who had become a good friend to both him and his wife.

"Go home, Joe," he said. "Madalyn isn't here."

"No..." he said, almost with a whisper. "She...has to be here. You're...I...wait a minute! There's something you're not telling me. She IS here, isn't she?! She's with you! I...I know she can't stand my drinking! The way I get! I know I'm not the easiest guy to live with! My tours and all! I'm used to commanding respect!

Obedience! Discipline! Please! Tell her it's all right! She can come back home! Please!"

"Joe, you need to understand," Fred said. "Your drinking and all, well...how can I say it? It's...gone beyond that."

Joe stood there, silent, with a puzzled look on his face.

"What?" he asked, after a brief pause. "What do you mean it's gone 'beyond that?' I'm perfectly fine! I attended the meetings like she insisted! Doesn't that count for anything?"

"Joe, walk with me and...I'll explain it to you."

"No!" Joe pulled away from Fred's hand on his shoulder. "It's a conspiracy! Everyone is against me! The army, my son, Madalyn, and...and...you! You want me put away, is that it! Well?""

"No, Joe, calm down, you've got it all wrong," Fred said. "Think back. Think back to when your problem began a few years ago. Your OTHER problem, not just your drinking. What Madalyn had to go through. What YOU had to go through and what you are STILL going through. Your excessive drinking pales by comparison. Remember what you were told when you were released. Things were not going to get any easier. And your son...your son...well...what can I say about him that you don't know already? It's been so long since he last came down to visit you."

Joe remained silent for a few moments. He thought back. Yes! Now, he remembered. The room. The room at that place where Madalyn had arranged for him to spend time in after that last, violent drunken scene in front of his son and their friends. The room which had been his home for many weeks. The room where Madalyn had visited him until the day when he had been released and declared fit to return home. He remembered...but...he remembered the other room as well...the other one...the one where she...NO! It all came back to him in a flash! Everything!

"I...remember now," he said. Tears flowed from his eyes. "I'm...so sorry. All I wanted... was to say...I'm sorry...for everything."

"I understand, Joe," Fred said. "We all do. Now...please...go home. Would you like for Estelle or myself to watch over you tonight?"

"No." Joe rubbed the tears off his cheeks. He turned and walked away as he spoke.

"I'm.all right, now. Really. I'll be fine." He dissolved into the foggy darkness.

Fred walked back to his motor home. Estelle waited for him at the front door. The once auburn locks of her fine, straight hair now glimmered in whiteness.

"Is he OK?" Her silhouette contrasted with the light that brightened the small living room. "Maybe one of us should stay with him."

"He'll be fine..." Fred sighed. "...for now."

"It's...not working out, is it?"

Fred gave her a skeptical look. "They were so sure!" he said. "They reassured us he could function and adjust on his own! It was such a relief for him to leave that place. He would have just vegetated there. Now, it looks like he'll have to go back, this time for good."

"How many times, now, has it been that you've had to remind him?" she asked. "He keeps coming back to the same thing. The demen---"

"Don't!" he interrupted. He lifted a finger and said, "Don't say it! Think of what it would be like if it were me or you! Would you be able to bear your twilight years that way?"

"I...don't know." Tears welled in her eyes. "But...it's... it's so not fair! All those years of serving his country, living a modest life with Madalyn, raising a son who doesn't care, and...for what? For this?!"

After a moment's silence, she wiped her eyes. "What did you tell him?"

"What I've told him every night," he said. "He always remembers how ill Madalyn became after he was released, how hopeless it all was for her. The treatments she went through. His OWN condition. It just added to his drinking problem. He remembers and then goes back home to sleep. Sleep. That is what WE should be doing. Don't worry. We'll look in on him in the morning."

"What about tomorrow night?"

"We'll deal with that when the time comes."

They switched off the light and went back to bed,

The night wore on.

Back in his own home, Joe lay awake. He stared at the empty, right side of his bed.
It wasn't right, he thought. Madalyn had gone away again. It had happened again. He was getting tired of looking for her whenever she left him in the middle of the night.

Sighing, he sat up in bed and took a drink from the beer bottle resting on a small table nearby. Well, he thought, let her blow it off for a while. Fred and Estelle would watch over her. Soon, she would return. She always did. Once she had calmed down, everything would be all right again.

Mouse in the House
Carolyn Ross

We believe the caper went down something like this:

The mice watched the house for us to leave early on the morning of August 5. By 9:00 a.m. they had found one entrance to the house via a drain hole next to the water heater. They couldn't all get in fast enough so they chewed through a wire behind the television to open up a larger hole to enter into the living room. They convened for their first meeting shortly before noon.

They decided the most effective damage could be done if they were organized. They divided up into smaller factions and worked up their plans, then came together as a group and elected a president to provide leadership so they could fully execute their devious plans.

One group was assigned to the train room and storage area, another to the bedrooms, other groups divided between the study and the living room. The largest group got the crème de la crème—THE PANTRY.

The pantry faction had the most fun! They crawled in, around, behind, and in some cases under whatever was in their path. Their excrement left a trail that could not be denied as their doing. They chewed into weak, defenseless containers and devoured the contents. They chose not to taste the sugar free Jello, those boxes were untouched. But they found the cornbread mix and a variety of other mixes in soft packages to be a special delight! Evidence revealed the pantry faction capped off many meals with a taste of coffee from Folgers coffee bags. They had even ingested two full packets of mouse poison I had positioned in the water heater area, but we did not find one dead mouse!

With proper nourishment, their troops multiplied! The younger mice grew to adulthood and joined in the fun!

It's always an exhilarating high for me as we get closer and closer to returning to our home in the Rio Grande Valley after an extended motor-home road trip. Three months this time on a 6,400 mile trek that took us along a rather circuitous route as we visited friends and family along the way, saw many new sights, and attended a 55th high school reunion.

As is my custom, I spent the last few days on the road working on my to-do list planning for the immediate tasks to be done on arrival and also formulating my longer term goals for the coming year. This year I added something new—I listed what I considered to be my accomplishments during the past year. This exercise seemed to bring new goals into better perspective for me. My plan was to hit the floor running. I'd have the immediate tasks done in a flash and then would be ready to begin on my plan for the coming year.

We pulled up in front of the house and off-loaded basket after basket of our belongings, everything required to insure our personal comfort for three months. The refrigerator holdings were immediately transferred to the house refrigerator, the other baskets lined up in the rooms where they would be dispersed to their former familiar spaces.
We moved the motor-home to the storage area. When we returned we began the arduous task of putting everything away with the goal of having the major work done by 4:00 p.m. when, in keeping with tradition, it would be time to sit back, sip a cool drink, and congratulate ourselves on a job well done.

Not!

I moved one of the baskets to the pantry, planning to get the kitchen squared away first. I noticed crunchy sounds coming from beneath my shoes as I stepped around in the pantry. I looked down and saw what looked like wild rice and cornmeal all over the floor. Indeed, some of the packages stored on the wire racks on the pantry door had spilled out onto the floor. I looked closer and realized it wasn't wild rice I was stepping on; it was mouse droppings . . . EVERYWHERE!

I heard a skittering sound coming from the wire rack which is fastened to the pantry door. I stepped back looking up near the top and spotted two tiny sets of beady eyes peering out from behind the gravy mix packages. I called out to my husband and he came running. We spotted two stringy tails dangling down between the wires . . . the two little mice hiding there didn't know we could see them! Bob banged on the door and we watched as they threaded their soft bodies down through the wire shelves and made a hasty retreat into a far corner of the pantry.

We stepped back as we began our assessment of just what a mess the uninvited house guests had made. The pantry is spacious, slightly larger than four and one-half feet by six feet with 60 running feet of shelf space, 18 inches wide. The pantry houses food items in one area, seldom used mostly over-sized kitchenware in another, and cleaning tools in one corner. Not one inch of this area went untouched by the invaders.

We walked through the house looking for evidence of infestation. In every room we found tracings of droppings, some heavier than others. Bob discovered where the little darlings had chewed through and severed the antennae wire which disabled our satellite radio system.
It appeared as though they had left no corner untouched . . . what a mess.

Bob and I decided the best course of action was to begin with the eradication process. I had first thought old-fashioned mouse traps would be the best way to approach this as I felt the glue traps were cruel – better just to snip their little heads off with a snap-trap. But after seeing just what damage the little ***monsters*** had done, I decided to glue them to the wall. And we did! We collected 21 dead mice in the first few days using mouse traps, glue traps, and little houses that go snap when disturbed. We also installed electronic sonic noise gizmos to repel whatever invaders survived.

When we had logged 24 hours with no new mouse cadavers to dispose of, we began the true cleaning process. Beginning in the far top corner of the pantry, every item was removed and was either tossed out or washed. As each shelf was emptied it was cleaned, sanitized, and adorned with a pretty new shelf paper. ALL 60 feet worth! I had to be careful while scrubbing the bottled and canned goods so that I didn't wash off the labels, but the cleaning process was a success and no container lost its label.

Each room of the house was cleaned, vacuumed, and sanitized which hopefully made them fit to use once more.

One of the last things I cleaned was the vacuum cleaner. We actually had three vacuum cleaners running most of the time: the Oreck upright, the canister-style from the motorhome, and the small portable Oreck that has the hose and all those handy attachments . . . a tool for every purpose.

The final indignity was when I found I had to clean even the cord on the portable vacuum and discovered that those little ***rascals*** had chewed through the cord, but luckily had lost interest before they chewed into the wire.

I could have been electrocuted!!!

Okay, now it's time to get back to my original plan and get myself organized and ready for the new year. Oh yes, and to revise my trip departure check-off list to include . . . ***properly store packaged foods and set up mouse repellents***.

NATURE OR NURTURE
Susan LeMiles

I wonder if you know
You gave me passion?
Does not your vision show
Our extra ration?
Of the love of striving,
For wisdom in books,
One love's long surviving
The risks that we took?

How did this come to be?
Through body's essence
Did blood, your womb to me
Ordain its presence?
Or was it the nurture
Of a mother's heart,
Projecting life's future,
Intentional art?

OFF A TRIFLE
Judy Stevens

The sign read, *"El Pueblo de Nuestra Sonora la Reina de los Angeles de Porciuncula."*

"How well do you know Castilian Spanish?" the man beside me quipped.

"Are you kidding?" I shot back, more than a little annoyed.

"My dear chap, before us lies the future Los Angeles. We merely overshot the date a trifle." He took a reading from the near-microscopic device imbedded in his wrist then grinned. "GIZMO puts the year at '1698,' so oops, a simple transpositioning of the number---could happen to anybody."

"Time Guides don't do math, I suppose," I said dryly.

He took my gibe so good-naturedly that I couldn't stay mad. I glanced again at the sign that someone had so diligently written, despite running out of paint and board towards the end.

"You said you wanted to see the city as it was in the old days," Pretov tittered. He was obviously enjoying this.

"I don't do seventeenth century," I said flatly.

"Shall we try again for the summer of 1968? It'll be a riot."

My groan was audible as we entered non-linear time.

Pretov's error might have gone unnoticed by history had we not just then inadvertently vanished in clear view of a peasant leading his donkey to market. That peasant's wild-eyed story to the local priest, accompanied by oaths that he hadn't touched a drop would eventually become the legend of two angry devils obliterated by the holy words on a sign. That same priest would later be forced to build a small chapel on the site to accommodate the many who came to pray for relief from their own devils. And after the priest went to his reward and was buried beneath the chapel he had built, the wealthy man who owned the land ordered a secret underground passage cut from its catacomb to his hacienda. And after that, the people went somewhere else to pray.

Eventually all of this would be so forgotten that by 1968, no one knew why that little stone building had a secret underground passage, only that some were glad it did.

We entered linear time the way we left it, materializing right in the spot where we'd stood moments—now centuries---ago.

“Yup,” Pretov said: “ 1968---right on the button.” He swung around then frowned. “What's <u>that</u> doing there?' he asked no one in particular.

Puzzled, I followed his gaze to a narrow stone building wedged in amongst more modern ones. It looked like it had been there all along and everything else had grown around it.

“We need to investigate,” he said.

“Investigate what?” I asked. I didn't like the look on Pretov's face.

A man met us at the door. “Hey dude,” Pretov said, “What's the deal on this pad?”

“Who wants ta' know?” said the dude, eyeing us suspiciously.

“My friend ‘n me, come in outa' Detroit,” Pretov lied. “ Hearda' somethin' goin' down ‘roun' here. Dis it?”

The dude relaxed a little. “Long as yer not da fuzz.”

“Whatya think, we're *crazy*, man?” Pretov roared, poking me in the ribs. I let out a cough and a fractured laugh. The dude cracked a faint smile. “Come on,” he said, “take a tour.”

We ducked inside what was once a one-room chapel. It was bare and bleak and musty and dark, and I tried not to notice the remnants that betrayed its many uses, none of which had been in the least holy.

The dude walked over to what had once been a stone altar and did something to the wall behind it. He triggered the floor to open and reveal steps of stone leading downward. It was obvious this place with its secret passageway had been heavily used down through the years by rum-runners, drug lords and who knew what else. Also obvious was the fact that this place would not be here, had Pretov not made that mistaken detour through 1698.

"Good place for stash," said the dude as he straightened up. "Good for bodies, too," he added with a jagged-toothed grin. "Makes no diff'rence ta' me if yer fuzz or not---Barney'll take care a' ya."

That's when I first noticed the other dude at the door affixing a silencer to his .38.

"We gotta undo this," Pretov breathed to no one in particular. I knew what he meant.

Just before we entered non-linear time the dude called Barney fired his .38 at us---or rather, the dude standing directly behind us. No matter - whatever happened then would soon be erased--- or so I fervently hoped.

We materialized a few seconds before we'd left 1698, which erased our previous visit. This time, the donkey saw us and the peasant didn't, which is all it took to unravel Pretov's error throughout all linear time. Thus the seventeenth-century priest was spared building, then being buried in an unsuitable place, the two dudes went their separate ways in the twentieth century, and---with some reluctance on Pretov's part---we returned to our own century.

I could understand why Pretov was reluctant to face the authorities at GIZMO. Time-travel is serious stuff, and a breach of protocol by a certified Time Guide usually means the poor fool has gone insane. So strict are the rules that it was a minor victory when I was at last able to convince them I hadn't been kidnapped; and an even greater victory when they decided I wasn't an accomplice and let me go. I learned later that after five long months in linear limbo Pretov was finally deemed innocent of misuse of non-linear time and reinstated to full Time Guide status. By then, GIZMO had pronounced the entire fiasco a simple transpositioning of numbers, and ordered a full review of its devices, as well as re-training in the basics.

I was just beginning to lose my fondness for dull linearity when I received an overly-friendly message from an all-too familiar source.

Now Pretov's got a side business unraveling other Time Guides' fiascos. Says he could use a partner. Says we'd make a good team. Says I'd be a fool not to invest in a sure shot thing.
I tried to keep my cool as I told him, "This 'fool' says next century, dude."

He said, "Funny, that's our next assignment, partner."

What can I say? The man's persuasive.

ONLY A MATTER OF TIME*
Frank Cortazo

"...But..., she IS real!" cried teary-eyed, twelve year-old Georgie Herbwell, lying on the dirt by the side of the road. He had fallen there after having been pushed and tripped by the three older youths surrounding him. "I've seen her! Everything she's predicted to me has come true!"

He squinted up at the silhouettes of the three leering muscular, blonde figures looming over him. The light of the afternoon sunlight surrounding them made them look gigantic. He struggled to pick up his fallen homework papers and school books lying scattered around him.

"Listen, loser," said Randy, the biggest of the three and the obvious leader. "Like I've told you many times, you watch too many movies. You're always reading your library books. What good is all that gonna get you? You don't like sports. You don't mingle with people. You're always writing gibberish in those notebooks..."

And no one would ever figure the things he wrote in it, thought Georgie, unless his specially-constructed code could be broken. Everything was there, his thoughts, his dreams, HER predictions, everything he----.

"... And you keep checking out that same stupid book from the library," continued Randy, interrupting Georgie's thoughts. "All your book reading's gone to your head! You really made a fool of yourself in class today by reading aloud that stupid story you wrote. I mean...come on...Who's stupid enough to believe someone could really exist who could predict the future?"

Gathering up his things as best he could, Georgie stood up. Adjusting his black-framed eyeglasses, he faced Randy, but not confident enough where he could look him in the eye.

"She IS real," he insisted,"and she predicted to me a few days ago that I would write a story about her and that I would get a high grade of 97 and...that is EXACTLY what happened."

The three older boys laughed.

"Yeah, right," said Randy. "Then, how come no one but you has seen her? Did you ever think of that, smart guy?"

Georgie remained silent. Randy had a point, he realized. No one else had ever seen her. He had been sworn to secrecy when she had first approached him. She had predicted he would cut his finger that night and it had happened. Another time, she had predicted his father would get a raise at his job and it had happened. Furthermore, she had predicted his pet cat would have three kittens on a specific time and date and it had happened as well, EXACTLY as she had predicted it. Just a few days back, however, she had predicted he would write a story about her, read it in class, and get a high grade of 97. She had told him her prediction would come to pass and it had. The odds of her predicting the exact number grade were phenomenal. No one else, however, had seen her.

"Call her," suggested one of the two other boys. "Let us meet her."

"Either put up or shut up," added the third boy.

"I...can't," shrugged Georgie. "She...appears to me only when she wants to."

"Yeah, that's what we thought," said Randy, pushing him aside. "You make her appear tomorrow, at school, if you know what's good for you. We'll all be waiting for it."

Laughing, the three older boys walked away down the street.

Georgie stood there for a while. He contemplated Randy's ultimatum before, at a slow pace, continuing to walk home.

Randy had made his intentions clear. It was only a matter of time until the confrontation took place. More than likely, there would be an audience. In front of everyone, Georgie would be ridiculed. If only she could appear, he thought. If only she could be with him when the confrontation took place!

He continued walking. As he was about to reach the last corner to get home, he heard a rustling of bushes next to him. A soft, feminine voice...HER voice..., called out his name. Turning, he saw her shapely, lithe figure illuminated against the light of the afternoon sun. Her long, golden hair cast luminous halos all around her. They covered the bright, skin-tight silver-colored jumpsuit she wore. Her fingers, as usual, were adjusting the metallic buttons on the panel of the small, rectangular device she had with her. It was attached to the left side of the white belt she wore around her waist. He still wondered what that device was.

She couldn't be more than a teenager, he thought, as he viewed her youthful face once more. She even reminded him of someone, now that he noticed her more.

She raised the palm of her hand upward, as if to halt him.

"I know all about it," she said to him before he could say a word. "It was not permitted for me to appear and interfere in your dealings with those three boys, just like it is not permitted for me to stand by you at your next confrontation. To do so would disrupt the natural flow of events in your life. Your better judgment, at that time, will persuade you to deny my existence."

"But..why?" he asked, a look of disappointment crossing his face. "You've...come through for me those other times, even when I doubted you. Your predictions all came true."

"Yes," she agreed. "They were predictions of what was yet to be. I had thought my presence at those moments had served to convince you of the good things to come in your future. I had been sent to persuade you to follow the course of a major turning point in your life However, the time has come for me to leave you. There are others who must, as well, be convinced."

"What others?" he asked.

She looked at him for a moment before responding.

"The others like you, " she told him. "THEY whose future is intertwined with yours. THEY who will make a significant breakthrough in this world. THEY who will become your colleagues in what will be one of the greatest scientific achievements of this world."

"What achievements?" he asked, confused. "Who...are you, really? Where are you from? I...you...you've...never even told me your name."

She smiled. "Who I am and where I am from are not important. What matters is what you do with your future. I appeared to you at this crucial time in your life. Now is when you must make a monumental decision to ensure you follow the correct path lying ahead of you. It... is only a matter of time."

Georgie stood there, thinking. What could she be talking about, he wondered.

"It involves Science, a subject which fascinates you," she told him, as if in answer to his silent question.

She looked toward his school things. "Have you not ever wondered," she continued, " why you continue re-reading that book...that PARTICULAR book...which your school library has made available to you?"

Georgie looked down at the title of his library book. After a brief moment, his looked back at her, a tinge of wonderment now evident in his eyes.

"You mean...I...I'm going to..."

"Yes...you...and those others. My prediction will come to pass. You will accomplish greatness. Now, however, you must let the seed of knowledge grow and develop within you until the day when all of those seeds unite and become as one. Our...my... the whole world's future depends upon it. I was sent to nurture that seed. Many times, great and grand, will you become."

Georgie felt better. His current predicament, at the moment, was forgotten. A look of doubt, however, crossed his face.

"Shed all doubt," she told him, as if reading his mind again. "You may, at certain times, attempt to deviate from your path, be it of your own free will or otherwise. You will, always, however, return to it. Record it all in the manner you have done. Now, George Herbwell, I must leave you. The future is yours. Do with it what must be."

"Wait!" urged Georgie. "How will I know-------?!"

At that moment, however, she placed her hand against the small panel of buttons on the device at her side. A brief flash of light burst from it and she disappeared.

Georgie stood there for a while, thinking of what she had told him. He looked around. No one had been nearby who would have seen them, no passing vehicles, nobody. At his usual, slow pace, he began walking home again.

He never did learn where she was from. Was she a prophet?

Her face had reminded him of someone, someone in his own fam........No. It was just too weird to be true,... and yet...there was something...some connection...or familiarity.

Some time during the night, however, while in bed re-reading his favorite book, the answer came to him. He thought of that story, of the traveler with his wonderful fourth-dimensional traveling machine.

At that moment, Georgie realized where she was from, who she reminded him of, how her life was linked to his. She DID say he would become many times great and grand...as in...great great great...etc. grand...uncle? Cousin? Father?

He wondered from how far ahead she had traveled.

Yes! His journals would survive the test of time! His code would be cracked along the way!

He himself and those many others he had yet to meet would bring about a monumental, historic achievement! With their combined efforts, their own similar invention would alter the course of history. Compact it would be, unlike that of the traveler of the story in his library book. It would be easy enough to be worn on the side of a belt around the waist. However, it would have to be for only a select few. After all, it WOULD alter the course of history but it would NOT be designed to disrupt its natural flow. That was what SHE had been most careful NOT to do.

Lying there, he looked up at the ceiling and smiled.

All he had to do was believe in striving toward that goal.

It would all come to pass, he thought.

It was only... a matter of time.

SEUSS-SUITED
Judy Stevens

I do not care what others wear
I hardly notice most the time
For it's just some cloth
And perhaps a moth
It all just suits me fine.

What others wear I do not care
Unless they point at me
Sancti-moni-ous-ly
And swear that what I wear
Has unsuit-abil-ity.

Then happily I scrutinize
Their every nook and cranny
For some fray thread
Or dandruffed head
To make me feel just dandy.

But what if I averted my eye
To meadow, to sky, to clover
Could then might we
Empha-ti-cally
Be more suited for each other?

SHROUD OF FAITH
Milo Kearney

Doubting Thomas had to see,
with his own eyes, the mystery.
He had to feel, he had to touch,
and what he asked was not too much.

He knew that faith must not be blind,
but should be of the reasoned kind.
In this he was completely right.
The proofs of faith must stand in light,
not make us stumble in the night.
And we, like him, have asked for proof
that Jesus Christ was not a spoof.

"I won't believe until I see
your shroud made in Antiquity."
"Come," Jesus says, "I have it here,
a weave made as they did back there."

"I won't believe until I spy
the pollen from the plants nearby."
"It's lain," says Jesus, "in the cloth,
since I was taken from the cross."

"I won't believe unless you show
how the bloodstains from your side did flow."
"See the stains run up and down again,
as I pushed up for air, then sank from pain."

"Surely any forger would provide
a spear mark going in your side."
"But measure the exact length of the cut,
the size a Roman spear would put."

"I won't believe unless you prove
it wasn't thought up afterwards."
"See the wound in the wrist or thereabout.
A nail through my palm would rip right out."

"Just how authentic can it be
without any thumbs, don't you agree?"
"People have only recently re-learned the fact
that nails piercing a wrist cause the thumbs to
retract."

"The whip marks could be added since,
It takes more than such things to convince."
"But, in the fourteenth century, who had known
that Roman whips were two-pronged, as here is
shown?"

"And the cloth that, since the twelfth century, has
remained
in Oviedo in the north of Spain,
which is claimed to be the napkin from your head?"
"Its stains match the Shroud's, showing where I
bled."

Doubting Thomas showed doubt no more,
He had the proof he'd been asking for.
And you, dear cynic, what of you?
You've seen the evidence hold true.

Will you say, "I will not believe,
though I see the nail's impression"?
Thomas rejected blind belief.
Will <u>you</u> choose blind rejection?

STORMY WEATHER ON PADRE ISLAND
Nelly Venselaar

Welcomed to the beach by

Terrifying noise of wind and storm.

Enormous white foamy waves slow down

Building up and up until foamy waves crash down again.

Forming quiet pools,

Allowing seagulls to look for food.

Never tired of their frolicking,

Coming back for more fun and games.

Occasionally one strays,

Soon followed by similarly curious ones.

An enormous freighter sails out of the harbor

Bobbing on the rhythm of this gale.

Stormy as it is, a shrimper glides out of the canal

Braving rough seas and risking life

To earn a living for his family.

SWEET MARY*
Leroy Overstreet

Sweet Mary was an orphan. Her father died in an accident while commercial fishing. Her mother died from pneumonia. She was very poor, wouldn't spend the money to go to the doctor until it was too late. Sweet Mary was 12 years old. She went to live with her aunt and uncle in the town where I met her. They owned a small restaurant and it was Aunt Bea who added the 'Sweet' to her name. Every time Aunt Bea introduced her to one of the customers. She would say: "This is my niece, Mary, isn't she sweet?" Soon, everybody was calling her 'Sweet Mary'. Aunt Bea loved her and she loved her Aunt Bea. She spent all her spare time, when she wasn't in school, helping out around the restaurant.

She was 19 years old when I first met her. There was a rodeo in the town where she lived. The rodeo producers asked all of us contestants and performers to parade through town just before the show. Aunt Bea's restaurant was on the opposite side of town from the rodeo arena and there was a large truck parking lot next to it and that was where the parade would start.

While I was waiting for the parade to get organized, I noticed Sweet Mary out in front of Aunt Bea's Restaurant. She was a pretty little thing and looked like someone I would enjoy meeting. I waved at her and she smiled and waved back. I rode my horse over close to where she was and tipped my hat. She came down off the porch and we introduced ourselves. She was very easy to talk to and I felt very comfortable and at ease with her. I said; "It's a shame you don't have long pants on, if you did you could ride behind me in the parade and could see the rodeo for free."

"That can be fixed in 5 minutes," she said. She dashed inside and came back in less than three minutes dressed in long pants and a short sleeved shirt that showed off her figure to perfection. I was amazed that anyone could change clothes so quickly!

"I'm going to the Rodeo Aunt Bea," she said. I kicked my left foot out of the stirrup and she swung up behind me.

Everybody in town knew Sweet Mary and she had something to say to everyone. She was so proud to be riding in the parade; you would have thought that she was the rodeo queen. She would say something like, "How do you like my new cowboy, Mr. Harris? I just caught him. Isn't he handsome?" Then she would rub my chest and belly with the hand that she was holding onto me with and lay her cheek up against my back. By the time we got to the rodeo grounds I was captured for sure.

I arranged a seat for her real close to the chutes and each time I was ready to perform she would blow me a kiss and cross her fingers for me. She would stand up and cheer and tell everyone around her, "That's my cowboy. Isn't he great?" After the show we went to Aunt Bea's Restaurant to eat and afterward we rode around the countryside and when I took her home at 2:00 A.M. I knew her complete life story.

She was nineteen years old and had been married the year before. The marriage didn't last but three months and her husband divorced her. When I asked her the reason, she was sort of evasive, "It just didn't work out." And it just didn't seem important to her at all.

Late Sunday morning, I went to Aunt Bea's Restaurant for a combination breakfast and lunch. Sweet Mary introduced me to all the customers that came in. She made them all promise to go to the rodeo and cheer for me. We laughed and told jokes until show time and when we got in the gate the whole section of bleachers near the chutes was filled with my supporters from Aunt Bea's.

After the show, we ate at Aunt Bea's and rode around until nine. I was working at a ranch about 75 miles from there and had to be at work at 5 A.M. There was another rodeo scheduled at a nearby town for the following weekend and I asked her if she wanted to go. She said; "Sure. I'll make arrangements for someone to work in my place. You can pick me up on Friday night and bring me back on Sunday night."

We spent every weekend together. Most of the time there would not be a rodeo close by that we could go to, so we would camp out on a secluded spot by a creek that I knew about. We would pack an icebox, barbecue ribs and go swimming naked in the creek. She would tell me risqué jokes. She knew hundreds of them. Every truck driver that stopped at Aunt Bea's brought a new one and she remembered them all. She was the most uninhibited person that I have ever met and she taught me things that I could not have ever imagined in my wildest dreams.

We were soul mates. I couldn't believe how much we enjoyed each other's company. We never once had a cross word. I couldn't understand how her former husband or anybody else could not have been happy with her. We bought matching outfits, boots, belts, shirts and hats, exactly alike. When we went to rodeos I brought her a horse to ride in the parade. I even got her elected rodeo queen at one show.

I usually worked until noon on Saturday if there wasn't a rodeo to go to. Sweet Mary usually worked until six. I could make it to Aunt Bea's Restaurant by about two. We would sit around, tell jokes and drink coffee until her shift ended.

Soon after we started going together, when I came in she said, "Aunt Bea, I need some medicine that I've got at the house. I'm going to get Jim to take me to get it. I'll be back in ten minutes."

We got in my truck and headed to the house which was about five blocks away. On the way, she unbuttoned my shirt and rubbed my belly. When we got to the house, she jumped out and said, "Hurry, we have to be back in ten minutes."

I followed her into the house and saw a string of clothes from the front door, across the living room that lead to the bedroom, shoes, socks, dress, slip, panties, bra. I entered the bedroom and she was sitting in the bed stark naked. 'Hurry, we only have ten minutes," she said. In five minutes she was ready to go back and when the ten minutes were past we were back at the restaurant.

I sat at the counter and drank coffee. She was happy as a lark. She laughed, told risqué jokes and giggled with all the customers. Her face had turned red as a beet and stayed that way all the rest of the afternoon.

When we were alone after she got off from work I said; "Sweet Mary, doesn't it bother you when your face turns red after sex?"

She said, "Why no, it doesn't bother me at all. Why should it? It just shows that I'm happy."

From then on, every Saturday, she would find some excuse for me to take her home and we got to where we could get back in less time than ten minutes. I would sit at the counter and drink coffee. She would laugh and giggle and tell risqué jokes, her face as red as a beet.

We had been going together for about six months. We had opened a joint bank account. We were each putting every cent we could rake and scrape into it. Soon we would have enough to get married. I could not imagine how I could find anybody more compatible to spend the rest of my life with. Sweet Mary felt the same way about me.

One weekend, I finished my work on Friday instead of Saturday. I couldn't wait to see Sweet Mary. I got to Aunt Bea's about three thirty, a day earlier than I was expected. There was a strange man that I had never seen before sitting at the counter drinking coffee and talking to Sweet Mary, her Friday man. She was laughing, giggling and telling risqué jokes. Her face was red as a beet.

THANKSGIVING
Eunice Greenhaus

Roast turkey's on the table

The pie is in the stove

Come on over Mabel

We've got a feast, by Jove

Creamed onions in the pot

Potatoes in the pan

Come eat it while it's hot

The rolls are nice and tan

Salad cut up crisp and green

Carrots swim in butter

Ice cream tastes so cool and clean

My stomach's all aflutter

My glass is full, the wine is poured

Now we can say we thank you Lord

For all the pleasures that you bring

For family, friends and every thing

THE CRIMSON VISITOR
Jack King

After he left the bar, John went home, opened the front door, and found a stranger sitting on his couch. The man was wearing motorcycle boots, black jeans, and a red leather jacket. His skin matched the color of the jacket, and two stubby black horns protruded from his bald crimson head. His eyes were set so deeply beneath his black brows that John couldn't see them.

"Who the hell are you, and what are you doing in my house?" asked John.

"Well, well, well, aren't you the brave one. You weren't the least bit startled when you saw me. Permit me to answer your questions. The answer to the question about who I am should be obvious, and the answer to your second question is that in exchange for certain actions on your part, I'm here to offer you a happy and everlasting life."

"My response to your first answer is that I don't believe in the devil, and my response to your offer is that I've heard it before, but not from anyone whose outward appearance even remotely resembles yours. How refreshing to meet someone so remarkably out of the ordinary. My name's John and I'd like to shake your hand."

Rising to his feet and extending a hand to grasp that of his host, the crimson one smiled broadly, and said, "Mine's Satan." A mutually enthusiastic handshake ensued. "I see you have a bar in the corner of your living room," said Satan.

"I get the hint," said John. "I'll pour us a drink. "Straight whiskey okay?"

“Whiskey’s fine, although I credit red wine for my vibrant complexion. Tell me John, do you believe in free will?”

“Why do you ask?” said John as he handed a drink to his guest and sat down with his own on the opposite end of the couch.

“Because you and I are going to arrive at a mutual agreement, and I don’t enter into contractual agreements with people who don’t believe in free will. Such people don’t feel responsible for the consequences of their actions.”

“But Sate, -- I hope you don’t mind if I call you Sate, Satan sounds so formal – all human activity has consequences, and often unpredictable, not always what the actor wants nor what society would prefer. Is this going to be a discussion about morality?”

“In part, yes. Do you believe people should be rewarded or punished for things they have done?”

“For what they have done? Of course not. We reward good behavior to encourage its continuance and punish bad behavior to prevent its recurrence. It’s all about the future; what one has already done cannot be changed.”

“But you mortals often incarcerate criminals or even execute them. You have not seen the future, so aren’t you punishing them for what they did in the past?"

“No, we’re trying to prevent them from repeating their crimes in the future. We use evidence recorded in the past to evaluate character and predict probable future behavior. It’s the future that we are trying to predict and influence.”

Satan took a thoughtful sip from his glass and replied in a confident, matter-of-fact tone,
“So it’s perfectly reasonable for me to shovel sinners off into hell, based on their past behavior.”

“You’re not listening, Sate. It’s about the future. A dead sinner cannot sin again, so dragging him out of the grave to punish him is like beating a dead horse so it won’t kick you again.”

“Hmmm, so if it’s all about what’s to come, you’ll commit all the evil deeds I ask you to if I reward you with eternal happiness in the future, right?”

“No, I’ve already examined all the evidence I could find and found nothing to suggest that anyone ever has or ever could experience eternal anything. Life is for living, death is forever, and you, Father Fordyce, should forsake these forlorn charades and go buy your own whiskey.”

Father Fordyce tore off his mask. “Damn you, John! Damn you!

THE DAY PATRICIA MOVED IN
Edna Ratliff

I remember the day Patricia came to live with us in Darrtown. It was a sunny day in April 1973 when my children, Charles and Sherry came in the backdoor. They had walked to Don's Carry Out to get a loaf of bread. Instantly, they wanted to know if they could have a puppy, because someone on Lynn Street was giving puppies away. I explained how much work puppies were, like potty training, water at all times, feeding, cleaning up after them, and baths. Sherry assured me they would take turns taking the puppy outside, feed, water, and they would faithfully clean up after the puppy. Charles agreed to it, too. The same story all children tell their parents about getting a puppy. I finally said yes, but it was up to their father, like all mothers tell their children. When their father also named Charles, known as Big Charles, came home the children gave him the same story they gave me. He told them as long as he didn't have to take care of the puppy it was fine with him.

After dinner, Charles, Sherry and I went over to check the puppies out. There were four puppies left to choose from. Sherry went straight to a brown short hair girl puppy with white on her chest. The puppy did look a little different but I wasn't sure what it was. Sherry picked the puppy up and asked, "Can we have Patricia." Of course, the owners said yes, and Charles also thought the puppy was the best out of the bunch.

After we got home, the children played with Patricia inside the house and out in the yard. They never left her for one moment. When it was time to go to bed who would Patricia sleep with? It was decided with a coin. Charles won, but the next morning Patricia was sleeping with Sherry. It seemed who ever Patricia started out sleeping with by morning she was in a different bed. I never said anything, but I'm sure Patricia had help changing beds.

The next day I made an appointment at the veterinarian for Patricia's puppy shots. As soon as we got into the examining room, Doctor Headily asked me if I knew what kind of dog Patricia was. I told him I didn't know. Then he went on to say he was sure Patricia was a Chihuahua, and she wouldn't get any bigger than seven to ten pounds. The only thing he could find wrong with her was she had a heart murmur.

Patricia and I drove Charles to his baseball practice, and Sherry to her swim team practices every day with one race each week. On the weekends the family and Patricia went fishing at Action Lake. I always kept Patricia on a leash. It was a good thing because she fell in the lake, and I was able to pull her out. Patricia liked to watch the geese and ducks, and tried to eat their poop, another reason to have a leash on her.

We had a small garden with several rows of strawberries. Patricia would walk up and down eating the strawberries. If you let Patricia pick between any kind of meat and strawberries she would choose the strawberries every time. Also back then I used to can tomatoes. The skin and seeds of the tomatoes were put on the compost pile to be used on the garden the next year. Patricia would roam back to the pile and eat the tomato skins when she thought I wasn't watching.

One day in midsummer I realized I was taking care of all Patricia's needs. Yes, I had a talk with Sherry and Charles about their dog. They did improve taking care of her.

Sherry and I were driving home from swim practice when we saw Patricia's brother. He was with another dog digging a whole. I stopped the car to watch. The other dog would dig for a couple of minutes then Patricia's brother would bark. The other dog jumped out of the hole and Patricia's brother would jump in digging as fast as he could. The two dogs kept taking turns digging. Sherry and I laughed and laughed at the comical dogs. Who would have thought dogs would have a system to dig a hole. Then I realized Patricia's brother must have gotten Patricia's head, because his head was too big for his tiny body. His head was so large he looked top heavy;

Patricia's head was way too small for her large body. No wonder she looked a little strange.

The next year I took Patricia to Dr. Headily. He said she weighed thirty pounds and wondered what kind of a dog she was. I reminded him, "last year you told me she was a Chihuahua and wouldn't get any larger than six to ten pounds." He just laughed and gave her, her shots.

When Patricia was two she became pregnant. The puppies were born early in the morning. My husband had gone to work and Charles had left for school. Patricia was in the kitchen when all this took place. I got some old ragged towels for her and tried to make her comfortable. Sherry didn't want to go to kindergarten; she wanted to watch the puppies being born. I let her stay home. After the first puppy was born Sherry said, "Oh, so that's how it's done." After two more puppies arrive Sherry jumped up and said, "I'm going to school. Today is share day and I'm sharing this." I helped her get dressed and we made it to the bus stop just as the bus pulled up. I sort of felt sorry for her teacher. I wondered what Mrs. Young would say about Sherry's news. Patricia had seven live puppies and one still born. We found homes for all the pups.

It was hard to grasp time. One minute we are giving puppies away and the next minute we are going to Charles' graduation at Talawanda. But it was even harder when Charles left for the Marines for three years. That was one of the worst days for all of us. We all missed Charles. Patricia checked every night to see if Charles was in bed before curling up on the end of Sherry's bed.

On October 23, 1983 Islamic Jihad used suicide bombers to blow up American and French Beirut Barracks. They killed 299 men of which 220 were American Marines. This was several days before Charles was to come home. He called to tell us he didn't know when he would get to leave because he was in charge of the Armory in California and he had to ship 1,000 M16 rifles, which had to be packaged in airlock bags for a six month cruise deployment. He would let us know later.

When Charles came through the door Patricia knew it was him and came barking and running as fast as her legs could carry her. Patricia lavished Charles, trying to give him licking kisses, trying to jump on his lap, and every night sleeping on the end of his bed. But after a year, Charles got married and moved to his own home. Sherry was four years younger than Charles and, later, graduated from Talawanda and went on to Miami University. Sherry decided to live closer to Miami University.

When Patricia heard the doorbell she would come running and barking in hopes it was Charles or Sherry. If it was one of them she would get their attention by jumping up and down until they petted her. Then Patricia would stick to them like duck tape. It was always fun when they came home to visit. But we realized the kids had out grown us, and I think Patricia knew it too.

One day in May when Patricia stood up, her body transformed into a slow motion movie as she slowly collapsed to the floor. Her breathing was shallow as Patricia passed out. I rushed her to a veterinarian. The veterinarian told me her body was wearing out, mainly her heart because of the murmur, but she wasn't in any pain. But if I wanted him to put her down he would do it. I couldn't do that to her. I wanted her to be at home with me when the time came. Patricia stayed one more month. The sun was warm like Patricia liked it on that Easter morning of 1991when she died. I'll always remember how she would listen to my problems, and always be there for me. I'll never forget those eighteen years.

THE DISBELIEVER*
Frank Cortazo

In magic, my young mind declines to believe,
For, nought do its tricks ever do but deceive
The eyes of a captive beholder to stare
At many things, not truly meant to be there.

The white rabbit, from a black hat, being pulled
And handkerchiefs with many colors leave, fooled,
Their audiences to, astonishment, greet
And to applaud at what is nought but deceit.

The flying doves, from nowhere, when they appear
And miniscule objects whose forms disappear
Are two more of those so-called tricks of the trade
Whose wonders, upon the mind's eye, are displayed.

These and many others, those with great skill know
How to well perform at a "magical" show
Where, eyes, they mislead and where, minds, they deceive
For, always, exists there, the need to believe.

The real magic, though, is how I am aware,
At five years of age with the rare gift I bear,
Of intellect, advanced, to truly perceive
Them to be mere ways, human minds, to deceive.

THE DOUBLOON
Judy Stevens

If there's one thing I've learned from life it's this:

imagination can either bind you or free you.

That summer, mine got jet wings.

I felt like Robinson Crusoe as I stood watching my only link to the world disappear in a cloud of red dust. I kicked my valise and wiped my nose on my red-caked sleeve and tried hard not to hate my parents who'd exiled me here at the end of nowhere—the place I'd be spending my entire summer.

I squinted in the harsh noonday glare at the barren landscape with its few odd-shaped trees then back at the only evidence of humanity in this place: a ramshackle house that looked as abandoned as I felt. I was Robinson Crusoe in the middle of Mars.

I shook off a tear—boys don't cry—and thought of what Mummy and Pop said, that this would be a great experience. They weren't fooling me any though; they must have failed to pay a ransom or something. I just knew I'd never see Sydney again.

Suddenly two things happened at once: Uncle Pete showed up from one direction and Aunt Mattie from the other. To this day I swear they just materialized, but the glare must have been in my eyes.

With a wide grin and twinkly jade eyes Uncle Pete wrapped a boney arm around me, practically squeezing my life out. He called me "May-Tee" and said we're in for a rip-roarin' time prospectin'. I was getting excited, until I looked up at Aunt Mattie, standing on the porch, arms crossed. If sour was a person, it was her. I determined right then and there that she was the warden of this prison, and felt a little pang of sorry for Uncle Pete: he looked like he had a few stories in him, and a child that needed to get out and play.

The first few days were awkward. I'd never hung around old people before, especially no-nonsense old people like Aunt Mattie. I soon learned that she was stern only on the outside, where she faced the world. I also learned that it was hard living in the Outback, where she'd lived all of her life; and, harder still, to be Aborigine—especially in those days.

Uncle Pete fancied himself a great prospector, but Aunt Mattie told me he was really an old magpie. I acted as if I knew what a magpie was, even saying the word aloud, secure that it wasn't a bad word, like the one Uncle Pete told me never to utter right after he did. I figured I had all summer to find out anyway, and maybe learn more unmentionable words, too. I was beginning to warm up to this magical pair.

My favorite times were our Walk-Abouts, especially when Uncle Pete found something strange and wonderful to bring home, like the shank bone of a wallaby. Then he'd give me his special wink as we walked all sweaty and grimy through the kitchen door to face Aunt Mattie's disapproving glare and some iced tea— and "the ritual."

"What have you magpies brought with you to clutter up my home?" she'd ask, as we emptied our pockets and gully-bag on the side table that always seemed to have newspapers covering it. Then she'd peer and pick at the trinkets with an air of distain, wrinkling her nose while scolding us for bringing such trash home. "Everyone else takes out trash," she would say; "You, my dears, bring it in." Then she'd tousle my hair, order us to wash up for dinner, and that was that.

It soon became a game to see how much we could disturb her, but it never occurred to me back then—being too young to matter—that these two old people were themselves playing a loving game.

It was a magical time; a time set apart from time; like Aboriginal Dream-Time. I wanted it to last forever, but it changed in a moment one day—a moment I've relived many times since.

It was late afternoon. Uncle Pete and I were making our way back home beside a gully when—without a word—Uncle Pete stopped. I stopped, too, for the Outback was laced with death in so many creatures that moved and so many plants, too. I peered into the fading glare of late afternoon but saw nothing. Uncle Pete methodically removed his sunglasses then cleaned them on his shirt, never taking his eyes off a particular spot at the bottom of the gully. Nothing moved in the red soil; no breeze disturbed the sparse vegetation. I hefted my snake-stick and waited for orders from my Captain.

"There, May-TEE. No—no, over there—yes, May-TEE, over there—mind that brush," Uncle Pete said, as I made my way gingerly down the side of the ravine, careful to avoid all the spots poisonous creatures lurked. I felt like a pirate in that nifty book Treasure Island, and wondered if I'd find doubloons—then wondered what a doubloon actually looked like.

I found it half-hidden in the rust-red dirt. As I crouched over it and brushed the soil away my shadow failed to lessen its luster, and I stared at it without touching, for I'd never seen its like. It seemed the universe held its breath, and time itself stood still just for this occasion.

Then I broke the silence with a war-whoop I'd learned from those American cowboy shows and jumped up and did a war-dance like I'd seen the American aboriginals do. I heard Uncle Pete's war-whoop, too. We grinned and gave each other a wink. Then he tossed me the gully-bag, which meant, "You're the captain, mate," and I felt all tingly, like we were going to open King Tut's tomb. "Remember the rule," Uncle Pete said. I reached in my pocket for a piece of rock, looked at that strange thing another moment, then picked it up and carefully put the pebble in its place so Uncle Pete's "equilib'rum" or something like that wasn't disturbed.

I held it for a moment in the palms of my hands. It was smooth, cold and shimmery-shiny after I spit the dirt off. It looked out of place here, like it was dropped from a spaceship or something. And it was heavy, real heavy; too heavy for its size, like all the gold in the world was jam-packed into it. I'd never seen that color before: it looked alive, like a blood-red golden heart the Aztecs took from their prisoners. Gingerly I put it into the gully-sack and made my way back up to the ravine's edge, where Uncle Pete lifted me back onto firmer ground.

"What'd we find—gold?" I asked him. Uncle Pete shook his head. He seemed distracted, as if I wasn't there, but if he said it wasn't gold, it wasn't gold. Uncle Pete knew his prospecting— he'd bought this land for Aunt Mattie from gold he'd found long before I was born.

I figured it might be a time piece, but we couldn't find a seam to open it. So, with the sun low in the sky, Uncle Pete dropped the strange thing back into the gully-sack, took my hand in his, and we made it home at twilight just as the dingoes cried.

Of course we caught holy terror from Aunt Mattie, brandishing her rifle and lantern, ready to go out after us. But when she saw the thing—we were calling it a doubloon by then— she suddenly changed her tune. After getting our promise not to scare the socks off her like that again, we settled in for the supper of our lives, and a lively rendition of our latest adventure, Pirates and all.

Funny how I forgot till just now Aunt Mattie looking at us wistful-like and murmuring that we *brought it home.*

The next morning I figured it had all been a dream, until I entered the kitchen and there it was: smack-dab in the center of Aunt Mattie's good table, kind of like a centerpiece. And there they were, all smiles like they were sharing some big secret, and I figured it was adult stuff and out of my reach—being young and all—so I just smiled back.

The next day we didn't walk-about because Aunt Mattie had

arranged family pictures. All I remember is the long, dusty trip to the outpost; and having to get squeaky-clean in a dirty washroom; then putting on some clothes I wouldn't be caught dead in, while the photographer pinched my cheeks to get some color into them. As I endured this torture, I caught Uncle Pete's wry smile and sly wink that said, "Even pirates suffer."

I don't remember much of the rest of that summer except that we never found another treasure as fine as that "doubloon." After that morning it disappeared off the table. Later, Uncle Pete had a man-to-man talk with me, saying he knew I wouldn't mind that he'd given it to "the Misses" for a keepsake of my visit. I felt pretty grown-up when he said that.

Then the years fled by and I grew up, and the world became my city and my "walk-about." But I never forgot that magical Dream-Time summer and the thrill of finding our "doubloon."

Now I stand again in Aunt Hattie's kitchen, lawyer's papers in my hand and fresh hurt in my too-adult heart, wondering where time went when it died.

They'd made a secret pact to go together, and it seemed Death was more than willing. Aunt Hattie died peacefully in her sleep at early dawn and Uncle Pete followed, just before sunset when the local coroner arrived. They'd left everything to me.

I stand in their kitchen —now my kitchen—feeling again too young to matter, with the weight of precious time, like the weight of that doubloon, heavy—like there was all the gold in the world jammed into it.

There's nothing I need here: I have the world and a great deal of its gold. What I really need no amount of gold could ever buy. What I really need is to see them again.

Still, perhaps a token from here—a "re-memory maker," as Uncle Pete would put it—so I might bring that long-ago magical Dream-Time place with me as I roam the world.

I know they had kept it—but where?

I find it wrapped in a note and placed inside a gully-bag in a drawer by their bed. The bed creaks as I sit and un-wrap the note. In the still air I read aloud Aunt Hattie's precise handwriting through tear-burned eyes:

"Don't grieve for us dear," it said. "Just know that our lives were full and long, and that we saw you far more often than you think—we really did. Do you remember the 'doubloon?' Its real name can't be spoken aloud, so I'll just leave it at that. Call it an ancient artifact if you will: you're the world explorer. You see, it's from Dawn-Time. Yes, dear, it's that old. Once upon a time, one of my ancestors loaned it out for a Walk-About; and, in due time, it found its way back home.

"My dear sweet boy, we've had enormous fun with it. It lets you return to earlier times. No, really—your Uncle just said this sounds like one of his tales. Anyway, you'll understand when you try it out. We left instructions for using it in your favorite hidey-hole. You didn't know I knew about that, did you?

"Burn our place down: take it back to brush and give it to the entire Aboriginal nation: they'll know what to do with it. Legal papers are in our hidey-hole, and I know you know exactly where that is. Love forever without time limits. —Aunt Mattie and Uncle Pete"

I sit on their bed watching the sun trace its pattern across the wall. Finally, with a heavy heart, I follow the letter's instructions as if these two lovely souls I adored hadn't gone stark raving crazy, and that time-travel was the most ordinary thing in the world.

The instructions read: "Place a marker where you are right now, then hold this 'artifact' just like the drawing says. Close your eyes and think of where and when you want to go back in time. It only works in your own life, so pick a good time. We know you've had a few. You're borrowing that time, you see—kind of like an exchange, except you're both in your younger body. That's all we understand; but don't worry: your younger self won't catch on to it.

"When you're done with the visit, come back the same way, and you'll show up exactly where you'd be, had you stood still all that time. Everything will be waiting for you here; no one will even realize you've been gone—imagine that. Then you can just go on living your life until the next time you need a break."

I reach into my pocket and pull out that real Spanish doubloon I always carry for good luck, thinking that in a life full of crazy risks, this is the craziest I've ever taken. I place my doubloon on the floor between my boots; and—feeling slightly foolish—hold the ancient artifact exactly like the drawing. Then, with another heavy sigh, I close my eyes on the day's waning light and all that lonely sadness enveloping me.

I open them to the fading glare of late afternoon. Nothing moves in the rust-red soil; no breeze disturbs the sparse vegetation. I see Uncle Pete methodically removing his sunglasses then cleaning them on his shirt, all the while never taking his eyes off a particular spot at the bottom of the gully. Hefting my snake-stick and with great joy, I await orders from my Captain.

THE FOX HUNTER
Georgia Tuxbury

Ed McCamber's death at sixty-five tore a jagged piece out of Birdie's life that she would tirelessly attempt to patch. It seemed as if she and Ed had been married forever, or as Ed often put it, "Since the man in the moon wore knickers."

Although Birdie did a remarkable job running the house and raising three daughters, she had never balanced a checkbook or pumped gasoline. Ed was the one who performed these tasks, as well as the one who made the decisions in their lives.

Twenty years before his death, Ed had said to her, "Our last filly has finally left the stable, let's pull up stakes here." The idea took Birdie by surprise; besides, she was never one to take a risk. So when he told her he wanted to quit his job at the Ford Agency and move to the country, the idea of leaving was frightening to her. When she expressed her doubts, Ed countered with, "Damn it, Birdie, it's not like we'd be heading west in a covered wagon. You got to learn to take a chance!"

"But ,Eddie, what would you do? You just don't retire at forty-five."

"I'm a good salesman. But I'd rather sell real estate than cars."

"But you've never done that."

"That doesn't mean I can't. I'll take classes, get my license and find a company that handles out-of-the-way properties."

"Oh, Eddie, that sounds really risky."

"Damn it, Birdie, it's always risky going after what you want in this world. You just got to make sure what you want is worth it.

And this is worth it, believe me." He left Birdie no choice but to believe him.

While still at the Ford Agency, Ed took night classes, received his real estate license and accepted the position of salesman for a company called Woods and Water. He and Birdie moved one hundred miles from home to a settlement close to Michigan's Pere Marquette River.

Theirs was one of the cabins dotting Poor Boy Creek. The meandering creek spilled its personality over the inhabitants—people who had escaped city life and now wandered about seemingly without purpose. Birdie settled into this life style as if she'd been born to it. After a year, she wondered why she ever had doubts about moving. Their cabin, sitting as it did where the creek joined the Pere Marquette River, had the best location of any of their neighbors. Ed told her, "We bought a million dollar view for pocket change."

Birdie loved to watch ragged sails of rain whip across the river, or the fog when it hovered ghost-like over the water, wrapping a shawl around the shoulders of the stately pines. And she gloried in the sun that would push its way in like a friendly neighbor. Birdie found beauty in all of the seasons. Even when winter draggled itself into May, she didn't complain.

Boredom may have hovered around Poor Boy but never nested at the McCambers. After living there several years, Ed found himself only dabbling in real estate; too many other activities grabbed up his days. Several times a week he and Birdie and their next door neighbors, Harvey and Toots Venable, headed for the hills or the woods or the river to enjoy whatever season it was. They would hike or hunt mushrooms, fish or swim, snowmobile or ski. Sometimes Birdie felt that anyone who didn't live at Poor Boy was deprived.

Residents of the settlement made do with a general store sporting two gas pumps that sat next to a tavern owned by Toots and Harvey. The Poor Boy Tavern was scruffy, rundown and comfortable—a place where customers could put up their feet on a chair and leave their boots on.

The tavern lagged unashamedly behind the times, its counter sporting hard-boiled eggs blushing in beet juice, over-sized jars of dills and pickled sausages. Deer antlers were nailed a bit off kilter on the paneled walls. Harvey offered venison jerky to his customers and must have gotten tired of hearing, "Who does the jerking, Harvey?" Whether they were long-time friends or strangers who pushed through the doors, they were greeted by Harvey's grand hello's and a sign above the bar: WELCOME TO POOR BOY—THE BEST PLACE ON EARTH. The McCambers and the Venables agreed that it was the best place on earth.

Birdie and Ed visited the Poor Boy nearly every afternoon. While Birdie sipped a draft, Ed drank Buds from a can and lit one Marlboro after another. On most days, Birdie would leave him sitting at the bar or playing pool to walk home the half a mile to prepare supper. As she headed to the door, he would tell her to just throw a hamburger in the frying pan. Though he wasn't a fussy eater, Birdie would already have a pot roast or chicken on slow bake waiting for him. It was one of the pleasures of life to see the gusto with which he ate her cooking.

Birdie knew that his unhealthy habits, only one of which was his over-zealous eating, would some day make her a widow, but it wasn't her style to nag. And it wouldn't have helped anyway.

The two of them never paid for a beer at the tavern; instead they worked off their drinks by helping out whenever they were needed, especially during deer hunting and trout fishing seasons. These were the times sportsmen threw off their coats to trade off-beat pointers over a beer. "You gotta wash your clothes in baking soda, then rub oil of cedar on 'em—even your boots. That way the deer won't smell nothing human." Or "Try Green Giant corn with half a crawler and when you're all baited up, spray the whole thing with WD-40." Then someone would invariably tell about old John Kaminski trying to bait up with creamed corn. "Just like a Polack," they'd say. Birdie, who was a Masarak girl, laughed at the Polish jokes, never taking offense.

Sometimes Birdie wondered how so many people found such an out-of-the-way place as Poor Boy. But they did, and every time a stranger pushed through the door, Harvey presented his own version of Welcome Wagon—offering hearty greetings and a beer.

One particular day Ed was humming back-up to the juke box's Merle Haggard and kibitzing while Toots and Birdie played a game of gin rummy. When Toots announced she was going down with six, Ed shook a finger at his wife. "Damn it, Birdie, you let a gin get right away from you when you discarded that last deuce. Look—rearrange all those twos, threes and fours." He pointed them out to her. "With that other deuce, you could have ginned."

"Gosh, Ed, I guess I missed it." She looked over Toots's cards, face up on the table, and played a three and four. "Hey, you're undercut! I gotcha for twenty-six!"

Ed hit his head with his hand. "I don't believe it! You're luckier than a three-peckered goat." Birdie knew it was a compliment.

"You know the guy over there, Ed?" Toots asked. "He just sat down at the bar." The man, alligator skinned and spindly, looked particularly tattered, even for the Poor Boy.

"Nope. Never saw him before." This was Ed's cue to walk up to the bar and start talking to the stranger. Toots and Birdie resumed playing cards. In the middle of the next game, Ed, his arm around the stranger's shoulder, ushered him to their table.

"Girls, I want you to meet Bert Stringfellow. He's a fox hunter."

Toots and Birdie said their hello's. "Now, Bert," Ed said, "I want you to tell these girls here how you catch a fox."

"Shit, it's easy as fallin' off a goddam log. You git yerself a shovel and jest find yerself a fox den . . . "

Toots interrupted. "How do you just find yourself a fox den?"

“Shit, thet’s easy, too. You jest look fer newly dug up dirt with lotsa bones around it. Bones and hair from him eatin’ a goddam deer.” Toots nodded and he continued. “So’s yer standin’ at the entrance of the den and you start shovelin’ ahead of yer feet.” The fox hunter pretended to be shoveling. “You keep a-movin’ up the tunnel shovelin’ as you do, until you git to the den itself. Then when you spot thet furry son-bitch, you grab him by the scruff of the neck and the middle of his back.” He grabbed an imaginary fox and threw it to the floor. “Quick-like. Then you gits down on him and crushes his rib cage with yer knee.”

“Geez!” Toots said, “why don’t you just shoot the bastard?”

“Shit, lady, thet’d ruin the pelts! I sell them things. They’re worth good money.”

Ed ushered the fox hunter back to the bar. “Lemme buy you a beer, Bert.” He turned to Harvey. “Hey, Harv’, how about giving my friend here one of those pickled sausages.”

“Shit, no, I ain’t thet crazy!”

Birdie and Toots watched as Harvey joined the two. They could see that the fox hunter was telling his story again, obviously enjoying its embellishment.

When Ed rejoined the girls at the table, he commented, “There sits a happy man, by God.”

“I’d say he’s just plain foolish taking a risk like that,” Toots added. Birdie agreed.

“Well, he’s doing something he wants to do, and he sure as hell is putting a new wrinkle to it. We should all be so lucky.”

Birdie had to smile. This was the same philosophy that moved them to Poor Boy.

“I think I’ll buy one of those fox pelts from him,” said Ed. “They’re only fifteen bucks.”

“What in the world for? Birdie asked.

“Just ‘cause I want to have one, that’s why.”

“Doggone it, Ed, no matter how cheap they are, we don’t have any earthly use for a fox pelt. It’s a waste of money.”

Ed sipped his beer, apparently persuaded. Soon afterward, Birdie left to get the pork chops breaded and ready for the pan. As soon as she heard the screen door wheeze open, she slid the chops into the iron skillet.

That night, as most nights, Ed retired to the bedroom while Birdie watched television. When the news was over, Birdie slipped into her nightgown, and by the red glow of the digital clock, found her way to bed.

As she folded back the sheet, she felt something furry lying on her pillow. She ran her hand across it. It reminded her of petting their old collie. Ah ha! The fox! She slipped the palms of her hands underneath the pelt and gently lifted it to the chair. Without saying a word, she climbed into bed and settled her head where the fox’s had been.

Ed raised up on one arm. “That was the biggest disappointment of my life. Damn, I guess we’ve been married too long.”

“Yup. Since the man in the moon wore knickers.”

Ed joined her in laughter as he skidded his chunky body across the sheet to put his arms around her.

Birdie’s youngest daughter, Sandy, who was closest to her mother both emotionally and geographically, helped Birdie with the funeral arrangements and all the paperwork that must be taken care of when a person dies. After the last farewell was said, Sandy stayed on and showed her mother how to write checks, balance a checkbook, change vacuum cleaner bags, pump gasoline. “All the things you need to know to have a successful widowhood,” Sandy said. And she went one step further: she urged her mother to sell the cabin. "It's too full of memories for you."

Birdie respected her daughter's judgment but was concerned. "What would I do then?"

"Move to an apartment. Near me."

"But what would I do then?"

"All the things you never got to do when Dad was alive."

"There was nothing I didn't get to do."

"Come on, now, Mom. Didn't you ever want to finish high school? Or travel? Do some of the things you couldn't do at Poor Boy."

"If I did, I must have forgotten about them" She thought for a minute. "I've always kind of wanted to paint, though. I guess I'd have to take lessons to do that."

"Oh, Mom, that's a great start!"

Sandy helped her mother get the cabin ready to sell and begin a new life. Harvey and Toots didn't want her to leave and tried to talk her out of it.

"I can't live on memories," Birdie said. "Sandy found me the perfect apartment. No keeping up a yard or worrying about repairs. And I've already had an offer on the cabin. You don't understand. It's just not the same since Ed's gone."

But they did understand and promised to visit her whenever they were in town.

After losing Ed, selling the cabin was the hardest thing she'd ever had to go through. She sold his possessions, after giving Harvey what he would accept: Ed's fishing poles, deer rifle, lawn mower. Harvey took the fox pelt, too, and hung it in the tavern above the welcome sign.

“What a lovely painting, Mother.” Sandy pointed to a water color of a frost-pink sun above a snow-framed creek.

“Thank you, dear, but it really isn’t. I’m painting from memory. It’s not the same as being there.” It had been three years, and she still missed Poor Boy.

“Gosh, Mom, why don’t you go back and visit?” Sandy had a guilty conscience. It was she who had moved her mother out of the place she loved. She often worried if it had been a mistake.

“I can’t. Visiting isn’t the same.”

“Have you seen Harvey since Toots died?”

“At the funeral, of course, then a couple of weeks after that he came by to see me, and we both just bawled. It didn’t make either one of us feel any better.”

“It had to be hard for him what with her dying so suddenly. He’ll come around when he’s ready.”

On a Friday in early May Harvey Venable did come around. He stood at Birdie’s door unannounced, his lanky frame in an “Aw shucks” pose, wearing the same smile that ushered strangers into the tavern making them feel like part owners.

“Harvey!” Thank God she had put on makeup that morning. “You’re a sight for sore eyes.”

He held up a paper sack. “I have a present for you.”

“Come on in. I’ve got the coffee pot going. What’s in the bag?”

“Close your eyes and take a sniff.” He put the sack to her nose.

“Mushrooms. Morels. I’d know that smell in a minute!”

“They’re out in all their glory.”

“I figured they were. Perfect weather to start ‘em popping. Warm and damp.”

“Birdie, put your blue jeans on. You were the best darned mushroom hunter at Poor Boy.”

“Sharp eyes. Good smeller.” That’s all you need.

“Naw, you need more than that. You need something called damned fool luck.”

“Well, I’ve had my share of that. You really want me to go with you?”

“I really do. Bring your fish pole, too.”

“I sold it.”

“No problem there. You can use Toots’.” Their eyes hooked briefly in a shared hurt, then flashed away.

“You’ll bring me all the way back here tonight?”

“No, I won’t. I’ll bring you all the way back Sunday night, though.”

Birdie’s eyes held question marks. “What do you mean?”

“My God, Birdie, we’re friends. You know my place. It’s got three bedrooms. Two baths. You’ll have all the privacy you want.”

“Are you sure you want me to come? There’ll be talk, you know.”

“So what. Let ‘em talk.”

After making a quick call to her daughter, Birdie packed a suitcase and gave it to Harvey to put in the car—the same one he’d driven four years ago. “Still looks the way it did,” Birdie noted.

"A hundred thousand miles and more to go before it dies. Just like you and me, Birdie." He squeezed her hand before he turned the key.

Words fairly leaped from her mouth. She told him how she took classes to get her high school diploma. How she and Sandy had visited the Grand Canyon. How she started painting.

"Are you any good?"

"I doubt it. At least not good enough to make money at it, but it fills in some of the gaps."

"What do you paint?"

"Mostly landscapes. Mostly Poor Boy. My soul's dug deep there, you know. It's the most beautiful place on earth."

"It is, Birdie, it is. And you're going back."

"How come you're not working on a Friday, Harvey?"

"I'm kind of retired. I sold the place to my son. Ron and his wife run the tavern now."

"Have they remodeled it?"

"Just a little."

"They didn't spoil the atmosphere, did they?"

"No, it's still down-at-the-heels."

"Good. I'd hate for it to get uppity."

They headed for a pull-off in the woods. "Like the car was aimed there," said Harvey. They eagerly set out afoot. She wondered if he was remembering how the four of them would go out to the woods in search of the elusive morel—Ed and Toots always lagging behind, always smoking cigarettes, pulling out a beer from their knapsacks while she and Harvey got right down to business.

"We were the ones who persevered, weren't we, Birdie?"

She laughed. His mind had followed the same trail as hers.

They passed a gathering of trilliums, and soon afterwards Birdie said, "They're right around here. I can smell 'em."

The two of them walked softly, as if sleeping mushrooms might be awakened to run off. Birdie tentatively brushed a hump of limp leaves with the toe of her shoe, uncovering the pointed umbrella cap of the morel. "Here's the first one!" She broke off the stem and held it up. "You owe me a beer!"

After several hours, they had two small sacks of the precious bounty. "Remember," Harvey said, "the more we get, the more we clean."

"I know. It's like fish."

Late afternoon they arrived at Harvey's cabin. From the porch she could see the house next door where she had lived for what she considered the twenty best years of her life. They walked to the water and onto the dock that Harvey and Ed had built one frustrating afternoon, neither one of them being a dock builder. The creek bubbled a musical welcome as Birdie tossed it stones.

"Does coming back hurt?"

"A little. But it's good to be here. I guess what I'm tasting is bittersweet."

"It's the flavor of the day," he said. He put his arm around her shoulder as they walked back to the cabin.

On Saturday morning they skittered around the banks of the river, dodging low-slung branches with fishing poles, and throwing lines into some of their favorite holes. But not a bite. At noon they built a fire to roast hot dogs and warm chilly hands.

"Any more luck like this and we'll have to buy steaks for dinner."

"It's the smart fisherman who already has them in his freezer," Harvey answered.

Another evening at Poor Boy and Birdie was confusing it with home. They played a game of cribbage in front of the fire where tangled ribbons of flame warmed the paneled room. After dinner they sat, blanket wrapped, and watched an old Cary Grant movie.

"And so to bed," said Harvey. "It's lonesome there, Birdie, besides being damned cold.
Why don't you join me?"

She knew it was coming. As the day wore on, the question had floated and dipped in the air like a kite. Birdie had prepared all kinds of refusals, but when she finally answered him, she found herself saying, "I'll see you there shortly."

Harvey's embrace was as comforting as a heated towel after a cold swim. It was like finding something precious that she'd lost. Besides that, it felt a lot like love. She ran her hand across his chest, twirling her fingers in the gray curlicues of hair. "You're only the second man I've ever slept with, you know."

"Yes, I know. You and Ed had a good marriage."

"There was a dark period. Before we moved here."

"There was?"

"Yes. For a couple of years had someone else. A young woman, the bookkeeper at the agency. It hurt so bad. The third worst thing I've ever been through."

"Let me guess. Losing Ed first. Moving away from here second."

“Right.”

“Did he know you knew?”

“No. I figured it would wear itself out, and it did.”

“Smart lady.”

“Pragmatic.”

“Hey, where’d you learn those big words?”

“I got me an edgy-cation, remember?”

“Yes, that’s what you said. How did you happen to do that?”

“Sandy wanted me to.”

“You’ve always done things to make everyone else happy. Have you ever done something just for yourself?”

Birdie lifted herself up on one elbow to look at him—a blur in the dusky light. “What do you think this is?”

“Yes, by God, that’s right.” He took her in his arms again and kissed her. But Birdie wanted more than that. She wanted it to last forever.

On Sunday afternoon Harvey opened the door of the Poor Boy Tavern for her. “Squeaks the same as always, “ she said.

“Been meaning to fix it.”

“For twenty years.”

“Some day.”

“I hope not.”

"You don't want anything to change, do you, Birdie?"

"I guess not. Bad fault."

"No, not bad, just impossible."

They drank their beers and talked to most everyone who entered, some whom Birdie knew and some she didn't. While Harvey was having a conversation with his son, Birdie went to the restroom. Both booths were occupied. She stood by the sink waiting.

"How about that Harvey," she heard one woman say.

From the other stall came the answer, "Yeah, the old geezer. At least Birdie McCamber's more his age than the others."

Birdie silently backed out of the room and returned to the table. She remembered the painful years when Ed was unfaithful and was pelted with a mélange of feelings—fear, jealousy, suspicion. What was she doing here? She didn't belong at Poor Boy now. Disappointment hung on her like a wet overcoat. When Harvey returned to his chair, she saw him as a stranger.

"What's wrong?" he asked.

"Oh, nothing. Just went to the bathroom and it was all filled up. There—they're coming out now. Who are those women? The blonde looks familiar."

"She ought to. She and her husband are the ones who bought your cabin. My next door neighbor."

"My God, that's right. Well, I only met her once."

"She's the town pump."

"How's that?"

"If you want to know the latest gossip, gather 'round."

Birdie needed go get away from him. She excused herself and returned to the restroom.

She looked at herself in the mirror. Ed always said she could subtract ten years with a smile. No matter what, she couldn't raise one. She gazed at her face, gone leathery from years in the sun and framed by silvery fluff. Harvey was right. She didn't want anything to change. But it had, and she had to accept it.

She walked out of the restroom. Dangling over the sign WELCOME TO POOR BOY—THE BEST PLACE ON EARTH—was the fox pelt. She remembered the fox hunter. How she and Ed had picked up stakes and made their way down a strange new path that led them here. And she remembered Ed's words, "Damn it, Birdie, it's always risky going after what you want in this world. You just got to make sure what you want is worth it."

She walked to the table. Harvey stood up when she returned. Such a gentleman. And such a handsome old geezer. She broke into a smile and made her way to the empty chair.

THE LADY BY THE SEA
Rudy H. Garcia

Mid July, mid sunny, breezy day,
By the emerald seashore was where you were
I shall not publicly describe the exuberance
Of the goddess-like beauty
Your body oozed that day

A Serena corpus, transforming
In me, such tan-talizing, arousing, erotic thoughts,
I will forever, selfishly, keep exclusively to myself.

You were the lady by the sea,
A freshly scenting flower
A blooming, scarlet red, impassioned sea rose.

Your spiraling jet, untamed emitting hair,
Came dancing in the wind,
Swooshing down below your curvy waist,
It netted me… It cast a bonding spell on me…

Your Doe-like soft and delicate steps upon the sand…
They caused a trance in me
I will not publicly nor privately divulge no matter how torturous the torment,
The love at first sight, I felt that beaching summer day,

Mer-Maiden By The Shore

You smiled at me
As provoking mermaids seductively smile at restless young mariners
And weathered seafaring old men, who spend their whole entire life
Sailing cupidity upon the sea

But unlike them,
Whose rum-induced inebriated spirits, raise an animated cup and toast
Falsely boasting of carnal rendezvous with such enchanting creatures…
I shall keep your bewitching and captivating smile private, and solely just for me.

De `Flur Of Eighteen Mays`

And than, like the shifting sands…
You inexplicably walk towards my direction
My knees, my legs, beget a wobbly state;
Suddenly, a jolting bolt of lighting strikes!

Piercing my virgin, untested heart!
Your devoted suitor, became my life-long fate
The inside of my stomach churns and burns and begins
To flutter with excited electricity!

Don`t no one ask me, what fantasia images
Erupted before my lovesick eyes.
Those sultry visions,
Of you smoothly, gliding over pearly white, Isla Blanca sands
Shall always and forever, be preserved for my memory only.

Perfumed Red, Red, Rose In Total Bloom

You pass me by and enter the cool, gentle, aqua-marine gulf water swells,
Barely knee deep, you rise on your pedi tippytoes
And skip your goose-skinned, sensuous-sensitive body over the surging tide
Skillfully, like the balletic, leaping dolphins do
You dive once, dive twice, dive trice, resurfacing, moist and glistering wet
With your mer-mane hair slicked back and floating atop the aqua blue water

Slowly, your lucent Rapunzel hair … fans open and wades mystically
Surrounding you with a million entrapping love petal tentacles
Laid out and waiting, to tangle me

Bathing Beauty

Sparkling in the mid-noon sun, you frolic fancy with the foam-crested waves
Right in front of me
And I transfixed and dumb-confounded be, remain catatonically hypnotized
What now, what now, what shall become of this novice lover now?
Now that my throbbing heart is penetrated through and true by you
What shall become of me, now that your flowers` perfume has my senses stirred!
Shall I shake myself free from this ecstatic state and pursue my new found love mate!
Or is this an enchantress nymph of the deep vast sea, my father often warned about?

Lovely Lady

Myth or legend, storied or real
I shall never ever tell a single other person or soul
How the pure existence of you does make me feel
For the very first time in my life
I learned how love feels… how it really feels…

My mind consumed races out of control
At a surreal warp speed!
My young buck robust body ruts uncontrollably
Desiring, only to be with you!

My father`s, bewaring and protective, experienced words of wisdom
Are foolishly purged from me and sent to travel aimlessly in the wind.
Because, the only thing that matters, the only thing that matters at all
Is the favorable good graces
Of My Lady by the Sea.

Royal Blue Tentacles of love

Submerged chest deep, you motion with slender firm desert tan shoulders and arms
And presumptuous me assumes you`re motioning me
Suddenly, my cemented feet began to wiggle
And with a love crazed giggle, I clumsily race against the wind
Splashing and hurdling awkwardly over the breakers towards
Your tentacles of love

Dolphin

My heart and my mind snap to and react for mere survival's sake
Transforming me, like her, into a love creation living by the sea
I too, shall love, but I wish her love for me
So now, I shall, I really must, like she
Convert myself to be a creature by the sea

But how and what, what kind of sea creature befits me?
How can I go forth and lasso her for me
A man-o-war!
That's what I shall me!
I spread my long and piercing tentacles and wrap her love for me.

Posing

Posing, barely knee deep, you turn half-way and grin at me
I take the pleasurable gesture as an approval and awkwardly splash in near you
I can not say, I shall not say, but because of you, I must remain submerged chest deep

You skillfully, like the balletic leaping dolphins do
Dive once, dive twice, than surface O` so near and right in front of me
Exposing yourself… with your dark long mermaid mane slicked back
Enough! Enough! I dare not say! How beautiful and healthy you were that day!

The lady by the sea
Was now swimming next to me!
And though we had actually known and grown by each other as friends since childhood
No one else must ever know, I will not say… what a women you were, that day I saw your nature by the sea.

THE MISTS OF THE HAUNTED PASSION

Frank Cortazo

As you stand alone within mists of despair,
You wait for she who always comes for you there
For a haunting passion within you to stir;
An uncontrolled, unending longing for her.

Unopened, your eyes must remain for your mind
To wander and search through those strange mists to find
She who appeared many times, daring to taunt
Your sanity, its serene calmness, to haunt.

You open your eyes and you see, standing there,
Her lithe figure in the white gown she must wear,
Her black, long hair flowing down, almost halfway
Upon her back to her slim waist, in display.

She stands tall and, at her fine figure, you gape,
Admiring the beauty of its perfect shape
As well as the youthful skin bearing no trace
Of aging lines upon her very smooth face.

You feel an ache burning within you to hold
Her for your fierce passion to, once more, unfold
But, motionless and quiet, you remain there,
Confined to the agony of your despair.

You see her eyes, chasms as black as the night,
And her soft lips, red like a bright, burning light,
The warmth of her presence engulfing your mind
As, for her, your deep love, she struggles to find.

You see her hands moving in silence to rise
And beckon you to her while her night-like eyes,
Like strong magnets, pull you with dominance and
You do not resist the force of their command.

You walk and approach her at a leisured pace
And, into your arms, she goes with an embrace
Whose warmth is surpassed by what, you are aware,
Is the scent of roses in bloom from her hair.

Your lips meet hers and, into a dark abyss
Of love you plunge, once more, consumed by its bliss
Whose power, unleashed, obtains total control
Of your body, of your mind, and of your soul.

For several moments, within your abyss
Of passion do you remain as her long kiss
Renews your fierce, undying love for her there,
The taste of its undying pleasure, to bear.

A while later, though, from her willing embrace,
You separate, great sadness filling your face,
As you see her figure begin to depart
And emptiness, once more, brings pain to your heart.

Back into the mists she goes, leaving you there
To suffer anew within depths of despair
Where you, in vain, struggle to utter a cry
But you do not hear it and you know not why.

You stand there as motionless as a hard stone
Within those mists where you remain, all alone,
Your true love gone from you with nothing behind
Of her brief existence, there, for you to find.

You feel the tears flow down your face as you try
To move and, perhaps to her, utter a cry
But, motionless, you remain as the mists tear

Through what little power of will you now bear.
You close your eyes and her face enters your mind;
A brief, fading memory left far behind
And bringing you torment within a great void
Of emptiness your thoughts can never avoid.

You open them and, at long last, a loud cry
Escapes from you, the silence there to defy
As movement returns to your limbs and you stare
At your bedroom for the mists, no more, are there.

A look of astonishment, your face obtains
And, for a brief moment, upon it, remains
When learning she, whom you love, always was kept
Within the depths of your own mind while you slept.

The dream now is no more but you do not resist
Your deep longing for it to, once more, exist
And if, truly real it could, once more, become
The next time you, into deep sleep, may succumb.

You feel the grief of her love left far behind
Within the place filled with mists within your mind
And nothing, there is, you can do until when
Your dream, when you sleep the next time, might
begin.

You close your eyes, hoping for sleep to pervade
Your mind, its full depths, to invade
So she may return for your love to exist
Through your haunted passion enveloped by mist.

THE NEIGHBORHOOD A&P

Marianna Nelson

A&P stands for the Atlantic and Pacific Tea Company. Back in the 1930s and 40s, everyone knew that name. From the small A&P in our neighborhood, we bought canned foods, winter vegetables, and packaged goods. In the summer, we purchased fresh vegetables from the Farm, a big produce stand on Grove Street, and also, during World War II, picked them from our Victory Garden.

The A&P was a short walk from our backyard to a dirt path that led to the store. The full-service store had no aisles and no grocery carts, just a grocer standing behind the counter getting customers the products they asked for.

The first time my mother sent me to the A&P by myself I was eight. I handed the list she'd written to the man standing behind the counter. He had a smile on his face, an apron tied around his waist, and a pencil behind his ear. "May I help you?" he asked.

I looked up at the high shelves behind him -- they were stacked with boxes and cans almost to the ceiling. To retrieve an item that was higher than the grocer could reach, he used a grocery store grabber -- a long wooden pole with a metal grabber at one end and a squeeze handle at the other. The grocer was an expert grabber. He looked at my list, then picked an item off the shelf with the grabber and deftly caught the box or the can with his other hand or in his apron. When he had retrieved everything on the list, he pulled out the pencil from behind his ear, wrote the prices on a brown paper bag, and totaled the amount. He put the items in the paper bag while I got out the money my mother had given me. He handed me the change and the bulging paper bag with the prices on it (my receipt).

I loved fresh vegetables, but in the winter, vegetables with long shelf lives -- carrots, potatoes, winter squash, turnips, parsnips -- were the only ones available at our A&P. I refused to eat turnips and parsnips because they tasted bitter. So, by March, I was sick of winter vegetables -- especially carrots because it seemed like we ate them every night. When my mother started to can tomatoes and string beans herself, they didn't taste the same or look as good as the fresh ones we had in the summer, but they sure were better than turnips and parsnips.

When my mother preserved food at home, she called it "canning." That didn't sound right to me because she put the vegetables in glass jars called Mason jars, not cans. Even though she canned for years, she always worried she might not seal the lids tightly enough and we would get food poisoning (we never did). On nights when we ate heated-up stewed tomatoes with toasted bread cubes in them or spaghetti with meatballs, it was my job to go down to the cellar and get a jar of tomatoes. The Mason jars were lined up in rows on our shelves and, as the winter progressed, the rows became shorter and shorter.

After WWII ended, manufacturers made more products and consumers had more choices at new stores like the Safeway supermarket that was built on Valley Road. It wasn't the same as the little A&P. It took longer to walk there and the friendly grocer with his grocery grabber were gone. Instead, we did the work, we took things off the shelves, and we put them in the grocery carts that we pushed up and down the aisles.

At first, the new way was a novelty, so it didn't seem like work to me – it seemed like fun. But, now that I look back on those years, I liked our little A&P and the friendly grocer with his grocery grabber.

THE OUTHOUSE*
Don Clifford

Ed Ledbetter choked on a plug of Copenhagen and dang near swallowed his store-bought upper plate. He glared at Jake Thatcher in disbelief. In between gasps for air he sputtered, "You want t'do what?"

"I wish to install a flush toilet in my outhouse," Jake said.

You could've heard a duck's feather fall to the floor. The usual hanger-ons at the Country General Store were rock still, waiting, so as not to miss a word. Even Granpaw "Stoneface" stopped his squeaking rocker and held it stiff as a statue.

The color in Ed's face graduated from eggshell white to flamingo pink, but the more Jake talked the redder Ed got. He thought he was being city-slicked. No one in Catfish Holler knew Jake very well, other than he got tired of racing after the rats in the City and decided to up and chuck the whole thing. He loaded his pretty wife, Thelma, two kids, and a host of family critters, and pointed the station wagon due West. They drove till they got plumb tuckered out.

They've been here ever since.

Jake was dead serious. "Yessir," he said. "I believe an outhouse is a great American status symbol for spacious living - something that we hi-rise apartment dwellers only dream about. I bought Old Man Caruthers' place because it is one of the few properties around that still had a standing monument to country essence. I don't mean to wax poetic, Boys, but I need to install a flush toilet for the comfort of the wife and kids. I admit I'm new to country ways, so I could use your help."

Granpaw got his rocker going again, the squeaks twice as fast. The conversational buzz swelled like an approaching swarm of bees. Any attempt to keep a straight face was well nigh impossible until Bud Lemming chimed in. “Jake, wouldn’t the flush toilet be more convenient inside the main house instead of the outhouse? After all, winter is coming, and…well, you know....”

That was the straw that burst the bubble. We ricocheted off the counters, rolled on the floor, and grabbed our sides splitting with laughter. Poor ol’ Jake stood dumbfounded. Being a city-boy, he had no inkling of the centuries of progress it took to move the comfort facility from outside to the inside. His face turned redder than Ledbetter’s.

Then the light dawned. A sudden grin creased Jake’s face, and with a mighty stomp that burped the pickle barrel, he cut loose with a booming laugh that set the smoked hams to swaying in the rafters. We guffawed all the harder; tears rolled down our cheeks. Even Granpaw “Stoneface” cracked his jaws and mumbled something about he thought he heard it all, until now.

From this moment, Jake Thatcher became a good friend. We could always count on him for at least one good laugh, even if the joke was on him. To this day, though, we still wonder what it would be like to have a flush toilet in an outhouse.

THE PAIN OF THE GUNSLINGER
Frank Cortazo

Shayne Blackburn knew another challenge awaited him when he heard the bellowing voice call him from the street outside.

"Come on out, Blackburn!" it roared. "I know you're in there!"

Blackburn leaned against the bar inside of the saloon and drank in silence. To any casual observer, he looked like a humble preacher garbed in black. However, he exuded an eeriness within the smoke-filled room with the long cloak and wide-brimmed hat whose ebony hue matched his suit and boots. It happened within each town the lawman -turned -gunslinger passed through.

"Come on out, old man!" bellowed the insistent voice. "Let's see if you're as fast as they say!"

The gunslinger was tired of these senseless, endless challenges. At over fifty years of age, he still wandered from town to town, attempting to escape from his past. He even tried assuming other identities and disguising himself. After a while, though, there would be someone who would recognize and challenge him. So far, luck was with him but...for how much longer? And...there was the arthritic pain afflicting his fingers...!

His thoughts drifted to his grandson, Stevie.

Would he ever see him again?

How long was it since the last time...ten, fifteen years? And...at a distance.

He sent Stevie to school back East to be cared for by friends. They were sworn to secrecy about ever revealing his relationship to the boy. Blackburn still felt responsible for the deaths of the toddler's parents during his final days as a lawman. He still heard the echoes of the bullets tearing through his mind.

Bullets fired at his daughter and her husband as they walked with Stevie upon a dusty street to greet him.

Bullets cutting them both down but one of them creasing the boy and leaving a permanent, lightning-shaped scar upon the right side of his face.

Bullets meant... for him.

For lawman Shayne Blackburn.

He remembered their bloodied bodies lying still while he gunned down the assassin who appeared from an alley nearby.

Those memories still haunted him, even now when he was known as one of the most feared gunslingers of the territory.

Blackburn missed Stevie. He remembered well the blond boy's innocent smile, his friendliness. He wanted nothing better than to reunite with him. However, it was best for the boy if he did not. If any of Blackburn's enemies ever learned of his family ties...

"I'm waiting, old man!" came the voice again, interrupting his thoughts.

Blackburn took his time drinking. Setting the glass down, he took his colt .45 from the worn holster at his side. All six chambers were loaded. As he placed it back into the holster, he turned and headed toward the bat wing doors. He ignored the wary faces of onlookers who sat or stood around him.

Stepping out into the board walk, he felt the heat of the afternoon sun against his weathered, rugged, face.

Waiting, at the end of the hot, dusty street, was his challenger.

He was just another kid dressed in a cow hand's plaid shirt with brown leather vest and dark jeans and black boots. A beige cowboy hat's brim drooped at the front. It covered the upper part of his face. Two guns were at the holsters at his side.

Another showoff, but a smart one, thought Blackburn.

This kid stood with the afternoon sun behind him.

"Go on home, kid," he said, stepping out into the street. "You don't want to do this."

"Draw your weapon, old man!" the kid said. "Let's see if you're as fast as they say you are in the dime novels!"

At a slow pace, Blackburn walked out into the street and faced the youth.

The sun blocked his vision.

To draw, from an uncertain angle, against the kid was not wise. And..., with the arthritis affecting his arm...

He was just a few feet away from the kid when his eyes took in the rest of the youthful face.

Why, he can't be no older than sixteen, he thought.

A good-looking kid, blond with full lips and... and...

His eyes widened when he saw...but...

Something distracted him.

It appeared to be...a figure..? .in the distance? A silvery-garbed...

He blinked and it was gone.

Maybe...it was ...a trick of the sun...a mirage.

His eyesight was not as good as it used to be.
It...can't be, he thought. It's...still there!

All of a sudden, the kid's hands moved!

They moved toward the guns.

In one split second, Blackburn drew his own weapon. The roar of two bullets being fired shattered the afternoon silence.

The kid yelled in pain as his guns fell to the ground without being fired. He clutched both hands to his chest as blood trickled from his fingers. Tears flowed down his face.

Blackburn held his smoking weapon aimed at the youth for a moment before he holstered it. "Go on home, kid," he told him. "You...do you know who I am?"

"Yes," answered the kid, holding back the rising tears of shame and anger. "Everyone knows who you are! You're Shayne Blackburn, the great gunslinger! Killer of men! The fastest gun in the territory. I grew up reading about you. I...spent many years learning how to use a gun but I...I never went up against anyone. I always wanted to beat you first ! I...someday...wanted to be the one who beat you to the draw! I wanted to be the one everyone would look up to as the fastest gun in the territory...!"

"...And the one who would inherit my reputation," Blackburn said. "You want to live the rest of your life being the target of every tinhorn wanting to be a gunman? If, of course, you survive past your teenage years!"

"You...you've murdered so many who drew against you!"

"All in self-defense," countered Blackburn. "There's no glory in it. It's not something I'm proud of."

"You...could've... killed me..." stammered the kid, "but you.....you didn't. Why?"

"Let's just say," interrupted Blackburn, "I'm tired of gunning down reckless, hot-headed kids who want to be sent to early graves. It pains me every time. I live with this pain day by day. You're too young to realize it now but, someday, you'll thank me for it. And...you can tell your grand kids how you went up against Shayne Blackburn and survived. In a way, I'm also trying to make up for all of my violent years..."

The kid, still holding his bloodied hands against his chest, remained silent, puzzled at this reply.

"...in my old age," finished the gunslinger, smiling.

He turned and walked toward the big, black sorrel tied to the hitching rail by the saloon. He mounted it, pulled on the stirrups, and rode away.

The mountains surrounding the town beckoned him. He would ride to one of them. Perhaps, there he would find the peace he searched for. Perhaps, there, he would be able to lessen the pain he felt...

The pain.

The physical and the mental.

And..., now...

Now, after this encounter, the emotional one as well.

As he rode toward onward toward the highest mountain, he thought about this latest incident. His reputation was preceding him down an even darker road. This was a close one. This kid survived. Not like so many others who...who never got the opportunity...

...And all for just wanting to make a name for themselves at his expense.

It was not clear whether or not this young man realized the truth of who he truly came up against.

Shayne Blackburn.

Fastest gun in the territory, as he was now known.

Never mind the days when, as a lawman, he cleaned up several towns of their outlaw element. No one remembered those days when the badge he wore stood as a star of justice. Now, he was known for his gun slinging days. In particular, everyone remembered his duel with the albino bounty killer, an event proclaiming his destiny.

This kid was fast but one thing was certain. His gun slinging days were over. He would not be fast enough to hold a gun in either hand. Blackburn made certain of it. The youth would live with this fact. He would be reminded of it if he ever tried to draw a gun again

Like a scar, it would remain with him for life.

Like a scar, thought Blackburn, teary-eyed.

Like the lightning-shaped, jagged scar the kid bore upon the right side of his face.

THE PARIS AFFAIR*
Jose A. Alvarez

Jane's soft voice woke Charlie up as the train came to a stop at the Gare du Nord. "Charlie, wake up. We just arrived in Paris; it's time to get to work."

"Christ Jane, I just woke up from a dreadful nightmare. Don't hassle me."

"Come on, let's go."

He rubbed his eyes and saw Jane's smiling face. She looked beautiful in a flowing peach silk blouse and a knee length blue skirt. She certainly looked better than in his dreams, wearing an oversize jacket and huge baggy pants as they sailed across the Atlantic in Bill's cruiser. And better yet, Bill was nowhere in sight.

Eloise greeted them as they got off the train. "Welcome to Paris, let's go home and get to work."

Elo gave directions to the taxi driver in fluent French.

"How far is it?" asked Jane.

"Depends on the traffic," Elo replied, "at this time of the day we should be there in half an hour."

Charlie remembered with a tinge of nostalgia the good times he spent living in Paris with Eloise a few years earlier. He had met many of her friends in the art world. "Too bad it didn't last," he thought.

When the taxi passed in front of Le Louvre and crossed Le Pont du Carrousel, he knew they'd soon be there. The ride to the fourth floor flat in the small elevator was noisy and slow. Bill was waiting for them and opened the door.

“Christ, I can’t get rid of this son of a bitch,” thought Charlie. “He is everywhere, from the middle of the Atlantic in my worst nightmare to the Rive Gauche in Paris.”

“It’s good to see you,” said Bill, “you guys look thirsty. What would you like to drink?”
Jane kissed him on both cheeks and accepted his offer. “It’s good to see you too Bill; I’ll have some Tequila”

“It’s not as good as what we had in Acapulco last December, but it’ll taste great after your long trip."

“Thanks.”

Eloise asked “How was your ride from Amsterdam?

“Very pleasant," Jane said. "These trains are fantastic.”

Charlie was pissed. What was Jane doing with Bill in Acapulco last December? “I hate that guy,” he thought.

Charlie asked for a glass of Scotch. Eloise poured herself some Chablis, and Bill prepared a Martini. Eloise brought a couple of baguettes and assorted cheeses to the dining room table. “Here, this’ll keep you busy while I prepare dinner. It’ll be ready in a couple of hours, so relax for a while.”

Jane chimed in. “You don’t need to bother with snacks Elo, we did not come here to eat. We have a job to do and we need to get on with it.”

“Now wait a second,” said Bill, “a little nourishment sounds good to me. Let’s try some of this cheese. What are you cooking Elo?”

“Well,” she said, “this is an old family recipe for Canard à l’Orange I learned from my grandmother Antoinette.”

"I can't wait to try it Elo. I am sure we'll love it," added Bill.

Jane looked at Charlie in disbelief. "What are these two doing? Don't they realize we have to finalize the plan for tomorrow?" she whispered to Charlie.

Charlie kept working on the cheese, spreading a generous helping on a slice of crusty French bread. "This is good," he said. "What is it?"

Bill explained, "This is Cabrales from the mountains of Asturias in northern Spain. I like it better as a dessert, but you are welcome to enjoy it as an appetizer."

"Gee, thanks Bill. I am glad I have your permission to eat some of this cheese before dinner."

"It just goes to show your ignorance, Charlie. As I always say 'once a boor, always a boor.' But that is fine; we need peasants too."

"Better to be a boor than an idiot."

"And who are you calling an idiot? I suppose I may need to teach you some manners."

Jane intervened. "Come on guys. Let's cool off. We still have to finalize the details for tomorrow's mission. Charlie, let's step out on the balcony."

Bill joined Eloise in the kitchen while Jane and Charlie walked over to the balcony overlooking St. Germain de Pres. "It is a beautiful evening. I hope the weather holds for tomorrow," he said.

Jane asked him "Why are you so tense? We need to keep our wits. Try to relax."

"Sure, how can I relax when I find out that you spent December in Acapulco with that jerk? I thought you had better taste than that."

“Relax Charlie, that trip, was strictly business. You don’t need to worry about him; I can’t stand him and his silly pranks.”

“Oh, really? What business were you taking care of in Mexico?

“You know we were gathering information on the Ambassador and his family. I can assure you it was all very professional.”

“Did you stay in the same hotel room with him?”

“Of course, you dummy. We were there as husband and wife. Did you expect us to sleep in separate rooms?”

Charlie returned to the living room and turned on the TV. He surfed through the channels till he found a sports channel carrying the Sumo wrestling championship from Osaka.

“Have you ever seen this Jane? It is really interesting. Let’s watch it.”

“You’ve got to be kidding. It’s just two fat guys in diapers throwing rice onto the ring and trying to shove each other off the stage.”

“No, Jane, it’s not that simple. There is a lot of strategy involved. It’s not just brute force; it is all a question of balance. A smart Sumo wrestler uses his opponent’s charge to make him lose his balance.”

“Well, you can sit here and watch the matches; I am going to get another glass of tequila. Would you like some more Scotch or more cheese?”

“No thanks. I am going for a walk as soon as this match is over. I think I’ll stop at Les Deux Magots.”

“What’s that?”

“That’s where the Ambassador likes to stop after the theater.”

“How do you know he stops there?”

“While you were cavorting in Acapulco, I was doing real research for this operation.”

“Jesus Christ Charlie, we were not “cavorting” in Acapulco, we were tailing the Ambassador. We even rented a sailboat to see if we could get near him at Pichilingue. But we could not get near him, there was too much security.”

“Yes, I read the report from agents “Bonnie and Clyde” after they returned from their assignment in Mexico. They could not get close to the Ambassador. I just didn’t know you and Bill were Bonnie and Clyde. You must have spent your time lying on the beach, next to your spying partner. How was it?”

“Oh, just stop it. By the way who’ll pull the trigger? I’d prefer it to be Bill, not me.”

“There’ll be no trigger to pull. We are planting a bomb under his car.”

“What do you mean 'we'? How are 'we' planting the bomb?”

“Eloise decided we should use a bomb and took care of all the arrangements. She’ll tell us the details after we finish the roast duck. In the meantime I am going out. It’s getting stuffy in here. I’ll see you in a while.”

Charlie took the elevator to the ground floor and walked into the cool Parisian Spring. He crossed the street by the church of St. Germain de Pres and headed for Les Deux Magots. A young couple approached him to ask for directions. They spoke in broken French and he could only understand a few words, “Le Louvre, Notre Dame, aujourd’hui.” He replied in English.

“I am sorry I can’t help you, I speak only a little French.”

The young woman replied. “Maybe you can help us after all, I speak English.”

"Her English sounds Scandinavian, and she is quite a dish too," he thought. "Let's give it a try," he said.

"We are lost and want to buy a map of Paris so we can find our bearings. Do you know where we could buy one?"

Charlie remembered spending a few hours at a bookstore along the Seine when he was living in Paris. It was probably still there. "Well I know of a nice bookstore not far from here, at least it was there a few years ago. Follow this street till you reach the Seine. Make a left and you'll find the bookstore a few blocks away. I forgot its name."

"Thank you very much. We appreciate your help."

"Funny," he thought, "she looks like one of the passengers who boarded the train in Amsterdam, though the woman in the train had dark hair."
Charlie sat at a small outdoor table at Les Deux Magots and asked for a beer and fries. He was sipping his beer, waiting for his food, when Jane approached his table. "Finish up Charlie; we need to find a place to talk."

"Not so fast Jane. I am waiting for some food. Relax a bit let's share the fries and then we can walk to the river to find a secluded spot."

Jane wanted no food and watched impatiently as Charlie finished his fries and beer. They left the cafe and walked briskly to the river. Halfway across the bridge, Jane stopped. "Let's stand here and watch the view for a while. I love watching the boats go by."

"What's this Jane? So now we are just a couple of tourists."

Some passengers on the aft deck of a tour boat approaching the bridge waved at Charlie and Jane as they sailed under the bridge. They waved back. A smaller boat rocking in the wake of the large tour boat appeared suddenly beneath them. As the boat moved away at full speed Jane looked at Charlie. "How I'd like to be on that boat right now. It looks like lots of fun." She pointed to the boat and added. "Look you can see the towers of Notre Dame Cathedral over there, right above the speed boat. Why don't you take a picture?"

"What's up Jane? I don't think we came all the way to Paris to take tourist pictures."

She sighed and said, "I am sorry Charlie. I am worried and don't want to think about what lies ahead. Better to daydream than to dwell on the problems ahead. Wouldn't you like to be sailing on the Seine with me right now?"

"Well, if you put it that way, of course I'd certainly enjoy being alone with you on any boat any day, as long as the weather is good. But we still have work to do. After the job is done we can play all you want." He went on, "what are you so worried about?"

"I think this operation is not well planned. There are too many loose ends."

"What do you mean? You know Eloise planned most of it," he said, "and none of her operations have ever failed."

"Well I am worried."

"Listen Jane, Elo has all the material in her flat. Everything is in place. We just need to go over some last minute details for tomorrow and we'll do that right after dinner. Tomorrow we execute the plan and then we can go sailing around the world."

"Charlie, don't be so flip. It is not the question of material that bothers me. I just don't think Bill and Eloise are serious enough about the project. This is a life and death matter, and they have been gawking at each other like teenagers."

"I see what the problem is. You are jealous."

"Christ almighty Charlie, of course I am not jealous. Is love and sex all you can think about? You are just as distracted as they are."

“Well somewhere I read that the only two things in life that matter are Eros and Thanatos.”

“Don’t get cute with me. The last thing I need is your pop psychology; I need you to take this matter seriously and take care of all the little practical details. Fuck love and death.”

"Like what little practical details?”

“Like, does Bill already know he must plant a bomb? He hates explosives. Give him a knife, or a gun, and he feels like a kid in a candy store. But he is all thumbs handling explosives.”

“What do you mean? Didn’t you guys train on the use of explosives?”

“Yeah, sure we did. But you should have seen Bill during training. He sweated like a pig, and at night he could not sleep.”

“Were you also sleeping with him during training?”

“There you go again. Of course not, we were in barracks.”

“That does not answer my question. How do you know he couldn’t sleep at night?”

“He told me. I could see he was distracted and short tempered. His eyes were blood shot every morning, I think for lack of sleep. I tell you I am worried about him.”

Charlie interrupted her. “Quick, let’s take a couple of pictures.”

“Don’t change the subject Charlie. This is serious. We need to deal with these questions.”

“I agree. But first some pictures.”

“Why are you suddenly in such a rush to take some pictures? I thought you did not want us to act like tourists.”

“Look behind you; see that young Swedish looking couple walking this way?”

Jane turned around slowly. “Yeah, I see them. They look like tourists taking pictures too. What about them?”

“Stand there while I take your picture; I want to catch them in the background.”

“Why, Charlie?”

“I think they are following us. I met them when I came out of Eloise’s flat and she asked me for directions to a bookstore. She is gorgeous and reminded me of another beauty I saw boarding the train in Amsterdam. Only that woman had dark curly hair. And here she is again, only this time in all her blonde Nordic splendor.”

“So you are back to love and sex.”

“Damn Jane. This has nothing to do with love and sex. This is serious and could be extremely dangerous for all of us. Yes, she is eye candy, and I would love to flirt with her in a different time and place, but not here and not now. What if they know of our plans?”

The Swedes stopped to take some pictures too. Charlie was sure that by now he and Jane were part of the Parisian landscape photographed by the Swedes. As they came closer, Charlie aimed the camera directly at them and snapped a couple of more pictures.

“What a coincidence meeting you here on the bridge. I guess you found the bookstore,” he said to the tall blonde. “Isn’t Paris beautiful in the springtime?”

“Yes, I love Paris in the springtime. But then I think Paris is beautiful year round. I’m glad that we meet again; I wanted to thank you again for your directions. We were able to find our way quite easily. By the way, my name is Marlene Bauer and this is my brother Hans.”

As they shook hands, Charlie completed the introductions.

"I am Charlie O'Shea and this is my friend Jane Norman. We were just getting ready to find a place to have a glass of wine on our way back to the apartment. Would you care to join us?"

"That would be delightful," said Marlene. "We'll be happy to join you. Do you have a particular place in mind?"

Jane jumped in. "One of the things I like about Paris is how easy it is to find a place to have a cup of coffee, a beer, or a glass of wine. Let's just amble back and find a place."

As they walked back across the bridge, Marlene inquired "What brings you to Paris?"

Charlie replied. "One of my old friends from when I lived in Paris a few years ago invited us to come and spend some time with her. What about you? What brings you to Paris?"

Hans spoke for the first time. "My sister and I wanted to spend some time together in Paris before our new assignments in the Americas beginning next month. I am moving to Boston, and Marlene to São Paolo."

"This looks like a great spot for a glass of wine," said Jane as they approached a small bistro, Chez Pierre. "Let's try it."

They sat at an outdoor table with a view of the Louvre across the Seine. Charlie opened a pack of Gauloises and offered them around. "Does anyone else care to smoke?"

Hans seemed offended, "No, thanks, we don't smoke."

But Marlene accepted the invitation, "I haven't smoked in quite a while; I think I'll join you. Thank you."

Charlie struck a match to offer Marlene a light. She guided his hand close to her lips and lit her cigarette, inhaling deeply. "These are strong," she said.

“That’s why I like them,” he replied.

A young waiter approached them to take their order, a bottle of Beaujolais some bread and slices of brie. While they waited, Jane picked up where Hans had left off. “You were saying that both you and Marlene will move to the Americas. “Will you be moving any time soon?”

Hans replied, “As soon as our Parisian holiday is over; we leave on Tuesday.”

“I am looking forward to living in São Paulo,” said Marlene, “I’ve never been to South America. I hear the state of São Paulo is the engine that drives Brazil’s economy, and the city itself is the main source of its economic strength.”

“You’ll love the people,” said Jane. “They are hard working, but they really know how to have a good time. And they are very sensual.”

“More than sensual, I’d say they are sexy,” added Charlie.

Marlene asked, “Is that the voice of experience talking?”

Hans joined the discussion, “Marlene needs to focus on her work. She won’t have time for much carousing.”

Charlie laughed at Hans comment. “Don’t be such a wet hen Hans. I’m sure Marlene will have time for both, and yes it is the voice of experience talking. As a matter of fact I plan to be in Brazil in a couple of months and if we happen to be there at the same time, I’d like to take Marlene out to some of my favorite hangouts.”

“That would be wonderful. I’d love to have you show me around, said Marlene.”

“Make sure to bring your dancing shoes. You’ll need them. We’ll be dancing the nights away.”

“Just remember dear sister, you are going there to do a job. That is your main responsibility. You’ll need to cast aside anything interfering with your work.”

The waiter brought their drinks and Jane used the interruption to change the topic, “What about you Hans, have you been to Boston previously?"

“Oh yes. I know it well. I went to MIT, just across the river in Cambridge, for my undergraduate degree.”

“Did you like it?”

“Are you referring to MIT or the city?

“Well, to both.”

“MIT was great, but the city of Boston was boring. It’s too Catholic for my taste; it was full of Irishmen.”

“Watch it pal,” said Charlie. “Remember my last name is O’Shea. What’s wrong with being Catholic and Irish?”

“It’s nothing personal; it’s just that they seem to wear their religion on their sleeves; always going to confession, praying to the Virgin Mary, and talking of sin and damnation. They are obsessed with sex, but their sex life is repressed. They have tortured souls.”

"It looks like you had no success wooing Irish ladies in Boston; they gave you the cold shoulder so you found them boring.” Charlie stirred the pot. “Jane what do you think, aren’t you from Boston?”

Hans backpedaled. “Well, of course, I also have very good Irish friends; I don’t mean to paint all Irish with the same brush.”

Sensing the awkwardness of the moment Jane asked Marlene “And what’ll you be doing in São Paulo Marlene?”

“I am a journalist specializing in finance. I’ll be in Brazil investigating recent financial transactions from Europe and the Middle East that we believe may be linked to terrorist cells operating out of Latin America.”

“That must be dangerous. I am sure if those terrorists moved their operations as far as South America they don’t want to be found,” said Jane

“Yeah Marlene,” added Charlie “that sounds exciting. What did those guys do?”

“I couldn’t tell you. I just was assigned this investigation last week, so I only have very sketchy information. But I do know that in addition to their financial skullduggery some of these terrorists are wanted for murder. When I catch up with them, they’ll be sorry. I’ll expose them.”

“What about you Hans? Are you also hunting criminals?”

“Nah, my work is less exciting. I’ll be teaching at MIT.”

“Well I hope you’ll have better luck with the ladies this time around.”

Marlene took a sip of the red wine and asked Charlie. “What does your Parisian friend do?”

“She is an art dealer specializing in Latin American paintings and lithographs.”

“How did she get into this business? She must be very good to succeed in this competitive market.”

“Her parents collected lithographs of Latin American scenes by Frédéric Mialhe; a French artist who lived in the early nineteenth century and she continued the family tradition. Eloise is very good at what she does. How she got started is a long story that would bore you to tears. I’m sure you’d not be interested.”

"I'd like to hear anyway. Do you mind?

Charlie continued "Our grandparents went into exile with their families when they lost all they owned to the communists. Both families settled in Washington where our mothers went to college. Both married right after graduation. My dad Patrick O'Shea, was, a medical student from Boston. Eloise's father, Louis La Fleur, was a doctoral student in Economics from Paris."

Jane asked Charlie to speed it up. "Charlie, we don't have all day. Get to the bottom line. We need to get back to Bill and Elo."

Marlene insisted "No, no, I am enjoying the story Charlie, please continue," she implored him.

"When they went into exile, Eloise's parents managed to smuggle their art collection with the help of the French consul, Monsieur Ribeaux, who kept the collection in storage until Isabel moved to France with her husband."

Marlene asked Charlie. "Are the people who confiscated your family's properties still in power?

"They sure are."

"Your family must hate them."

"Of course we do. They imprison torture and kill their opponents. They should be shot."

"We should be going Charlie," said Jane. "It is time to meet with Eloise."

Charlie hailed the garçon. "L'addition s'il vous plait." He went on "Let me treat." He added

"Marlene, I'll be at the Maksoud Plaza in São Paulo in early June. Give me a call and we'll go out."

She replied, "I'll call you for sure."

After leaving Chez Pierre Charlie asked Jane, “What did you think?”

“I can’t believe you. You’re upset because I was working with Bill in Acapulco and yet you make a date with Marlene in Brazil. You’ll do anything to get her into bed.”

“Don’t be silly.”

“What if they are trailing us because we’re the 'bad guys' they are after? Perhaps we should cancel the operation.”

“You’ve got to be kidding Jane. We’ve come too far to cancel now.”

“I am sorry Charlie, but I am getting more worried by the minute.”

“Are you seriously thinking of aborting the mission in a fit of jealousy?

“Charlie, we should reconsider the whole operation with Bill and Elo. Let’s hurry back.”

They walked in silence back to the flat as a soft rain began to fall.

THE RAPE
Bidgie Weber

In the 1800's Saturday nights in a camp filled with roughnecks and drillers meant anything could happen and most Saturday nights it did.

Housing for the oil camp workers consisted of a combination of "tent" and "wooden shoe box" fixtures. The top portion of the structure was made of stiff canvas that had been coated with some sort of oil mixture to help keep out the biting cold wind during the winter months.

There were wooden poles at the corners to reinforce the canvas walls. Of course, that meant the cool air of the blistering summers was also blocked. Some of the men in camp had cut holes in the sides of their "house" making it possible to roll up sections of the wall in hopes of what summer breezes blew might make the nights bearable. Summer brought insects and sickness so it was a choice of heat or bugs. Tenie liked neither, but Big John preferred bugs to heat so he cut "windows" for them.

A hand made wooden slat door was not, by any stretch of the imagination, a barrier to keep out evil. At best, a would be intruder would be forced to knock down the wooden door, giving the intended victim scant moments to arm himself. At worst, the canvas that covered the top half of the door could be cut with a sharp knife and allow an intruder quiet access to do his mischief.

This July Saturday night seemed like the hottest night in years. Tenie was feeling the heat as it seemed to bake the sweat from her body. It was like a hot, muggy, damp, sticky wool blanket had been thrown over her head and made breathing a chore. In a daring moment she decided to roll up the "windows" to allow what little breeze there was cool her flushed face.

The results of this careless move would prove to be a life altering event for Tenie and Big John. Worse, it would be a fatal mistake for one roughneck. Big John had not returned from town where he had to make a small delivery. Tenie knew she had time to haul a few buckets of water from the river for a quick spit bath. She grabbed the tin bucket from the corner and slipped out into the night.

Anxious to enjoy a nice cool reprieve from the brutally hot day she forgot about the rolled up windows.

Big John had purchased a size ten wash tub so she could wash what dirty clothes they owned plus, she could bathe in the tub. The one concession which reminded her she was truly a lady in a man's world was the small wild flowers she had painted around the bottom of the tub. This was her reminder that true beauty of God's bounty did exist. Each time she took her "standing spits bath" she would have her "lady moments" in her field of flowers. Tenie reached for the gourd they used for a dipper and slowly poured the cool water over her body. With the lye soap she had made and the added flower petals, the cool water skimmed down her body and left a gleaming sheet of beauty in its path.

As she transported herself to a dream world, she was unaware that just outside her tent stood the real world.

Buford Bingham, mesmerized by the surreal sight in from of him, stood outside the "window" in the real world. As it happened, the roughneck was staggering his way across the grounds when he noticed something strange.

A woman! A woman who had nothing on except soap and water! He watched as Tenie stood in the one luxurious item she owned.

Buford's "rod and staff" were certainly no comfort to him. In fact, he was fast becoming aware that they were demanding his attention…quickly!

Buford was a backwoods cedar chopper, the equivalent of today's "poor white trash". He was used to taking what he wanted when he wanted it and from anyone; he decided that this was the time! What he wanted stood right in front of him. Without a thought beyond self, Buford jerked his huge hunting knife from his boot, jabbed it through the canvas and opened a slit big enough for him to dive through.

The moment Tenie stepped out of the washtub she saw the silhouette of a man standing in front of the window. For an instant, she thought Big John had returned from the day's work.

The odor of sweat, dirt, oil and arousal hit her full force. In the time it took to digest what had happened, fear stepped in. She knew the scent of fear, she had smelled it often enough…just not her own!

The outside world was reduced to the size of her little tent. Tenie not only heard her heart pounding, she felt it in her head, behind her eyes, her ears popped with the rhythm of her racing heart. She knew, if she did not act quickly her world ceased to exist. Time did not stand still but she could not seem to move. She felt as though she was trying to run against a sea of mud. Her mind raced ahead of her body. She knew what she had to do but could not get her mind, body movements and directions working together.

Fear is not cowardice, it is common sense, and she just had to apply it in this case. Endurance has its limits, not to be tested too much, too often. Tenie had reached her limit. Her immobile state suddenly gave way and her strength stepped in.

Suddenly she was as inhuman as this monster on top of her. There would be NO rape this night. NO good time for Buford G. Bingham, for this night would see another bastard setting up camp in HELL.

Tenie inched her way closer to her pistol. Buford was lost in the expectation of what it would feel like to enter the pearly gates of this wild thing he had come upon. He could almost feel his relief as he imagined it bursting free. He forgot it was a person he was ravaging, a person with just as much purpose as he had.

He quickly parted Tenie's legs and moved in between them, prepared to enter her. Just as he thought he could feel himself enter the gates of heaven and hear the heavenly choir, he realized the choir sounded more like a gun shot.

This was NOT her Big John making tender love to her, this was an animal in rut.

Tenie's hand latched on to the pistol, her lifeline. Fear, endurance and strength took over, as she shoved the barrel in Buford's gaping mouth. The four of them pulled the trigger.

Blood, bone, teeth, meat and what little brain Buford had stored, poured down on Tenie's face.

Naked, lying on the floor covered with kibbles and bits of Buford G. Bingham is what Big John saw when he burst into the tent.

Big John was just as sure by this time, Bingham was in Hell begging for a glass of ice water and his chance of getting one was just as dead as Bingham! By the time Big John managed to throw a blanket over Tenie and roll down the windows, a crowd had gathered in front of their tent. Big John and Tenie both knew they would have to leave camp immediately. As was the way of early days, they had to leave camp not because Tenie had killed a man, who deserved it, but because she was a woman in camp who dressed like a man, rolled and smoked Bugler, and spit with the best of them, all of which was taboo!

That very night was the start of Tenie and Big John's life on the run. They had heard about the Rio Grande Valley, then known as Six Shooter Junction, and thought it might be just the place to start a new life…far from roughnecks and roustabouts. Tenie could be a female. She could become a real wife. She would be able to make a real home, have lady friends to talk with. She would be able to sit out in the beautiful cool evenings in South Texas and enjoy life.

NOT LIKELY!

THE ROPER

Hugh Barlow

The Roper stands alone.

Feet together, he swings the rope above his head.

His victim jumps—the rope goes 'round his feet.

Toying with him, The Roper untangles his victim.

Once again, the rope goes 'round—this time to land on Victim's neck.

Back to reality.

I hate jump-rope!

THE SPEED LIMIT
LeRoy Overstreet

A man is driving through a small south Texas Town on his way to the city for an appointment with a doctor. The speed limit through the town is 30 miles per hour.

After passing through the town the driver begins to increase his speed a little but notices a pickup truck, up ahead facing toward him, turn on a flashing blue light. The pickup has a big sign painted on each side with the name of the town, and above that, in much larger letters, "POLICE".

The man pulls over to the side of the road and stops. The police pickup drives past, makes a U-turn and stops right behind. A Cop gets out of the police pickup, walks up to the driver and asks to see his driver's license. The driver hands the Cop his driver's license and also his concealed handgun license as is required by Texas law.

The cop walks back to the police pickup, reaches in through the open window, picks up the radio microphone and calls someone. He stands there an awfully long time talking on the radio with the microphone in his right hand while waving the two licenses around with his left. The driver wishes he would hurry up because time is getting short and he doesn't want to be late for his appointment.

Finally the Cop walks back to the driver's window with his yellow ticket book and the two licenses in his left hand and his pen in the right.

"You were going 42 miles per hour in a 30 mile zone."

But Officer, I was looking right at a sign that said 40 miles per hour."

You have to go past—You have to go past that sign before you can go 40 miles per hour!"

"Well now, that doesn't make sense to me because the sign right opposite on the lane going towards town says 30 miles per hour and, by your reasoning, it would be alright to go past it going 40 miles per hour while going TOWARDS town in the exact same zone that you say it would be illegal to go 40 miles per hour while LEAVING town?"

"Well--- uh--- You may have a point. I'm going to let you go. What kind of a gun is it?"

The driver caught somewhat off center by that one says: "Uh--- Why--- Uh--- It's a Smith and Wesson, .357 magnum revolver loaded with hollow point bullets."

"Have you got it with you?"
Of course I've got it with me. If I hadn't have had it with me I wouldn't have showed you my concealed handgun license."

"Where do you keep it?"

"Right here under the seat by my right foot where I can put my hand on it." And he reaches down and puts his hand on the gun.

"Oh no--- no! Don't take it out! Don't take it out! Here's your licenses. You can go now."

The driver heads toward the city and says to himself: "I'd better set the cruise control 2 or 3 miles per hour faster than the speed limit if I'm going to get to the doctor's office on time.

THE TEMPTRESS*
Hugh Barlow

I find myself walking down a street that I knew from when I was a child. I do not remember how I got here, but I know the street well, and I can see that it is about mid spring. The hedges have lost all their verdure, and fresh buds have yet to bloom on the dead looking twigs of the shrubbery. There are scraps of litter mixed in with the leaves that had fallen from the last autumn. Candy wrappers and cigarette butts are woven into what looks like rat's nests under the hedges, and the snow of winter vanished long ago. The leaves are the dun color that comes with age and decomposition. I see the red of a Kit Kat wrapper, the green of Wrigley's chewing gum, and the silver tinsel of some foil that was discarded some months ago adorning the detritus under the hedges like Christmas decorations left out to weather long after the season is gone. I feel an errant breeze teasing me with the touch of a chill, but the teasing is just a hint. The bite of winter is gone.

In the distance, I see a form that I know well. It is a blond woman dressed in tailored slacks, a white frilled shear blouse, and a black form fitting jacket that is open in the front and accentuates her body. Oddly, while I can see the woman's striking blue eyes clearly, I cannot make out her face. It is as though she is wearing a mask made from nylon stocking that blurs the features of her face enough that they are indistinguishable. Although I know I should know this woman well, just by the shape of her body, I am curiously unable to recollect exactly who she is.

My mystery woman smiles a hidden smile through her mask, and attempts to seduce me with her eyes. She says not a word, but brings up her hand and beckons me with the classic one finger curl that says, "Come hither." Her eyes make promises, and she turns. I become excited by the promises and I follow. The mystery woman walks toward the lobby of the most expensive hotel in town.

The building has a tower of ten or so stories with two wings to each side that are about three stories tall. The central tower juts forward from the main structure and is supported by several large pillars where the driveway tunnels under the building on the ground floor. Instead of walking toward the automatic doors, I am surprised to find that the mystery woman begins to climb on the trunk of a black stretched limousine that is parked under the tower.

She climbs on the roof, and triggers a trap door that is set in the ceiling above the entryway. Again, she beckons me with the crook of her finger, and I climb onto the roof of the car and help her enter the trap door. After boosting my mystery woman, I grab the edge and pull myself up into a dark space. The woman reaches down, closes the door behind us, and I find that the place where the door once gaped has become indistinguishable from the marble floor that we crouch on. Feeling about with my hands, I cannot find the joints where the door once was.

I look about to see where we are, but all I can see is that we are in a darkened space. The only light comes from the distant exit signs to my left and right, and several dim, blood red bulbs set in fixtures on either side of a very long hallway.

The mystery woman stands, turns, and walks down the hallway. She seems to peer at each door to see the number, but I am unable to tell one number from the next except by feel. She goes from door to door in the darkened hall until she reaches the one she is searching for. She fumbles for a key, and I ask myself, "If she has a key, why did we have to sneak in?" The door unlocks, and the mystery woman turns on the lights to the room that I have yet to see.

The light from the room floods the hall and shows stained, torn and ruined wallpaper. It seems to have aged several hundred years or so, but the building we are in is only a few years old. The decay that I see is not possible in the amount of time that this building has existed. I shrug that off, and follow the mystery woman into the room after she enters.

The room that I see is very different from what I saw in the hallway. The walls are antiseptic white and everything looks freshly painted and scrubbed surgically clean. Instead of seeing the bedroom set that I had expected, I see one wall of the room bracketed by a row of gleaming glass tubes that go from floor to ceiling. The tubes are large enough that a person could stand inside and not touch the gleaming glass. The windows of the room are curtained with heavy white drapes that do not allow the daylight through, and in the center of the room is a stainless steel console with many lights and switches. There is a computer monitor embedded in the console, and an antiseptically white keyboard on the stainless counter. At the console is a black plastic swivel chair with rollers.

The mystery woman walks to the stainless steel console, puts her jacket on the back of the chair and then brushes the chair out of her way. She then uses the keyboard, and flips a few switches. Two of the glass tubes make a popping sound, and sigh with the sound of a vacuum being filled with gasses. Two glass doors pop open, and the mystery woman walks up to one of the tubes and enters.

I stand rooted to the spot as I watch the woman enter the tube. She turns and looks at me as the door sighs shut behind her and seems to ask, "Won't you join me?" as she gestures toward the empty and open tube next to her. I shake my head no, and a look of sadness enters her eyes as the machines that run the place start the floor of the tube spinning in a clockwise direction. The floor shakes as my mystery woman turns like a ballerina in the center of the glass tube.

The air is quickly evacuated. Blood pours out from her body through the pores on her skin, her mouth, ears, and other body orifices as she snaps her head with each turn to look at me just like the dancer she so recently resembled. The look in her eyes is one of pity as the vacuum chamber centrifuges her blood up against the walls and I lose sight of her. Eventually, the machinery stops, the woman falls limp to the floor in an unrecognizable mass of flesh and bone. The blood on the glass walls of the chamber flows to the floor to puddle while the pink mists of blood in the chamber slowly coagulate and drop to the floor, drawn by gravity.

Although it is mid summer, and sweltering hot in my camper, I awake in a cold sweat, with the acrid stench of fear in my nostrils; with it burning in my eyes. I shake as the adrenaline courses through my blood. While it is still very early in the morning, there is NO WAY that I am going back to sleep! This is why I do not like to dream.

THE THIN MACHINE
Caroline Steele

Think thin, think thin.

Where to begin?

Cut out goodies,

Eat more woodies,

No midnight snacks,

No pudding packs.

Be fat or lean -

A thin machine.

How do I pick?

ANOREXIC!

THE TRADE WAR
Travis M. Whitehead

Juan Hinojosa only wanted to help the boy. Jose Chapa seldom came to his science class, he never turned in his work, and all Jose had in his grade book was straight zeros.

However, Jose, a stocky young man with thick, dexterous hands and a nervous energy, never gave him any trouble, and he seemed to Juan to be very bright. So when Robert Larsen asked Juan to just let the boy come over to his mechanic's shop everyday, he was inclined to agree.

"Juan, nobody in his family has ever graduated from high school," said Bob Larsen, a tall, blond fellow with a large, hooked nose and a high forehead.

"The way I see it, he's going to be a mechanic, he's never going to use the science," Bob Larsen told him. "He'll just drop out of school if he fails science. Why don't you just let him come over to my shop during your period and you can give him a passing grade."

It seemed like a good idea to Juan Hinojosa, his thin wiry frame standing in a sweeping curve in the door of Bob Larsen's shop. Several students were trouble-shooting a broken-down Camaro, another was turning brakes, and a third changed piston rings.

Juan felt a little weary from a late night of solitary drinking. He wasn't so young anymore, and he could feel it. Bob barely seemed to notice his bloodshot eyes, and in his customary fashion said nothing. Juan appreciated that, but in any case he wasn't concerned. It was with clear heads that both men discussed the future of one of their students, always a grave issue. Jose had fixed Juan's car several times and mentioned going to a vocational school after high school. If he did not have his diploma he was not going anywhere. He was not losing anything by skipping science, and what Bob said was true; Jose Chapa would drop out. He was that stubborn.

Juan agreed with Bob's suggestion, and over the next few months Bob Larsen reported that the young man was doing well. When Juan's car suddenly seemed to not be getting enough gas, he let Jose take a look at it in Larsen's shop.

"It sounds like maybe the timing belt," Jose said when Juan explained the problem.

"You might need some spark plugs too, I think," Jose added.

"You want me to just leave it here?" Juan said.

"I think so," Jose Chapa said. "Maybe if you come back this afternoon I can have it ready."

"Well, son, I'll need it back this afternoon," Juan said. "Can you have it running when I come by? That's the only car I've got."

"Well, I got this Buick I have to look at first, but I don't think it's a problem, and I'm rebuilding a carburetor, and then I have to go pick up some parts, but I think I can have it ready," Jose Chapa said.

Juan knew for a fact the car would be ready, because when Jose said "I think," or "maybe" it was as good as done. When Juan came back in the afternoon, the car was ready.

"O.K., it's good as new," Jose said. "You've got a new timing belt, new spark plugs and new spark plug wires. It's running like a million bucks."

Juan was always happy to see students, any student, doing well. He was delighted that Jose was doing so well, too, and then rumors began circulating that he let Jose go to the mechanic's shop everyday so he could get free auto service. There were rumblings and whispers for about a week, when he was called to the superintendent's office along with the principal of the high school, Mr. Aguilar. They sat across the Superintendent Gomez's big oak desk. Mr. Gomez, leaned back in his chair against a backdrop of John F. Kennedy pictures, and began his inquisition.

"Mr. Hinojosa, I'm sure you understand why you're here," Mr. Gomez began, twirling a pencil in his fingers.

"No, I really don't," Juan answered obstinately.

"We've got information you've been sending a student to Mr. Larsen's class," Mr. Gomez said. "You've been giving him grades."

"He's just getting rid of problem students because he doesn't want to deal with them," blurted Mr. Aguilar.

"I don't know what the hell you're talking about," Juan said. "This student has never, ever given me any problem at all."

"Right, because he's never there," said the principal.

"How do you know he's never there!?" Juan said. "Were you there in my class everyday? Where the hell have you been!?"

"Are you telling me he's been coming to class everyday?" Aguilar said.

"No, he's not there every goddamned day-"

"Mr. Hinojosa, you will watch your language in this office." the superintendent said.

"Don't give me that horseshit!" Juan snapped. "The kid's old enough to make up his own mind about what he wants to do, if he wasn't in my class it was his decision, not mine."

"So, you're telling me you didn't give him permission to go to Mr. Larsen's class?" asked Mr. Gomez. "Because we have witnesses who said you did."

"I'm telling you this is supposed to be a free country and whoever told you that is a liar!" Juan said. "You think you're teaching these kids, you're not. They're supposed to be learning how to think for themselves and all you're worried about is the goddamned TAAS."

"Mr. Hinojosa, did you, or did you not, give that student permission to go to Mr. Larsen's class?" asked the superintendent.

"I am telling you right now I did no such thing," Mr. Hinojosa said. "If he did that, he went of his own free will, and I encouraged him to build on what he does best and to find his own way in life."

"We can't allow that, we could get in trouble with the state," said the superintendent, now that the truth was out. "What's the kid going to do when he takes the TAAS?"

"We are supposed to help these kids prepare for their future," Juan said.

"The school board hired me to prepare them for college," the superintendent said. "That's what I intend to do. You say you're trying to help him, but you're not. We could get in a lot of trouble."

"You could get in a lot of trouble, what about the kid?" Juan asked. "I also hear you're getting rid of the trades. Is that true?"

"We're making room for other classes, in technology, computers, engineering," the superintendent said calmly, sitting up now and leaning over his desk.

"What if they don't want to do that?" Juan asked. "What if you've got a kid who likes to work on cars and engines and refrigerators?"

"I'm not going to debate that issue," Gomez said. "That's none of your concern. You've violated several school district policies and given a student grades he didn't earn. You've also jeopardized his future."

Juan resigned -- more out of disgust than any prodding from the school board. He packed his bags, locked up the house, and left for Mexico City where he got a job managing a hotel on Cinco de Mayo Street. It was just a temporary job until he found something else.

Bob Larsen came to see him after school let out for the summer. The school had eliminated the mechanics classes so Bob had also resigned. Juan put him up in the hotel and took him to the zocalo, first to the National Palace, then into the cathedral.

"You like it here?" Bob asked as they took a late breakfast at La Pinata on the zocalo.

"Oh, absolutely," Juan said as he dove into a ham omelet.

"Think you'll ever come back to Orange City?" Bob Larsen asked half seriously.

"Oh, hell no," Juan said. "By the way, what happened to Jose Chapa?"

Bob Larsen shrugged and shook his head. "Dropped out, like I knew he would," he said. "The superintendent says it's because we gave up on him."

"Oh, that's a bunch of horseshit!" Juan said leaning back with eyes wide open and putting down his fork. "We did everything in the world for that kid! And look at him now."

"I think he'll do O.K.," Bob Larsen said. "He's got a lot of talent, he could get a mechanic's job anywhere."

"Either that or his cousin," Juan said.

"His cousin?" Bob Larsen repeated.

"Yeah, you know, the one that's been stealing lawnmowers?" Juan said. "Maybe Jose can fix them up for him and sell them at a profit. Real good career for him to get into, courtesy of the superintendent."

THE WALL OF INFAMY*
Frank Cortazo

Rodrigo Reyes looked up from near a huge stone wall within a desolate, war-ravaged village. He saw a lone eagle hovering over the area. Smiling, he thought of the peaceful freedom the bird possessed. Rare and sought by the people of this impoverished country, it was a prize worth fighting for. Therefore, what was about to occur might serve to balance the long struggle between the powerful, military government and the people it sought to subjugate.

Rodrigo stood with his back against the tall, forlorn wall. Even with the heat of the rising sun, the hard surface felt cold and bare. It was not any ordinary wall. It was what remained of an old adobe building demolished by a stray cannonball during a battle between revolutionaries and government soldiers. Its battered structure was scarred with bullet holes. The blood stains of many who fell beside it still adhered to its rough surface. Rodrigo could almost hear the echoing cries of those who fell before it.

His eyes glistened as he looked back at the eagle overhead, flying with majestic glory. Perhaps, one day, this land would possess the peace and freedom its people craved and ---

Coronel Cruz's approach interrupted his thoughts.

"Well?" asked the military man, resplendent in his dark, military uniform. "How does it feel to stand at the place where so many of your compatriots fell?"

"I am honored," answered Rodrigo, perspiration running down the side of his face. "It is not every day a person with my reputation gets such an opportunity."

"I am glad you approve," said Coronel Cruz, smiling.

His shiny front gold tooth was as bright as his impeccable attire.

How could Rodrigo compare beside one such as he? Garbed in white, cotton shirt and pants and faded, straw sombrero, Rodrigo appeared to be the lowliest of beggars. His hard, bearded face was solemn. It masked the scars and the hatred of oppression looming over him and his people.

No.

He could never attain the style of elegance of Coronel Cruz. The soldier exuded a natural, charismatic attractiveness envied by other men. It was why the senoritas always were after him like honeybees!

"You know, Rodrigo," continued the coronel, "you have come a long way to get here. Who would guess? A *peon*! A mere *peon* would rise to become the most feared bandit in all of---"

"Not a bandit, Coronel," interrupted Rodrigo. "A *revolucionario*. A guardian angel for the oppressed and for the poor. A soldier of the people."

"Perhaps..., in your eyes,..." Coronel Cruz agreed, "...and... in the eyes of those whom you call your followers. However, there comes a time when even the greatest of heroes falls. The shadow of death looms over you, Rodrigo."

Rodrigo stood silent. He turned his head to look at the wall. It stood there like some silent giant waiting for the next barrage of bullets to strike it. He looked back at Coronel Cruz and said, "This wall is your solution, is it not?"

The coronel smiled but did not respond.

Anger rose within Rodrigo. "It always is with you military types! A simple bullet in the heart or head is not enough for you! No! You must make a spectacle of it! You must show everyone just how merciless and intolerant of rebellion your government is!

You must make an example to them!"

Coronel Cruz remained silent. He waited until Rodrigo calmed down. "It is the way things are," he said. "Higher authorities than I are in control. You know it to be true, Rodrigo. We live through dark times."

Rodrigo stared out at the emptiness of the street. Nothing moved except for a bit of dust rising with a slight breeze. He looked up and saw the eagle still hovering in peaceful silence, like an angel spreading its wings, and giving us hope. "I know," he said, teary-eyed, as he looked back at the military man. "I...I just do not see any other way we can---

"There is no other way!" bellowed the coronel. "You know that! For the love of God, this must take place! It is the only way this country can continue having a hope for the future! You cannot escape from this, Rodrigo. The firing squad awaits you."

He pointed to the group of armed men standing nearby.

Rodrigo moved away from the wall. He stepped away from its shade, into the heat of the morning. He stared at the mountains bordering the village in all directions. In the distance, a brief flash of light, almost shaped like a person, captured his attention. *Alucinaciones,* he thought. The morning heat and the tenseness of the situation were beginning to affect him.

He walked away a short distance and felt the eyes of Coronel Cruz burning into him. The military man now stood in front of the wall.

"Very well," Rodrigo said. "However, the pain awaiting me will be worse than the damage made by any bullet."

He stepped aside and stood away from the six men to whom he issued orders. Like himself, they looked like peons, all dressed in cotton white shirts and white pants. Unkempt and unshaven, however, they did look like bandits beneath their wide-brimmed, straw sombreros.

"Preparen!"

The sounds of rifles readied for firing tore into the stillness of the morning.

"Apunten!"

The sounds of those rifles aimed at their target added to the tension.

"Fuego!"

The sounds of those same rifles that fired at their target broke the silence.

A frightened bird flew away from a nearby tree. As the sound of its flapping wings receded, a grim silence filled the area.

Tears flowed down Rodrigo's face. He walked over to the bloody form that lay motionless by the huge wall. The smell of spent ammunition greeted him. Thin wisps of smoke danced over the blotches of red splattered over the impeccable uniform. The eyes stared at nothing while the gold tooth gleamed in the sunlight from a mouth frozen with a smile. Behind the prone figure, fresh blood and more bullet holes were now scattered upon the wall.

"A voice behind him broke the silence. "Why?"

It was his friend, Emilio Robles, one of the six members of the firing squad.

"Why do you weep, Compadre?" He placed a hand upon Rodrigo's shoulder. "He was an enemy of la revolucion, just like any other. You did your duty."

Rodrigo stood there, still staring at the dead man. "Yes. I did my duty. There is still hope for this country to obtain its freedom. However, the road to regain it just became a bit sadder. You see, Coronel Cruz was a soldier, one of the highest ranking, a valuable asset to his government. He was not just any ordinary soldier. His superiors were unaware he aided la revolucion.

"For a long time, our forces needed to strike a major blow at our oppressors. It was Enrique's idea we do this. With the demise of a high-ranking officer of the army, our cause would, for certain, move forward. He rode all night to arrive at this place and surrender himself."

Emilio looked from Rodrigo to the dead soldier.
"Once word of what took place here today reaches la capital," Rodrigo continued, "we will know if it was not a waste."

"*Perdoname, Rodrigo*," said Emilio, "but...you called him...Enrique? Did you know this man?"

Rodrigo hesitated and looked away, grief-stricken.

"His name was Enrique Angel Cruz," he said, "a *patriota* of this country. He joined the military at an early age. He was husband to Amalia Rosenda and father of Luisita and Jaime. All three were killed at the outbreak of *la revolucion* by troops of soldiers. They were the victims of a crossfire, or so it was reported. And...last of all...he was the brother...the brother of Rodrigo Reyes Cruz..."

Emilio's face filled with realization.

"...Rodrigo Reyes Cruz, who, as a poor peon, left home while still a boy to search for fortune across the world. The boy who became Rodrigo Reyes..., bandit..., and..., *revolucionario*."

He turned and walked away.

Emilio stood silent. A moment later, he ordered the rest of the men to remove the body of Coronel Cruz. The man would be given a decent burial as befitted a hero and soldier of *la revolucion.*

Once more, the huge wall stood silent. Its tall shadow spread across the ground like a grim specter of death.

Above, in the sky, the eagle hovered no more. Instead, it flew away, taking with it the majesty of its own peaceful freedom. Soon, it vanished in the distance as it glided toward the highest mountains.

THIRD TIMES A CHARM*
Ann Greenfield

"Found thee out even in the arms of thy paramour."

Sir Walter Scott, Ivanhoe

"One word frees us of all the weight and pain of life: that word is love."

Sophocles, Oedipus at Colonus

Greek tragic dramatist 496-406 BC

I don't know how long I sat in the restaurant, dejected, blinking back tears. The words hurt so much. I want a divorce. I don't love you anymore.

I wasn't prepared. Can anyone ever be prepared for this kind of news?

His words weren't said with malice or hatred, only a disconsolate resignation. An acceptance to the words as matter of fact, like he was telling me something he saw on the evening news, like an everyday occurrence. Not even a hint of sadness to his voice.

After he said those four hurtful words, all the tension drained from his face into mine. He looked years younger. I felt years older. His posture was now straight. Mine slumped. I felt like a failure. The worst part was that I felt unlovable. At my age there was slim chance of finding someone who would love an old woman like me, a slim chance of a third marriage.

Not that I would want one. Men are swine!

But I didn't want to be alone for the rest of my life, with no one to share the little things: a warm body next to me on a cold night, a person to laugh at my poorly delivered jokes, to make coffee in the morning or pat me on the arm just because, to kiss the back of my hand in the car to let me know he's thinking about me. I even wanted someone to be a guinea pig while I practiced cooking new gourmet recipes without gagging or to tell me white lies about my weight and assure me that I'm still sexy and desirable.

Apparently I'm not sexy or desirable or loveable. I'm unwanted.

"Ma'am, can I get you anything else." The waiter placed the check on the table.

Damn! That S.O.B. left me with the check. I paid the bill and quelled my anger and resentment. I had a style show fitting at one-thirty. I headed back to the shop and picked several outfits for my model to try on. I worked with her before and she was quiet and didn't talk much.

Thank goodness! I didn't feel like talking anyway.

My mind drifted while I worked. I thought we were okay after his affair. Every marriage has its ups and downs. Right? We worked hard on building up a new trust, especially after his paramour stalked me. This crazy woman called the shop twelve times a day to immediately hang up disrupting my sales clerks. She returned jewelry to the store. She came to my house during my daughter's graduation party.

In a final act of desperation, this mentally unstable woman called my house and whispered threatening things. My husband and I combined forces to take out a restraining order against her. I thought things were finally back to normal, that we had worked through this betrayal.

Apparently not.

I could get through this. Maybe. I did when my first husband filed for divorce after I stuck with him thought a stint at an alcohol treatment facility. I was strong then and I would be strong now, so I kept repeating in my head, “I can get through this.” I put up a good front. I dressed and went to work. I exercised. I ate nutritiously. Nothing in my routine changed.

But thoughts of abandonment and rejection crept in when I lay in bed at night, alone. Even with a glass of wine before bed, I didn’t sleep well. I woke several times. I stared at the ceiling in the dark watching the reflection from the light of the digital clock. Tears stained my pillow case. I had to work harder and harder to cover the dark circles under my dull and listless eyes. My skin was paler than usual and gray hair roots peeked through at the part. I’m sure no one noticed. I didn’t smile much, but I was polite. I hardly ever cried, anymore.

Once a week when my bookkeeper came to the store, she asked, “How are you feeling?”
And once a week I replied, “Fine! Thanks for asking.”

I didn’t elaborate on “fine.” Everyone is familiar with the acronym.

Freaked-Out Insecure Neurotic Emotional.

And I felt exactly that way, my emotions raw and on edge.

Still, I made it through the Winter Texan season of style shows, Easter, Mother’s Day, and the wedding season.

September, my slow time of the year and four months after the divorce was finalized, one of my friends, Julie, insisted I go with her to the beach. “You look awful. You need to get away and to quit feeling sorry for yourself. He was an unfaithful bastard and this weekend is about a new start.”

“Why are we going to the beach? I hate the beach. Sand. Skin cancer. Heat. Let’s go somewhere else besides Padre Island.” I proposed.

“No. I’m taking you away from here. Somewhere you wouldn’t choose for yourself. We’ll give ourselves facials. I’ll dye your hair. You look like an old woman and you're not. We’re going to relax, eat sea food, drink wine, watch sun sets and ogle young nearly naked men!” Julie flicked her eyebrows up and down. “Who knows? You may even get lucky. No strings attached.”

Julie was one of those happy, energetic, easy to be around; the glass is half full kind of people. She laughed and gave great hugs. Julie was not going to take no for an answer. Thankfully she didn’t, because after that weekend I slowly worked my way back to the living, granted it took a year.

Over the next year Julie insisted I socialize. Get back up on the horse so to speak. We went to the annual fund raising events of both the International Museum of Arts and Science, Collage, and Museum of South Texas History, Heritage Days. College had men dressed in Tuxedos. Very handsome, but no single men. Heritage Days had men in pressed jeans, boots, and western shirts. Not really my cup of tea. And again no single men. I informed Julie that single men didn’t go to these kinds of events. Their wives dragged them there to spend their money on auction items.

Each time Julie enticed me to go to some social event with, “Tom will be there.” Then she’d proceed to give me different tidbits about Tom. “He’s a widow and owns and farms citrus. You’ll like Tom. He’s got all his hair. He’s kind and funny. He’s tall with mahogany eyes.”

“Oh great! Mr. Personality.”

“Is that code for ugly? Does he have all his teeth?”

“Beggars can’t be choosy.” Julie grinned.

I rolled my eyes.

“No, really Tom’s got that clean country boy look. You know the ruggedly handsome cowboy type. You need someone completely different from the men you’ve married. Someone like Tom, for instance. Be brave. Take a risk. Stop by his orchard on the way back from Weslaco. Introduce yourself."

I blinked my eyes in disbelief. I couldn't respond to that. Cowboy. Country. Words that conjured up unfamiliar images. Unfamiliar lifestyles. My mind raced through scenarios of Tom. Tom and me. Me and Tom.

Humm. Could Julie be right? Do I need someone like Tom?

"Maybe I should invite both of you for dinner," said Julie, interrupting my day dreaming.

"No match making!" I said in a firm dignified voice. "I hate blind dates."

Julie just laughed at me. "Loosen up. You need to have more fun. Try someone new. Be a risk taker."

And so this went on for a year, Julie telling me how great Tom was and threatening to fix us up, and me refusing to play along giving every excuse. We attended art walks and she even dragged me to the symphony. I began to feel better, even hopeful. I went out on a few dates, but no one I wanted to kiss, much less share my bed with. The next time I was going to be picky. Gradually, I was making my way back to the living.

Driving back from a style show in Weslaco, Julie's words echoed in my head. "You'd like Tom. Stop by his orchard. He's perfect for you."

Could someone really be perfect for me? I'd given it several tries. My record was piss-ant poor. I wanted Julie to be right. I wanted her words to be true. My heart ached for someone new. I wasn't a risk taker. I played it safe, by the rules, all of my life. Look where it got me. Maybe I should take more risks. Be more spontaneous. Loosen up as Julie put it. I used to be fun. What had happened to that girl, I wondered.

Then a crazy thought hit me as I drove past orchard trees, Julie's words still embedded in my psyche. I'd show her. I could be spontaneous, risky. I pulled off the road and headed into the orchard. Grapefruit were delicious. No one would miss one or two. Would they?

That's when it happened. I wasn't expecting it. I didn't go looking. I was minding my own business, sort of. Love bonked me on the head and sliced its way into my heart. Love found me in the most unlikely place.

"Are you dead?"

Of course I wasn't dead. What a dumb thing to ask. Why would I be dead? I gradually opened my eyes to see a man with mahogany colored eyes and a huge grin on his face beside me. One arm bent over a knee, the other on the ground next to my body.

"Can you get up?" He patted my hand.

"I think so. Why am I down here?" I was flat on my back in the middle of an orchard surrounded by grapefruit.

"Well, you were stealing grapefruit. One fell off the limb and bonked you in the head and you went down like a sack of potatoes."

I slowly sat up and looked around. "I was stealing grapefruit?"

He nodded.

"Humm. That's not usually something I do." I frowned. "Do I look like a thief?"

He ran his eyes from my face to my shoes and back. "No. Not really. Most thieves wear more sensible shoes. Shoes they can run away in easier if they get caught." We both stared at my shoes. "I don't often see high heals, hose, and designer dresses out here in the orchard. Pert' near never!"

I struggled to get up. He grabbed my arm and jerked me to my feet. He picked leaves out of my red hair and dusted me off. Then he held me at arms length and ran his eyes down and up again, reappraising. The corners of his eyes crinkled.

“Okay, thanks I’m fine. A little embarrassed, but nothing is broken.”

He held out his hand. “Tom Daniels.”

My eyes widened with recognition. This was Julie’s friend.

“I’m Brenda Martin.” Apprehensively, I shook his hand. “Um, Thanks for helping me up.” I began walking toward the road and my car. Tom matched my pace.

“Mind if I ask? Why were you in so far? Most people take the grapefruit off the ground closest to the road.”

“None of the ones on the ground looked good.”

“Um-hm.”

“I just wanted to do something a little risky, something daring, but not hazardous or dangerous.”

“You didn’t choose very well did you?”

I spun to glare at him and crammed my hands on my hips, but my heel caught in some soft dirt and started sinking into the ground. My arms began to flap and my body weaved and bobbed and I fell on top of Tom.

His arms secured me tight against his body leaving no space between us and I could feel every contour of his hard, muscular body touching mine. He chuckled. I squirmed my arms against his chest and up on my elbows. I lifted my eyes past his neck, then his chin and stopped at his mouth. I stared at his mouth. His lips were full and smooth. I wondered what it would be like to kiss those lips. Tom slid his hand up my back to the base of my neck. My breath caught.

"Are you married? You're not wearing a ring."

I stared down at his mahogany-colored eyes. Tom had seen me for only a few minutes and already he noticed my clothing, shoes, hands, and had given me a compliment. I wouldn't have used cute exactly, but still, it was a compliment. He recognized designer clothing, which was more than most men. He'd patted me and showed concern, and he hadn't condemned me for trying to steal a grapefruit.

Tom was good looking. He had an olive complexion and a great body. He smelled of grapefruit. He smelled delicious. Possibilities danced in my head. Was this really Julie's Tom? Tom the cowboy?

"No. You?" Again, I stared at his luscious lips.

Tom parted his lips into a wide grin showing white straight teeth. He rolled me onto my back and cradled my head in the crook of his arm. Then he pressed his knee between my legs. My dress inched up towards my waist. His warm thigh rubbed the inside of mine and I could feel his desire. Fire ignited somewhere south of my hips and I started to have hot flashes. I swallowed and gasped for air. He ran his thumb across my lips and whispered, "You're pretty damn cute." And then, he kissed me. With tongue and more passion than any of my previous husbands ever had. My head began to spin and I arched up to him. My hands tangled in his thick dark hair.

I couldn't help myself. I kissed him back.

THROUGH THE GLASSES*
Bidgie Weber

What? My precious baby must wear glasses?
Won't they hide his lovely long lashes?
Oh, dear, oh dear, he is only three!
Oh my, oh my, what will people think of me?
I must have done something to affect his sight.
I sang to him…I read to him…I told him stories every night!
I tried, oh how I tried, to do things just right.
Nothing I could say, nothing I could do would change what was.
It just was! Nothing more, nothing less, it was! It was…just because!
I cried. I begged. I even argued with God.
He does big things, small things…all things with just a nod.

How do you tell a boy of three
That these funny looking things will help him see?
Oh woe! Oh woe! All I could do is feel sorry for me.
I never once thought how unclear and fuzzy, things seemed to be
For my little boy of three.
The wire frames fit snug behind his tiny ears…
I tried hard to be brave and smile through my tears.
But my baby didn't seem to mind.
And I thanked God…
He was not blind.

Many years have come to pass
Since the "year of the glass."

Hundreds of frames have perched on his nose,
But his most favorite from all of those
Is the very first pair we got when he was three.
For the very first time he was able to see
A doodlebug digging a hole for her young…
To see how a spider web was hung.
He saw for the very first time
The dew on a rose petal sparkle and shine;
He saw rainbows and the colors that abound;
He saw a whole new world all around.

I saw a mother so vain…how absurd!
My child's vision wasn't blurred.
All through his life my son showed me things I would have missed…
The goodness in people, the kindness all around…too many things for me to list.
I realize now, when my son was three…
He needed glasses so I could see.

THIS OLD HOUSE
Nellie Venselaar

Driving through the country side
There is this old ruin of a house
Without windows, drooping sideways.

Windowless walls are like sightless humans,
Casements are in a blind, unseeing framework,
Looking so forlorn and lonely.

What could this old house tell us?
What does it see through windowless openings?

Who broke the glass? Why?
Maybe vagrants or hoboes lived here?

Maybe young boys played target shooting,
Or used it as a clubhouse as boys like to do.

What have these blind staring windows seen?
Maybe an artist painting this old house?

Who lived there?
Where did they go?

What did they see?
A love scene or a crime?

A group of shiny horses standing in the shade,
Partly surrounded by gorgeous trees
And flowering bushes in the last light of the setting sun

Giving a rosy shine to the lifeless, sightless house.

THE VALLEY OF THE SHADOW OF DEATH*

Milo Kearney

Who ever knows what is truly going on in the world around us?

The Rio Grande Valley, in the 1970s and 1980s, held out a promise of a simple life, far away from the hectic race for materialist success of mainstream American life. Here a semi-tropical Candide could tend his cenizo-and-arbor-vitae garden and escape the Great American Dream-Lie of Forrest Gump. And yet, who knew what dark gar-shaped shadow moved under the resaca-like calm of Valley society?

It was like a scene out of a Garrison Keeler "Guy Noir, Private Eye" radio skit. I was working at my desk in the Tandy Building, on the campus shared by Texas Southmost College and Pan American University at Brownsville, when "Annette" (as I will call her) came to my office door. In her early thirties, she was a long-haired svelte beauty in high heels and an incongruously dirty white trench coat. I invited her to take a seat, expecting to give the usual counseling about university course planning. Instead, Annette poured out a story of murder and woe.

She told me how she had made her way, perilously (she claimed), from Central America back to her native United States. Central America, at the start of the 1980s, was shaken by social conflict. Archbishop Oscar Romero of San Salvador had been punished for his criticism of the government's human rights abuses by being assassinated, in 1980, while he prayed at a hospital chapel altar. In Nicaragua, after 1981, the Contras had led a revolt against the Marxist Sandinista government. In 1982, over 45,000 Indians and *paisanos* had fled for their lives from rightist death squads in Guatemala to refugee camps in Mexico.

Annette asked if I realized that Oscar Romero's assassination had been ordered by a graduate of the CIA-sponsored School of the Americas. She denounced American support for right-wing movements, and decried the horrors being inflicted on the poor. I was acquainted with the plight of the Central American region. My family and I were involved, through our church, Portway Baptist, with helping the homeless, and had taken street people, from time to time, to shelters, including the Catholic Church's Casa Romero, named for the assassinated Salvadoran Archbishop. When a tsunami of Guatamaltecan refugees poured across the Mexican-U.S. border, our church coordinated with St. Mary's Catholic Church to give them a place to sleep and to provide meals, while helping them to head on to relatives or prospective jobs in the interior of the United States.

Annette then told me her personal story – how she and her husband had been involved in helping the Central American poor, in tandem with liberation theology priests. Their efforts had brought them to the attention of rightist groups, and Annette's husband had been kidnapped and murdered. She had fled for her life, but was afraid that she was still in the cross-hairs of "nefarious" forces, in which she principally counted the CIA.

I never understood how Annette thought I could be of use to her, but, for the next few weeks, she would drop by my office, from time to time, to speak of her misfortunes and fears. One of her worries was that she was being followed by a certain individual of the Brownsville scene. Let's call him Hubert. Hubert was a mysterious fellow. With no visible means of sustenance, he nonetheless managed a life, renting a room in a boarding house and wandering around the town and the university scene.

Somewhat seedy, like the down-and-out-yet-glamorous Annette, Hubert nonetheless managed to pop up at virtually all of the town's social functions. He was always sharing the most surprising insights into the lives of the local social and political lions, and he amazed us all with his detailed knowledge. Indeed, some of us had engaged in idle speculation that Hubert was being paid to be a government informer. So my ears pricked up when Annette surmised that Hubert was a CIA agent.

She not only insisted that Hubert had been following her at a distance, but declared that she felt sure that he wanted to murder her, just as her husband had been murdered. I couldn't buy it. Her claims had just gotten to be too wild. After all, this was the Valley, our wonderful sleepy little community, by-passed by the outside world. "Hubert is known for walking around town a lot," I explained, "He must be just going the same way, or maybe he likes you. He is a strange fellow."

"What corner?" I asked, confused.

"Go around the corner of the hall outside your office," she said. "He's been following me all morning, and he followed me here. I'll bet he's still here." I hesitated at such a bizarre suggestion. "Go ahead," she insisted.

So I got up and walked outside the office. I turned left, and followed the hall as it turned right, and then, at the first intersection, I turned right again. And there was Hubert. He was not just there, but he was standing plastered stiff, right up against the wall, next to where it ended at the intersection. Embarrassed, I said, "Hello," and returned to my office. I could not understand why anyone would stand in such a self-incriminating position.

"See what I told you?" Annette charged. After she left, I sat for a little, and then went back out into the hall. Hubert and she were both gone. Whether he had followed her or not, I had no idea. Yet the whole episode seemed so strange, I had to ask myself whether both of them were in cahoots to make me fall for such a ridiculous whopper of a tale. But to what end?

I would probably still come to the same conclusion today, if it had not been for Jack. Or so I will call him. Jack was another American who, in this period, fled up to Brownsville from Central America. Annette had introduced him to me. Like Annette, he looked shabby, but he also exuded a mood of wholesomeness. He was in his early twenties.

Jack told me that he had been doing mission work in Central America, when his mission center had likewise come under attack from rightist forces. I listened sympathetically to Jack's equally harrowing story of oppression and assassinations. I took him along with our family to services and activities at our Portway Baptist Church, and he started to show up there on his own, as well. The way to the church was far out along International Boulevard, but (like Hubert) he had a taste, when not riding with us, for walking long distances.

Jack seemed to be a wonderful addition to our church group and to its eleemosynary programs. It was a pleasure working together with him, and I began to forget Annette's fears that dark forces in Brownsville were out to assassinate those who had won a reputation for radical liberalism in Central America.

Then it happened. The Brownsville Herald broke the news that Jack, while walking at the side of International Boulevard (not far from Portway Church) had been hit and killed by a car. The vehicle had totally left the street to run him down, and then had immediately swerved back onto the highway and sped away. Spectators had seen what had happened, but nobody had caught the license plate number. Case closed.

Was it a coincidence? Several years later, I was speaking with a retiree from the CIA. He had not heard about Jack, but he immediately knew Annette from her name. He told me that she was a well-known political agitator, and that she had moved on from Brownsville to the North-east.

Perhaps things were not as innocent in the Valley as I had assumed. But the dark shadow submerged, the ripples dissipated in the water, and my family and I returned to our resaca-calm existence of those halcyon days.

VAMPIRES SUCK
Hugh Barlow

The little clapboard church sits stiffly in the sun. It's steeple marks time with it's shadow on the sidewalk. It is the last place most people would think to look for a vampire, but I am sure that one is in there. Contrary to popular opinion, there is no such thing as a noble savage. There is also no such thing as a noble vampire. I get angry when I see all the vampire based novels in the science fiction section of my favorite bookstore. Twilight has it all wrong. Dealing with vampires is more like the movie *The Lost Boys* than the TV show *Forever Knight*. I ain't no scientist, and I don't have a degree in biology, but I do have some practical experience in dealing with these suckers (pun intended). I discovered my first vampire quite by accident. Actually, it wasn't a human vampire, but was one of the animal variants most people don't realize are related. I have come to find out that the old stories of werewolves and were-cats are actually based on facts. Oh, the stories are twisted and exaggerated all out of proportion, but they are based on fact none the less.

I had the misfortune to run across one of these critters when I was out deer hunting back home, and the damned thing nearly got me. It seems that it and I were tracking the same prey, and when I shot the deer, the werewolf decided to go for me. After I shot the werewolf, I took it to a vet because it certainly looked odd. I thought I had killed a *chupacabra*, but instead I found that I had shot a wolf that had been genetically modified by a virus. You see, the vet was a friend of mine, and HE was trained in molecular biology. He got quite excited when he discovered the mutation, and he charged me with the task of going out and looking for more of these modified wolves. Once I knew to look for them, they were not hard to find. I just wish my buddy had simply left the task to ME. Instead, he tried to create some himself, and it cost him his life.

What I learned from him before his death was that the virus seems to thrive in animals that hunt for food. Carnivores are it's primary target. It doesn't seem to work in herbivores. At least I have never seen a were-cow or were-rabbit. The virus does cross species lines, and a human can become infected by a werewolf or other were-animal. My buddy suggested that it was some kind of space virus, and that it was acting like something from the movie *Invasion of the Body Snatchers* in that it was designed to take over the host body and completely re-program it to create more of itself. At least this is what I was able to understand from what he said. He used a bunch of science lingo that I did not understand, but he simplified it for me. I have discovered that it not only re-programs the body, but it seems to re-program the mind as well.

If what all you know about vampires and werewolves comes from books and movies, then you have been fed a boatload of misinformation. While vampires don't LIKE garlic, it will not kill them. It seems that the virus makes them slightly allergic to it. Vampires also have a sensitivity to onions, shallots, leeks, and chives. I don't know what's in these plants, but when exposed to them, vampires and the like get a severe rash. Holy water has NO effect unless you mix it with garlic. Wooden stakes are effective only because anything will die if you put a stake in it's heart. A cross? Oh, SOME vampires might shy away from one but only for comic effect. I find a cross most effective if you sharpen one end and use it as a stake. Daylight? Oh, yeah. THERE is a bit of exaggeration for you! While vampires are sensitive to sunlight, they can certainly go out during the day. They use plenty of sun screen, cover up, and use really dark glasses. The sunlight does hurt their eyes. Bright light from any source can make them skittish. I always carry a bright LED spotlight with me when I go hunting now. It has saved me on more than one occasion. Silver bullets? Use lead... it is cheaper and just as effective. Which is to say, not much effective unless you use a LARGE caliber gun.

Something about the virus makes the circulatory system much more effective in the affected creature, animal or human. The virus also makes them much more aggressive and intelligent. One of the key indicators that someone has been affected by the virus is a marked increase in intelligence. If Uncle Bubba all of a sudden gets smart, stay away! If you notice that he takes off coon hunting more often and doesn't use the dogs, there is another sign. Bubba suddenly buying stock in Cover Girl and getting flesh tone base when he ain't even got a girlfriend? That greyish pallor that he has started using makeup to cover up? Sign number three. Drinking Bloody Marys instead of beer, and there ain't a can of tomato juice in the house trailer? Sign number 4. All the dogs under the porch getting lean and mean? Well, that may be a sign or not. Maybe Uncle Bubba liked mean dogs to begin with. Maybe he infected them, or they infected him. Hard to tell.

Something about the virus causes the victim to crave fresh blood. The modern vampire can beat this by using refrigerated blood--my buddy did--but they often use that as a last resort. There is something about the fresh kill that makes the blood more satisfying. They need the thrill of the hunt. Sucking blood from a cow just doesn't quite satisfy. Oh, you know those animal mutilations that always seem to get blamed on aliens? Usually, that's Bubba and his dogs gone wild on a tear. That's why he doesn't take the dogs coon hunting any more. He doesn't want the competition. You get a pack of coon hounds turned werewolf out on a tear, and people are going to notice. Usually Bubba just kills the dogs after he gets infected. He knows that he cannot afford the competition or the accidental chance of exposure. Infected animals will not attack each other for blood... there is something about the infected blood that makes it unpalatable, but they will kill each other to survive. That is the name of the game for vampires... survival.

The autopsy that my buddy did on the infected wolf showed that the heart and brain were completely remade. So was the intestinal tract, the musculature, and the entire cardiovascular system. The lungs were also redesigned. That was why he was so excited about the discovery. He wanted to see if he could use the virus to do some gene engineering. He figured that with a bit of splicing, he could remove the aggressive tendencies and the need for fresh blood, and help people who had genetic pre-dispositions to illnesses of all sorts. Unfortunately, it was his experimentation with animals in his care that did him in. He was not as careful as he should have been and he was infected himself.

Attacks from a vampire rarely lead to a successful conversion from human (or were-beast) to vampire (or were-animal). The reason for this is that the attacker usually does not leave a living creature behind after the attack. In order to have a successful conversion, there needs to be enough blood left in the body for the victim to survive the attack. This rarely happens. Unfortunately for my buddy, it wasn't a case of him getting his blood sucked out. An errant needle is what did him in, or maybe he stuck himself on purpose, I don't know. Even when the victim does survive the initial attack, the virus doesn't always run true. It often mutates into something else. AIDS? My buddy suggested that AIDS may have been a mutation of the vampire virus. I will probably never know, though, since I have dedicated my life to wiping this scourge from the planet. I started with my uncle, Bubba, but I just took out my buddy. His is the body in the church. In a little while, the preacher will come and tell about what a great man he was, and how it is a shame that he was cut down in the prime of his life. Everyone will be weeping for their loss except me. I know his secret. I saved him.

VOODO TAGS*
Judy Stevens

Young man, of course I'll explain. You see, it all started with a washcloth…

Wait—there's a tag on your uniform—let me tuck it back in. There. Now, don't we all feel better?

Where was I? Oh yes. Well you see, no matter how I folded it—the washcloth, I mean— that white tag—you know the one along its seam? It seemed a coincidence that it always faced me—you know the tags they put on everything today? It faced me, all exposed, ruining the effect—do you realize how such a thing simply ruins the looks of one's guest bathroom? I'm sure you do.

Oh. Yes officer. Of course: I'll get to the point.

As I was saying, I began noticing other tags and labels, facing me. <u>Exposed</u>. Why, I could see them on my couch pillows from across the room. And my closet—don't get me started! It was all so—untidy.

I tried to ignore them, I really did. At first I simply refolded or turned them over and went about my day. But the tags were always there, facing me. It was unnerving It was like I'd been cursed.
I removed them. I even cut off the ones that said, "Do not remove under penalty."

But I could still see that little white remnant sewn into the seam—always facing me.

So I unlaced every thread so that no remnant of their whiteness showed. It took hours—but I did it. I broke the curse.

Then, just the other day I noticed the frayed edges where I'd carefully removed all traces of the tags—were facing me. They were always facing me.

I knew then that I had to destroy them.

Oh, hello, Doctor; nice to meet you. Have you met this fine young man? You're taking me where? Oh, that's so sweet of you. You know, I can't use my house just now. I had to burn it to get rid of…

Wait, you have a tag showing. Here, let me....

WILEY COYOTE
LeRoy Overstreet

Wiley's story began some weeks before April 29, 1999 and ended for Wiley about 10:00 o'clock the night before. I had been seeing its tracks on Green Island for several weeks and called David Trevino, who was the U.S.D.A. nuisance animal control trapper for Cameron County at that time. I told David that there would be an unusually high tide in Laguna Madre on April 28, 1999, and that we would be able to go around Green Island by boat without any trouble, so we decided to try our luck.

We found Wiley working the shoreline on the back side of Green Island so I ran the boat as close as I felt was prudent and stopped the boat with the bow against the shore. As soon as the boat stopped, Wiley started trying to slip away from us. David squeezed off a shot, but missed. Wiley picked up his pace a little bit. It was running from left to right on an angle away from us. David shot again and missed again. His third shot missed also, and by that time, Wiley was running flat out. David's fourth shot drilled old Wiley dead center! It was truly a remarkable shot.

I stepped it off the next morning and found that it was 180 yards from where our boat was stopped to the dead coyote.

The three shots that missed cause me considerable discomfort every time I think about them. Because the manufacturer of these high-powered bullets warns that they can skip across the water for six miles or more and change direction every time they hit the water.

The next morning when I made my rounds I noticed that old Wiley was a female and was very fat and her belly was very full. I thought she might be full of pups and my curiosity prompted me to open that big belly to see what was in there. And that is when I went back to the boat and got my camera. When I emptied out the stomach of that critter, I found 27 little baby wading birds in there!

27! And that was just what it had eaten in one day! They appeared to be mostly reddish and snowy egrets.

Now, an ancestor of Wiley is on Green Island. It is Wiley also. I first noticed its tracks on January 8, 2009, more than 18 months ago! Jody Palacios and David Trevino, The U.S.D.A. trappers, have tried every trick they know to try to catch it. All to no avail. If a coyote was killed with 27 little undigested birds in its stomach, how many would you guess it would eat in two seven-month nesting seasons?

There is one sure way to catch old Wiley, and that is with an air boat. Boats run by coyotes all the time. They don't pay any attention to a boat unless it stops. With an air boat you can run right up to a coyote, blind it with a handheld flood light and shoot it with a shotgun from 20 feet or less with no. 4 buck shot. Jimmy Paz, The U.S.D.A. trappers and I have proved this method many times. It always works. The shotgun has a range of about 100 yards and we don't have to worry about the bullet from the high-powered rifle skipping six miles across the water and endangering the life of some fisherman on the Lower Laguna Madre. I can't imagine anything any more devastating than to learn that one of the bullets intended for a coyote had hit someone.

If we had an air boat, we could have eliminated this coyote many months ago. If I had the money I would buy one myself. It wouldn't have to be a new one. A good used one would work just fine. We need one with 300 horsepower or more, with a wide blade propeller, capable of stopping and starting on dry land and the bottom of the hull covered with polymer. Such a boat could be bought for $10,000 to $15,000. Or, better yet, the TPWD and other public funded entities give away their used ones every year when they replace them, but I can't get anyone from Audubon to even apply for one of them.

Old Wiley spends most of its time in the wooded part of Green Island but about every week or ten days or so it comes out to work the shoreline. I think it probably feels like, after a steady diet of poultry, a seafood platter goes good from time to time.

If we had an air boat, we would make a run around Green Island every night until we could find Old Wiley working the shoreline and shoot it with our shotguns. I feel confident that we could end its existence in less than a month's time.

WHO IS THIS OLD LADY?
Bidgie Weber

Who is this old lady who gets up each morning with me? She sleeps late then drags herself out of bed accompanied down the hall by a symphony of melodious sounds. The woodwinds make themselves heard with a crescendo of cannons that introduce moans, groans and grunts resonating from within, followed by creaks, cracks pops, aping Chinese firecrackers, each punctuating every step of the morning's journey.

This old lady is not completely unwelcome but I would like to establish protocol. Waking each morning half dressed is such a surprise. She must get hot during the night and remove a portion of our sleepwear. The girl who used to occupy this space never experienced "night flashes." There was no disrobing during our sleep!

These mornings there is no hitting the floor barefooted and ready to run. Feet must be careful now. Feet are stiff, swollen, and seem to need a ten minute warm-up period before attempting to take a step.

The young girl and I shared exciting dreams. We would ride horses, race cars, dance 'till dawn, and meet gorgeous young men who flirted shamelessly with us. Lively children would play hide and seek with us. We raced on legs that flew. That young girl would jump out of bed each morning to see what new adventures awaited. We had so much fun and energy - nothing ever slowed us down. We were *simpatico.*

The old lady and I now dream of butterflies in the garden. We visit with old friends who have long ago moved on to another life in a world beyond. Dreams of dancing the night away have been modified. Now we observe others dance to the tempo while we sit and softly hum with the melody. Children are no longer rowdy and wild; they gently comb thru our hair and bring us iced tea while we rock.

Now, this old lady gets up each morning with me and stays. These new days come to us with magical gifts. Surely, it was not always like this. Orange blossoms smelling so sweet we can taste the fruit. Sunrises and sunsets unequaled in nature. Has it always been this way?

Now we start each day with quiet appreciation and gentle acceptance for whatever a new day might bring.

Who is this old lady who has become a part of me? We just might learn to accept, welcome and love each other.

YOUR LOVE*
Rudy H. Garcia

I do not love you as others love theirs
I love you always and genuinely true
And though some may say, my way of loving
Is considered old and perhaps even out of date
I say to them… listen carefully, and in earnest.

The wind I say, is older still
Much, much, older still… and yet…
It still persists, it still continues blowing true!

I do not love you as others say they love
I love you around the clock and even in my dreams
And though the fad of passing time, is to disguise
one`s lust as love, I say to them… be silent and
reflective for a moment,
Tonight the stars shall sing with light!

Then wait for morrow till dawn renewed
And soon thereafter the ancient sun shall reappear
To warm the heart and spirit too
To radiate Gods` love for you

I do not love you as others think they love
I love you with my all breath and my cosmic
universal mind
And too with every tiny grain of clay that molded
me!
And though some may say that I a silly dreamer be
I say to them… for that, be certain, yes, rest
assured…
And with a flawless guarantee!
That just as sure as the river flows, cutting into the
living earth

Your love carves deep in me.

Waaaat
Judy Stevens

Dottie said this book'd raise the hair on my neck. Said not to read it alone at night. Thinks I'm a silly old scaredy cat. Well, pish-posh to her.

Favorite chair: check. Coffee mug on table: check. Lights out; reading light on: check.

Oh, almost forgot—doors locked: check.

Nice, quiet house. Just the way I like it. Neighbor's kids all tucked down for the night. No noise from them —'till dawn. Got the world to myself.

Gosh-dang, but this book's creepy. Two murders before the fifth page. But good. Dottie's right: it's a rip-roarer. I need a sip of coffee.

"Waaaat..."

Yipe! I liked to jump a foot! What in Tarnation is that? I wiped the spilled coffee and set the mug down with shakey hands. Then I laughed nervously at my silliness. Sounded just like the ghost of Scrooge, it did. Imagination'll kill, if you let it. I went back to my murders.

"Waaaat..."

This time I didn't jump: I froze. Clear as a bell, it was. Came from the far end of the hall. Memory kicked in: I'd forgotten to close the bathroom window. Yipe.

I was alone at night with a maniac in my one and only bathroom that I'd cleaned the living daylights out of just this morning. My gun was in the bedroom and my telephone was in the kitchen. I hefted Dottie's book. She wouldn't mind if I got a little blood on it, I'm sure. It'll enhance the reading.

I stood slowly so my joints wouldn't tell the world where I was and tip-toed to the front hall. I glanced at the front door and made up my mind not to race out. Probably another maniac on the porch. Instead, I scooted across the hall to the kitchen and grabbed my trusty three-pound flashlight. It would kill a mule. Big Beam, I call it. I flipped it on and trained all its wattage down the hall.

Big Beam says nobody there, scaredy-pants.

"Waaaat..."

I grabbed the biggest knife I had, trained Big Beam on the noise and snuck down the hall. The sound came from my spare bedroom, where the grandkids would sleep when they came to visit. I slithered up to the door and paused.

"Waaaat..."

I did what all the good guys do in those detective thrillers, only I didn't break my own door down—that'd be stupid itself. Still, I felt like a fool, standing there knife all ready and Big Beam showing what all the fuss was about.

The kids had left a toy on the dresser by the window. Beside it a little fan moved slowly right-left-right. Caught in its guard was the string from the toy. Bemused, I watched as every so often the toy let out a *"Waaaat..."*

Grinning from ear to ear, I unloosened the string, turned off the fan and the lights and closed the door.

I returned to my roost beside my still-warm coffee mug, thinking this book won't be half as hair raising as what I just lived through.

Twelve pages and one more murder into it I heard—

"...Wuuuu..."

THE GREAT SEQUOYAH MYSTERY

The Cover-up Stretched From The Cumberland Mountains to The Rio Grande Delta

Don Clifford

In late 1842, a small group of self appointed emissaries set out from Cherokee Indian country and headed south for the river called by Spaniards and Mexicans the Rio Bravo Del Norte. Ostensibly, they sought a legendary lost band of Cherokees who emigrated to Northern Mexico during the mid-1700's in order to preserve their tribal ways from the adverse cultural influences of the white man.

According to the prevailing literature, the leader of the group was an elderly man named Sequoyah. He is celebrated as an illiterate who invented the Cherokee alphabet -- a 92 symbol syllabary that depicts the sounds of the language in readable form. Supposedly, the adaptation of the alphabet was so simple that any Cherokee who studied it became literate in the language within a very short time.

For many days they traveled an old Indian trail from Fort Gibson, Arkansas, to San Antonio and onward through the Wild Horse Desert. Enroute, the old man became sick, complaining of strange chest pains that radiated throughout his body. After a prolonged rest, the old man's health improved enough to continue the journey

In early 1843, the group arrived at the Rio Bravo (Rio Grande), crossed over near Mier, [1] worked their way down river and visited kinsmen at several rancherias on both sides of the river including El Zacatal, Carrizales, El Capote, La Paloma and Los Indios. [2]

The rigors of travel proved too much for the old man. In August 1843, he died in a Mexican village named San Fernando. Thus it was that an unlettered man, who devoted his life for the betterment of his people, died during one last act of service while seeking to reunite his lost tribesmen.

Or so we are led to believe.

Actually, also according to the prevailing literature, Sequoyah died on three different occasions. First, Traveler Bird, a direct descendant, claims that Texas soldiers killed his ancestor Sequoyah/George Guess in June 1839 during a skirmish on the Brazos River. Grant Foreman, a respected chronicler of Cherokee folkway, and James Mooney, a noted anthropologist for the Bureau of American Ethnology, quoted from the Cherokee Advocate newspaper an elaborate description of the journey and the 1843 death in San Fernando. Traveler Bird claims further that another man who assumed the role of Sequoyah -- George Guest -- died of a bullet wound in 1844.(3) Third was Thomas Maw whose portrait is said to be that of Sequoyah. His demise is unclear.(4)

So who was this elderly traveler to the Lower Rio Grande? And why was the Cherokee Advocate account so painstakingly detailed? More importantly, if this was a cover up to a conspiracy, what was involved and who stood to gain from it? The answers are not readily apparent but a time line of events helps to reveal some of the mystery.

During the mid-1750's, ancient secret written symbols were placed in use against the Anglo invasion of black robe missionaries who preached peace and brotherhood in one breath but who endorsed war and slavery in the next. The symbols were kept secret only from the whites and misbegotten mixed bloods. In 1766, Sogwili, meaning "horse" in Cherokee, was born into the Anisahoni Clan and raised as a warrior-scribe of the Seven Clan Scribe Society. He learned and became adept in several versions of writing systems. (6) Also, he warred against the whites.

When a young man of twenty, Sogwili captured and scalped a

white man named George Guess in retaliation for the murders of his father, mother, and sister. Since the doomed man had no further need for the name, Sogwili took it in order to deal with the whites.

In 1794, the Cherokee Nation fell but Sogwili/ George Guess refused to make peace and resisted U.S. government efforts to "civilize" himself and his people. In 1797, he led a group of Cherokee dissidents beyond the Red River into an area ruled by Spain. Within two years they were well established on the Brazos River.

During several years of relative peace and comfort Sogwili communicated with his clansmen in the Cumberlands via the secret syllabary. In 1806 he returned to the Cumberland Cherokee to tell them of lands to the West and of his peaceful settlement on the Brazos. 812 more emigrants followed his lead to the West.

In the summer of 1816, tribal police captured Sogwili/George Guess during one of his return visits to the southeast. In October, a general council of mixed blood Cherokee judges, tribal police and warrior chiefs -- the New Order of the Nation -- tried him for witchcraft and denounced his syllabary as a work of the devil. He was charged, also, with encouraging emigration beyond the limits of the United States to Spanish Texas. The council branded him and his wife on the forehead and back. They chopped off the fingers of both his hands between the first and second knuckles. Just before his brother Whitepath rescued the tormented couple, Sogwili's ears were "cropped" -- the mark of a traitor to the Cherokee Nation.

Up until the year 1821, the syllabary had been concealed from the American public. However, word of an unusual writing system leaked out through missionary reports of a communication breakthrough for teaching the Gospel. This created a dilemma for the Cherokee Progressives under Principal Chief John Ross. Worried that the American public would someday find out about Sequoyah's torture and mutilation, the missionaries' revelation forced them to grudgingly acknowledge the existence of a well defined writing system. But because the whites considered anything of Indian origin as repugnant and savage, it was, therefore, necessary for Cherokee conspirators to establish a "civilized" credibility.

The fake name of "Sequoyah" was created and became a symbol of intellectual achievement -- fake because the word "sequoyah" has no meaning in the Cherokee language. It is derived from the Anglo inability to pronounce "Sogwiligigageihiyi", which was bastardized to "Soquee" or "Skeequoyah", meaning the Devil's Gang Place, a reference to the headquarters of the Scribe Society. "Civilized" because such intellectual achievement was simply "not possible" for a non-white.

The Progressives could not hide the fact that Sequoyah/George Guess developed the syllabary for use among the Cherokee, but they could the disfigurement of a traitor by creating a front man to be Sequoyah. Thus came into being Sequoyah/George Gist, allegedly a half-breed(7) whose father, Nathaniel Gist, fought in the Revolutionary War against England. The sound alike name was enough to divert from Sequoyah/George Guess and at the same time provide the needed infusion of white blood.

Meanwhile, within the Cherokee Nation, Sequoyah's name became a resistance symbol for Cherokees opposed to the Progressive New Order of mixed blood Cherokee leaders and "traitors" friendly toward Anglo-Christian civilization. The Progressives considered nonconforming Cherokees as savages and stumbling blocks to assimilation into the United States.

Out West in 1822, Sequoyah/George Guess and other relocated Cherokees visited the Province of Texas Governor Trespalacios in San Antonio and, along with Baron de Bastrop, signed articles of agreement for a land grant. Before the agreement was ratified, Emperor of Mexico Augustin Iturbide was overthrown in 1823, and the grant became moot. By this time, Sequoyah refused to travel to Mexico City with the others because the Spanish agreement simply imposed new laws on the Cherokee. According to Guess, the Spaniard was just another white man.

Back East, the conspiracy gained momentum. In 1824, the Cherokee General Council voted to award a medal to

Sequoyah/George Gist in recognition for the great gift of literacy. Four years later, Thomas Maw sat for a painting that was passed off as a likeness of Sequoyah/George Guess.

By 1825, the flood of white American settlers into Texas brought new troubles to the Western Cherokees and other tribes. It was the same land-grabbing pattern that forced the removal of the Cherokee from the East. Seeking peace and noninterference, Sequoyah/George Guess and several families moved 200 miles further west and settled on lands that bordered the Comanche in what is now San Saba County, Texas.

In 1829, a Cherokee circuit rider preaching the white man's proposal kidnapped Sequoyah's daughter, Gedi, who with her mother, Eli, were visiting with clan relatives in the Cumberlands. Eli attempted to negotiate Gedi's release, but Eli herself was captured and hung with the traitor's brand for all to see. George Guess, several hundred miles away, was unable to set up a rescue because the turmoil of the Mexican revolt against Spain had begun.

In June 1831, Sequoyah/George Gist and sons arrived at a Cherokee settlement on the Colorado looking for scribe Sequoyah/George Guess. Gist was the emissary of the Chief of the Western Settlement who wanted Guess to teach his people to read and write the native syllabary. George Gist became an adept pupil. This suggests that Guess tacitly accepted Gist as a Sequoyah alter ego.

By now, the Cherokee Progressives considered Sequoyah/George Guess an embarrassment and ordered his assassination. Gist warned Guess in time and the assassins themselves were ambushed. Apparently, George Guess had "converted" George Gist to his way of thinking. Only then did Gist show the medal he had received from the General Council seven years earlier.

For the next few years the Cherokee People became embroiled in a series of catastrophic events. First, in 1835, came the forced removal to the Oklahoma Territory resulting in the infamous Trail of Tears. A year later, Texas revolted against Mexico, and the resident Cherokee were pressured into the Mexican Army. In 1838, Texas President Mirabeau Lamas enacted his Indian removal/extermination policy.

Apparently, Sequoyah/George Guess was not caught up in some of these events, because in February 1839, he left the San Saba area to rescue a Cherokee emigrant group stranded on the west bank of the Mississippi River. The group included his daughter, Gedi, whom he hadn't seen for eleven years. A company of Texas volunteers must have just missed him when on February 15, they attacked a Comanche camp near the mouth of the San Saba River.

But, alas, events did catch up to Sequoyah/George Guess. On June 9, almost home while leading his daughter's emigrant party, he was killed in a skirmish with Texas soldiers on the Brazos. By July, the Texan war against the Cherokee was in full scale. A young John Salmon "R.I.P." Ford (future mayor of Brownsville, Texas) tasted his first action against the Shawnee, some of whom were allies to the Cherokee.

Meanwhile in Oklahoma, disputes between the Old Settlers and the New Progressives bordered on civil war. History records that Sequoyah (in all likelihood George Gist) greatly influenced the negotiations. The result was a document that declared the two factions as "one body politic, under the style and title of 'The Cherokee Nation'." On July 12, 1839, Sequoyah signed the document as President of the Western Cherokees. Two years later, for reasons unknown, Sequoyah/George Gist was run out of the Cherokee Nation. The following passage suggests another phase in the cover up:

"Sequoyah...had become seized with a desire (italics mine) *to make linguistic investigations among the remote tribes, probably with a view of devising a universal Indian alphabet.*" His mind dwelt also on the old tradition of a lost band of Cherokee living somewhere toward the western mountains. In 1841 and 1842, with a few Cherokee companions and with his provisions loaded in an ox cart, he made several journeys into the West, received everywhere with kindness by even the wildest tribes. Disappointed in his philological results, he started out in 1843 in quest of the lost

Cherokee, who were believed to be somewhere in northern Mexico; but now an old man worn out by his hardship, he sank under the effort and died -- alone and unattended it is said -- near the village of San Fernando, Mexico, in August of the same year. Rumors "...having come of his helpless condition, a party had been sent from the Nation to bring him back, but arrived too late to find him alive...."

Again, with no explanation, Traveler Bird claims that in 1844, Sequoyah/George Gist [6] died from a bullet wound. Had Gist become an embarrassment, also?

The March 6, 1845 edition of the Cherokee Advocate, a newspaper controlled by the Progressives, reported that Sequoyah was alive and well and living with countrymen near Matamoras, Mexico.

The following April 21, Chiefs Standing Rock and Standing Bowls returned from the "Spanish dominions" and certified that Sequoyah died August 1843. The statement was witnessed by Daniel G. Watson and trail guide Jesse Chisholm,[7] himself half Cherokee. Were these historical persons a part of the conspiracy, also?

News traveled slowly. A month later, a Chief Oonoleh organized a search expedition for Sequoyah but is informed of his death by Jesse Chisholm. He is told that Standing Rock attended Sequoyah during his last sickness and had witnessed his death and burial.

With Guess, Gist and Thomas (portrait sitter) Maw dead, the principle stumbling blocks to accommodation with the white man were gone. Relatives of the deceased were too weak financially and emotionally to continue any organized resistance against the New Order. Those who had fled were scattered and too far removed to cause further trouble.

While Indian and non-Indian alike freely acknowledge the Sequoyah/George Guess legacy to the Cherokee, the prevailing literature does not accept that he had used an ancient writing system against the white man's encroachment. Thus the myth prevails that the Cherokee learned the syllabary within a very short time, when in actuality, many Cherokees had been using the writing system all along.

Meanwhile, what about that journey to the Rio Grande? Did it actually take place? Probably, yes. Someone made the trip because the descriptions of locations along the route, especially of Mier, are too accurate to be false. Did an old man purported to be Sequoyah travel to the Lower Rio Grande Valley and later die in San Fernando? We may never know. From a conspiracy standpoint, San Fernando was a perfect place for dying. At least three communities with the same name were in existence - one in Coahuila just west of Presidio/Ojinaga; the second, about half way between Matamoras and the Rio Soto La Marina. The most likely third candidate is the tiny river crossing community on the San Fernando Creek, about six miles northeast of today's Santa Gertrudis headquarters of the famous King Ranch.

Is a "Sequoyah" buried at a "San Fernando"? If so, who? If George Guess was killed on the Brazos in 1839, and George Gist died of a bullet wound in 1844, then who traveled throughout the Rio Grande Valley as Sequoyah, and now lies dead and buried in San Fernando since 1843?

Author's Note: According to the internet website, *www.cherokeenationmexico.com*, the cave in which Sequoyah died and was buried was discovered in 2001. It is on private land near Zaragosa, Coahuila, Mexico. San Fernando is present day Zaragosa.

End notes:

1. Neither Foreman nor Mooney identify Mier as the place where the Sequoyah party first crossed the Rio Grande River. Foreman describes a conversation with a Mexican Army officer who brags that a short time before, some 300 Texans were defeated in battle and captured. This probably refers to the ill-conceived battle of Mier and the subsequent Black Bean incident.

2. Brownsville pioneer William Neale reports in W.W. Chatfield's *THE TWIN CITIES OF THE BORDER,* 1893, that back in the 1830's, the Indians in the areas mentioned were "...thick as blackbirds." Neale also relates that in 1828, a Cherokee chief had an agreement with the City of Matamoras that he would not make depredations against Mexican citizens. Supposedly, the chief took the city's money, anyway, and ambushed any Mexican found outside the city.

3. Gist had to leave the Cherokee Nation in 1841 during the guerilla war in Indian Country. Before he could return to the Nation in 1844, he died of a bullet wound. *Cherokee Renaissance in the New Republic*, William G. McLoughlin, 1992, Princeton University Press.

4. How Thomas Maw died is unclear but his absence in the prevailing literature suggests that he, too, was assassinated. He was a minor chief, the son of Chief Hanging Maw who fought during the Revolutionary War with George Washington. Thomas Maw's name does not appear on any documents after 1838. Both he and "George Guess" are signers to the Proclamation of 1828 which deals with the removal of the Eastern Cherokee to the Arkansas Territory. Traveler Bird claims that a John Lowery signed Sequoyah's name to the treaty - signing another important Indian's name to a white man's paper was a common joke for the Western Cherokee. Did Lowery sign Maw's name as well?

5. The Cherokee alphabet takes its place among other writing systems that existed long before Columbus set foot on San Salvador. The written forms of the Mobilian Trade Language and the graphic symbols on the Michigan Newberry Stone are but two examples.

6. Traveler Bird provides no explanation for the death of Sequoyah/George Gist.

7. The same Jesse Chisholm after whom the Chisholm Trail is named.

8. Bird states that George Gist was no half-breed but a full-blood Cherokee.

SELECTED BIBLIOGRAPHY:

Traveler Bird, *TELL THEM THEY LIE: THE SEQUOYAH MYTH*, 1971, Westernlore Press publishers, Los Angeles, CA 90041

Dianna Everett, *THE TEXAS CHEROKEES, A PEOPLE BETWEEN TWO FIRES, 1819-1840*. 1990, University of Oklahoma Press, Norman, OK 73091

Grant Foreman, *SEQUOYAH*, 1938 Vol. 16 in the Civilization of the American Indian Series, University of Oklahoma Press, Norman, OK 73091

James Mooney, *MYTHS OF THE CHEROKEE AND SACRED FORMULAS OF THE CHEROKEE, from the 19th and 17th Annual Reports Bureau of American Ethnology.* Reproduced by Charles and Randy Elder Booksellers, Publishers, 2115 Elliston Place, Nashville TN 37023

W.W. Newcombe Jr., *THE INDIANS OF TEXAS* 1961, University of Texas Press, Austin, TX 78713-7819

THE LONG WALK
by Joan Soggie

It was a quiet Sunday afternoon in 1999 when the phone call came. At first I did not recognize the high-pitched voice and stuttering words.

"Yes, I'm sorry, who is this?"

"This is K-Keo, M-Missus Lorrie, how are you?"

"Keo! How wonderful to hear from you! Are you still living in Vancouver? How are you? How are the children?"

"They are OK. But I am very sad. My sister Veo is dead."

Veo? Dead? It seemed impossible.

After hearing as much of the sad story as Keo could tell … her sister's decision to pay for her parents' condo by taking a job in New York, a sudden illness, the desertion of friends, the call from some anonymous official to inform the family of her death … I promised to tell other friends here, and she promised to call again with her parents mailing address. It would be no good to phone them. Twenty years in the country had not been long enough to learn much English.

Twenty years!

And my thoughts turned back twenty years to the Veo that I had known.

Late winter, 1981.

Veo's family had been in Canada for a year and a half. Coming as refugees from Laos by way of a refugee camp in Thailand, their lives had been in chaos for most of that decade … most of Veo's short life.

An exuberant, active twelve year old when she and eight other family members arrived in our town, she had communicated with vivid pantomime. Now, seventeen months later, Veo seemed comfortable speaking English. Her eagerness to communicate, her hunger to belong, fired her superhuman energy. Nothing was too daunting. When given a pair of ice skates, she pushed a chair around the rink a few times until she got the hang of it and then, with her characteristic grin, struck out to catch up with friends. She brought the same determined enthusiasm to her school work, and by the end of that year her teacher expected that she would have caught up or passed her own age group.
Bright, adaptable, mischievous, Veo had adjusted to life in the prairies with an outwardly carefree aplomb. You might have thought she had grown up in this land of hockey and 4-H, instead of in a house on stilts overlooking rice fields half a world away.

But she carried that faraway home within her.

"It is so beautiful there," she told me in her eager way. "Very beautiful flowers, and it smells so good! Someday you should go there. I could show you!"

The complex political reasons for having to flee that bright land were, to her, frighteningly simple. She had little to say about the communist government, but did tell of being afraid of soldiers and police. Her sister Keo had been old enough to understand more exactly the bitterness of that Asian war and the danger that hung over her family if their father's former life should be exposed. Maybe that was what caused Keo to stutter, especially when confronted by anyone in uniform … even a nurse.

So this March day when I took Bouakham, mother of Keo and Veo, to her doctor's appointment, it was young Veo who came with us. Bouakham sat silent beside me as the miles of flat prairie and hummocky sand hills whizzed by. She responded with a smile and a nod to any remark addressed to her. But since neither of us knew more than a few words of the other's language, it was a relief to us both when I spoke to Veo instead.

"I hear you and Keo walked all the way home from school, Veo!"

The girls generally rode the school bus to the high school eight miles away, as did most of the other students in our little town. A senior student might drive the family car, some of the boys even had their own half ton. Occasionally, someone might go by snowmobile, or bike. But to walk that long, cold, dusty road? Unthinkable!

Until Keo and Veo, one sunny, cool March day, told their bus-driver that they would walk home.

"Oh, that was a good walk!" exclaimed Veo.

"But a long one."

"Long? No, it was not long. You want to hear about a long walk?" Veo laughed. "I'll tell you about a long, long walk!"

She settled down with her chin on the back of the front seat, inches from my ear.

"We were in Laos, on our farm, and my Mom and Dad wanted to get away. Some of my Dad's friends had been taken away, at night, by soldiers. We thought they were killed. It might happen to us, too. My Dad wanted to take all our family out of the country to Thailand. But we needed money to get a boat across the river, and money in Thailand, too. But the police watched us. If we sold anything, they would find out and maybe put my Dad in jail. Or they might find out he had been a paratrooper with the French army on Ho Chi Minh trail. If they knew about that, they would kill him for sure.

"We had our farm, our house, our water buffalo. We couldn't sell our farm or our house, but my Dad came up with a plan to sell the water buffalo. You see, when the dry season came, sometimes people would move their buffalo to another part of the country where the grass was better. My Dad had a friend who lived a long way north. He decided he would take our buffalo to him and get him to sell them for him. He told me and Keo that we should go with him.

"So we set out, Keo and me walking behind the water buffalo, my Dad leading the biggest one. We walked and walked and walked, and saw lots of towns and people we had never seen before. Whenever we came near a town, there were police all the time. Sometimes soldiers were driving down the road, or had checkpoints where everyone had to stop and show their papers. My Dad had papers … the police at our town had given him permission to move the water buffalo … but whenever he saw soldiers or police he would tell me and Keo to climb up on the back of a buffalo, so they would see right away it was just one old farmer and his daughters moving their buffalo to pasture.

"So we walked and walked, riding the buffalo sometimes, but most of the time walking. Keo and I liked to walk. We did not wear shoes, the dirt was soft and warm, not cold at all, the country so beautiful and green, not brown like here. When night came, we always found a place to sleep, someone would say, come here, sleep at my house. We walked for four days like that. Sometimes we were scared, when the soldiers stopped us and asked questions, but they always told us to go on.

"Sometime I think I will go back there, and walk there again. Maybe someday, after I am a doctor and rich, I will fly back to Laos! It would be fun to go back with Keo … you could come, too! It is very beautiful. You would like it there."

"What happened when you got there, Veo?"

"Oh, my Dad sold the buffalo, and paid money to his friend to make up the papers in another name, and then we took the money and walked home. Then he talked to a man with a boat who would take us across the Mekong River. And he told Nou and Khantaly to come with their kids, and told Amphay she could come too, and we just went for another walk one evening, leaving everything in our house as if we would be back right away. All we took with us was the money from the buffalo."

How many other stories did you have, Veo? What other adventures have you never told?

After that long walk, and the midnight flight across a river patrolled by soldiers, when a sneeze, a splash, or a crying baby could trigger a blast of machine gun fire, after that came the long two years of waiting in a Thai refugee camp. How did that feel, that seesaw between hope and despair? Did you see your parent's pain, weighed down by the daily annoyances and petty grievances of a thousand other like them lost in limbo? Then the exciting news of a sponsor, and another strange adventure, re-inventing your life in a small prairie town.

And after that, your struggle to find your place as an adult, the realization that your dream of becoming a doctor must be exchanged for the quick money needed to buy comfort for your parents.

How must it have felt to realize that you never would go home?

Yes, dear Veo, yours was indeed a long walk.

MY SOAP OPERA
By Eunice Greenhaus

There's nothing like the new age of technology! I bought a new VCR?DVD player. It came complete with all the wires needed for installation and an instruction book on how to do it. My sister and I tried until we were both out of patience and all we could get was a light on the player showing that it was plugged in and a display saying "channel 3". We had a problem because I had a TV cable box which the DVD wiring had to somehow go through. I needed someone who knew what they were doing. AHA, THE CABLE COMPANY!

At 9:00o'clock the next morning I was on the phone with them, talking to a menu robot. As soon as I gave it my telephone number it told me that there was no service in my area. I owe $217 and do I want to pay it now or my service would be cut off. Since it couldn't understand what I replied to this I was switched to a real live person.

Before I could even bring up the problem with the wiring, I had to find out how I could owe them any money since the bill was automatically put on my credit card each month. It turned out that I had received a new card with the same number on it ..but a new expiration date. Somehow this interfered with my payments. Meanwhile the cable company never notified me that the card was no longer valid or that I had any overdue payments. My card was updated, the amount due was paid...and "yes, there was service in my area".

We finally got around to the reason for my call. I explained that I needed a technician to wire the DVD set to my television and cable box. "No problem at all" he told me. "Someone will be there tomorrow between noon and 5:00PM. I was delighted. This was great service. It was well worth the $35 they were charging to come to my house.

At 2:00 o'clock the next afternoon the serviceman, Joe, arrived. He examined all the wires, looked them over half a dozen times, looked at the schematic book when I shoved it into his hands and hooked up the set.The DVD said "channel 3" and the TV had only snow. Joe changed some wires. He got the same result. He changed some more wires, same thing. Now he called a fellow worker and was talked through what to do...same result. He called someone else, no better. Now he called his boss and asked him to send someone to help. I gather that the boss said "No", Joe went out to his truck, I figured either to flee or to cry, but in ten minutes he came back. "They're sending reinforcements," he informed me.

Soon Mac arrived. Confidently, he pulled the TV farther out, asked for a DVD disk and put it into the machine. He switched wires. Now the DVD said "channel 3" and the snow on the TV said "weak or no signal". Mac switched some more wires, and then some more, and more. Finally, Look at that!, my movie was showing on the TV screen, but it was a silent movie. Joe and Mac were both perplexed. Now John arrived to see what was taking them so long. John was the expert and he soon had the DVD playing and the movie talking. He took away my one do-it-all remote and programmed every remote I had.

After three hours my DVD player was hooked to my television and cable box....and in order to play the DVD I needed to push buttons on three remotes, one to turn the TV and cable box on, one to put the TV in the right mode and finally the DVD remote to operate it.

Three hours, three technicians and three remotes.

They also wanted to charge me for three service calls. How great is the age of modern technology!

THE FACE OF THE ENEMY
Frank Cortazo

Private First Class Danny Romo ran in the night into what he thought was enemy territory. Panic! His rifle lost...in the muddy ground of a rain-drenched darkness. He ran! He ran until...he was lost!

Within the maze of winding, glistening trees, the smell of recent rains lingered. It mingled with the stale humidity permeating the air.

The enemy was nearby. Footsteps approached behind him and—

The voices!

His pursuers.

He must move on!

He stumbled. It was only a matter of time before the enemy confronted him. With desperation, he crawled and hid behind the cover of some bushes.

Fear gripped Private Romo. Raindrops pounded his face and blond head—his helmet was missing!

Helpless!

He was out there by himself, the sole survivor of a squad sent to reconnoiter the area. By mere luck, the bullets missed him when his group was ambushed, and now...now, the pursuing enemy was determined to finish him off, as well.

No weapon, but —

His knife was still by his side!

The long army-issued weapon capable of slicing through the thinnest hair with deft precision. Danny gripped it. He felt its sharp, serrated blade. He clutched the weapon harder; the voices were louder.

"Come on..." he muttered. Any moment now—

"Come and get me, you slanty-eyed—!?"

Perplexity crossed his face.

The voices were gone. Only the splat-splat of falling rain—

"Where are you?" His head swiveled in all directions; his eyes tried to pierce the gloom.

Bushes rustled somewhere in the darkness ahead. He could not distinguish anything...the rain fell harder.

One hand held his knife, the other wiped the rainwater battering his eyes. He continued to stare ahead until he saw...a shape!

An enemy soldier...walking toward him, holding a rifle!

Danny could see the person's small frame outlined beneath the rain-splattered uniform and under the helmet he wore. He heard the soldier's boots squish, with slow, careful strides over the rain-saturated leaves. As the soldier approached where he lay hidden, Danny saw the face.

Why...he's...he's just a kid!. A kid of no more than —

But...he was the enemy!

Here.

Face to face.

It was a matter of kill or be killed.

Danny broke his cover with a loud yell! He rushed at the enemy soldier.

Before the youth could fire his weapon, Danny wrenched it from him and threw it aside. He fell over him and pinned him to the ground. He swung his knife-blade to the soldier's neck.

"Daaa...! Daaa!" The enemy soldier yelled as he struggled to escape.

Danny's grip tightened as he looked into the soldier's pain-stricken, bulging eyes.

Kill! Kill! Kill!

The word raced through his mind, his hatred of the enemy evident upon his frenzied face.

"Daaa...no!!!" screamed his victim. "eeeee.....meeeee!"

Danny blinked, a puzzled look—?

The young soldier's face...it...it...was changing!

It changed into...the blond- haired, freckled face of—

"No, Dad!" screamed the youth. "It's me! It's me! Let...me gooo!"

Danny loosened his grip as he recognized his eighteen-year-old son's face. He saw Little Dan covered in mud, his soaked beige t-shirt and blue jeans stuck to his body with the splashing rain. Confused, he looked around and saw the rain-drenched bushes of his back yard. A flash of lightning illuminated the area for one brief moment and—

That's my house!

No! It...it happened again!

And this time...this time...Little Dan almost—
"Little Dan!" he cried over the noise of the rain. "Son...I'm...I'm sorry! I'm so sorry this happened! I didn't know...are...are you all right?"

The boy sat up coughing and crying.

"Why, Dad?" The tears streamed down his face. "Is this why Mom—"

Danny thought about Evelyn. Where would she be? How long was it since she walked out on both of them? A year? He remembered her wanting to take Little Dan with her, the boy refusing to go because...he loved and was so *much* like his father.

"Son," Danny told the boy. "I...your mother, she...was right in leaving me. I...I thought I could control this but...it's...the memories. The memories of my whole squad not making it back except for me and —"

He paused as he looked out into the darkness. A brief flash of light illuminated the darkness and vanished, almost as if someone...

No!

His condition was becoming worse. These hallucinations. They were becoming —

"They called me a hero," he said. "They honored me when I got back. Gave me a medal. But...what good is a medal? How is it going to bring back all of those guys who died back there? And... their families. What about *them*? Their suffering and—"

He stared at the dark, wet ground.

Another flash of lightning illuminated the area. Danny saw his own tormented reflection in a small puddle of rainwater.

I see the face of the enemy!.

"Dad," he heard Little Dan say. "It wasn't your fault. You gotta let it go and move on. You gotta—"

Before the boy could finish, Danny hugged him as he wept over the boy's shoulder. Little Dan was right. Danny needed professional help.

He would seek it tomorrow.

Tomorrow, he would drive to Corville. There, he would make an appointment for a visit to Dr.Steinmetz's office. He would follow through with this before...before it happened again and he hurt Little Dan...or...someone else.

He hoped the psychiatrist would cure him before he went insane. Otherwise, he might be sent to Radcliff Sanitarium or—

"Don't worry, Dad, I'll help you get through this."

Wiping the tears from his eyes, Danny let his son help him stand.

"Are...are you OK, Dad?" asked the boy as they walked back to their home.

Danny hesitated, looking out into the rain-drenched trees. "I...I am—" Raindrops glistened on his face. "I—"

He stared at the trees. A flash of lightning lit up their swaying shapes.

He gasped!

The enemy!

"Let's...let's get out of here!" With fearful determination, he pointed toward their home.

"Into that abandoned building!" he said. "We can hold them off from there until reinforcements arrive!"

HEROES
Mary Jane Coder

In my office sits a broken man.

One of many who hide behind superficial smiles,
Or behind tears too long held back.

They tell me their stories –
Stories of incomprehensible horror.
Stories of loss, grief and despair.

For over 30 years the experiences, everything, have been held in, hidden.
I listen, careful not to say things like, "I understand."
It is not possible for me to understand – I have never been in a war.

Again and again, I listen to the stories as I watch the wounds heal.
I see changes in the men and say a quiet prayer of thanks.
I know that God is healing them.

They are still damaged but no longer broken.
They go home to their wives and families.
They do things they haven't done in years.

The broken men are heroes.
They are the soldiers who go to war to protect everything and everyone in this country.
In the process, they've lost so much,
A piece of their soul, maybe…
I try to help them find it.

Another broken man walks in;
We begin again.

BIRDS, ROCKS, MURDER
Edna Ratliff

Sheets of rain splattered the windshield like large wet kisses while wind rocked the truck. Harry's knuckles turned white as he fought the steering wheel for control. In spite of the tension, he smiled. "You know, Helen, I'll be top bird now at the Robin Bird Club back home. Because I'm the only one who has seen the Olive Backed Warbler, and I even have a picture to prove it. Plus, I even found a large geode rock. I think it weighs about a pound. What a remarkable day." The wind shook the truck with its last breath; then the rain stopped.

Helen stared straight ahead. "I've been thinking. Maybe we should separate for a while." Helen glanced sideways at Harry while her body faced forward. Her mind told her maybe this wasn't such a good idea to ask Harry while she was alone with him.

"Forget it! I'd rather see you dead than listen to the chuckles about you leaving me." The truck jerked to the right fishtailing down a dirt road. Harry's boot hammered the gas pedal to the limit causing the truck to bounce wildly up and down over the large ruts. Helen clung to Precious, her Rottweiler. The truck stopped suddenly throwing Helen and the dog forward as Harry reached for a .45 revolver from under the truck seat. Helen grabbed the geode and slipped it into her jacket pocket. Harry swung the truck door open and pointed the revolver at Helen. Once out, he slammed the door shut, still waving the gun at her. He walked around to Helen's side.

"Get out! Slow! If that dog moves, I'll kill her."

Precious tried to get out of the truck, but Helen pushed her back and said, "Stay." As soon as Helen shut the truck door Harry grabbed her by her hair and threw her to the ground. He gave a horrendous kick to her stomach. Helen screamed. Pain coursed through her body. A screeching sound came from the dogs claws scratching at the window while barking ferociously at Harry. Harry raised his foot to kick Helen again, but instead he turned and yelled “Shut up. I’m so sick of that damn dog.” The dog still barked intensely and scratched faster trying to get through the window. Harry walked toward the clawing, barking dog with the gun pointed at Precious, while Helen struggled to get up. Helen reached into her pocket for the geode as Harry put his hand on the truck door handle.

At the Weslaco police station, Lt. Garcia bellowed out, “Detectives Martinez and Cruz, a man’s body was reported off of 1015 south on the road that goes into the orange grove just across from Fat Daddy’s. Two boys riding their bikes discovered the body. The boys are home with their father George Remiroz. The boys said they only saw the body, and rode home as fast as they could. According to Mr. Remiroz the boys will be home all day so you can question them there.” Lt. Garcia handed the boy's address to Detective Martinez.

Detective Cruz put the flashing light on top of the unmarked 2010 black Tarsus and drove to the scene. He pulled onto the dirt road and stopped before they drove through the tire tracks in the dried mud.

Martinez got out of the car and inspected the marks. “There are two different tire tracks here," he said. "We need to get impressions of them.” He looked up and noticed the vultures circling overhead. "We better head down the road."

"Do we have to walk?" Cruz wiped the sweat from his face. “It sure is hot, must be near a hundred.”

About three tens of a mile later, the detectives found a man's body lying close to some fallen trees next to the orange grove. He was lying on his stomach with his face turned to his right side. The back of his head was smashed in. The blood, mud and flies made it hard to see his face. A .45 revolver lay within the victim's reach.

"Two sets of prints, here," Cruz said. "One appears to be a hard sole and the other, maybe a tennis shoe."

“This is definitely a homicide.” Martinez put his cell-phone next to his ear. “I’ll call it in.”

The detectives secured the area and waited for the Medical Examiner to arrive. After the pictures were taken of the body, the M.E. reached into the victim’s pocket and retrieved the man’s billfold. He handed it to Detective Martinez.

Martinez rummaged through the billfold. “Well, it wasn’t robbery," he said. "He has a hundred and seventy two dollars. His driver's license says his name is Harry J. Martin. And, here is a receipt for a lot at Sunshine Villa RV Park, just right down the street on Airport Dr. He looked up and said, "Got anything else for me, Doc?”

“Remember, I just got here.” Doc examined the man’s head, “He was hit with something hard and round several times.” The M.E. shouted to his staff, “Everyone, look for anything that’s round that you could use as a weapon. Check it for blood.”

Doc turned back to the detectives, “From the dried mud on his face, I’d say he was killed yesterday, shortly after the two inch downpour.” He stood up and snapped off his latex gloves. “After I get him back to the morgue, I’ll be able to give you a better time of death.”

“Thanks Doc. One other thing, can you do the impressions of the two tire tracks and the shoe prints while we check out the Sunshine Villa RV Park?” Detective Martinez asked.

"I’ll get my men on it.” Doc smiled. “Remember, you owe me.”

Detective Cruz parked at the office of the Sunshine Villa RV Park. The two talked to the owner, Mr. Goodman, who told them the

Martins lived on lot 122. He also said the Martins had left early morn Tuesday and were gone all day, and Mr. Goodman hadn't seen Mr. Martin since then.

Cruz moved the Taurus across from the Martin's lot 122. Two trucks were parked in front of the RV. Both trucks had mud on their wheels and mud had even splattered up on the sides. The Ford truck had an Ohio license plate and the Chevrolet had Kentucky plates.

Both detectives walked past a picnic table that had a fishing pole, a dog grooming brush, a bucket with geodes in it, wet tennis shoes and an old cup of coffee. Martinez tapped lightly on the door of the large motor home.

The door opened. "Gerrr! Arf! Arf!" A Rottweiler barked. Saliva dripped from his huge white teeth. Martinez reached for his revolver. His heart raced. He backed away from the door and prayed the dog wouldn't come through the screen.

"Precious! Sit!" The woman pointed to the wall behind her. The dog stopped barking, turned and sat next to the wall. "It's okay Precious!" She opened the screen door, stepped outside and closed the door behind her. She stood about five foot eleven, about fifty years old with thinning copper-red hair, blue eyes, and freckles. Her chin and forearms had bruises and scratches.

"I'm Detective Martinez and this is Detective Cruz." They flashed their badges. "Are you Mrs. Martin?"

"Yes, I'm Helen Martin."

"Where did you get those scratches?" Martinez asked.

"Precious, my dog, decided to chase a rabbit, and she pulled me through the cactus." Helen rubbed her forearms.

"We talked to Mr. Goodman and he said you were gone most of the day yesterday, could you tell us where you and Mr. Martin went?"

"Yes, we got up early and drove to the nature center in Port Isabel because we both wanted to see the Olive Backed Warbler. They are a very rare bird in the states. We wanted to add the Olive Backed Warbler to our bird list because we belong to a bird club back in Ohio. The member who has the most rare birds on their list wins a hundred dollars.

"After we saw the bird, Harry wanted to stop at The Nature Rock Shop to look for some geodes. But they didn't open until twelve thirty, so we had lunch and went back. Harry collects geodes and he found one he really liked." Helen bit her lip and hesitated a minute.

Detective Martinez raised an eyebrow. "Did anything else happen?"

"We got into an awful argument. I wanted to stop at the Walmart in Weslaco to buy some yarn because I need the same lot number to finish a shawl. He told me we would stop at the one in Port Isabel where he had already picked out a fishing pole the last time he was there. I informed him we could stop at both Walmarts. That made him angry. He insisted we were only going to one Walmart and it was Port Isabel.

"After we parked at the Walmart in Port Isabel, I told Harry I would wait for him. I was so angry. When he walked away I locked the doors, put my key in the ignition and yelled out the window telling him he could hitch-hike home, and I could do whatever I wanted to do, and I left." Mrs. Martin looked down. "So I got my yarn in Weslaco and drove home. Harry never did come home."

"About what time did you get home?"

Around three, I think. Why all these questions? Is there something wrong with Harry?"

“Was that the last time you saw your husband?” Detective Martinez stared into her eyes, but she broke eye contact and looked at the ground.

“Yes. Tell me what’s wrong?”

“I’m sorry to tell you, Harry was murdered.”

Helen’s eyes welled with tears. “Who could have done this?”

“That’s what we're going to find out. Did Harry have any enemies that you know of?”

Detective Martinez waited patiently for her response.

Helen wiped her tears on the sleeves of her blouse. “Nobody liked Harry after he came home from Vietnam. He was an angry man. But I don’t know of anyone who would want to kill him.”

“Do you have a picture of Harry we could borrow?”

“I’ll go get one.” A few minutes later she handed a picture to Detective Martinez. “Here’s Harry's latest photo.”

Martinez handed her his card. “If you hear from him, call me. Meanwhile, I’ll be in touch.” He started to walk away but turned to Helen. “One other thing. What size shoes do you wear and which truck is Harry’s?”

Helen opened the door. “I wear six and a half, and the red candy apple Ford 250 belongs to me and Harry.” She waited on the threshold with the door open.

“Who owns the green Chevy?” Martinez asked on the way out.

“Jimmy Miller.” Helen disappeared into the house and shut the door.

As they walked away from the house, Detective Cruz said, “Martinez, I’ve been watching that fellow next door,” He nodded towards the neighbor who sat on his porch, carving on block of wood. “Maybe we should talk to him. I’m sure he has heard things.”

Martinez and Cruz introduced themselves to the man, and showed him their badges. The block of wood turned out to be a wooden horse.

“What did you say your name was?” Detective Martinez asked.

The man stood up towering over the detectives. He must have been at least six foot three, very thin frame with thick salt and pepper hair, and a mustache to match. “My name is Al Grant.” Al started coughing and had to sit back down. “Sorry guys, sometimes I just can’t stop coughing.”

“Have you seen Mr. Martin or heard from him these last few days?”

“I saw him a couple of days ago when he came home drunk. Thought we were going to have to call you guys, but Precious stopped him in his tracks. If it wasn’t for Precious, Helen would probably be dead.”

Al coughed again, but this time he put a lozenge in his mouth. “Harry always has an argument going with someone, not just Helen. The people in the park feel sorry for Helen as I do. I think she is too afraid to leave him.”

“Mr. Martin was murdered. Do you think his wife could have done it?” Detective Martinez watched Al's face for a reaction.

"Helen is too kind hearted to kill anyone. Besides, she has Precious.” Al started coughing again. “Now Precious is a different story. That dog would kill him.”

“Do you know of anyone who would want to harm him?”

“Everyone wants to harm him, because he makes everyone miserable, but to murder him, I don’t know.” Al put his tools and horse in a box. "I'm sorry guys I have an appointment in thirty minutes. Besides, here comes Jimmy." Al stood up and waved to a young man walking towards him. "Hi, Jimmy."

Jimmy was about five foot nine, copper-red hair, blue eyes, not a drop of fat on his body—just all muscles.

"Where are you going, Al?" Jimmy asked.

"To the doctors, like always." Al shook Jimmy's hand. "You and Helen are much better off now, see you later."

"You must be Helen Martin's son, am I right?" Detective Martinez asked.

"Nephew, Sir. My name is James Miller, but everyone calls me Jimmy. My mother was Aunt Helen's sister. When I was three, my parents died in a car wreck. Aunt Helen took me in and treated me like her own. She told me Harry was murdered."

Jimmy scratched his head. "You know it could be anyone. He does bet a lot on the horse races back home, and I know for a fact his bookie had to nudge him to pay up. But then again, he makes enemies everywhere he goes, so who knows?"

"I take it you didn't like Harry?"

"Me and the rest of world couldn't stand him, but Aunt Helen loved him." Jimmy shook his head. "Why, I don't know."

"Did you ever have a problem with Mr. Martin?"

"Not since I came home from the Marines. Harry would just say hi, and not much anything else." Jimmy smiled. "Excuse me, I need to help Aunt Helen with the funeral arrangements."

The detective handed Jimmy a card. "If you think of anyone let me know. I'll be in touch."

Detective Martinez's phone rang as he and Detective Cruz got into the car. He answered.

"Martinez….

"Is that right…uh…Thanks, Doc."

He turned to his partner. "Doc said they didn't find the murder weapon, but he was positive it was some kind of round rock; also the tennis shoes were a size six and a half and the other shoe print was the victim's. He thought Mr. Martin died around 2:00 PM Tuesday, and...good old Doc has the tire tracks and shoe impressions ready."

We've got her." Cruz grinned. "We know she's lying. But we have to find the murder weapon. You check out Mrs. Martin's alibi about being at Walmart in Port Isabel. I figure they would have been there between 12:30 PM to 2:00 PM. Walmart's security tapes run in a forty-eight hour loop. I'm sure you'll be able to pick out Harry's Ford. I'll check out the back ground on the Martins, and Jimmy Miller."

Martinez winked. "I think Jimmy was smiling way too much. I'll get a search warrant because I think I know where the murder weapon is. We'll meet back at the station."

Cruz dropped his partner off at the police station. Two and a half hours later, he returned.

"Martinez, you're right. They never stopped at the Walmart." Detective Cruz smirked. "I told you we got her."

"But maybe it wasn't her. It could have been smiling Jimmy. I got a report back saying he was arrested for beating a man severely. From the report, this man and Jimmy never did get along. Then the man killed Jimmy's dog for no reason, and that's when Jimmy attacked the man putting him in the hospital. A week later, the man dropped all charges against Jimmy. I think the man was paid off to drop the charges. As for Mr. and Mrs. Martin, they've had a violent marriage until about four years ago."

Detective Martinez looked up from the report. “I think that’s when she got her dog, Precious. Also, I got to thinking how Al Grant spoke up for Mrs. Martin, so I checked him out, too. The only thing I could find was, about three years ago, his wife died in a car accident. It was a foggy night and her car veered off the road over a cliff. She was killed, instantly. Al Grant, himself, doesn’t even have a speeding ticket.”

Martinez held up a piece of paper, “Here’s the warrant. Lt. Garcia said he would send a couple of officers over in case we would need them. We have to pick up Fred Moor from Medical Examiner office. He will check for blood on anything that’s round that could be used as a weapon.”

They arrived at 122 Sunshine Villa RV Park. Detective Martinez banged on the door.

“Police! Open up.”

Mrs. Martin called out, “Just a minute. Sit, Precious.” She opened the door.

“This is a search warrant.” Martinez handed the paper to Helen. “You’ll have to put a leash on Precious and bring the dog outside with you. We need to search the area.”

Helen and Jimmy took Precious over to Al’s place. The three stood and watched the officer search everything. They heard Detective Martinez tell Fred Moor to make sure he tested the geodes in the bucket for blood. And look for anything that was round that could be used for a murder weapon.

The detectives searched inside the trucks, and they concurred that the truck tires matched the tire tracks taken from the murder scene. Helen’s tennis shoe was a perfect match from the murder scene too.

“Like you, I thought for sure we would find blood on one of those rocks. Now, what are you thinking, Martinez?" Cruz asked. “We know they were at the scene, their tires put them there. Let's take them in."

Detective Cruz with several officers walked over to Al Grant's place. "Mrs. Martin and Jimmy Miller, we want the two of you to come with us." He turned to Al Grant. "Can you take care of the dog?"

"Sure." Al looked astonished.

At the police station, Mrs. Martin and Jim Miller were placed in different interrogation rooms. About fifteen minutes later, the two detectives entered the interrogation room where Helen sat.

"We know you lied," Detective Martinez said, as he sat down across from her while Detective Cruz stood. "Your truck was at the scene and you left your tennis shoe print. Also, Detective Cruz checked out your story and you never were at the Walmart in Port Isabel. What are you hiding? We want the truth." His fist hit the desk with a hard bang. "No more games!"

Startled, Helen blurted, "I can't stand living this lie anymore. Being married to Harry was like being married to an angel one second and the devil the next. The truth is, it had been raining hard, and Harry seemed to be his old happy self. This gave me the courage to tell him I wanted a divorce. But Harry went wild, driving crazy and ran off the highway and slammed on the breaks throwing Precious and me almost through the window. He had a gun and pointed it at me. I figured he was going to kill me. I was so scared. I grabbed the geode just before he dragged me out of the truck. I knew I was going to die when he threw me to the ground, and kicked me. But Precious was going crazy and Harry turned on her."

Tears ran down her face. "When Harry reached for the truck door, I hit him as hard as I could with the rock. He fell to the ground, and while he was trying to get up I grabbed the keys and got out of there. On the way home I called Jimmy. He told me not to worry. He would take care of Harry. Jimmy promised he wouldn't hurt

Harry. Later, when I saw Jimmy, he said Harry was gone when he got there. You have to believe me."

"Why didn't you tell the truth?" Detective Cruz asked, "Because the courts would have believed you, what with all the violence in your marriage"

"I have my reasons," Helen sniffed.

"Is it because you believe Jimmy Miller killed Harry?"

Helen covered her face with her hands, "I don't know."

"We'll be right back." The partners went to the other room where Jimmy was.

"Your Aunt said after she knocked Harry out she called you. What happened then?" Detective Martinez asked.

"Al was with me when Aunt Helen called. He said it would be best if he talked to Harry. I guess he figured I'd kill him." Jimmy wasn't smiling. "Later, when Al got back, he told me Harry had used his phone to call someone. Al didn't know the guy's name. But Harry was going to stay with someone then go back north for good. I lied to my aunt; I told her Harry was gone when I got there."

"How did the mud get on your truck?" Detective Martinez asked.

"Al's muffler had fallen off of his truck so he borrowed mine," Jim rubbed the back of his neck. "I should have known Harry would never leave."

Detective Cruz pulled his partner aside. "I believe I saw Al Grant sitting in the waiting room. I'll go get him." He headed out the door. Detective Martinez asked the officer at the door to take Jimmy Miller to a holding area.

Cruz brought Al Grant into the interrogation room. "Have a seat."

"I been waiting for you to pick me up, then I thought I'd save you a trip. I guess you want the truth." Al coughed.

Detective Martinez said, "Mr. Grant, Jimmy Miller told us you borrowed his truck to go talk to Harry. Is this true?"

"Yes. When Jimmy told me Harry tried to kill Helen and Precious, I knew if Jimmy went, he would kill Harry for sure. When I got there, Harry was sitting on a log planning how he would kill Helen. He offered to pay me if I'd help. I got so angry inside I picked up a rock. As he started to get into the truck, I hit him again and again. I couldn't stop the anger inside me knowing he wanted to kill Helen."

Al wiped his eyes on the back of his hands. "Helen is like a breath of fresh air to me." He coughed and put a lozenge in his mouth. "Now Helen doesn't have to live in fear and can be happy. I want you to know there's nothing between Helen and me. I wish there had been, but there wasn't. I have lung cancer with only about three months to live, and then I'm gone. I asked God's forgiveness for killing Harry, but I'm not sorry he's dead."

Al reached into his jacket pocket. "Is this what you have been looking for?" He handed a geode rock to Detective Martinez.

Al Grant, you're under arrest for the murder of Harry Martin."

ABOUT THE VALLEY BYLINERS
Marianna Nelson

In 1943, the year the Rio Grande Valley Byliners was founded, newspapers were written and managed mostly by men. Few women were journalists. So, given the male-dominated field at the time, it was unusual that the Byliners was started <u>by</u> women, <u>for</u> women. Minnie Gilbert of San Benito and Lucy Wallace of Mission were among the founders. Minnie wrote mostly the society pages for the Brownsville Herald and the Valley Morning Star, and Lucy for the Mission Times.

The Byliners was started to encourage women to become more professional in their writing and to find opportunities in the writing field, as well as to get to know each other. They wanted to exchange ideas and have fellowship with other women writers and wanted to concentrate on women's interests without the men feeling they were the only ones who could write. Thus, for many years the Byliners had a "women only" rule for members.

This changed in the early 1980s when Ann Washington's husband, Tom, became active in helping with the books the Byliners had published. So, the "women only" rule was dropped and men were invited to be members. Gradually, over the years, more men became interested in and joined the group. Now, the membership is fairly even between the sexes.

Starting in 1975, the Byliners began writing and publishing their own books. The first, *Gift of the Rio*, was spearheaded by Lucy as part of the 1975 Bicentennial activities in Mission. She managed to get a grant for the publishing costs from the Mission Bicentennial organization. Single-handedly, she rounded up the writers, helped come up with subjects, and pushed the project to completion. Each chapter, which was written by a different writer, told of places and events in Valley history. Minnie and Ann Washington edited the book and Ann did the index. Marge Johnson recalls all of them sitting around her dining table, going over the galley proofs and laying out the pages. The book came out and was very well received. About 3,000 copies were printed. It sold well and the Byliners ended up with some money in the bank.

After a while, Lucy got a second wind and decided that the Byliners should write another book, this one about the people who settled the area and those who left a special mark on the Valley. Someone came up with the name *Roots by the River*. The press run was 3,000 again. The book was also well received and eventually made some more money.

A third book was conceived when it turned out that a lot of people were left out of the "Roots" book who deserved recognition. The book was called *Rio Grande Roundup* because it "rounded up" others who had done much for the area. This time, the press run was 5,000 and was paid for by the monies made from the first two books. It did not move as fast but enough copies were sold to pay the printing expenses.
Both Lucy and Minnie wrote several chapters in each of the books, as did Ann Washington. Their work was always well researched and well written.

Lucy died in the late 1980s, and Minnie lived to age 99, leaving her writing days behind in the late 1990s. Marge Johnson remembers them as bright, interesting ladies who pursued their own careers, as well as the goal of creating these publications to leave a lasting legacy to the historical literature of the Valley. Others participated by writing a chapter or two, but Lucy and Minnie did the real work.

The Byliners had a period of low membership, perhaps because a potential member had to be a published writer and had to be invited and recommended by two members to join. After the rules were changed in the late 1980s, membership increased again.

Since then, Byliners leaders included Eileen Mattei, Adrienne Ostmann, Mona Sizer, Jeff Harris, Ruth Harris, Sandra Vela, Janet Wilder, Verne Wheelwright, Jack King, Don Clifford, and Sue Groves. All helped the organization continue its high level of achievement – with Excellence in Writing Contests and publications of the winning entries, monthly newsletters, annual Writers Workshops, monthly Writing Challenges, attainment of non-profit status, and publication of two more books: *Tales Told at Midnight Along the Rio Grande*, edited by Mona Sizer and published in 2006, and *Collected Tales From the Rio Grande*, edited by Don Clifford and published in 2010.

The Byliners meet at the Harlingen Public Library on the second Saturdays of the month at 1:30 p.m., except for July. Writers and would-be writers seeking to perfect their craft and meet others who are doing the same are invited to attend a meeting and to join.
This is the Byliners' sixth book. Who knows? A seventh may be in our future!

ABOUT THE AUTHORS:

Jose A. Alvarez is a first generation immigrant to the United States. He grew up in Havana, Cuba and left the island in 1960 to attend college in the United States where he settled after graduation. He began writing personal essays and short stories after his first trip back to Cuba in 1997. He has lived and worked in Puerto Rico, Brazil, Mexico, Israel and the Netherlands and enjoys writing about his experiences living in different cultures. Recently he moved to the Rio Grande Valley where he has been an active member of the Valley Byliners since 2010. He has also been a member of the Narciso Martinez Cultural Arts Center in San Benito, where one of his stories was published in the 10th Anniversary Anthology.

Hugh Barlow is a stay-at-home father who has worked in a number of industries, such as a truck driver, gas pump jockey, junkyard mechanic, electrician, cook, and meat cutter in a packing plant. He has worked on road crews, and has his own business doing home and house trailer repairs. He collects Volkswagons and currently has four air-cooled VWs. He loves reading and writing Science Fiction and Fantasy. For fun, he repairs computers. He has been published in his college newspaper and had one poem published nationally. He hopes to go back to college and finish his education.

Mary Jo Bogato has taken her love of nature and turned her South Texas ranch into a natural outdoor classroom. With lots of love and hard work, she took an over-grazed ranch and turned it into a balanced and natural habitat for native species. She was featured on Texas Parks and Wildlife TV for winning a Lone Star Land Steward award. She is an avid outdoorswoman, nature photographer and angler. Wildlife photos including alligators have been taken on the ranch and published in books and articles for years. She has been recognized and known for being passionate about outreach and education. As a master naturalist, hunter, angler, instructor or guide, Mary Jo is a model of how to motivate people about conservation of wildlife and habitat.

Don Clifford is a retired U.S. Air Force officer whose non-fiction articles appeared in various archaeological journals, UT/Brownsville Historical Studies and Valley newspapers. His first published fiction is *The Outhouse,* a short story that appears here as the first-time winner in the history of the Jack King Writers' Challenge. In 1995 he served as editor of the prize-winning NEWSLETTER of the Cameron County Historical Commission; in 1996 he co-edited *A Blast From The Past* for the Brownsville Historical Association; in 1998 he coauthored *A Kid's History of Brownsville*; in 2008 he published his first novel, *Ben Solomon in Destiny Diverted.* In 2010 he was the chief editor of the Valley Byliners book *Collected Tales From The Rio Grande.* His latest work is a children's book *Zoo Nonsense*, a zany collection of rhymes with crazy animal antics illustrated by Olga Cruhm. Anticipated in 2014 is *Squeaky, The Littlest Angel.*

Frank Cortazo , a retired elementary school teacher and part-time dance instructor, wrote his first short fiction story when he was nine years old, a crime tale patterned after a 1940's television movie serial. His earliest influences were western movies from Mexico with characters similar to the fictional swordsman Zorro. They led to his interest in super-hero comic books, classic Hammer Films and Universal Studios horror and science-fiction movies. Since high school he wrote rhyming narrative poetry. Some of his poems were published in several anthologies during the late 1990's. He uses comic books, paperback novels, videos, and other items pertaining to the super heroes, horror, science-fiction, western, and mystery genres as sources for his writing. He credits authors Louis Lamour, Stephen King, Edgar Allen Poe, Ian Fleming, Robert E. Howard, and many others as influences in the creation of his own works of fiction.

Marge Flados is a retired registered nurse who has authored two books. *The Road From Spink,* published in 2005, is a perspective on life while growing up in the rural Midwest during the Great Depression and WWII. *Retro Parenting* was published in

2013 and offers methods of parenting that 21st century parents no longer employ but would work better than the organized lifestyle children endure today. According to Marge's resume, she has moved 28 times, lived in 20 towns and cities, 10 states, the Panama Canal Zone, and served in the U.S. Navy. She and her now deceased husband, Norman, eventually settled in Harlingen, Texas. Her story, *A Cat's Tale,* is a Jack's Writing Challenge winner.

Rudy H. Garcia lives in Laguna Vista, TX., and he and his wife Rita have four daughters. His poems appear in *Telling Tongues*, Calaca Press, Northwestern University; *poets of the east village* N.Y./N.Y.; and *poetry pachanga*, Border Senses.

Pete Gray grew up in Kearney, New Jersey, at the end of World War II when rock and roll was popular and times were prosperous. He intended to become an automotive design engineer but fate drew him to California and an initial career in photography. His photographs won prizes, were published in magazines, and sold in two art galleries in Orange County. His embellished career included computer programs, fiction, poetry, travelogues, essays, self-help books, instruction manuals, business plans, technical reports and a few letters. Since retirement, Pete has had articles and photographs published in such magazines as *Messing About In Boats, Trailer Life, RV Life,* and *Escapees*. In 2007, he married journalist Grace Guido and when they are not writing about their travels across North America, they spend the winter at the Fun N Sun trailer resort near San Benito.

Eunice Greenhaus was born and raised in New York City. She went to school in Massachusetts, lived in Connecticut, California and Texas. She settled in a San Benito, TX trailer park where she teaches Mah Jong and writes. Her memoirs and poems appeared in two previous Valley Byliner books, *Tales Told at Midnight Along the Rio Grande* and *Collected Tales From the Rio Grande.* As a member of the Writers Group at Fun N Sun, she wrote for and helped edit *Fun N Sun Then and Now*, a history of the RV resort, its residents and activities.

Ann Greenfield is a native Texan, born in Austin, raised in Amarillo, and lives in McAllen with her husband and two cats. She received a B.S. in Education from Texas State University, and is a member of the Writers League of Texas and Valley Byliners. Ann has attended the WLT Summer Writing Retreat, Jodi Thomas' Writers' Academy and Sandi Ault's Wild Writers' workshop. Ann's career began when she took a local writing course in order to help her son with college English. During the course, she had an opportunity to submit a ghost story to a the Valley Byliners who accepted and published her first story: "The Hanging Room," in *Tales Told at Midnight Along the Rio Grande.* Ann writes romance, mystery, and fantasy. Published writing credits include: "Winter Traditions" and "They're Heeeere!" in Valleysong; and "Ghost Sheriff" and "Entertaining Angels Unaware," in Haunted Texas Highways.

Sue Groves is an Emmy-award winning photojournalist, who moved to the Rio Grande Valley in 2011, after spending many years in broadcast journalism and the entertainment industry. She worked with the West Coast Bureau of NBC Network News and the Walt Disney Studios. While in southern California, she wrote and produced several documentaries, industrial and music videos, and traveled extensively throughout Europe and the Soviet Union. After graduating Magna Cum Laude with a B.S. in Mass Communications, Groves spent her junior year in London, studying British theater, film, literature and politics. She later pursued her masters degree in Cinema at the University of Southern California in Los Angeles. Currently, Groves is a contributing writer/photographer for *Beyond ARTS* and the *Church Reporter* magazines in the Rio Grande Valley, and volunteers as a pastoral services lay minister, lector and elementary school teacher for the Catholic Church. She enjoys softball, fencing, and horseback riding, and can kick-start a Harley.

Susan LeMiles (Holmes) has authored a novel, an historical brochure published by the South Padre Island Bureau of Conventions and Tourism, and is a featured columnist for the monthly magazine, Valley Business Report. The poetry, she writes for herself.

A romantic suspense novelist, she sets her stories in the rich historical context of the Rio Grande Valley. *Touch the Mayan Moon*, reflects her understanding that The Rio Grande Valley is neither Texas nor Mexico, but a land of its own, with its own history, its own people, mingled in a cross cultural environment. This book is available in paperback and Kindle formats through Amazon or her author website www.susanlemiles.com. Her next novel is set in Port Isabel in 1865. She plans publication to coincide with the 150th anniversary events of the Battle of Palmito Ranch, the last battle of the Civil War.

Milo Kearney is a Professor Emeritus of History at the University of Texas at Brownsville. He and his wife, Vivian, now live in San Antonio, Texas, in order to be near their daughter Kathleen and son-in-law Danny Anzak, their son Sean and daughter-in-law Lisa, and all their grandchildren. Milo has published nine books as editor and eleven as author, including *Stories that Brownsville Told Its Children* and *Border Walls, A Musical About Redbeard of the Rio Grande.* His latest work, published in 2013, is *Man, God, Satan, Jesus, and Holy Spirit,* a collection of poems that comment on our spirituality, the meaning of life, the roots of Faith, and the role of the Church.

Jack King was born in 1936 in Raymondville, Texas, and after some moving around, he went back to Raymondville and finished high school. He pulled a three-year hitch in the Army, then worked eighteen months in heavy steel fabrication and 5 ½ years in gas pipeline construction. He started college at the age of 29 and earned an A.A. in architecture at San Antonio College, then a B.A in Humanities at U.T. Austin. He worked for the Texas Department of Health for ten years, taught high school English for two years, and art classes for more than 20 years. Some of his short stories appear in *Collected Tales from the Rio Grande*, for which he designed the book's cover. Jack is a Byliners Past President, lives in Harlingen with wife, Nina, and daughter, Miranda. His son, Cody, is in college.

Bruce & Marianna Nelson sold their Connecticut home in 1997 to travel in a 26' house on wheels. Their on-the-road adventures plus tales of their present life in the Valley are chronicled and photographed in a blog called "Nelson's Notes" (www.otr.studoio221.net). Three of Marianna's previous stories appear in *Tales Told At Midnight Along the Rio Grande* and *Collected Tales From the Rio Grande*. Her contributions in this book come from her stories about growing up in the northeast. Bruce's creative bent finds outlet in several videos including "The Computer Fix-It Shop" which won Best Technical Achievement from the WILD's Film Contest in 2008. *Fog* is Bruce's first appearance in a Byliners anthology. Bruce served as Byliners Vice President for Public Relations and Newsletter Editor while Marianna served on the Byliners Board of Directors.

LeRoy Overstreet writes mostly about his unique adventures that began during the Great Depression and continue today. His stories include experiences on some vast cattle ranches of central Florida, rodeos, alligator hunting, inventions, and many other subjects Most of these stories are contained in his latest book published in 2013, *Adventures and Escapades with Friends, Foes and Renegade.* It's a collection of personal incidents told in a true tall Texan style as would be expected of someone who now lives near Rio Hondo, Texas. And if you ever wanted to catch and skin an alligator, in 2012, LeRoy published details in his *How to Catch an Alligator...and what to do with it when you catch it!*

Kamala Platt, Ph.D., M.F.A. is an author, artist, profesora, and independent scholar in South Texas and at The Meadowlark Center in Kansas. In her poetry her teaching and her life, she engages ecological and cultural borderland traditions and "green rascuache" life ways, to find footholds of environmental and social justice & well-being amidst the crises of a feverish planet. Following a community compilation *Kinientos* (Wordsworth, 1992) and first collection of poetry, *On the Line*, (Wings Press, 2010), she is currently encouraging preorders for a current and historical borderland chapbook, *Weedslovers: Ten Years in the Shadow of September* for Finishing Line Press, publication in Spring, 2014.

Edna Ratliff was born in Columbus, OH across from the Ohio State Football stadium. At the age of six, Edna's family moved to Pickerington, Ohio. While in the third grade she wrote a play about being kind to one another, made hand puppets out of socks, a stage out of a huge cardboard box, and put on the play for her class The teacher asked her to do the play for other classes too. Ever since then she has been writing stories for children. Also, fiction mysteries fascinate her as she figures out where to leave clues for who did it. Her publishing credits include an article on "Tecumseh" for *Ohio Magazine*, "Bridging the Gap" for *Good Old Days* magazine. She and her husband, Ed, moved to Mission, TX in 2012. Since then, she serves as moderator and collector of the short stories submitted for Jack's Writing Challenge.

Joan Soggie travels the full length of the Great Plains each Spring and Fall with her husband, Dennis, from their forever home in Elbow, Saskatchewan, to their adopted home in Harlingen, Texas. Little wonder that her writing draws from the landscapes, histories and personalities of the prairies. Her stories have been published in *Saskatchewan History and Folklore*, the *Saskatchewan Archaeological Society Newsletter*, and online at virtualsaskatchewan. Besides reading and writing, Joan enjoys kayaking, hiking, dancing with her partner of 50 years, and just being Grandma. Joan and Dennis have four grown-up children and eleven nearly-grown-up grandchildren.

Caroline Steele returned to the Valley after an absence of 20 years. She considers herself a world traveler and teacher, enjoys reading and writing, is involved in community activities such as Scouting, church, library and is a cat whisperer at the animal shelter. She says her best publishing efforts are "Letters-to-the Editor." Her poem, *History Lesson*, was published and taped for the blind, and presented here as a Jack's Writing Challenge winner. Although she won a newspaper contest in Honolulu with a holiday story in 2002, she does not see herself as a truly published author - college magazines hardly count when they showcase various talents in the school. She did have a short story published in the *Saltwater Papaya* in Canal Zone, Panama.

Judy Stevens finds time to be a rock hound, potter, cartoonist, and eclectic collector. Originally from Minnesota by way of Southern California, she came to the Rio Grande Valley in January 1977 with her husband and daughter. Nowadays, she delights in watching the grandkids grow and hanging out with Grandpa. Judy is a multiple-repeat winner of Jack's Writing Challenge. Her stories also appear in *Tales Told at Midnight Along The Rio Grande* and *Collected Tales From The Rio Grande.*

Georgia Tuxbury retired from public relations and advertising in Michigan and moved to South Texas where for seven years she was the Rio Grande Valley reporter for Southwest Farm Press. She is currently a freelance writer, who writes plays, short stories, poetry and novels. Alamo Country Club, where she lives, has presented more than a dozen of her plays. For nine years, she has led a class in "Writing Your Life Story," and leads a weekly critique group that meets at the Pharr Library. She and her husband Bob live in Alamo and have five children and eight grandchildren.

Bidgie Weber was born and raised in the Rio Grande Valley. She has a deep abiding love for the area and enjoys writing poems and stories about her childhood. Fiction is a relatively new endeavor for her and, like everyone else, waits to write that novel that hovers at the edge of her mind. Her first experience in writing was drafting commercials for KELT-FM radio. She says she hopes to keep writing "...till my fingers are too stiff to hold a pen." Bidgie's short stories appear in all three recent Byliner books.

Verne Wheelwright, PhD. is an internationally recognized professional in the field of Foresight and Futures Studies. He is the author of *It's Your Future, Make it A Good One!* as well as *The Personal Futures Workbook*. He has published articles in a number of professional journals and other publications. He has addressed audiences in major cities across the U.S. and in several international cities about how to explore and plan for the future. His web site is **www.Personal Futures.Net**. Verne's short stories appear in all three recent Byliner publications.

Travis M. Whitehead is a Valley resident employed as a reporter for AIM MEDIA Texas, formerly the Valley Freedom Newspapers group. His stories and articles have appeared in the Valley Morning Star, the McAllen Monitor, and the Brownsville Herald. Travis developed an early interest in the culture of Mexico. "I am drawn to the liberation of uncertainty south of the Rio Grande River," he said. "The unexpected flashes of color and human impulse energize me, and I take inspiration from the unabashed individualism that flourishes there." He studied English and Spanish at Texas State University and traveled extensively through Europe and ended up in Mexico for the purpose of writing a biography about a bullfighter. Instead, he was overwhelmed by the beautiful handmade works of Central Mexico. The result is a book published by **Otra Voces**, *The Artisans of Michoacán: By Their Hands,* which he wrote "... to provide an introduction of the artisans to the rest of the world."

Janice Workman claims she is "...a Texan since 1986, Yankee for life. Writing since I could put crayon to paper. Published in *Tales Told At Midnight Along the Rio Grande* and *Collected Tales From The Rio Grande*. Enjoy various hobbies and adventures that keep me in writing ideas. Live with my husband and dog pack, not so quietly, in Harlingen, Texas, and await discovery, fame and fortune."

Nellie Venselaar passed away in 2013 after living an exciting 94 years. As a child in Holland, she pledged that she would see the world, which she did...England, Holland, Indonesia, USA, and Australia with visits to 60 more countries. She is a published author whose short stories and poems appeared in two previous Valley Byliners publications, *Tales Told at Midnight Along the Rio Grande* and *Collected Tales From The Rio Grande*. One of her first published novels, *A Musical Journey*, is a fictional account of one family's escape from Nazi-held Holland---which may mirror her own departure from Europe during World War II. In her later years, she divided her time between a home in Canada and Harlingen, Texas. She held no Byliners office but contributed immensely to its success with her willingness and volunteer spirit.